To Desmond
Best wishes
from
Barbara M. Javel
November 2

A Little Piece for Mother

A Little Piece for Mother
By Barbara Towell

Spinetinglers Publishing
22 Vestry Road,
Co. Down
BT23 6HJ,
UK
www.spinetinglerspublishing.com

Published by Spinetinglers Publishing – July 2012

ISBN - 978-1-906755-46-1

Printed in the UK.

For my husband John, my parents Ladislav and Tita (Claire), my daughter Caroline and my son Jan.

Dedicated to the victims of the Holocaust and its legacy; especially my grandparents Gyula and Margarette and my father's sister Gabrielle, who died in Auschwitz-Birkenau.

The mask begins to crack and the shadows creep through the fractures like tiny beads of blood seeping from an untended wound. It happens so slowly that no one notices until the mask shatters to reveal a monster too dark and deadly to defeat.

PART ONE

Chapter 1
1950s
Reflection on childhood

Mother wore a cardigan even on the hottest of days, and I have no recollection of her wearing any garment without sleeves. She was what I'd describe as a handsome, rather than pretty woman - tall and slim with fine high cheekbones and a straight nose too long for a classic beauty. She never wore powder, and only a touch of lipstick on what she considered formal occasions such as a visit to the doctor or an appointment with the headmistress at my school. Her thick lustrous, raven black hair was harshly folded into a French roll, held tightly with a cumbersome clip. No wisps of hair were left untamed to stray across her face. I think if they had, her expression would have been softer. The only times it fell freely around her shoulders was in the mornings before she got dressed. I thought then that she looked beautiful - but I never told her.

When I was a child Mother had dark moods, inexplicable moods; they were unpredictable and made me feel afraid. At these times I'd often catch her staring at nothing; standing motionless, a statue with shards of cruelty sparkling in her eyes, and yet in truth she was never deliberately unkind. However, I have to admit that she was rather out of touch, and sometimes even mildly ridiculous, mood or no mood.

The much-hated hat she bought me when I was six, says it all. That broad brimmed, brown felt hat I wore with sufferance and a great deal of protest, because at school it made me a figure of fun. Although children in the 1950s weren't obsessed with fashion, there were certain things even a six year old wouldn't wish to be seen dead in, and that hat was definitely one of them. I absolutely loathed the thing.

"Please Mummy," I begged one winter morning. "I don't want that hat. I don't like that horrible hat."

As I was about to throw it back into the coat cupboard, Mother smartly grabbed it, and it was back on my head before you could say Jack Robinson.

"The big girls keep laughing - saying things..." I began to cry, but tears changed nothing.

"What things do they say?"

I whimpered, "That I look stupid. They keep pointing at it - and laughing."

"Now Child, you are being silly. You take no notice. Huh! Such a fine hat to keep you warm. Makes them jealous. They want one too."

They want one too! How wrong could Mother have been.

So desperate was I not to be seen in that pudding basin, a few days later I took matters into my own six year old hands. It was a Friday afternoon playtime when I noticed one of the huge refuse bins containing the pigs' swill was wide open. First, checking that nobody was looking, I tossed in the hat; and there it lay with all the school dinner that we kids wasted. I knew later in the day the County Council truck would arrive at the school to take away all that revolting macaroni milk pudding, lumpy mashed potato and greens for the pigs to eat - and the hat. Well, I hope the pigs got more enjoyment from the hat than I ever did.

Of course Mother was furious, as I knew she would be and when she came to collect me at 3.15, I was forced to lie. The hat had been on my peg one minute and gone the next.

While the other mothers asked their children, "And did you have a nice day?" or "What did you have for lunch?" she spent at least ten minutes marching up and down the cloakroom tutting and clucking like a hen as she searched the rows of pegs for it. I pretended to help her, but knew with certain satisfaction she'd never find the monstrosity since it was miles away by now.

Swiftly pen was put to paper and a letter sent to Miss French, the headmistress, demanding the theft be fully investigated. Would you believe it? Mother was convinced that the unsightly hat had been stolen by one of those jealous pupils. Throughout the rest of the term, she lived in hope that the thief would be discovered, reprimanded, and the hat returned to its rightful owner. If pigs could fly, I thought to myself.

Even now, fifty years on, I hear the jingle of an ice cream van and I'm drifting in a sea of loneliness. Instantly, I become that little girl standing by myself on the kerb of our suburban avenue on Sunday afternoons watching the neighbourhood children being bought ice cream cones by their grandparents, aunties and uncles while I stare empty-handed. Why did my family have no other relatives to share with us, those 4 o'clock English teas of ham salad and tinned peaches? I vaguely knew from an early age that it was something to do with the war.

The ash tree in our garden was a magnet on summer Sundays. It swayed and sighed as I aimlessly pedalled my bike round its thick trunk. From the adjoining semi-detached house where my best friend Lisa Harris lived, often there could be heard laughter and raised voices in easy, unthreatening challenge; typical of family gatherings. But for me it was like living in a museum on Sundays. The door was always closed. I was never allowed anyone in to play, on Sundays.

"It is day of rest," Mother would remind me. But Father was the only person who worked six days a week and needed to rest, yet he never spoke a word on the matter.

I didn't understand why Sunday was so special because we weren't Christian, or religious in any shape or form. When I asked if I could go to the Baptist Sunday school with Lisa, Mother answered, "Martina, do not be so silly."

"Why so silly?" I asked.

"Do you not read fairy stories, Child?" She refused to be drawn into any further discussion. I was left confused.

The Diary of Anne Frank remains a significant book to many people. To me it has more significance than to most. It was our 4th Year Junior class reader. During a lesson in the school library one Thursday morning, our teacher Mrs. Carlson, having first instructed the class to read specific pages, took Ted Gilling out into the corridor to deal with his incessant disruptive behaviour. *The Diary of Anne Frank* obviously held no appeal for him.

Once the library door was closed, Susan Rawlinson turned to the photo on the back cover of the book and said to me, "You don't 'alf look like that girl Anne Frank. "'Ere look you lot," she continued, stretching out her arm. The book wavered in her hand as she pushed it in sharp stabs towards her gaggle of mates who obediently gathered round the table where she sat in the centre of the library.

"Really," I whispered nonchalantly, trying not to sound annoyed and wondering why I was, because she had not really spoken unkindly. All the while I kept my head down, looking at the pages of my copy, but no longer concentrating on Anne's plight in the attic.

"Are you Jewish?" Lisa asked me later in the playground after we had just eaten roast pork for our school lunch.

"I'm English!" I snapped back. "Well - Polish English."

Her quizzical expression did not escape me. Quickly I chimed up with, "Would you like a Spangle?" and offered her the manky packet that had been festering in my gymslip pocket for a number of weeks. That was the end of that - for now.

In the evening when I broached the topic with Mother, she ignored my words and carried on polishing the dining room table. I bit back the temptation to yell, "You know that I'm Jewish - and so are you and Daddy. Why didn't you tell me?" Instead, I chose to say it in a calm and collected manner. Her silence told me everything, and at the same time told me nothing.

My parents had been naturalised by the mid-1950s and were extremely proud of their new passports. Mother longed to be British and insisted that *I* was - after all I was born in London. In spite of their striving to be accepted as English, and Mother's attempt to make the language her own, my parents more often spoke to one another in Polish, although never to me. They said it was unnecessary to teach me their mother tongue. "It is the future we should be looking to; the past it should stay in past," Mother often said.

Once I overheard them discussing whether life wouldn't be easier all round if they changed our surname, Kalinski, by deed poll. Maybe not to Smith or Jones, but Kalin or Kalinson perhaps. However, I lost track of the conversation because of their constant hopping back and forth from Polish to English as immigrants frequently do. But Father remained Mr. Kalinski, a respected Polish pharmacist, and Mother Mrs. Kalinska, a respectable Polish housewife. Their earlier decision to anglicise my name to Kalinski[1] continued to lead me into awkward explanations for years to come.

As far back as I'm able to remember the neighbours were friendly, but where we lived, there were few foreigners after the Second World War, and we were still considered quaint outsiders. Well, so Mother maintained. She was always on the defensive, always on her guard, always taking people with a modicum of suspicion.

I want to be clear about this. I did have friends - yes I did. Loneliness manifested itself in the way that I always felt different, apart. Apart from the English world Lisa lived in. I was born in England, it's true, and indeed could speak no more than a Polish phrase or two in those early days. But I didn't feel English; and I didn't feel justified in calling myself Polish. I was Jewish, but "not Jewish". We celebrated Christmas, even though Mother seemed to despise God, and the word 'Jesus' wasn't in either Mother's or Father's vocabulary. I definitely wasn't Christian. But who was I? Where did I belong? Nowhere. It felt as if I was an outsider peeping into a familiar house without having the right to enter any of its rooms.

To my delight, when my bedroom was to be redecorated, Father said that I could choose the décor, and Mother agreed providing I promised not to choose shades of brown, characteristic of homes soon after the Second World War.

Mother preferred bright shades. Even though our furniture was heavy and made of dark wood, her favourite colour was red; and she was therefore pleased with my choice of wallpaper, patterned in tiny dark pink rosebuds; and a new maroon carpet was purchased for my room.

I'm still able to visualise the red Formica table by the window which overlooked the garden and was always referred to as my desk. I see the contents on its surface changing with rapidity as the years pass - like a film fast-forwarding. Frames containing colouring books roll on to refocus as sketch pads. *Beezers* melt into *Bunties*;

---

[1] Polish female surnames normally end in 'a' and male in 'i'.

then as the 1960s arrive, the *New Musical Express*. All the while the hands of the alarm clock move with frightening speed. On the right-hand corner of the desk by the lamp, there's always a diary. First a small navy blue Enid Blyton pocket diary, then a series of girls' red Letts ones, and finally the turquoise Five Year Diary complete with silver padlock.

If it had been within my power to remove one item from my bedroom, it would've been the imposing wardrobe opposite my bed. When it was light, it posed no threat, but once darkness fell and the curtains were drawn, the electric light cast eerie, fluid shadows across the floor and walls. I feared to turn my back on the monster, and was too afraid to stay in the room until I'd checked no burglars were hiding inside.

When I tried to explain to Mother how scared I felt, she refused to entertain such nonsensical fears, and was flippantly dismissive. "Burglars sneaking into wardrobes!" she scoffed. "If the child's reading matter makes her believe these things, Stefan, then her books must be censored."

I'd no idea what censored meant, but I knew it couldn't be good. Terrified that I'd come home from school one day and find my bedroom bookless, I refrained from any further attempts to share my fears with Mother. But a night-light appeared on the landing after the weekend.

My bed flanked the long wall of the bedroom where at its foot stood a hefty mahogany chest of drawers. Over the years a variety of different dolls and teddies sat on the top, keeping guard. By the time I was twelve there remained only two. Mr Bear, whom I adored and would never part with. I loved his fat, round wholesome gold body and those gentle glassy eyes. The other was Polly, my traditional Polish doll given to me by Marek, a friend of the family going back to my parent's childhood days in Kraków. He lived in Ealing, a popular suburb for immigrant Poles, and was the only regular visitor to our house.

On these occasions, almost without fail, Mother would roast a joint of beef or lamb. As I grew older, I suspected she did this to make a point. The point being, that the Kalinskis were very English now. In return Marek always greeted us with "Cześć" to remind us, we were essentially Polish.

Marek was fun. Marek was jovial. Marek brought a breath of fresh air into our house. He tousled my hair as if I were a lad, played Snakes & Ladders and Snap with me. He was tall and thin, giving the impression that he was rather undernourished. His unruly thatch of dark hair and shadow of a beard completed the illusion of self-neglect.

Mother frequently sighed after his departure and said, "That man he needs a good woman, wife to care for him. He needs good food. An iron for clothes. Is it not so?"

She would persist until, with exasperation, Father would reply, "Hania! Marek, he owns delicatessen. And has he not lived with Bronia for many years?"

"But not married. She is not wife."

Yet Marek was Marek - a bit of a Bohemian who played the piano quite badly and painted quite well.

On Mother's better days she'd sometimes surprise me by accepting Lisa's mum's invitation to join them for a picnic. (I called Lisa's mum Auntie Anne and her dad Uncle Greg. In those days children called adults they knew well auntie and uncle - the exception being Marek who said that it made him feel old.) Anyway, picnics then didn't involve fair rides and swimming pools with humpy bumpy slides. No, our picnic spot was a slightly overgrown field surrounded by a band of trees. We chose to call it a wood, but in fact it was not.

Lisa had a brother, Peter, who was almost three years older than us. He was kind and generous with his time, and quite often played with Lisa and myself at the expense of being called "sissy" by some of the local lads. I was glad he wasn't like those tough nuts, stealing girls' berets and chucking them into the bushes. He was Peter, and I liked him.

Picnics meant playing cricket on a wide, open space rather than in the confines of our back gardens; and taking delight in climbing the craggy branches of the trees that knelt down, inviting us to clamber up. I recall on those long ago summer picnics, the sky being always azure blue - and Mother laughing.

Tea was a simple affair - orange squash from a striped blue and white thermos flask; ham and cheese between white slices of Mother's Pride; Swiss roll or custard creams and crunchy apples. In the early 1950s rationing of butter and sweets was still in existence. Therefore, throughout the decade sweets were a rare treat and not expected on every outing. But Auntie Anne wanted these picnics to be special - so after the healthy apples, she'd plunge her hand into the picnic basket and pull out a sixpenny bar of chocolate. Then after a little hesitation, her other hand would dive in, and a second bar would appear. Our eyes were glued on the chocolate, ripe with anticipation. Yet Mother had stopped laughing and always looked away. It was as if the sunlight of her day had disappeared behind black clouds. Her eyes remained averted as her fingers tore petals from daisies, or tugged at tufts of grass.

Auntie Anne would toss her blonde curls and call, "Who's for chocolate then?"

"Me!" we children would cry out in kiddie excitement.

Each child was given an equal share and Auntie Anne broke what was left and offered half to Mother. Even as a child I was embarrassed by the way Mother, without making eye contact, refused in that chilly, distant voice. Luckily Auntie Anne didn't appear to be offended. "Okay. All the more for me," she'd say laughing, and popped the tasty squares into her mouth.

I wasn't forbidden chocolate, nor was it banned from the house, but Mother simply never bought it - ever.

"Mummy," I inquired one day after a picnic, "Why don't you like chocolate?"

"What is there to like or not like?"

At a later date when I asked again, she answered, "And why is it then Child, that you do not like liver?"

Whilst Tommy Steele was singing the blues and the simmering Cold War with Russia fuelled my nightmares, I was encouraged by Father to have opinions on current affairs. Such dilemmas as whether Britain should possess nuclear weapons were discussed over Sunday lunch. I knew that Harold MacMillian was the Conservative leader and Prime Minister. I had more than an inkling as to why the slogan, *You've never had it so good* rang true; but still I had no answer as to why Mother had a number printed on her arm which would not wash off. She always sidestepped the question I eventually no longer dared to ask.

With the arrival of television, the radio, which had previously taken pride of place in the sitting room, was relegated to a corner in the dining room. Mother still followed *The Archers* at quarter to seven on weekdays, but other than that, the radio was largely condemned to silence.

Television was magical there are no two ways about it. And it was television that initially opened my eyes to my own family background. The windows were unlocked, and at last the truth so long denied me began to unfold.

PART TWO

Chapter 2
2008

I'm sitting by the Cloth Market in Kraków sipping my first coffee of the day. As the morning sunlight cuts across the square, I spot a dark haired girl of about eleven. She's wearing a navy blue coat similar to the one I wore at Our Lady of Lourdes. Instantly, I'm back in 1960.

1960

It's my first day at Our Lady of Lourdes. I'm almost ready to leave home and feeling nervous as I'm the only girl from Manor Lodge Primary to have won a free scholarship to this private school with such a good reputation.

"It only takes two girls a year on scholarships, all other pupils must pay," Mother proudly told everyone she met on the day the good news arrived. And the next day, and the next - and the next.

Never mind that it's a Catholic school and all the girls, whatever their religion, must attend Religious Instruction lessons as well as every religious service held during school hours. "I wonder if girls without a religion have to attend too?" I ask myself while adjusting the knot of the unfamiliar navy and white striped tie.

The bus ride to Our Lady of Lourdes will take about forty minutes, and then there's a tedious ten-minute walk to follow. Unlike Manor Lodge where a rough match of bottle green skirt and jumper suffice, the uniform policy at this convent school is strict. I need to get going, but first I must check in the full-length mirror that my navy blue pleated skirt is just below the knee before putting on the regulation coat and the hat which pupils must wear at all times, both to and from school. It's much the same size and shape as the ghastly brown pudding basin cast to the pigs many moons ago. The difference now being, that all the girls, other than sixth formers, are required to wear them.

My new brown leather satchel lies on Mother's twin bed. It contains the brand new equipment, which doubtlessly will soon look worn and shabby. My shiny black fountain pen yearns to write its first words on those clean pages of the new exercise books; the ones I vow to keep neat and tidy until the very end, but feel certain that I'll not quite manage to do. The geometry set is a stranger I have barely acknowledged; but I love the Lakeland pencils lying cosseted in their tin. Twenty perfect unused pencils in a range of different shades. They were bought at Smiths over a fortnight ago and I've resisted using them. However, I have opened the tin daily to admire the collection - like a connoisseur of art does a great painting.

So busy am I thinking about those fine pencils, that I almost forget to pick up the shoe bag, containing my new PE kit and the black indoor-shoes I'm obliged to change into once in the school building. I'm considering what the punishment will be if I forget when Mother calls, "Hurry, Child. It would not be good to be late on first day, would it?"

I think to myself, we're only leaving half an hour earlier than we need to.

Mother insists on accompanying me in spite of us having made a trial run yesterday and the day before that.

"Why does Mum have to take me? I'm not a baby," I moaned during supper last night, hoping to win Father over to my side.

"It is a long way, we worry," he says.

"First day, and such a long journey."

"So why did you make me go to that dumb school which is miles away in the first place?" I butt in. "Then you wouldn't have all the drag of having to go with me, would you?" I say rudely. "I wanted to go to Leven Hill anyway. It *is* a grammar school, you know. And I did pass my eleven plus, remember? But oh no! It's good enough for Lisa and all my friends, but not good enough for me."

Carried away by the injustice, I mimic Mother, "Private school."

"Let us hope this private school does something for the child's manners," Mother says to Father, then sips a little water from her glass.

"Let us all be calm. I think she is nervous perhaps, Hania."

Father turns to me. "But that is not an excuse to be rude. So, all this excitement the night before a big day is not good. No more speaking to your mother like that. She will go with you this once. Now, we eat, right?"

"Not right," I whisper under my breath.

I know they've heard, but they pretend they haven't and we return to the business of dinner.

The front door closes behind us, and I look up towards Lisa's bedroom window. She's getting ready for school, but nevertheless takes the time to wave and mouth good luck. Her term began last week. Like most private schools Our Lady of Lourdes begins during the second week of September. If only I'd gone to Leven Hill Grammar with Lisa, I wouldn't have to be starting a new school today without knowing a soul - and I definitely wouldn't have to suffer the humiliation of being taken to school by my mother.

We set off promptly at 7.15am as planned. We pass the billboards with fresh adverts. Five Boys, with fixed expressions, stare at me across the street; chocolate is the only constant factor in their lives. The chocolate looks delicious, real enough to pluck out and eat. I think of our picnic with Lisa. Only three weeks ago. It feels like an eternity.

After a tedious bus ride and a brisk walk, we come to an abrupt halt at the wrought iron gates which gape open like a receptive open-mouthed whale. The huge rusty brown building with its round towers loom high, reminding me of those Enid Blyton school stories I used to read. In that instant I'm overwhelmed with uncertainty. Should I go in alone? Dare I? I'd made Mother promise to leave me once we reached the entrance. My courage unexpectedly has deserted me. I'm afraid and I feel very small. Instinctively, I slide closer to Mother and look into the vast playground where a huddle of girls stand chatting and giggling - the stamp of friendship. I'm envious. I'm alone.

Too proud to ask Mother to accompany me, I remain glued to the spot and say nothing, hoping against hope she'll conveniently forget her promise and walk with me as I step across the threshold into this new phase of my life.

The playground is bathed in sunlight. A girl with shoulder length, dark hair appears in the doorway of the main school building and strides in our direction. Her arms swing in time with her confident marching. From a distance, I think she bears a resemblance to me, although when she gets closer, I see she's nothing like me. Not only is she smiling broadly, but is much taller and has that curvy shape of a young woman.

"Good morning, and welcome to Our Lady of Lourdes," she says as if she were the headmistress. "I'm Christine Barton, senior prefect. Do come with me."

"Good morning," Mother replies.

I try to smile.

"Come on," Christine says beckoning.

I hear Mother's voice, but am afraid to look at her in case she sees my fear.

"Goodbye," she says, her voice almost inaudible.

"Bye," I whisper back, and then force myself to take a giant step into an uncertain future.

Moments later as I'm trotting behind Christine, I look over my shoulder and catch a glimpse of Mother as she heads for the bus stop. I can't see her face, but her shoulders are hunched and her head bent low. I wonder how she's feeling.

I'm no longer Martina Kalinski, Junior 4 pupil at Manor Lodge Primary; and later in assembly, when the headmistress, Sister Mary Paul addresses us, my head, if not my heart tells me that I now belong to Our Lady of Lourdes.

"From the moment you entered these gates this morning you became First Year students of Our Lady of Lourdes. You are now young ladies of this establishment and we will expect you to behave as such. At this school you will be given every opportunity to succeed. Indeed, the staff and I wish every girl success." She continues in a haughty tone, "Wear your uniform with pride. And always remember young ladies, to study hard and play hard. When times become difficult, as of course sometimes they will, remember our Blessed Lord is always with you."

Standing on the school stage dressed in her black habit, she looks down at us as if from the heights of heaven. With penetrating eyes, she scours each line of girls while she speaks. It's as if she's weighing up each and every one of her new acquisitions. Attentive to every word, I try not to move a muscle in fear of being noticed.

After the pep talk, Sister Mary Paul begins the "Our Father". Without hesitation all the girls and teachers join in. Here I feel safe. We used to say that prayer at primary school. Pleased to be 'one of the crowd' I begin proudly, "Our Father, who art in heaven…" As the chanting proceeds I hear my own voice growing ever louder, until suddenly in horror, I realise that it's the *only* voice. "For thine is the kingdom, the power and the glory. For ev…" Immediately I stop. Heads are turned, all eyes focusing on me. My cheeks are on fire, my heart cold. In a few minutes I will learn that only Protestants pray these words at the end of the "Our Father", but for now I'm baffled and deeply embarrassed.

At last assembly is over, and as we sit waiting to file out, I think how dreary the place looks without brightly coloured posters or pupils' paintings on the walls; only a picture of Mary on one side of the hall, and on the other some saint. I guess he's a saint since he's got a halo thing above his head. High above the stage, just below the ceiling, is a large crucifix with Jesus hanging on it. He must be our Lord, poor thing, I think as I rise from my chair to follow the girl beside me out and onward to what's to be my form room.

When I return home, I unpack my heavy bag and take out a thin booklet which contains all the prayers I'll need to know. The "Hail Mary", the Catholic version of the "Our Father" and the "Angelus" plus the appropriate grace said before eating lunch. I set myself homework that evening; and it's to learn all these prayers off by heart in order to spare myself any further embarrassment.

Friday morning means mass at Our Lady's. I'd in fact not been inside many churches; neither did our family indulge in outings involving this kind of visit. Surprising as it may seem, I'd never sat through a religious service of any kind other than school assemblies or carol services. Most children by the age of eleven would have been invited to a wedding or two, but not me, since I had no extended family, and we had few close family friends. Therefore mass came as quite a shock during my first week, and it amplified my sense of alienation within this Catholic environment.

After registration we form a crocodile behind our form teacher Mrs. O'Sullivan and begin to troop across the grounds towards the chapel. I'm worried about mass, but don't like to ask anyone what it will entail or how long it will last. Krysia, who's rapidly becoming my friend moans, "Hope there's not going to be a long boring sermon."

"God, same here," says Sinéad from behind.

They chatter on as we walk along the winding pathway to the chapel. In front we stop by the flowerbeds. Noisy conversation continues while I admire the deep pink roses and wait for the prefects to tell us when to go in. Once inside, the talking stops immediately. Sister Mary Paul appears and leads us to the front pews where our form will sit for the duration of this academic year.

The silence is razor sharp. I like the stillness, and as I look around the chapel, I'm overcome with its ornate beauty. What a contrast to the school hall. A huge stained-glass window in shades of reds, blues and purples provides a stunning backdrop to the altar. The brightness of the sunshine creates the illusion of the pictures being three-dimensional. And only yards away hangs Jesus Christ dying on the cross. It dawns on me as I notice the sad expression on Jesus' face, that it was the Jews who were responsible for killing him. In dismay I squirm in my seat as I think about me being a traitor amongst all these Christians; and I hope no one here will ever find out that I'm Jewish.

Luckily, so far no one's even hinted that I might be.

While this worrying thought careers around my brain, I hear the bell for the start of mass. Quickly I leap up with everyone else. The elderly priest, garbed in decorative green robes is coming out of the door on our side of the chapel, right in front of me. As he walks past, I'm overcome in a different way - by a revolting, pungent smoke puffing out of a tarnished bronze vessel dangling at the end of a chain. The nun with him, who carries it, waves it in the direction of my face. Trying to suppress the urge to cough, I take out my handkerchief and pretend to blow my nose. Noticing that no one else seems surprised or troubled by this "smoke", I wonder where the other non-Catholics are sitting. (I discover at break-time that the "smoke" is in fact incense.)

In the meantime, everyone else's faces are deadpan while they wait for the start of the mass. I kneel, I sit, I stand, I mumble what I hope sounds like the correct Latin responses, and all the while I'm cursing Mother and Father for sending me here. They could have at least taught me a few basic things about the religion before I started. I feel like an alien uncomfortable in my disguise.

I observe a silver cup being raised by the priest, and the nun who assists him, rings a small bell. From nowhere a wasp appears. Soon it's buzzing round the priest's head and shoulders. Unaware of the danger, he continues praying and lifting the cup up and down. This provides me with a welcome distraction. No longer paying attention to the proceedings, I conjure up the hilarious scenario which entails the wasp stinging the priest. I bow my head, trying to stop myself from laughing as I imagine what could ensue. The priest, in my mind, would be leaping in agony, pulling at the robes harbouring the trapped wasp. My imagination is on a roll now, and the wasp, angry at being imprisoned, is stinging its way around his body. The cup flies through the air landing with an almighty crash. The little white, round wafers shower in all directions; and best of all is the expression of horror and dismay on Sister Mary Paul's face. Oh what joyous chaos!

Another ringing of the bell brings me back to earth, and I feel a pang of guilt for wishing such a dreadful thing on anyone - especially a priest. By this stage of the mass, Holy Communion is being distributed to those who are entitled to receive it; and that definitely doesn't include me.

With the words "Ite, missa est", the mass is over. Like an elderly cuckoo returning to the cubby-hole in a clock, the priest vanishes through the side door and we girls are being herded to lessons.

In less than a month, I realise with amazement that I've grown quite accustomed to the strange Catholic rituals. Sitting with me on a bench beside the netball courts are my three special friends, Krysia, Mary and Sinéad. I'm looking forward to playing goal attack in the new First Year netball team. In primary school, although loving the sport, I'd never even been considered for reserve. With disappointment now a thing of the past, I wait pleased as Punch for Mrs. O'Sullivan, who's both our form mistress and PE teacher. She'll be taking our very first netball practice of the season. I'm so happy.

Sinéad, with her gentle Irish lilt says to me, "You're a super shooter, so you are. Goal!" she cries as she leaps into the air imitating my shooting technique.

"Yeah!" cries Krysia jumping up to defend the imaginary goal.

Mary, who is short, skinny and a bundle of energy, plays centre because she's incredibly fast at darting around the court and dodging opponents. At present she's quietly seated on the bench, smiling at these antics as she munches her apple.

I'm delighted with these friendships, and find myself praying that they'll last. It's my dream that by the time we make Third Year, we'll be just like the Four Marys in the *Bunty* - friends forever; friends through thick and thin.

Our Lady of Lourdes, ironically, begins to feel more like home than my real home. I look forward to the approach of Mondays. The lessons are generally more interesting than those during my last two primary years. English, History, Music and of course PE are my favourite subjects. Most of the teachers are pretty strict, although fair and usually pleasant. Mrs. O'Sullivan, I adore, she's the best. She's quite young; yet she manages to be both motherly as well as a brilliant teacher. Some of my classmates are perpetually falling out, but Mrs. O'Sullivan somehow always manages to find the time to mediate, and miraculously, they're friends again. Fortunately, falling out isn't a thing that's happened to me so far and I'm determined to avoid it at all costs. I want nothing to spoil these halcyon days.

Chapter 3
1960

October 29th 1960. Today is Lisa's twelfth birthday party and I've been invited even though we haven't exchanged more than a few words for several weeks. Since we've been at different schools our paths rarely meet. I leave early and return home so much later than she does. Then there's the pile of homework which takes up a great deal of my time - and Sundays are still a "no go area" with regards to inviting friends to the house.

It's Saturday, and I find myself rushing through the front door at 1.45pm having returned from playing my first netball match against another school, St. Bede's. I'm jubilant until I see Mother with sour expression, standing arms folded in front of the cooker.

"And why you are *so* late?"

"I told you ages ago I might be. St. Bede's is miles away. And the coach didn't pick us up on… Oh never mind. Actually, I'm lucky to be home *this* soon," I say tugging off my school tie and kicking my PE bag into the corner by the kitchen cupboard. I edge towards the door planning my escape to the bathroom before Mother calls me back for lunch; but I grow tentative when I realise she's ladling spoonfuls of vegetable soup over the sides of the bowl.

"Mum!" I call out. "Watch what you're doing."

The soup by this time has begun to flow across the table and is trickling down the side onto the floor.

"It is all your fault."

"Oh!" I exclaim seizing a cloth and beginning to mop it up, now resigned to the prospect of having to sit and eat what she has spent hours cooking. She's really angry, I can tell, far angrier than a little spilt soup should warrant.

"What's wrong?"

"What is wrong? What is wrong? You are late Child. That is what is wrong…"

"But you knew…"

"Do not interrupt when your mother speaks. Sit. Eat."

"But it's Lisa's party and I haven't even wrapped the bath salts and talc..."

"Eat, Child eat," she says banging an empty bowl hard on the table laid for two. "Good soup is not made to be wasted."

It's not untypical of Mother, to be in a good frame of mind at breakfast and by lunchtime utterly in the dumps. Inwardly, I sigh and just get on with the supping of soup and remember how very pleased Mother and Father had been when I told them I'd been selected to play in the First Year netball team.

After a few minutes Mother says less harshly, "It is party of your friend, so do not worry. Lisa understands it is honour to represent your school this way." (Mother pronounces the "h" in honour - in spite of me perpetually correcting her.) But today I let it go. I've noticed a letter with a Polish stamp lying on the far side of the table. "Who's the letter from?" I ask. "Didn't think you knew anyone from Poland anymore?"

"I do not," she snaps. The letter vanishes into her apron pocket. Suddenly she recognises the urgency for me to rush. "Less talk and more eating, or you will be very late. It is not polite to be late for party. Come on hurry, Child."

Hiccupping, I gallop up the stairs, quickly bath, wrap the present, scribble my signature on the birthday card and pull my red tartan tunic over the soft white jumper Mother knitted. Ready, and only half an hour late, I leap over the low bushes that separate our front gardens. At last I'm rapping on the front door.

"Hello!" greets Auntie Anne in her usual friendly manner, not at all put out by my lateness. She shakes her blonde curls in the direction of their back room. She looks so pretty, like Doris Day I think. "They're in there, love."

"Thank you Auntie Anne," I reply wishing Mother were more like her.

Singing, or to be more accurate, screeching rings from behind the closed door. I grow more and more reluctant to intrude as the chorusing of "Seven Little Girls" continues. I'm still in the hall when Auntie Anne reappears.

"You okay?"

"Fine," I fib.

"Mum okay?" This makes me curious as to why Mother shouldn't be.

"Fine," I repeat opening the door.

In front of me are five girls dressed in the latest flared skirts. As they sing and sway these bob up and down over stiff petticoats. Their legs boast silky stockings and there are no home-knitted jumpers for them. Lisa and another girl Norma, who'd attended Manor Lodge Primary, are wearing identical machine knitted v-neck air force blue cardigans without blouses underneath, whereas the three girls who I don't know, are wearing tiny, clingy baby pink cashmere sweaters. I picture myself standing there in my tartan tunic and long white socks wishing the earth would swallow me up. They've grown into mini teenagers and I'm not part of their world.

It's not hard to see Lisa's embarrassment as she turns down the record player and hastily introduces me to her new friends from Leven Hill Grammar.

"This is Martina. She lives next door." She emphasises the *she lives next door* wanting everyone to understand the reason why it was necessary to invite this real baby.

Trying to sound casual, I say, "Happy birthday. Sorry I'm late. It was because I was playing netball against another school and I didn't get home 'til quarter to two."

With that, I hand Lisa her birthday present and sit down on the nearest chair. I want to run away, but inner stubbornness prevents me from acting like a baby even if I look like one.

"Ooh, netball," mocks Norma.

"And did you win?" asks Carol, the one with brown hair fashionably backcombed into a beehive. When she turns slightly to her left, I think it looks remarkably like a hedgehog.

"Three one to us," I say with pride.

"Smashing," says the strawberry blonde who's sitting on the floor flipping through Lisa's pile of 45's.

"Yeh, smashing," echoes Norma.

All Lisa does is nod. I'm not sure what that's meant to signify.

Mandy, too busy swinging her mousy ponytail and dancing to the rhythm of the music, doesn't even acknowledge my presence. She's miming the words of "Seven little Girls". All she needs is a microphone in her hand and she'd be a pop star on TV. In her dreams!

"You go to that Catholic school now, don't you?" inquires Norma pretending she doesn't know.

"Yes, Our Lady of Lourdes," I answer cautiously, curious as to what will come out of her mouth next.

"But you're not Catholic?"

"There are tons of girls at the school who aren't Catholics," I exaggerate. "You don't have to be Catholic to go there, you know."

The record's finished and the other girls suddenly become attentive.

"Well, what's the point of a Catholic school if it takes any old person then?" points out Hedgehog.

I can't think of a good reason so just blurt out, "It's just a school." My answer sounds pathetic even to me.

"You're Jewish anyway aren't you?" says Norma putting me in the hot seat.

"Jewish?" echoes Strawberry Blonde.

"I've never even been in a synagogue." I'm looking to Lisa for help here, but she's busying herself with the choosing of the next record.

Fortunately for me, Auntie Anne sticks her head round the door to tell us tea's ready and we should be moving through to the lounge very soon. The dining room table, which is normally in the back room, has been put in the lounge for the party; and on this, a buffet has been placed. A year ago we would've been on our feet and through the door like cats to a fish supper, but twelve months on, nobody wants to appear keen, so we all just sit there. Auntie Anne returns, "Hurry up you lot. I'll have eaten all the best food myself if you don't get in there quick."

There's the usual party fare of sandwiches, cocktail sausages, iced fairy cakes with hundreds and thousands, biscuits and my favourite chocolate cornflake cakes. In the centre is the pink and white birthday cake with twelve candles.

At the sight and smell of the tempting food, sophistication and maturity are quickly forgotten. Food is piled onto the plates and the hungry girls flop down into either the sofa or a deep armchair. Strawberry Blonde is in such a rush to sit beside Norma on the sofa that a couple of egg sandwiches and a fairy cake slip from her plate, ending up in a mound on the new beige carpet. Lisa, who hasn't noticed, treads on this little pile, squelching it into a mush. Auntie Anne, without a smile, rushes over with cloth in hand; and I'm betting that she's regretting this adult buffet idea.

I sit on the stool in the corner by the television. Lisa's opposite. She's hardly spoken to me since my arrival. The present I gave her is left unopened in the other room. I guess she was afraid to unwrap it in front of her pals in case I'd bought her a doll, or something equally childish.

The tea-time conversation is centred on boys. The ones they fancy from their school; and then a less animated diatribe follows about some stupid teacher who keeps forgetting which kids have done, or not done, their homework. It's impossible for me to join in, and to be frank, I don't really want to. In the middle of all this, Lisa looks over at me, and she smiles sheepishly as if to apologise for needing to be so stand-offish.

The food disappears quickly from the table. It's amazing to realise these girls can eat like gannets yet remain so slim. Auntie Anne offers round what's left over. Even though I've little appetite, I'm unable to resist my favourite chocolate cornflake cakes. Savouring the three I've taken, I try to make them last by breaking off the flakes, one at a time.

Uncle Greg, already dressed for work comes into the lounge when it's time for the birthday cake. Yesterday morning, on my way to school I bumped into him coming home from the hotel where he works as night manager. In his hands he held a box containing Lisa's cake, made by the chef. He told me he had very nearly forgotten to collect the blessed thing from the kitchen. Apparently, there had been "panic stations" due to a boiler breaking down, and no hot water in some of the bedrooms.

When Peter appears, I'm particularly pleased to see him. I hardly ever see Peter these days. He's getting on for fifteen now, and as a Fourth Year has better things to do than spending his time with First Years.

"Happy birthday!" calls Uncle Greg. Peter repeats this in a gruff squeaky voice, which makes me wonder if he is starting a cold. He turns to me and says, "Hiya! Your school still all right?"

"It's nice," I reply while Uncle Greg lights the candles and Strawberry Blonde turns off the standard lamp. Once "Happy Birthday" has been sung, I feel a burning need to escape. The cue comes when Lisa announces that we're going to prepare a dance routine to Tommy Steele's "Little White Bull" of all things.

"I'm feeling a little bit sick," I say to Auntie Anne.

She smiles. "I'm not surprised love, after all those chocolate things you ate."

With that, I call out, "Bye" to anyone who cares to listen and flee without waiting to hear if anyone replies.

This day, which had begun so well, grinds to a gloomy end. I sense the tension as soon as I enter the house. Mother's alone. She's not cooking; neither is she watching television which is her usual practice after preparing the evening meal. Her expression is stony as she sits at the dining room table knitting in steady robotic rhythm. I recognise *that* mood. The one I dread.

"Hi!" I say cheerily pretending I've not noticed her surliness.

She looks up at me, "Hello," she says without enthusiasm and produces a weary smile. Then, as if feeling obligated, she enquires if I'd had a nice time.

"Yes very, thanks," I answer spotting beside Mother's wool basket, the letter from Poland, the one I'd seen earlier. A tiny corner of paper is peeping from the envelope.

I don't want to venture into the darkness of my bedroom, so instead I go into the sitting room and switch on the television. *Six-Five Special* - I love that programme. As I snuggle into the armchair I hope Cliff Richard will sing my favourite song "Living Doll".

Father comes home soon after. He's keen to know the score of my netball match; and then he asks how Lisa's party went. I'm glad he's home. That's until he declares *Six-Five Special* to be rubbish. Pointing at the television set, he remarks scathingly, "They look ridiculous, all that waving of arms. Why do they not stand still and sing properly?"

He then turns over to ATV in hope of catching the *News*. Like everyone else in the world these days, he wants an update on the American election; how the handsome young Jack Kennedy's presidential campaign is getting along.

But there's no *News*, only a preview of a programme soon to be broadcast. It's a clip of a city being bombed. Warsaw. I do know that my parents' families died in Poland during the Second World War. The following shots are of masses of distressed people on a platform being herded towards railway freight carriages. Father's looking most uncomfortable. He begins to rub his left cheek. I want to ask him questions, but I don't know where to start.

Shortly he's up and BBC is back on screen. "You can have your programme," he says leaving the room. "Hania, when is it we eat?"

The final credits of *Six-Five Special* are rolling up, so I switch off the television, and watch the silver dot grow smaller and smaller until it disappears altogether.

Chapter 4
1960
Next day

The door is ajar. I can just about see them. I'm hiding in the cupboard surrounded by Wellington boots of different sizes. The soldiers have their backs to me and are searching slowly and systematically. Their boots are heavy and their bodies thickset. I'm terrified. It's like being in a silent film, for they're speaking, but I can't hear a word they say. They have not as yet opened the cupboards on my side of the kitchen, but it'll not be long. There's no escape. The long rifles are viciously prodding anything and everything in view. Sugar streams from a pierced packet; saucepans crash to the floor, and then from nowhere fly potatoes, leeks and carrots. One of the soldiers has a letter in his hand. It's the one from Poland, but much fatter, almost a parcel. It's being ripped apart; now thrown aside. I feel it in my bones; they're after me. And when they find me, I'm certain they'll kill me. One of the soldiers turns, and Norma looks straight at me.

I wake up with a start. It's 3 o'clock. No. I look at the clock again and see in fact it's already 8 o'clock. My heart is pounding and cold tears begin to trickle down my cheeks. I lie without moving, rooted in the nightmare until I become aware of the heavy rain pelting against the windowpane. I'm trying to rally from the dream when the memory of yesterday's dreadful party surfaces. I hear movement downstairs. Usually on a Sunday morning, I like to stay in bed a while and read; however today I'm in no mood for *The Lion, the Witch and the Wardrobe*, so instead I get up.

It's good to find Father at the kitchen sink filling the kettle - and no soldiers.

"Morning," I say surprised to see him up before Mother.

"Mum she has some stomach pain today. I think it best she stays in bed."

Once Father has taken Mother a glass of warm water, still in dressing gowns, we share a pot of tea and some toast with the wonderful plum jam Mother made last week. Father thumbs through the Sunday paper while I stare out of the window at the denuded trees, furiously waving their branches in the gathering wind.

After breakfast I'm asked to throw the tea leaves into the dustbin. Teapot in hand, I open the back door, lift up the metal lid, and there it is - the letter from Poland. Its envelope is rent in two whilst the pages seem to have been shredded into a hundred or more pieces. They lie scattered like tiny snowflakes across this week's refuse.

Chapter 5
1960
The following Tuesday

In English we're studying Shakespeare. At the beginning of term we studied *Tales from Shakespeare* by Charles and Mary Lamb, and now we're embarking on a more in-depth study of *The Merchant of Venice*.

Having already flicked through the pages, I'm pretty sure that this is the play with a Jewish character. I feel apprehensive.

"Girls, put everything down, just look up and listen." Irritated by the dropping of pencils and shuffling of books, Sister Ingrid tosses aside her own copy of Charles and Mary Lamb then proceeds to narrate, in fairy tale mode, the story in her own words.

"Many years ago, hundreds of years ago, in Venice, there lived a nobleman. His name was Bassanio. Before long, like most young men who have too much money and little sense, he's squandered all his wealth and has virtually nothing left." She pauses and asks a really obvious question. "Put your hand up girls if you think he's going to regret such foolishness?"

Without exception every hand in the class shoots into the air.

"Certainly he does, just like the Prodigal Son."

Her slow delivery of the story, peppered with comparisons from situations in the Bible, is almost sending me to sleep, until I hear, "You see girls, Shylock the Jewish money lender, hates Antonio for spitting on him in the Rialto. Like most Christians at that time, Antonio despises Jews…"

"And why would they be hatin' Jews, Sister?" interrupts Sinéad without putting her hand up.

"Yes. Why?" demand others in the class.

Sister Ingrid is anxious to provide background, so she establishes silence then proceeds to explain that Jews had been hated for many centuries - for two main reasons. "Firstly," she declares, "because Jesus was crucified by the Jews; and secondly you see, in Shakespeare's day it was considered sinful to lend money with interest, and Jewish money-lenders did precisely this. Of course, all bankers would be sinners today if this was still the case, wouldn't they girls? They all charge interest."

She's laughing now, amused by her own little joke; but she fast resumes a serious demeanour. "Yes, Shylock was hated by Christians, like all Jews were at that time. Now girls," she hastens to add, "what you've got to remember is, that it's not like that today."

"But Sister, the Germans hated the Jews, didn't they? And the war wasn't *all* that long ago," calls Sonia from the back of the classroom.

"Yeah, that's why they gassed them," chimes up someone else.

"Uh! That was the Nazis," states Mary.

"Same thing. Germans. Nazis - whatever," says Sonia.

Sister Ingrid coughs and it's clear to me that she's not comfortable with the way this is going, so immediately she stops any further discussion and resumes her rendition of Shakespeare's tale.

During the last ten minutes of the lesson we read through the speech from Act 1 scene 3 in which Shylock rants at Antonio about being spat upon in the Rialto:-

Signior Antonio, many a time and oft, in the Rialto, you have rated me...

We're set the task of writing the speech in our own words for homework.

When we arrive at the bus stop after school that afternoon, every bus that comes along is already crowded with pupils from the nearby secondary modern. We groan and protest as there's a real nip in the air. But actually I'm pleased, because it provides me with a great excuse to carry on gossiping with Krysia, Sinéad and Mary. Krysia lives less than half a mile from Our Lady's and doesn't need to travel on the bus, but hangs back to chat anyway. The conversation returns to the English lesson. She pipes up with, "Hey, you know what Sister Ingrid said about people these days not hating Jews?"

"Yeah!" Sinéad and Mary answer in unison.

"Well, actually I think that's rubbish."

"I don't see why it's rubbish. I mean after all the gas chambers and vile things the Nazis did to the Jews in the war, Krysh. I'd think most people feel dead sorry for them," Mary says.

"That's a load of trash actually, 'cause a couple of weeks ago, I overheard my dad talking to my mum, and he was telling her that Dr. Lieberman, who lives across the road from us, wasn't allowed to be a member of the golf club. Why? 'Cause he's Jewish. That's what Dad said anyway."

"What 'cause he's a Jew? Blimey, that's unbelievable, isn't it Sinéad?" says Mary.

"Crackers."

This is the moment to unburden myself, reveal my guilty secret. Weeks ago we made a pact never to keep anything from each other. Best friends - no secrets. And all the while I've been hiding the greatest secret possible - my Jewishness.

I'm at the point of spilling the beans when Sinéad comes out with, "To be sure those golf fellas sound just like me da, so they do. Da hates everyone who's not a Catholic."

Krysia glowers at her and surreptitiously nods in my direction.

"Sinéad!" blurts out Mary.

Hand covers mouth. It's plain to see that Sinéad is mortified. "Oh sorry, Martina, I'm so sorry." And there she is giving me a bear hug.

"It's a porky anyway, because Sinéad's dad's really nice," puts in Mary.

Sinéad is smiling at me. "Oh yeah, as long as you're a *Christian* that is." She's now laughing so loudly that half the bus queue is looking at her.

My secret remains untold.

It's already dark by the time I turn the corner into Woodland Avenue. The wind is up, whining through the bare winter branches. I know I'm late and wonder if this will mean trouble.

Hurrying down the road, I'm debating whether to tackle the Geometry questions before Shylock's speech, when I see an ambulance. It's parked outside Lisa's house. On second thoughts I think it might be outside our house. Fear cuts me like a knife. I'm petrified. What's happened? Who has it come for? I'm running, running so fast.

Chapter 6
1960
Same day

As I approach the ambulance, I see that our front door is the one wide open; and within seconds two ambulance men appear carrying a stretcher. Lying on it is Mother. “Mum! Mum!” My voice sounds miles away, as if it belongs to someone else. I love Mother as I’ve never loved her before.

“Where have you been?” Father scolds the moment he sees me.

He carries on speaking, but just like in so many of my dreams, the words are incomprehensible.

“Mum,” I whimper walking alongside the stretcher as it journeys to the ambulance. Looking down at her, I see she’s very pale; her face taut, skimmed with a damp film. She opens her eyes, looks up at me. Her hand reaches from under the red blanket and takes mine. She manages a smile. “It is all right Child, only appendix.”

Uncle Greg had his appendix out a few years ago, so I know that appendicitis isn’t too serious. “Oh!” is all that I’m able to say as I watch Father follow the stretcher. He tells me to stay with Auntie Anne until he gets back from the hospital. Mother holds her smile as the stretcher is lifted up into the back of the ambulance. Pain fits her like a comfortable glove.

Auntie Anne is by my side as the ambulance pulls away.

“Don’t worry love, she’ll be fine,” she says. “Let’s go inside, it’s getting really cold.” Her comforting arm is round my shoulder and I snuggle up to her as we walk towards the house.

Lisa’s in the back room doing her homework. She’s filling in a map of the British Isles - the cities and the physical features. We’re on equal ground, both wearing our school uniforms. Our exchange about homework is easy, and we even laugh heartily at the twin *Whitmarsh 1* French textbooks lying side by side on the table. For a while we’re back to our primary school friendship. That’s until Norma shows up.

“See you in a bit.” Lisa’s tone is decidedly chilly as they disappear upstairs into her bedroom, and I’m left with Shylock’s speech.

Thankfully, Norma leaves before we eat. To my surprise I'm very hungry and gobble down several slices of leftover roast beef from Sunday's lunch, and accept seconds of potatoes and green beans.

"When will Dad be home?" asks Peter. "I need to ask him if he'll be able to come to my school carol concert. Got to order tickets by next Wednesday."

"Are you singing then?" Lisa laughs.

"Don't be daft, 'course I'm not singing, I'm reading a poem."

"A poem?" she sniggers.

"Yeah, you might've seen them in books. Written in verses, they have rhythm…"

"For goodness sake, stop it you two. Dad's working double shifts until Christmas, so unless it's his day off, it's unlikely, love. But check with him tomorrow."

After supper I return to Shylock. My version is coming along quite well.

You say I am not a Christian and a horrid person,
Then you spit on my clothes.
All because I take interest for the money that I lend to people
And now you want my help…

I'm really getting into this speech when Lisa enters. Now Norma is no longer here she's anxious to be friendly again. Oblivious to the mound of books in front of me, she begins to gossip about some boy in her class she fancies. Not wanting to be rude I listen and make, what I hope, are the right noises; but all the while I'm concerned about getting this homework finished. I've still got the Geometry to complete before tomorrow, and am worried about finding time to fit in some violin practice because I have a lesson tomorrow during lunchtime. I really enjoy playing the violin, and all of us beginners have been told that if we don't come up to scratch by the end of our first term, we won't be allowed to continue. Besides, Father has promised me private lessons if I show promise.

Emergency Ward 10 saves the day. Today of all days, that's the last television programme I wish to see; however Lisa's off her chair in a flash, leaving me to finish the speech before making a start on the Geometry.

Tired, I find it hard to concentrate when I get to the Maths. It's been a couple of hours since Mother was taken into hospital and I'm wondering if she's had the operation by now. Father hasn't phoned. Is this a good sign, or a bad one? During one episode of *Emergency Ward 10* I recall a woman dying, and it came as a tremendous shock to everyone because as Dr. Rennie told Sister, "It was only a routine operation."

Shortly after the current episode of *Emergency Ward 10*, Peter comes into the room. "You okay? Want a drink or anything?"

"No thanks."

Immediately he tunes into my anxiety. "Auntie Hania, I mean, your mum, will be fine, you'll see…"

"It's not that. I'm stuck on a blasted Geometry question."

"Not like you."

"Yeah well, I'm a bit tired tonight."

To my relief Peter sits down and helps me.

It's not long before there's a knock at the front door. Father I hope. But no, it's Marek. It turns out that he'd been invited to supper; and with all the drama of Mother's emergency, no one had thought to phone him and tell him not to come. It's becoming like Piccadilly Circus on a Saturday night, for within seconds there's another knock, and this time it is Father.

Father, horrified at having forgotten Marek's visit, apologises; then with no further delay, breaks the good news that Mother's operation went well, although, there was a complication because the appendix had been fused to the bowel. No wonder Mother had been in poor spirits for some time; she must have been suffering a great deal of pain over a long period.

"You two need a little drink," says Auntie Anne after rebuking Lisa for still being glued to "the box" and not having made a start at drying the dishes.

"No, thank you," replies Father anxious to get home.

Half an hour later however, I'm still working on Geometry with Peter, and through the wall we can hear the three of them talking.

The grandfather clock chimes 9 o'clock as we enter the house. Father's keen for me to practise the violin and then go to bed as soon as possible, although first he wants a quick word. The sitting room's freezing, so he at once lights the fire while Marek dashes into the kitchen to make hot drinks.

"Soon be warm," he declares more merrily than perhaps the occasion merits. But that's Marek, always trying to make the best of things.

"So," says Father as we sit before the roaring fire, "Mum she will recover, therefore there is no need for you to worry. But the situation is this. You must not come back to empty house after school. You see, after work, I will go to hospital. Auntie Anne, very kindly has said you can go there until I return."

"I don't need to go next door. Just give me a key, and I'll let myself in…"

"No, you are only eleven years old. You will not come back to empty house, be alone. And then there is question of supper…"

"God, I'll be twelve soon. I'm not a little kid, you know."

Father's tired and irritable. "No more discussion!"

Here I play my trump card.

"You don't know how difficult it is to get my homework done properly next door. Lisa keeps talking to me, so I can't concentrate.(I don't mention Peter's help.) And what about my violin practice?"

He suddenly appears more sympathetic. In truth, I don't much relish the thought of coming home to a dark, lonely house, but it's preferable to the alternative. Marek comes to the rescue. "I have suggestion. As you know Bronia has gone to visit her daughter in Toronto, so I help out with this problem." Father does not silence *him.* "You see, Margot she can look after shop. So without problem, I can leave, and be here in good time for Martina when she comes home from school. The supper too is solved. A man who owns deli will never starve - nor will his friends. What do you say, Stefan?"

A weight lifts from my shoulders when I hear Father agree, but in the same instant I worry that Auntie Anne may be offended. "Who will tell her?"

"You always worry. Auntie Anne she will agree it's easier all way round." He then turns to Marek. "You like to stay here? You know there is spare room."

"It makes sense. Yes, I stay. From Thursday though. I have some arrangement tomorrow in evening."

"Good, it is decided. Please now, violin Martina, then bed."

Wednesday evening, after netball practice, I don't hang about chatting, but hurry to catch the bus before rush hour. I've found it hard to concentrate all day and am now eager to learn how Mother is. Wednesday's half-day closing so Father's able to go to the hospital and still be home before me.

It's perhaps not hard to guess that he must have phoned the school, because Sister Mary Paul made a point of approaching me in the dining hall, and to my embarrassment asked if I was, "Holding up all right."

Even worse, during afternoon registration, Mrs. O'Sullivan excused me from netball practice. I told her I'd be there.

Today is colder than yesterday. The frost lies thick like glinting snow. In spite of the pavements being slippery I walk fast, trying not to slide. I hurry past the Five Boys poster, the Baptist church, and speed up into a trot as I turn into Woodland Avenue. Our house comes into view. Seeing a light in the sitting room window makes me feel safe. It's good to realise Father will be there and I'll not have to face darkness alone.

While I drink a glass of milk he informs me that Mother's still feeling pretty groggy. This, he says is only to be expected after abdominal surgery. She's on a drip and will be unable to eat solids for a while. Nonetheless, the doctors are satisfied with her progress so far.

I don't have much homework tonight because the Geography teacher was away. The Science homework, drawing the water cycle will take approximately ten minutes, and the diary for History, written from the point of view of a Medieval Lord of the Manor, doesn't need to be handed in until after the weekend. I sit at the kitchen table and copy the water cycle from the textbook while Father heats up Hungarian goulash from a jar and slices the remains of a loaf of bread. Once I've finished, before packing away, I show him the diagram, then go to dump my school bag in the hall.

Lying on the carpet by the front door is a letter boasting a Polish stamp. I'm pretty certain it wasn't there earlier, but who knows? Gingerly I pick it up; it's addressed to Mother.

I recognise the writing. If I could read Polish, I'd open it, but since I can't, I decide to dispose of it instead. The last thing I want is to risk Mother coming home to it and being upset. Father, wearing Mother's apron, is standing in the kitchen doorway calling me to supper. Quickly I dive down, seize it and stuff it into my school bag. "I'll chuck it in a bin on my way to school tomorrow," I say to myself.

Chapter 7
1960
Same evening

Eating supper without Mother feels strange. Father takes the lead in telling me to eat all the meat. I spread butter on my bread while he prefers it dry; and later I ask if I may spread a little plum jam on the last slice. Usually I'm not allowed to unless my dinner plate is clean. But today he says, "Why not?"

We linger at the table discussing my progress on the violin and my ambition to play in the school orchestra. He asks about netball, and for once Science and Maths don't feature in the mealtime conversation. As we peel our oranges he says, "You seem to like this school. I am glad. And I think you have good friends."

Warming to this topic, I proceed to talk about Krysia, Sinéad and Mary until at last he points to his watch, reminding me that I still have violin practice. I feel relaxed and happy as I sail through the scales and a couple of Grade 1 pieces.

The *News* has finished when I venture downstairs, and there in the sitting room I find Father glued to the programme previewed last month. I recognise some of the sequences, Warsaw being razed to the ground. The commentator remarks that other Polish cities suffered massive devastation too, he mentions Kraków. An interview with a survivor follows. The woman describes how she was a small child during the bombings in Poland; and how in the middle of the night her house was destroyed.

I lay there in my bed with what felt like the whole world toppling upon me. So scared was I, that I hid beneath the covers. When I dared to look across to side of the room where my brother and twin sisters slept, all I saw, it was a cloud of dust curtaining the sky. I remember screaming, fleeing to my mother's room. "Mamusiu! Mamusiu!" I cried. It was useless because she was lying beside her bed, muttering, barely conscious, and in minutes she was dead. Terrified, not knowing what to do, I ran out into the street; however it was hopeless, for everyone in the houses on either side of road had been killed. The houses they were in fact little more than rubble. My beloved family - almost the entire neighbourhood buried under debris.

Even after so many years the woman on TV still weeps.

For how long exactly I stayed alone, she says, *I cannot be certain, but my memory is, that during those following days, I wandered up and down many streets, howling for my mother, my brother and sisters. While all the time, even at four years old, deep down, I knew I would never see them again.*

The programme continues showing other horrific scenes and painful interviews. For the first time in my life I see film footage of Auschwitz. A voice-over sounding very much like Hitler's, shouts in German. Words I am unable to understand, but it doesn't take a genius to work out that *Judenschwein* is not intended as a compliment. There's a knock on the front door. This breaks the spell of horror.

It's Mrs. Carr, the elderly lady who lives next door, at number 62. "Sorry to disturb you dearie," she says as if she's come to ask a favour, "but I was wonderin' how your mummy is?"

I assure her that she's doing fine, and with that, she hands me a box of chocolates, then hurries back down the path.

The television screen is blank when I return to the sitting room. Father declares, "We have seen enough for one night. Not good to watch such things before going to sleep."

We're touched by Mrs. Carr's kindness and indeed delighted with the chocolates. With a devilish glint in his eye Father lifts the lid. "Come, we eat. Mum, she won't want them."

I'm on to my third chocolate, a strawberry cream when out of the blue I feel courageous and say, "Tell me what happened to you and Mum in the war. I don't know why you won't ever talk about it. It's not a big secret, everyone knows about the Second World War. Oh, and I'm not completely stupid. I do know we're Jewish, known for ages actually - Dad, don't you think I'm old enough to know what happened to my own family?"

Silence. Father scratches the side of his nose.

"To bed."

I remain firmly planted in the chair. "No, I'm not going. It's so unfair. I need to know. Can't you see that? Please, Dad."

To my amazement he relents; but carries on to tell me what I already know - about my parents being childhood friends; his father managing the local post office, and Mother's being a bank manager in the Kazimierz Quarter. He clears his throat, and then states that he met up with Mother again in Kraków after the war.

"Yes, yes, I know that." I'm longing for him to talk about what I don't know.

"This question you ask about why Mum and I do not speak of our Jewish background." He hesitates. Sighs, and sighs again. It's plain to see he's finding this difficult.

"You have read *The Diary of Anne Frank*. I saw this book with you when you were in junior school."

I nod.

"Then you must know how people felt about Jews, and how life was for them. And before Second World War, all over Europe, it is also true that Jews they were not always liked so very much. Many were quite rich, had good businesses; often they were clever, intelligent - you know how it is Martina - even with children in school. Sadly, success breeds jealousy. So, it was in Germany, the Nazis they brought in laws of segregation - Jews to be in separate schools, shops, buses. Jews they must have their own doctors and so on. Gradually houses, properties, as well as jobs they were confiscated - stolen by Nazis. Anyone who was even suspected of being Jewish was in danger. Of course, you know this."

I nod again.

"But it was not only in Germany where such things happened. This hatred spread across to many countries in Europe - all those Hitler conquered; and this included Poland. Yes, it was an extremely difficult time to be Jewish - to survive. People did not advertise the fact. And you see, old habits, they die hard. It is not so very easy. You must know such a saying - it is hard for leopards to change spots."

"Yeah, but nowadays..."

"You are young. You did not live through these times."

"But Marek doesn't make such a great big secret of being Jewish, does he?"

"That is true, he does not. But everyone is different. This you understand when you are older."

He's no longer making eye contact, but staring at the wall as if it were a cinema screen. "So, I tell you what you want to know." A pause. "In 1938, it was not so long since I graduated from University of Kraków. Such a dangerous time to be alive. Czechoslovakia it was soon to be invaded by Germany; and Poland it saw invasion too was inevitable.

"As student I had been activist in anti-Nazi organisation - meaning Martina, that I was working openly against Nazis. Of course such a situation was very dangerous for me; especially later once German invasion had taken place. The repercussions - that means results - would mean certain death - and very likely death for my parents also. In meantime, supporters of Hitler were working away in background, and my role in this organisation had, as I said, not gone unnoticed."

Father moves from his armchair and sits on the sofa beside me.

"My cousin Basia she married Czech boy. They were living in Brno in Czechoslovakia when invasion took place. One day my mother she received letter, a warning. You understand it was brave and noble of Basia, for she risked her life writing such a thing. So anyway, she described the disbelief and terror all Jews felt as they witnessed German soldiers marching into the town - Nazi flags being raised - and their hearts they chilled to hear cheering and music of triumph. Life for Jewish people under Hitler's regime… this is not so very easy to talk… but I try… vast numbers of Czech, and Slovak Jews they escaped as the regime tightened around them. Many they find their way to Kraków where there was refugee transit centre. This arranged for many people in danger to be transported, escape to safety - a great number to England. I had friends, mostly not Jewish, who worked on this committee; and these men they advised me to get out of Poland this way while still it was possibility.

"My father he warns me to stop, for I was endangering safety of both our family and our Jewish community, but stubbornly I refused. Many neighbours they worried, were angry, and told me so to my face; but I was young and idealistic. You probably find this thing hard to understand, but I could not so easily give up - give in to those Nazis. I simply could not."

"Oh God!" I say looking down at a chocolate melting in my hand.

Father passes me his handkerchief.

"Also this. As I have told you, I had not so long qualified as pharmacist. With German invasion, it would be impossible to find job. After… well… I decided, with blessing of my parents, to get out of Poland."

"Leave your parents?"

"Yes. This was very hard; a most painful decision to make; for I was an only child, and like you, a precious child to my parents."

Never before had I heard myself described as a precious child. I blink away the tears.

"So, I leave Poland with party of refugees. From Kraków we travelled by train to Gdańsk, where we were transferred to ship which took us to Stockholm. Maybe this does not interest you?"

"Yes, yes it does. Go on."

Before resuming his story he takes the atlas from the bookshelf and turns to a map of Europe. "Of course it was a dangerous journey because German Intelligence knew about movement of refugees, so we could not sail directly to England across Baltic Sea, but took route via Skagerrak - between Norway and Denmark. See here on map. When we finally disembarked at Tilbury and set foot on English soil, another Pole, who had travelled with me, described it as the "Promised Land." And for us all, it was true. So, with others, I went to Westbourne Grove, a school - being used as refugee camp. From there…"

The phone begins to ring. Father answers it. It's Marek confirming the time he'll be here tomorrow. When Father puts down the receiver, he's no longer in the mood for World War Two. I've long stopped kissing my parents good night, but tonight I make a point of it.

Before reaching the top of the stairs, I hear the phone ring again. This time it's Auntie Anne. A fuse has gone in her house and as Uncle Greg's at work, she wonders if Father would mind coming to the rescue.

Chapter 8
1960

Mother's been in hospital for two weeks, and it's been suggested that she has a week's convalescence. A pleasant little place with a sea view has been booked in Eastbourne. Father says it's ideal as their old friend Wojciech, who lives in the area, will be able to visit. I'm thinking that she should be arriving about now as I walk past the shops on my way home from school. Netball practice has been cancelled today because Mrs. O'Sullivan has flu, therefore I'll be home at least an hour early.

I walk slowly admiring the Christmas lights already twinkling in some shop windows and think that they bring a touch of magic and promise to this season.

Proudly, when I arrive home, I take from my purse, the shiny new key I've recently been given, and let myself into the house. There's an unfamiliar quiet. Is there no one here? From the street I saw a dim light glowing between the drawn curtains.

I put down my bag in the hall and am just about to call out, when through the half-opened sitting room door, I see them. They're pressed against the far wall. They are so preoccupied that my entrance remains unheard. I can't believe it. His hand's inside Auntie Anne's blouse. He's kneading her breast like Mother does the dough when making bread. Her head tilts back, her eyes closed and her arms are wrapped around his waist. She looks as if she's in heaven as he kisses her neck. Now I can hear her deep breathing and odd guttural noises coming from him. Horrified, frozen to the spot, I watch their hips move in gentle unison as if in a dance. How could they? I'm shocked, deeply shocked. Without making a sound, I grab my school bag, leave the house and run to nowhere.

Chapter 9
1960
Next day

Gone to school.
Early violin lesson.
Forgot to tell you, sorry.

Martina

I place the note in the centre of the kitchen table. It's not quite 7am and still dark outside. I don't want breakfast. I can't face sitting and looking at him across the table. Neither am I able to cope with making polite conversation just as if nothing's happened.

Quietly, I unlock the front door and creep along the path which shimmers in the frosty moonlight. I don't believe it. There's Auntie Anne putting out her empty milk bottles. Her dressing gown is loosely tied, and as she bends down, her breasts become visible. The image of them being kneaded immediately leaps to mind. She spots me, and smiling, calls out in that voice she uses when talking to children, "Morning love! You're an early bird today, aren't you?"

I don't want to see her, let alone speak to her, but in spite of myself I mumble, "Yes." My eyes are down, my back is already turned, and I'm on my way to school.

Heading up the street I pass the familiar billboard, where instead of the Five Boys, grins Santa Claus. He's waving at me, and inside the bubble at the bottom of the poster, it reads, "Have a very Merry Christmas."

"Very funny," I scoff. Pulling a face, I stick out my tongue at him, only to see a ruddy-faced clergyman looking daggers at me as if he's come across a child of Satan.

The bus is almost empty when it finally arrives. I'm glad that I don't have to stand or squeeze in beside some stranger, and am able to sit by a window for a change. The Christmas lights have lost yesterday's magic. Instead I prefer to watch the dustcart trundling down the road. But soon I'm blind to whatever's passing, for I'm replaying scenes from the previous afternoon. The repulsive image of them groping and pressing against each other remains etched on my brain. It won't be erased, however hard I try.

I picture myself dashing from the house. "Martina!" A voice rings out when I'm about a third of the way down Woodland Avenue. Peter. I bolt round to see him coming towards me; his brown hair is shiny with sweat and he holds mud-caked football boots by the laces.

"Hiya! Do you know where my mum is? She's not indoors," he says, the boots swinging and twisting against his thigh.

Not wanting to divulge the fact that she's in my sitting room kissing someone who's not his dad, I tell him that she's probably shopping. Standing still is excruciating, like not being able to scratch an aggressive itch, so wasting no more words I'm off. Running, running until I'm panting and almost winded.

The green, dating back to village life, is roughly a mile from our house. Thankfully, it has a bench. Having collapsed on to its hard, cold wooden slats, I sit in a daze whilst getting my breath back. A myriad of feathery snowflakes begins to float down from the sky. With an icy pinch some land on my face, melt, and flow like the tears I'm unable to weep. The flakes twist and waltz like a flurry of ballerinas in tutus. It only takes minutes for the view to become a patchwork of grass and snow. Impervious to the cold I sit and watch the lights in the distant houses flicker on and off. Each house a home with its own set of stories.

Later, an old man with a scruffy black and white terrier puffs his way to the bench. He flops down letting the dog off the lead to exercise. Although he looks quite harmless, he's closer to me than I would choose, so I shift further along the bench and ignore him. An unpleasant smell of beer wafts my way as he lifts a bottle to his lips.

"Bit late for you bein' out, girlie, ain't it?"

"Really." I pretend to be surprised.

"Yez, nearz six."

This is my cue to make a move.

The trees create silver silhouettes against winter's suburban sky. I skim my foot over the icy puddles and avoid walking on the pavements' cracks. Someone opens a front door and a marmalade cat rushes inside. My breath billows between my lips like smoke. It's bitterly cold; nevertheless I walk at snail's pace. Home is definitely not where I want to be. I'm indecisive. Don't know what I want. Don't know what to do.

Should I speak to Father about it? Or perhaps talking to Marek would be the better option? Confrontation. What will Uncle Greg do if he finds out? What will happen then? Gee! And what about Peter and Lisa?

By the time I near home I've come to the conclusion silence is probably the best policy; after all Mother will be home in a week, then life should resume a semblance of normality.

I'm prepared for wrath. The front door opens, and Father, coat unbuttoned, is about to step out when he sees me. Before I'm up the garden path it starts. "You are here!"

I'm both surprised and pleased to hear relief in his voice. But the tone quickly changes to anger, "So, where have you been?"

"The - the library - after netball practice."

"The library? All this time, the library?"

A plausible reason occurs to me, one that may, I think, appease his fury.

"I was looking things up about Poland - you know the Second World War. What we were talking about… and, and um just sort of forgot the time."

Not able to handle an inquisition, I throw off my coat and begin to climb the stairs.

"Why not tell Marek? Come home first? Not go off in this way."

Marek appears from the sitting room and quickly jumps to my defence. "It is a difficult time for her, Stefan." He winks at me. "Anyway, I too was a little late," he adds. "With Margot off with flu, I had to close deli today myself. Had to rush - so have to say, no time to think about food for the evening." He crosses over to me, tousles my hair and says brightly, "Never mind, all is well that ends up well. Come. Martina is safe, no more fuss. I told you she would be Stefan. Now, let's think what we eat."

But Father is deaf to excuses. "Martina, you know to leave note. What with Mum being sick, you should not be worrying me so…" He carries on, but I'm not listening, not until his voice becomes quieter and he says, that because Marek was late, we will get a fish supper from the fish and chip shop. Fish and chips is my favourite, especially I adore the chips with vinegar and tomato ketchup, but tonight I'm not hungry. "Not for me," I say. "Don't get any for me. I've a bad headache, so I'll just go to bed."

I check inside the wardrobe for an intruder, take Mr.Bear off the chest of drawers, lie on the bed and hug his rotund, furry body close to mine. Leaving the light on not only helps me to feel safe, but this evening it will serve to prevent me from falling asleep. I long to blot out today, but I'm sure that sleep will only bring bad dreams. Day, night - nightmares in both; there's no avoiding them it seems.

I must have drifted off, in spite of myself, and awaken an hour or so later to the smell of fish and chips. Polish is being spoken downstairs and some Polish folk tunes thumped out on the piano. Laughter punctuates Father's and Marek's conversation, and I'm aware this house has never experienced so much jollity.

It's gone 9 o'clock when my bedroom door opens, and there's Father holding a plate bearing half a piece of fish and a small portion of chips.

"Headache better?" He shifts the books and puts the plate down on my bedside cabinet. "Here, I thought you might be hungry."

"Thank you, but I'm not - actually I'm feeling a little bit sick."

He remains sitting on the bed however, and reaches out to feel my forehead. "You do not have fever; but yes, you are pale. All the upset, I know this."

He sits. I lie down. I say nothing. He says nothing. Then out of the blue he begins, "When I left Westbourne Grove I went to work at Bourneville chocolate factory in Birmingham - to learn English, you understand. It was not possible to work as pharmacist in this country until I could do this."

Now my headache is real, and I'm in no frame of mind to focus on Father's story. He says he understands when I explain I need to get some sleep. Switching off the light, he leaves, reassuring me that I'll be as right as rain by morning.

The bell rings. I snap out of my reverie and am annoyed to see that I've missed getting off at my usual bus stop. Fortunately it's early, so instead of crossing the road and waiting for a bus going back the other way, I walk to school.

As I amble along I begin to realise that I really am feeling sick. I put this down to no food having passed my lips since yesterday lunchtime. In my bag is a rather elderly orange which I keep meaning to eat at break times, but never do. I sit on the next suitable garden wall and begin to peel its tight, tough skin. It weeps down my sleeve. Old it may be, but still juicy. I bite into its sourness. The orange's sharp tang is painful to my tongue and cheeks, yet I suck hard and long. I bite again and again. And I feel the same satisfaction as when I worry an open cut with the hard corner of a railway ticket.

By the time I arrive at school I feel sicker than ever, so when Krysia meets me at the gate, she's shocked - says I look like a ghost.

"Go home, silly. I'll tell Mrs. O'Sullivan you're ill."

"No Krysh, I'll be fine." And with that I throw up on the grass verge.

Krysia passes me her hanky. "God! I'd better get a teacher."

"No," I insist. "Don't you dare! I'll be fine in a minute or two."

The morning is cold so we venture inside the chapel and creep into a back pew. I let Krysia copy my Maths homework while I stare at some nuns who are at the front, praying. We sit silently for a while before starting to whisper.

"Can you come to my house Saturday week? For my birthday," says Krysia handing me an invitation. "I know it's a bit short notice, but Mum said I can invite some friends over for tea. And by the way you won't need to worry about getting home; my Dad said he'll take you in the car."

"Oh! Well, my mum's coming back home around then - so I'm not sure," I say feeling sorry because I like Krysia so much and would love to go to her house, but at the same time I'm relieved to have a genuine excuse. If I accept her invitation, I must reciprocate, and then what might my friend learn about me?

Two of the nuns are scowling at us, so we get up and slip out of the door.

I feel marginally better, but decide to go home anyway. The possibility of vomiting over the floor in assembly isn't all that appealing.

A golden retriever is urinating on the base of the billboard as Santa continues grinning unperturbed. No longer feeling sick, I'm beginning to feel a fraud until I acknowledge my desperate tiredness, and know that after the events of yesterday evening I could really do with a good sleep. I feel hungry again. How strange. Fortunately, in my purse is my pocket money, two shillings. I walk into the newsagents.

"No school today?" asks the nosey shopkeeper.

"No." I think what an accomplished liar I have become.

Not being able to face chocolate for once, I buy a packet of potato crisps. I don't want the salt, so I drop the little blue bag into the nearest rubbish bin and enjoy crunching the crisps all the way home.

Not a soul in Woodland Avenue. I'm grateful for that. I hurry along the road, and in spite of the house being so chilly, it's pleasing to get indoors unchallenged by neighbours.

The sitting room fire hasn't yet been lit. Ash fills the grate, waiting to be cleaned out before a new fire can be built. I don't know how this is done because Marek has been making up the fires since staying with us. So without taking off my coat, I go into the kitchen and I run myself a glass of water. The kitchen boiler provides welcome warmth. In winter, the first thing Father does when he gets up in the morning is to bank it up with fuel. I stand close, warming my marble-blue hands and I think about Mother. I decide to make her a welcome home card. She seemed to like the ones I'd made her. How proud I felt to see, displayed on the windowsill of her ward, those Get Well cards with my own drawings of roses, right in front of the shop-bought ones. The materials I need are in my bedroom, so I run upstairs. With frustration I try to find the light green sheets necessary for the task. I know the cards are mixed in with comics under my bed. Sifting through the pile I'm almost reaching the bottom when I hear a key in the front door. Who could it be at this time of day?

It's Auntie Anne, I recognise the way she clears her throat. Even though we have a weekly home help, while Mother's been away, she's been popping in to bring the odd item of shopping, or the laundry, temporarily being collected and delivered next door. I don't want her to know I'm home, so I stop what I'm doing and keep absolutely still. Within seconds another key is turning in the lock.

"Got the house to ourselves," I hear Auntie Anne's triumphant cry. A giggle follows. "And Greg was fast asleep when I left."

"Lucky."

"Um."

Only the sound of movement, and I've got a pretty good idea what they're doing.

"Oh my God! How am I going to escape this time without being seen?" I say to myself.

It doesn't take long before I hear footsteps on the staircase. They stop before they reach the landing. They're close. Close enough for me to hear the sighs, and the slobbery kissing.

"Slow down. A little patience," I hear Auntie Anne say in a way which means "Don't stop."

Thankfully, my bedroom door is almost shut, but from where I'm sitting on the floor, I can just see them through the chink. It's as if they're eating each other. It disgusts me. They're at the top bend of the staircase leaning against the wall, locked in each other's arms. They begin to sway a little and I wonder if they'll soon fall down the stairs. But to my consternation, they move upwards onto the landing, right next to my door. My head drops between my knees. I just don't want to see them, nor hear their grotesque groans.

"Anne, um, that feels so good. Ooh, what a body you have."

I hear shuffling, and then it's relatively quiet.

"Oh my God!" I say again. This time it's more like a desperate prayer. How long are they going to be there? I wonder. This is nothing like the kissing in the old Ginger Rogers and Fred Astaire films I enjoy watching on television.

Tentatively, I open my eyes. And they're still at it, more frantic than ever. I think that soon they must get tired and go downstairs for a coffee or cup of tea.

Slowly, not wanting to make a sound, I snatch the nearby cushion. Still wearing my coat, I lie back waiting for them to get bored. I'm pleading with God not to let them find me, to help me think of a way to escape as soon as possible. The unwelcome noises are growing louder and louder so I press my hands over my ears until they're burning. This doesn't entirely do the trick.

After a while I become aware that the noises have stopped. Have they now left? No, they're still in the house. A giggle. Then a distant whisper. Coming from exactly where, I'm uncertain. Can they still be upstairs?

I sit up. Ears alert. This is so much like one of my nightmares. Should I pinch myself in the hope of waking up? I wait until the house is completely silent. Even then I'm as scared as Mother is of Alsatians and don't move for at least another ten minutes.

Cautiously, I poke my head out. I'm beginning to think they must have left the house after all. But when? It's then that I see them. The spare bedroom door is wide open. And there they are, fast asleep on top of the red blanket. Naked! Marek is half lying on top of Anne, his hand resting on her breast and his head is on her shoulder. Her Marilyn Monroe curls are partially covering his face. They're dead to the world. I make a dash for it.

Where to go? The library. It's warm. It's safe and it's free. I'm so relieved to have escaped unseen - and with my school bag which would've certainly betrayed my presence. Detached from reality and devoid of emotion, I no longer feel the child I was, and wonder if I ever will again.

On my way to the library, I feel sure that they must have been doing what Mother told me only married couples do. The thing described in that little book. I'm repulsed. Well, I suppose Auntie Anne is married - but to Uncle Greg. Will Auntie Anne have a baby in nine months? What will Peter and Lisa feel about having a new baby brother or sister?

I can hardly forget the shocking diagrams in the little book that Mother gave me. This was after I'd asked her about periods some weeks prior to her appendix operation. Having decided it was time for me to learn about "growing up" she explained the process of periods without embarrassment, but next day I found on my pillow a little book, *Facts of Life*. When I read through it, I couldn't believe that men and women could do such rude things to each other. There were so many questions that I wanted to ask her, but I couldn't bring myself to speak about the shocking act of love as described in those pages.

Several days later, during a wet lunch break, Mary brought up the subject of sex. The confusion surrounding "*doing it*" had become a current topic of conversation. After the joking and embarrassed giggles had subsided, Mary declared that her older sister had assured her that babies are a result of a man and woman *sleeping* together.

"*It* happens when they are *asleep*," she emphasised with great authority.

Well, I thought, how did Father get across to Mother's bed if he was asleep?

I dismissed the thought instantly, not being able to entertain the horrific image of Mother and Father doing something so revolting.

"But then, where did I come from?" I asked myself later during Maths.

Sinéad said with certain logic, "Well, to be sure, it can't be that horrid else no one would be doin' it, would they? And there are millions of babies bein' born every day all over the world. In Ireland, in the town where me da was born, there's this family with eighteen children, so there is. So they must've done it eighteen times."

"Yeah," agreed Krysia. "Suppose you just get used to it."

I'm thinking as I hover on the library steps, Auntie Anne and Marek must be used to "*doing it*" all right. I make my mind up to speak to Father about what I'd witnessed. And I'm resolved to do it tonight - even if there are only a few days left before Mother comes home.

Chapter 10
1960
Same day

The library is like a public toilet without lavatories. If the council would only paint the pea-green walls a coral pink or a primrose yellow, it'd cheer the place up no end. Like the school library, the shelves are filled with rows of dull fusty, dusty hardbacks instead of the appealing bright paperbacks as sold in Smiths. I note from where I'm sitting, in the reference section, the majority of visitors are housewives who arrive with their baskets on wheels. Once having chosen their fortnightly read, they're on their way within minutes. An elderly man hunched over today's Times, and a young oriental woman taking notes from an encyclopaedia, are the only other people in this area. It may not be the most popular place to be, but I like its warmth and silence.

Before going our separate ways, Lisa and I used to make a trip to this library our weekly treat. Often on Saturday mornings, having exchanged our books, we'd wander back down the road to the newsagents with armfuls of fresh reading material and buy gobstoppers, sherbet dips, penny chews; sweets that would last. The nosey shopkeeper would always ask us if we had enough money to pay for all of them; then once we had handed her the money, she wanted to know the titles of the books we'd chosen.

Nowadays, I walk up and down the children's section and find little there that takes my fancy; although I have made a start on *Sue Barton Student Nurse* which seems promising. The librarian who smiles as she stamps the out-going books reminds me of Sue's picture on the cover. The older librarian, with greying hair, who's been stacking the shelves, joins her colleague at the desk. She's eyeing me; her expression severe. I feel sure she's questioning why I'm not at school. I resist challenging her stare; instead I look down at the book on the table in front of me. *A History of the Holocaust* by Yehuda Bauer.

I read for the third time... *even leading church figures such as St. John Chrysostom (c.347-407) declared that the Jews sacrifice their children to Satan and that they are worse than wild beasts.*

"Worse than wild beasts... sacrifice children to Satan!" I whisper in horror and despair.

This seems to override the problem lying in the spare bedroom at home. Wild beasts. Jews, wild beasts? I must discuss the matter with Father as soon as possible. Perhaps even before raising the other issue? Then intrudes another replay of Marek and Anne kissing - the grotesque involuntary gruntings - naked - on the bed. These pepper my thoughts and destroy my concentration. I change my mind. This has to be my priority. Nonetheless I still fear the consequences. But I've every confidence that Father will know how to deal with the matter.

But how to broach the subject? How should I start off? What words should I choose? "Today I felt sick. I came home from school and I found Marek and Auntie Anne asleep. They were lying on the spare bed, together - and they were naked."

I think that this might be enough. Because if they were on the bed, and sleeping together, then Father will know "doing it" must have happened. Perhaps it won't even be necessary to mention the embarrassing fact, that they were naked? Father, by then, will have grasped the ghastly picture.

Satisfied with the plan, I turn to the second of the reference books and focus on the term *anti-Semitism.* This, I learn, was derived from Wilhelm Marr, an anti-Jewish agitator who founded the anti-Semitic League as well as the journal *Antisemitische Hefte* in 1879. I read on, but realise by the time I reach the end of the chapter that I have absorbed little else of significance.

When I glance up at the clock at the far end of the library, I see it's only a quarter past one, and much too early to return home; however the library no longer feels a safe sanctuary. I'm becoming paranoid because the older of the two librarians so frequently eyes me with accusation. I see neighbours in every face entering the door, and fear that they will recognise me and ask the inevitable question. Why am I sitting in the library if I'm off school sick? My backside is numb, almost as numb as my mind has become. I cannot stay here any longer.

Desperate for the toilet, I make my way to the public lavatories situated opposite the taxi rank and near to the pet shop. They stink. And the walls are that hideous pea-green. There's no toilet tissue, so I'm forced to use my embroidered handkerchief which I then throw away into the small metal bin within the cubicle.

Having discarded most of the sixpenny bag of chips bought from the fish and chip shop, I wander into the pet shop. It seems a good place to waste a bit more time. A white mouse with twitching silk whiskers and tiny pink toes stands up in his cage to greet me. His black beady eyes plead for my attention. I think he's very sweet and how lonely it must be to spend your life caged behind bars like that - even if you're only a mouse. It occurs to me that Father might buy him for me as an early birthday gift.

I envy the goldfish swimming in the large tank. Round and round they go, in and out of the weed seemingly unaware of me, each other or their own existence. In the next tank are masses of neon fish. They swim at the same speed and in the same direction. It's as if they are in a trance, swimming endlessly from right to left, left to right. I tap the glass with my index finger. Instantly, as if one body, they turn and swim the other way. Flicking the tank again, I'm taken aback to hear, "Hey, you stop that. Get out of my shop, you cruel little beast!"

Beast! He's addressing me.

I don't need telling twice.

By half past two I'm ensconced in St. Joseph of Arimathea, the Catholic church off the main road, in a side street. It's surprisingly warm for a building which is not so very small and has a high beamed roof. There's no one else in the church. I'm surprised by its simple décor - no stained-glass windows, but all around the whitewashed walls is a series of oil paintings portraying the story of Jesus' crucifixion.

The echo of my footsteps is eerie as I walk down the centre aisle towards the side-altar at the left of the sanctuary. I sit mesmerised by the glowing candles on the stand in front of me. With a three-penny bit, the last coin in my purse, I buy one and recall what Sister Mary Paul told us about lighting candles for personal intentions. The flames dance in the dusky light and I pray. At once I say sorry to God for me being a wild beast, and then I ask Our Lord for help with the problem of Marek and Auntie Anne.

I'm wavering now as to whether my decision to "let on" about Marek and Auntie Anne really is for the best. No, perhaps I won't mention this to Father after all. I read once in the newspaper about a husband who killed his wife when he found her in bed with another man. The judge called it a "crime of passion" and therefore the murderer got off scot-free. That was in Italy though, where apparently the law is quite lenient on matters of the heart - according to Father anyway. But we are in England. What if Uncle Greg kills Auntie Anne? Does she really deserve that? I wonder what Sister Mary Paul would advise? I feel certain what they did is the sin called adultery. Sister Mary Frances skimmed over that one when we were learning about the Ten Commandments during an R.I. lesson.

"Sister, what's adultery?" Sinéad asked.

"Never you mind, young lady," she replied." Just take it from me it's a mortal sin. And as you all know, a mortal sin means hell."

I revert to my original decision to speak to Father, and beg Jesus to help in being able to stop what's going on between the two of them before anyone gets hurt.

However, thinking about these last weeks, it's both sad and ironic to realise that home has never before been such a happy place. Along with Marek and his Polish sausages, German sausages, Bratwurst sausages and Frankfurter sausages, came fun. Meal times have become times for laughter and light-hearted discussion. The sound of Marek playing the piano has raised the roof, and there I sat doing my homework, simultaneously tapping my foot to the rhythm of the music. One evening, the three of us *really* listened to Brahms Violin Concerto. Marek said he'd chosen the piece specially, knowing how much I enjoy playing the violin. Although I wouldn't admit it, especially to my friends, I like it almost as much as Cliff Richard's songs.

On those Saturdays without netball fixtures, Marek has been taking me to the deli, allowing me a free reign to help either on the shop floor or in the storeroom. A couple of Saturdays ago after a morning match, Auntie Anne took Lisa, Peter and me to see, the *Two Way Stretch* at the local cinema. It's impossible for me to dismiss Auntie Anne's warmth and kindness towards me. Nevertheless, it annoys me to feel this surge of gratitude. I'm baffled, really baffled. How can such nice people do *those things* to each other?

"Please, Jesus, I know what they've done is a terrible thing - disgusting, but I really don't think they deserve to burn in hell for ever and ever," I pray.

My brain is a colourless Kaleidoscope. I'm unable to make any sense of it all. I look for inspiration in the eye of the quivering candle flame and simply hope for the best.

To kill time, I get up and wander round. The Christmas explosion is everywhere except in St. Joseph's where there's still no sign of the approaching festivities. I've learnt about Advent, and know that soon, when it comes, there'll be a nativity crib and a Christmas tree here, but for the moment I like the starkness, it suits my mood.

Intermittently, people "pay a visit", as Sister Mary Frances calls it. "Whenever you pass a Catholic church," she stresses, "you should pop in and say a little prayer to Our Lord. It doesn't take more than five minutes or so out of your time. Just remember how much Our Lord loves you, girls."

But does he love me? I stop beside another picture hanging on the wall. Glaring down at me is Mary with a smiling baby Jesus on her knee. I notice the small silver plate at the bottom of the frame. *Our Lady of Częstochowa - Poland.*

"Polish," I whisper, and think she must be truly angelic to have such a bright gold halo. How odd for someone so holy to appear so disgruntled.

It's 3.45pm, I'm bored. I decide to go home. I feel sure they can't still be sleeping together. If Marek asks about my early arrival, I'll bluff my way out of it by spinning the old chestnut about feeling sick and having been sent home from school. This may indeed help in getting an absence note out of Father.

Chapter 11
1960
Same day

All is quiet. There's as yet no fire burning in the grate of the sitting room. My heart sinks. Surely they can't still be on the spare bed? I'm debating whether to retrace my steps to the church when I catch sight of a note lying on the hall table.

Dear Martina,
Have to work late.
Auntie Anne expecting you for supper.

Marek

I'm surprised that he had the energy to go to work. Although relieved at not having to face Marek, the thought of going to Auntie Anne's for supper is gross. I'll have to think up an excuse. In the meantime I recognise an advantage. With a bit of luck Marek's lateness should make it possible to speak to Father alone.

Before I get a chance to phone and excuse myself from supper next door, Auntie Anne lets herself into our house. "Hello love!" Her eyes are bright and her voice cheerful. "Saw you coming in. You're a bit early today. Everything okay love? Got the note I see. Come on. Brrr it's really cold in here."

Lost for a plausible excuse I find myself sitting in front of the Harris's fireplace making polite conversation with Uncle Greg. He's very late for work and gobbling down a cheese and tomato sandwich.

"Be nice when your mum's back home, won't it? Bet you can't wait."

That's an understatement.

He chomps a bit more sandwich. A piece of tomato falls off the plate onto his shoe. He picks it up and eats it anyway. I feel sorry for him - for what he doesn't know, so I smile at him.

"It'll be Christmas before you know it. Any ideas about presents?"
"A mouse would be nice," I reply without a lot of thought.
He hoots with laughter. "A mouse? Did you hear that Anne? Martina says she wants a mouse for Christmas."
Auntie Anne comes in from the kitchen drying her hands on a tea towel. "A mouse? Didn't know you liked mice?" She too is chuckling.
"Well, if you're desperate for a mouse, there are plenty under our shed - and you're welcome to the lot of them," Uncle Greg says.
I watch as they exchange smiles.
"A white pet mouse," I emphasise feeling very much the outsider.
Auntie Anne removes her husband's plate. When she returns a couple of moments later, Uncle Greg's in front of the mirror taming his brown curly hair. Auntie Anne offers him a slice of her homemade chocolate sponge.
"Not now love, I'm already running late. Must rush."
"Shame," she says placing her arm affectionately round his shoulder.
"You have it love," she says turning to me.
"No thanks."
"But it's your favourite?"
"No thanks, I'm not hungry," I insist, not wanting to accept anything from her.
They kiss, and he's on his way. I'm puzzled. This normality leaves me feeling decidedly uncomfortable and confused.
It's too awkward not to eat anything at the supper table, so I take a couple of spoonfuls of Shepherds' Pie. Lisa heaps her plate and proceeds to wolf down the food. Although Peter appears a little sullen, he chats to me more than Lisa. But I'm lost for words and respond in monosyllabic sentences. However, not wanting to make my displeasure too obvious, once again I use that tired excuse of feeling sick and add, I have a tummy ache, as the reason for being so quiet and having little appetite.
Auntie Anne seems genuinely concerned about this recurring ailment of mine, and while I'm helping to bring the dirty dishes into the kitchen, she offers to accompany me to the doctor tomorrow. Then suggests it may be *that* time of the month, and wants to ascertain if I know all about *that* kind of thing. I assure her I do

know about, *that* kind of thing, and will be fine in a day or two. All the while I'm listening to the unfamiliar coldness in my voice.

Lisa asks me in a friendly, but smug tone, if I've any homework to do.

"You can come in the back room and do it on the table with me and Peter."

Of course, I have no homework today since I wasn't at school.

"It's okay, I'll do it later - thanks anyway."

With a flick of her curly blonde ponytail she's out of the door.

Relieved to be free of Lisa, I watch the television news, feigning interest in the debate concerning the proposed new airport at Castle Donington near Derby. Aiming to get a man on the moon is a bit more engaging. The handsome pair, John and Jackie Kennedy wave with gusto from their shiny car; but all that really matters to me is Father getting home before Marek, and me being able to speak with him alone.

When the opportunity presents itself, I freeze. It's 7 o'clock. Still no Marek. Father has scrambled some eggs and is sitting eating them at the kitchen table. I wait. I convince myself that it's better not to share bad news when a person is hungry. I can actually feel my heart beating and my throat's tight. In these last weeks it's become unusual to sit and eat a meal in silence. We've already had, "Have you completed your homework?" as well as several convoluted explanations from me as to why it was necessary to come home from school early.

The eggs are disappearing fast. It's time. Father's now standing by the sink easing off the cap from a bottle of beer. Now. It has to be now. How did I decide to begin?

"This morning…" No, can't say this *morning*, I've only just told him I left school a little early. So I'll say, "When I returned from school, I found Marek kissing Auntie Anne on the stairs" - or did I decide to miss that bit out and go straight onto the sleeping together part? And what about what I saw yesterday? Should I include that?

Father is up and out of the kitchen. Some of his scrambled egg remains on the plate. He's back with the *Radio Times*. He opens the pages and begins to say something when I leap in. “Dad.” I’m impressed with the power in my voice.

“Yes?”

“Dad,” I repeat. “I’ve got something I must talk to you about.”

“You look so serious, what can it be?”

“It is serious, very serious.”

I stall.

“Well?”

Closing the TV paper, he returns to the table, sits, but ignores the remnants of his supper. He looks worried; probably thinking I’m on the verge of confessing to some awful crime.

Okay. Here goes. “Dad - please may I have a white mouse for Christmas - or maybe for my birthday?”

I don’t believe the words which have just escaped my mouth. Neither does Father who’s laughing. He gets up, puts his hand on mine. “Oh is that all! If it is a mouse you want, then you may have a nice plump white one. Providing, of course you make promise to feed it - always clean cage yourself - without being told of course.”

He resumes eating the now stone-cold eggs. I’m furious with myself. Five minutes later Father’s still at the table. Plate empty. Glass empty. He gets up. I summon up courage. “Dad.”

The phone rings. Another opportunity missed. Perhaps when the call’s finished, I think.

Marek appears in the hall.

Now there’s a double reason for not wanting to see the man. Exasperated, I reply to his dramatic, “I am home!” with a quick hello and brush past him.

“For you,” he says throwing me a bag of boiled sweets.

I don’t look at him, but politely smile. Inside I’m so angry; angrier with myself than with anyone else.

Chapter 12
1960
Next Wednesday

Mother is on her way back home. It's half-day closing for the chemist. Yesterday evening there was a phone call from the convalescent home. Mother doesn't like it there. She hates the food. She says her bed is uncomfortable and that she's always cold because they refuse to light the fires until lunchtime. Matron spoke to Father first; then Mother came on the line and demanded that the necessary arrangements be made to collect her as soon as possible.

Good old Marek comes to the rescue. He's recently purchased a new car and has volunteered to take Father down to Eastbourne. I'm in Geography with the map of England in front of me wondering whereabouts the three of them are at this moment.

When I arrive home, I find to my surprise, on the table, two pounds beside a note from Father. It says the money is for me, to buy a white mouse. Yes, two pounds should cover a small cage, the necessary food and sawdust. He says that this is a gift. It's for me being so good while Mum's been away.

There's a P.S.

Peter has agreed to go to pet shop with you. As soon as you get home, knock next door.

P.P.S. Sandwiches and banana in pantry in case of delays. If we are very late home go to Auntie Anne's

Whiskey is established in his cage. Nose and whiskers are happily twitching as he treads the little red wheel in a cage quite a bit bigger than the one he used to live in at the pet shop. I've never had a pet before, and I love him already. Not knowing where the cage will live, for the moment it's placed on the coffee table in the sitting room. Half watching his antics and half learning French vocabulary, I hear a car pull into the drive. I'm at the front door waving before Marek has even switched off the headlights.

Mother looks happy. She's smiling, and I'm smiling back. Auntie Anne comes out in welcome. Nodding politely at Marek, she hands Father a Victoria sponge cake. "Hania," she says, "how lovely to see you home."

I wonder.

Mother moves around the kitchen like a stranger. Marek stays for coffee and cake, then to my relief slips away leaving the three of us to make awkward conversation round the kitchen table. But he doesn't go before presenting me with a brand new LP recording of Brahms Violin Concerto.

"One day I want to come to hear you playing this music, in concert hall," he says smiling.

I don't know how to respond, but make up my mind that in spite of everything, I will write him a letter of thanks.

"Do widzenia!"

"Do widzenia!" Father replies.

"Goodbye!" says Mother. "Have you eaten, Child?"

I tell her I have.

"She looks a little thin, Stefan."

"She's had sick bug. But she is better now."

Once Marek has left Mother gets up and goes to the cupboard. She scours the shelves and begins to rearrange the crockery. I hope she's not going to complain because I know how hard it's been for Father while she's been away.

It's not very long before she feels tired and says that she needs her bed, but before going upstairs, she steps into the sitting room. I'm standing behind her as the scream fills the house. "A mouse!" she yells. "Stefan, a mouse!"

"A pet mouse, Hania. It is Martina's."

"No mouses! No! I will not have mouse! I have told you I hate mouses. They are dirty things. Small rats."

"Mum it's mice - and that's Whiskey. He's a tame mouse, my pet mouse. I've only just got him."

"Well, you can only just get rid of him. No mouses…"

"Dad said…"

"No! No mouses."

She's quite hysterical; and I know things are back to normal when Father doesn't say a word.

Chapter 13
1960
New Year's Eve

Be tidy, I write in my new diary. This is to be my New Year's resolution. I try hard to keep my writing neat, and slanting to the right. Sister Mary Frances took me aside after R.I. during the last week of term, and told me that handwriting slanting backwards is a sign of a person's bad character. *Wild beast* immediately sprang to mind. In trepidation, I thought the evil flowing through my veins must be manifesting itself through my handwriting.

"Now, I'm sure this isn't the case with you," she added, "but it would be wise to do something about it while you're still young."

I'm working hard to develop a style which is not only neat, but leans to the right.

The two words I've already written under January 1st look pretty okay in my estimation. Flicking through the diary, I wonder what'll be written on each page by this time next year.

The second resolution is to write in this diary every day. At least a couple of sentences. Each year I begin well, but by February or March the entries become, not only extremely short, but spasmodic: *Saw Cliff on TV* or *Ate two whole bars of chocolate today.*

I hear Mother's footsteps coming towards my bedroom. I'm stretched out in the middle of the floor on my stomach, and leaning on one elbow as I write. Ten past ten in the morning and I'm still in pyjamas.

"Not dressed, Child? And getting those nice blue pyjamas dirty I see."

But she seems pleased that already I'm writing in the 1961 diary, the red *Letts School-Girls' Diary*, a gift in my Christmas stocking. "You like diary then? That is good."

"Yes," I say and tell her my two New Year's resolutions.

She's been baking for tonight's party at the Harris's, her contribution to the fare. The delicious smell of freshly baked plum jam doughnuts and cherry cakes wafts upstairs. As yet this morning, I've only had a cup of milk and a slice of buttered toast, so I'm delighted when Mother tempts me down to sample the cakes. The sight of them makes my mouth water and I congratulate her on being such an excellent cook. It's good to see her eyes light up with pride.

I have to admit that the Christmas season turned out better than I'd expected. The anti-climax of Mother coming home from hospital was almost too much to bear, but things surprisingly picked up as my birthday, December 23rd, drew near.

"What about your party? Who will you invite?" Mother had asked.

"I don't want a party this year."

"No party?"

I waffled on about me being a bit too old now.

"Nonsense," replied Mother as her knitting needles clicked their way to another winter cardigan for me.

But I stood firm; there was no party.

Apart from the big Jewish secret, I go hot and cold just imagining Lisa with my new friends. What might she say to them about me? What would they think of her back to front jumper and pearly pink lipstick? Yet there's no way Lisa could have been left off my invitation list, even though no one would consider us best friends any longer.

Krysia's definitely my best friend. That's a fact. The four of us, Sinéad, Mary, Krysia and I openly discussed this. There's no confusion now. Mary and Sinéad are best friends, and Krysia and I are best friends.

In revenge, when Mother was in hospital, I told Lisa this on the bus on our way to see the *Two Way Stretch*. That is after she had told me, Norma was her best friend, and I'd only been invited to the film because I wasn't allowed to stay in the house alone for a whole afternoon. Why's Lisa so mean to me these days? It's really hard to understand.

Whilst enjoying my second cherry cake, I savour the memory of my birthday outing - the trip to Bertram Mills Circus in Olympia. Much better than a party. I envisage the clowns chucking water at each other; the nubile trapeze artists taking their lives in their hands, and recall the sheer thrill of the coloured lights and…"Martina!" My daydream ends. "Here. Your school bag," Mother says holding it out to me. "Look, such a mess. Tidiness it is your New Year's resolution, so why not start a day early and clear it out now?"

"Oh Mum! I've still got my room to tidy. I'll do it later," I say in hope that she'll forget."

"Better now. I think perhaps a little rest will be necessary before such big party tonight. It will be past midnight before you sleep."

"Don't fuss. I won't need a rest."

"Thank goodness it is Sunday tomorrow, and no work for your father. He's not so very keen on parties, and if he has to work next morning, well…"

Mother fills the cake tins until it's almost impossible to squeeze down the lids. She's verbose today, and I really believe she's looking forward to this party. I certainly am not. Flashbacks of Auntie Anne with Marek are never far from my mind when I'm with either of them.

"So strange," she continues, "that in Scotland there is Bank Holiday for New Year's Day, but no holiday for us English."

In truth, there's little to tidy in my bedroom. The wardrobe door's wide open. No one has mentioned anything about clothing. What shall I wear tonight? I hope Mother won't insist on choosing for me. I'm *not* wearing the red dress with a Peter Pan collar. I'll have to be sick again and stay at home if that happens I decide.

The new Sue Barton book I'm reading is plonked back on my bedside table. I put the Lexicon cards back into their pack. Then I gather up the pen and pencils from beside the bed and slip them into the pencil case. Protruding from beneath the bed is Cluedo; lid half off, pieces and cards higgledy-piggledy. I'd asked for a tennis racket for Christmas, to replace my old Woolworths' one, but as I'd been given that for my birthday, instead I received the much desired game on December 25th. I've been trying to play it with Mr Bear, but as it involves outwitting your opponent, and is not a game of chance, it's proved to be an impossible waste of time.

We don't celebrate Wigilia as most Polish people do, but follow the English Christmas traditions, although Jesus is never mentioned, and even the token gesture of going to church on Christmas morning like the Harris family do, is not on our agenda.

On Christmas Eve, Father brings in the Christmas tree, planted in a bucket. Mother places some red crepe paper round the base, and it's my job to decorate it with baubles and tinsel. The smell of the pine needles is intoxicating - I love it. As I take the glinting glass balls from the folded tissue and hang them on the branches of the tree, I listen to the radio - children from across the world sharing their Christmas traditions, and in between each rendition, carols are sung.

The same as Christian children, I'm excited on Christmas Eve, and eagerly await the opening of a small stocking left at the foot of my bed. The gift inside I cherish most is the Father Christmas made of honey cake, elaborately decorated with icing and silver balls. This I know is Father's contribution.

After breakfast there's an exchange of family gifts. Mother usually buys Father a new shirt and tie, and Father almost always comes up with some kind of household gadget for her. This year it was an electric potato peeler. It looks like a fairground rotor, but made of clear plastic. Its rough flat inner base whirls round tossing the potatoes up and round until they are smooth and white. Well, that's the theory.

Dinner's always at 1.00 sharp - roast turkey with chestnut stuffing, potatoes, but no sprouts. Mother stopped cooking those years ago because she prefers carrots. She makes her own Christmas pudding, which according to Auntie Anne, bears some resemblance to its English counterpart. I prefer the fruit compote she makes as an alternative. We have to wash the dishes and be ready for the Queen by three.

Usually Marek and Bronia join us for Christmas Day lunch, having spent Wigilia with other Polish friends. The prospect of my Christmas improved this year when I learnt that Marek would be staying with them in Croydon for the whole Christmas period.

Father tells me this "disappointing" news shortly before the big day while he and I are heading back from the local shops - precisely as we pass the grinning Santa Claus. This time, I return his smile, and am unable to refrain from giving him a little wave of joy.

While I put away the Cluedo board and pieces, I picture myself playing with Mother and Father on Christmas afternoon; and wonder why they only play games with me once a year when they seem to enjoy it so much.

4.55pm, dusk. The sitting room curtains are drawn and I'm lounging on the soft maroon rug in front of the glowing fire. Shadows, cast by the flames, dance on the walls like witches round a cauldron.

Mother's taking a nap before the New Year's Eve "do" while I listen to the Brahms Violin Concerto. Tonight I'll adore Cliff, Adam Faith and Brenda Lee, but for now I prefer Brahms. At the same time I'm noting all the helpful information included in my *Letts School-Girls' Diary* - Tables of French and Latin verbs. Logarithm tables. They definitely will be useful. I settle down to the crossword. 1 across: Egyptian sun god. *Ra* I write in the little squares.

All the while the shadows grow higher, wildly dancing up the walls and across the sepia photo of Father in his British Army uniform. Gradually they eat away the room's cosy spirit, and I'm contemplating what it must be like to leave the country of your birth, not knowing if you'll ever see your parents again. How must it feel to arrive in a strange land where you're unable to speak or even understand the language?

The witches dance on and the violins crescendo. My thoughts turn to Mother. I'm wondering what is her story. I know now the number she hides under her sleeve is due to her having been in some concentration camp or other - but she remains silent, Father remains silent and of course, I remain silent. Will I ever learn her truth?

Unwilling to stir when the record comes to an end, I lie there thinking.

"Martina!" Peace is broken.

Mother stands above me clutching my school bag.

"Here you are, Child. Doing nothing I see."

She sits down on the fireside chair and tips the bag's contents onto the rug. Two small wrinkled apples tumble out on top of exercise books, textbooks, stray pencils, a rubber and lots of crumpled sheets of paper. I see her pick up an envelope.

Oh no! I think, remembering the letter from Poland, the one I'd intended to dispose of on my way to school. That *thing*, having travelled with me to and from school for weeks, only has to come to light on New Year's Eve. The eve that is supposed to herald the promise of better things to come - that's what John F. Kennedy, president elect, has been saying to the world anyway.

Through the walls of the semi, I hear sounds of preparation for tonight's party. Dull thuds suggesting the movement of heavy furniture is followed by the Brook Brothers' "Warpaint" at full volume.

"Turn that noise down!" Uncle Greg bellows.

To my relief, however, I see the envelope in Mother's hand isn't the Polish letter, but my invitation to Krysia's birthday party. She's now removing the card from the envelope and reading it. She asks me why I didn't ask to go since Krysia and I are such good friends. Intent on retrieving the other letter before Mother notices it, I'm eyeing the pile on the floor while blabbing on about the party being too close to her coming home from the convalescent home.

Mother's still reflecting on the invitation when I spot the Polish letter partially covered by the atlas. I move slowly but decisively so as not to alert her. Then I grab it along with some other sheets. I start to crush them into a ball, but quickly change my mind and tear them into narrow strips. Without delay I jump up, flee through the back door, and scatter the pieces throughout the dustbin.

When I return, Mother complains that she's just discovered a note from the school which includes important dates for the Easter and summer terms.

"Sorry," I say beating a hasty retreat upstairs.

I'm weighing up my appearance in the full-length mirror, and for once it meets my approval. The flared dark blue skirt, although a little plain, at least doesn't make me look like a six year old; and the white blouse with its fashionable three quarter length sleeves completes an acceptable picture.

Turning my head to see what I look like from behind, I realise how lucky I am to be tall and slim; and then feel a touch of pride in watching my high ponytail swish around my shoulders. I have to admit that my thick dark hair is my best feature. And, I think, now that it has grown long, I bear less resemblance to Anne Frank.

It's too early to go to the party, and indeed, Father's still in the bathroom getting ready. Mother's watching television. I don't want to join her and risk any further discussion as to how I should, or shouldn't dress for this party. Never has it been a problem before. I used to be content to wear whatever she put out for me. I sigh as I think about how uncomplicated these traditional New Year's Evening gatherings once were. Whatever day of the week, these occasions had always been a simple, but a special pleasure for only the Harris and the Kalinski families. This year, because the party is on a Saturday, it's grown out of all proportion.

You can never pretend that something hasn't happened once the die has been cast. I do so wish I could erase from my mind those images of Auntie Anne with Marek. I have tried, but failed. Therefore I vow this evening to avoid her as much as possible.

The crossword I began earlier remains incomplete. 12 Down. Chinese religion. Haven't the foggiest. I cheat by looking up the answer on a back page, *Tao.*

"Never heard of it," I say aloud becoming aware of knocking at the front door. Father comes out of the bathroom, a towel wrapped around his waist. He sees me on the landing and says, "It must be Marek."

"Marek?"

"Yes, Marek. He comes for drink before party." He adds, "You look very nice."

"I didn't know he was invited." Disappointed to learn that Marek's on the invitation list, I forget to thank Father for the compliment.

"Of course, he knows Uncle Greg and Auntie Anne quite well since staying here with us."

"Yes, at least one of them *very* well," I almost say out loud.

The front door is eventually opened.

"Hania. Cześć!"

"Good evening, Marek."

Father hurries into his bedroom, I return to the crossword. My bedroom door's open. The television is switched off so I'm able to hear the raised voices.

"Letters?" Mother says in English. "I do not open letters from Poland…"

I prick up my ears. What a coincidence! The letters are forgotten for weeks then rear their ugly heads again twice on the same day.

They change to speaking Polish, but surprisingly I pick up the gist of what's being said. "Mamusia wrote on her New Year card that she met her by chance in Kraków... Hania, I do not know what happened... but for God sake, why not after all these years?"

Her? Who is this *her* that Marek's mother met by chance in Kraków?

"I have no words for her - neither for you on this matter. It is the past. That is where it belongs, and that is where it *shall* stay... I will *not* see her if she comes."

Marek matches Mother who has reverted to speaking in English. "That is ridiculous Hania. Just letters. You know it is not a possibility to come. She is living behind Iron Curtain, not New York."

"Letters suddenly are possible. What next?"

"But what is..."

"No Marek. I say no. And that is finish of conversation."

"I do not understand. Why not to send simple New Year's greetings. What harm in that?"

"You were not there - not there with us in Auschwitz. You were safe here in England," she persists with a spiteful edge to her voice.

"Auschwitz!" I gasp.

Father's dressed, rushing down the stairs.

"Flying planes in the air force, Hania, I would hardly call that safe."

"What is this?" Father interjects. I know from the way that he says it that he means STOP.

"It is nothing," Mother bites back and flounces out the room into the kitchen slamming the door behind her.

Father pushes the sitting room door shut, and I'm no longer able to hear what's being said. I've no idea what Mother's doing in the kitchen, but I reckon the party is doomed as far as we're concerned.

Chapter 14
1960
New Year's Eve Party

The house is hot, filled with colourful balloons. The music rocks, and the smell of sausage rolls is welcoming as we arrive at the party - and not late.

Earlier Mother surprised all three of us. After about ten minutes, the door of the kitchen was flung open and, as if making a dramatic entrance on stage, she declared, "We have new American president. This is soon to be new era. New times of hope are ahead for all people in our world. No time to be thinking of past. 1961, it will be a good year."

She sounded like the president's ambassador. I had to curb the temptation to laugh, as much from relief as from this extraordinary performance. Father got up from the armchair, walked to where she stood, lightly touched her hand and smiled. Soon we are on our way, and if nothing else, I'm looking forward to seeing Whiskey.

Uncle Greg greets us at the door and a bubbly Auntie Anne comes from behind, vivacious as ever. She's dressed in a new bright yellow skirt with white dots which bounces up and down over the stiff petticoat. The belt is tight showing off her waist. She says, "Hania, do you like my new white cashmere jumper?"

By Mother's standards it's very skimpy; however she says that she does, and hands over the cake tins. Auntie Anne flirts a little with Father, telling him he looks so much more relaxed without a tie. She dismisses Marek with a quick hello ignoring the fact that he's already passed her and is accepting a beer from Uncle Greg.

There are even more people here than I'd expected. I recognise Mr. and Mrs. Drake and Mr. and Mrs. Jones who live down our road. In the corner sit an uncle and auntie of Lisa and Peter who I've met on several occasions; they acknowledge me with a friendly wave. At first I can't see either Lisa or Peter. Then I spot Lisa, and I wonder how she'll receive me with her cousin at her side. Susan's a year younger than us, and when she's visited in the past, the three of us have played together happily.

Susan comes towards me, smiling, “Hiya! Haven’t seen you for ages.”

“I know. Hiya!” I simply reply.

Lisa’s decided I’m a friend this evening and shows me the silver bracelet her cousins gave her earlier.

“It’s a late Christmas present,” she tells me pouring me a lemonade without having asked me first what I’d like to drink.

We sit in the dining room listening to Lonnie Donegan singing “Ham ’n Eggs”.

“It’s awful, isn’t it?” laughs Lisa, and we agree.

“Let’s go and play some records in my room,” she says, and I’m happy she’s her old self, well at least for tonight.

As we’re about to leave the adults for a while, I catch a glimpse of Peter coming through the front door. He tells me he’s been to his friend Ricky’s house. “How’s Whiskey?” I ask. The cage isn’t on the back room shelf where it has been ever since Peter offered to look after him for me. “He’s not dead, is he?”

“No, ’course not, silly. We’ve put him in the garage for the party. You know how much your mum hates mice, or mouses as she calls them. And Auntie Joy is almost as bad. I’ll take you to see him soon. Okay?”

“Yeah, thanks Peter, I’d like that.”

Lisa also has Cluedo. Susan sees the game and immediately asks if we could play it. I suspect Lisa will act all superior and pretend that it’s too childish to play board games on New Year’s Eve, but she doesn’t. We listen to 45’s and play for some time. Then Lisa moves Colonel Mustard and says to me, “Martina, would you go down and get us all more lemonade?”

“Oh! Do I have to? You go,” I say as if we were best friends again.

“Come on, it’s my house, so what I say goes.”

I’m not quite sure how serious she’s being, but to avoid conflict I go anyway.

The atmosphere downstairs is stifling, not only is it very warm and high with the smell of alcohol, but my eyes begin to water as I make my way through clouds of smoke to the soft drinks’ table. It reminds me of the lay teachers’ staff room at school.

One or two couples are attempting to jive in the centre of the room. Behind them, on hard chairs, with backs to the wall, sit Mother and Father. Mother’s legs are crossed; one hand is on her lap whilst she holds an almost full glass of white wine in the other. She stares at the dancers, looking thoroughly bored. Father's posture is awkward as he chats with Mr. Jones. I don't think he finds this exchange very engaging for he nods more often than he speaks, and he keeps sipping his beer at very regular intervals. I know this isn't their kind of party.

I need to be very slow and careful carrying the drinks back across the room since I have already been nudged and pushed by the dancers at least twice. Marek comes into the room; he takes the hand of Susan's pretty eighteen year old sister Jennifer, and spins her into a jive. They dance a little, laugh a little; and make eyes a little. Mother is glancing at Father, communicating her disapproval. He looks at his watch. But it's only 11.35.

Unable to manage three lemonades, I return for the third. Auntie Anne is now on the floor stealing the show as she dances with Uncle Greg. They've cleared the limited dance space, and almost everyone in the room is admiring their action. But I'm not blind to the way she looks at Marek every time she swings in his direction. Her hair is hanging across one brow, and once again I recognise that Marilyn Monroe look. But Marek's not responding; he only has eyes for the skinny young brunette.

Serves her right, I think, delighted that their "love thing" is over. I do feel sorry for Bronia, who according to Marek, is due back next Thursday. I leave them all to it, anxious to get back to Cluedo before the other two get tired of the game.

At ten to midnight, Peter comes into Lisa's bedroom. Before summoning us down for Big Ben striking the hour, he manages to trip over Lisa's lemonade glass.

"Hey you!" admonishes a soggy Lisa. "You're fifteen years old, and you can't even hold your drink."

"Very fuddy," replies Peter.

Without tidying up we trundle down to join the adults. The television is on and Andy Stewart is singing his heart out.

"Champagne everyone," calls Uncle Greg. To me, it seems that *everyone*, apart from Mother and Father, is rather the worse for wear and would be better off forgoing more alcohol.

"Here girls, champers." He offers each of us kids a glass.

I'm standing beside Mother. She jumps into action. "Not for Martina. No alcohol for the child," she says.

"Come on Hania," Marek puts in. "Crack your face for once."

"What you say?" she retorts in fury.

Father is up. "Marek!"

Gently, but firmly he pushes Mother back down on to her chair.

"Let it go. Foolish words, that is all. He is a little drunk, you can see it."

But it's too late to do anything about my champagne; I've already drunk more than half a glass.

Mother's about to speak when Big Ben strikes midnight. The focus is now on the television, and the champagne's disappearing fast. Taking a few more sips, I realise that it's not really to my taste, so I swig down the last dregs in the sure knowledge Mother's looking. When I switch my gaze to Father, I catch sight of him pecking her on the cheek and then he turns and does the same to me.

Adults are speedily doing the rounds, wishing each other Happy New Year and giving everyone in their path a quick, sometimes not so quick kiss. Auntie Anne is managing to do her round at a terrific pace. Marek's busy pouring himself another glass of champagne when she reaches him. I think he's teasing her. I've seen it on films; the way a man will ignore a woman whom he really likes. She waits a moment, bridles, and then moves closer. He casually turns. I think he's going to kiss her, but he pretends he's not noticed her, and offers the glass of champagne to Jennifer.

Holding hands in the ring, everybody begins to sing,

"Should auld acquaintance be forgot and never brought to mind…"

Then Marek begins some sort of Jewish folk dance and almost everybody joins in. But not Mother and Father who are restless and anxious to leave; however I remind them that I've not seen Whiskey yet. Peter's not in sight, so they puff a little and reluctantly sit down again on the same chairs.

Having had nothing to eat so far, I wander off into the back room to grab any leftovers. There are a couple of tired looking ham sandwiches, a plate of rejected cocktail sausages, an almost full bowl of peanuts plus a couple of misshapen mince pies. I help myself to a curling sandwich and sit on the footstool waiting for Peter to reappear. Lisa tells me he's gone to the toilet. She laughs as she whispers in my ear, "Not feeling good."

She's in the mood for dancing now, so is Susan, but I'm not. I figure if I sit here long enough he'll eventually come. If I return to the front room, Mother will surely insist on leaving straight away.

Half past twelve. I'm feeling tense and consider giving Whiskey a miss when Peter comes down the stairs, entering the room with a little swagger. He says a girl from his class phoned to wish him a Happy New Year. I think he looks decidedly pale. "Wh-Whiskey," he says as if he's having a job to remember my mouse. "Blimey, I promised to take you ages ago, didn't I?"

"Never mind," I say walking through the kitchen and out into the garden. Peter staggers a little as he takes the back step.

"Are you sure you're okay?"

"'Course," he reassures me.

I shudder with the sudden impact of the freezing air. Many houses stand in darkness, and I feel very grown up being out here after midnight when so many people are already fast asleep. As the garage is attached to the house, access is easy.

The door's slightly open. It's dark inside. Peter goes in first. He turns on the light.

"Jesus!" he exclaims. "What the hell?"

The tone of his voice is really frightening me. I'm looking now. And I see them quickly breaking away from one another. Auntie Anne is fumbling with her bra and little jumper. Marek stands gaping like a frightened rabbit in the headlights.

"You bastard!" I've never heard Peter call anyone that before. "You bloody fucking bastard!" he yells at Marek, then strides towards his mother and spits in her face. "And that's for you. How could you, you bitch?"

"Look, er - we just came in here to get some more beers," says Marek.

"You what?" shouts Peter, "Typical! Bloody typical! What else would you expect from a stinking rotten Jew? Now, get out of here."

Auntie Anne is whimpering and begging Peter to keep his voice down. But it's too late. Uncle Greg is there, standing in the doorway with Mother and Father behind him, open-mouthed.

Chapter 15
2008
Kraków

The trumpet sounds from the Basilica of the Virgin Mary. 7 o'clock in the evening. It beggars belief to realise the tradition of a trumpeter calling the hour, night and day, has continued for eight hundred years - a watch system to ensure the safety of all who live in Kraków. We could have done with a system like that in Woodland Avenue all those years ago. A box, just like Pandora's, had been opened, and what had escaped could never be put back.

Sticks and stones may break my bones, but words can never hurt me.

"What nonsense," I say to myself, as I leave Market Square and pass through the narrow streets on my way to the new Jewish Museum. It should read:

Sticks and stones may break my bones, but cruel words shatter the very heart of me.

The performance of Klezmer music is late in starting, so I wander round looking at the photographs displayed on the museum walls. I particularly concentrate on those victims of Auschwitz. I try not to, but I can't look at photos of that place and not search for Mother.

The band is ready, and since I'm one of an audience of nine, I take a seat in the front row. When the music begins I'm excited and entranced by the sound of the strings. It touches me in a way that I'd not expected. As if from nowhere the words *typical, what else would you expect from a stinking rotten Jew?* dart into my head.

Who would ever have thought such a thing of Peter? More than four decades have elapsed since then, and when I think of that New Year's Eve, it still hurts like a knife being twisted in a wound.

My world at Woodland Avenue was shattered. And yes, Pandora's Box was well and truly opened on New Year's Day 1961.

Chapter 16
1961
New Year's Eve Party

A stunned silence follows before the storm erupts. Mother appears dumbfounded and Father gapes, unable to believe his ears.

"I'll give you stinking rotten Jew." And Marek is lunging towards Peter with fists clenched.

Uncle Greg snaps into action and is between them before a blow can be struck. "Hey! What's all this about?"

Party guests have gathered round, sobered by this display of violence. Peter Sellers in the background is now singing "Goodness Gracious Me".

Peter Harris, however, is cherry red and on the brink of tears. His voice takes on a girlish quality as he points to his mother, who is sniffing and dabbing her eyes. Then he stabs the air towards Marek, now being restrained by Uncle Greg and Mr. Jones.

"Ask them. Go on bloody ask them. They were kissing… all over each other- disgusting - they're disgusting."

Marek shakes himself free. "For God's sake, you idiot little pup!" He sneers at Peter as if he's been done a grave injustice, then turns to Uncle Greg. "I don't know what he thinks he saw, but it was a peck, just a New Year's Eve kiss. Look around you, a couple of minutes ago everyone was at it. Didn't you ask me to go and get more beers from garage?"

"Yes," replies Uncle Greg.

"It was nothing mate, just a peck, that is all. Don't make mountain out of bloody mole hill."

"You bloody liar!" Peter shouts.

"Anne?" Marek asks.

"Yes, yes, that's all it was, really Greg. A New Year's Eve kiss." Auntie Anne is at her husband's side. She appears relieved and has regained control.

I'm standing there, despising the pair of them, thinking, "You liars!"

Peter holds the trump card. “Yeah! In the dark? So why didn’t you have the light on then?”

“What? Of course it was on.” Marek is frighteningly convincing.

Peter looks at me. “It wasn’t was it?”

All eyes are on me now. I hesitate. Then say, “I can’t remember.”

“Well, you saw the way they were kissing too, didn’t you Martina? And it wasn’t just a peck, was it?”

I’m still so angry, feeling bitter and betrayed by Peter’s insult to Jewish people that I lie. “No,” I say to punish him. “I didn’t see anything.”

“You did too!” he shrieks, and then vomits where he stands.

“I don’t know what the boy thinks he saw, but if you want my advice,” Marek says to Uncle Greg, “I would keep him off alcohol.” With that he pushes passed the voyeurs and disappears.

Chapter 17
1961
New Year's Day

I lie awake until sunrise. It's just as well sleep escaped me, because I dread to think what I'd have dreamt. I still can't believe the venom that came out of Peter's mouth. I thought I knew him. Peter, who apart from his sister, never has a bad word to say about anybody. It just goes to show what's lurking beneath the surface. Indeed, I savour a sadistic satisfaction at what I did in vengeance. Serves Peter right.

Revenge does not taste so sweet when I realise what I've actually done by lying is to let Marek and Auntie Anne get away with it yet again. In the chink between the curtains I see a metallic grey sky and the rain pelting down. As I keep going over and over the events of last night, the rain splashes incessantly against the windowpane. "Happy New Year," I mutter to myself, and feel a tear roll down my face as the burden of guilt descends upon me. Looking across at my *Letts School-Girls' Diary*, I recall yesterday's question - What will be written in the diary by this time next year?

When I brave it downstairs, Mother and Father have finished their breakfast and they are discussing the evils of drinking too much alcohol. "And Peter so young. Ah! Yes, a disgraceful performance was it not?" Mother continues to pontificate. "And they laugh at me when I say no alcoholic drink for the child. See where it led to with Peter." She's still got more to say on the subject, "Not the boy's fault. Is it not the adults who are to blame?"

Father nods. "Tak, tak."

I hook on to, "It's not the boy's fault."

Mother sees me, "Breakfast Martina?"

Her mood is better than I'd expected under the circumstances, whereas Father seems truly down in the dumps. He's the one who today appears far away and distracted. Dismissing Mother's offer of another coffee, he bolts up from his seat and heads for the door, telling her he's going to phone Marek, check he got home safely. "Hania," he says, "Peter was not the only one who overdid the alcohol."

"Breakfast?" asks Mother.

"No." I'm very curt. Too curt, so I tack on a quick thank you. I've made my mind up to do the right thing and don't want any delays. I've definitely not forgiven Peter, but nevertheless am determined not to let Auntie Anne (Ridiculous now to call her that) Anne and Marek off the hook yet again.

It's not going to be easy. Here I am again, asking the same questions. How should I do it? What shall I say? What will be my opening words? If only I'd told Father when I'd seen them kissing and canoodling in our house. But it's too late for self-recriminations. I just have to get on with it, and now.

On reaching the Harris's front door, I can hear music playing; ironically it's "Warpaint". I wait in the pouring rain until I summon up the courage to knock. Lisa appears. Now out of friendly mode, she greets me with, "Oh! It's you." And she stands in her pyjamas looking straight through me.

The smell of bacon and eggs wafts through the hall. Anne pops her head out of the kitchen wanting to know who's at the door. She sees me, averts her eyes and momentarily drops the smile. In that split second her eyes betray her. She knows I saw them last night, and is worried.

"Hello love," she says, her voice overly friendly. "Greg darling, one or two fried eggs?"

"Two," he calls back. He sounds cheerful enough.

But not for long, I think.

I must speak with Peter soon. Explain. Explain why I lied. Tell him, how hurt and angry I felt - make him realise how his words insulted all Jewish people. In that moment, I wonder if Peter is in fact aware that our family is Jewish. After all it's never really come up - except at primary school when we were reading *The Diary of Anne Frank* - and Peter wasn't there.

"Yes?" asks Lisa nibbling away on the corner of her jammy toast.

"Can I speak to Peter, please?"

She smirks. With sudden camaraderie says, "He's not feeling too bright today. Remember?"

Peter appears at the top of the stairs wearing creased blue jeans and a loose unironed carrot coloured shirt which looks more like a pyjama top. His face is phantom white. "It's okay." He dismisses his sister with the wave of a hand.

"See what I mean," hoots Lisa looking up to heaven.

I'm not invited in. Even though it's cold and the rain is lashing down, we stand on the doorstep with the front door ajar.

"What do you want?" he says icily. Peter is a different person.

"I think we need to talk. I need to explain," I say very quietly, and suggest that perhaps this is not a good place - the bus shelter round the corner, on the main road, might be better, more private.

"No need."

"But - I need to explain. Why I lied, said that I didn't see them, you know, kissing and ..."

Peter interrupts, "You saw nothing. Nothing. I was drunk."

I hear Uncle Greg's footsteps padding down the stairs. "Breakfast ready yet? I'm starving, love."

"But Peter, they were..."

His whisper is a hiss, "You saw nothing! Right? I told you, too much to drink. Just leave it. Bye."

The door promptly shuts.

I'm standing alone soaked to the skin.

Chapter 18
2008
Kraków

It's late, but I'm reluctant to return to the hotel after the wonderful concert, for the pulse of the Klezmer music still haunts me. Having ordered a coffee and a plum brandy, I take my phone and text:

Gr8 concert. Hope headache betta.
Having qk coffee. C u soon.

M xx

Content to be alone, I watch life carrying on around me. Glass after glass of wine, vodka and beer are being knocked back. I ask myself, what will be revealed as a result of all this drinking? *In vino veritas.* In wine there is truth. Today, I saw this quotation scrawled on a wall of a bar, and I recognised it from my student days. I'm thinking about these words while sitting at a round table in Market Square close to the entrance of Wislna Street. The April breeze whispers through the city and the temperature's high considering the late hour. Kraków is buzzing. Animated conversation and laughter come from every quarter.

A busker, with eyes shut, plays loud reverberating old Cream numbers on an amplified electric guitar. No one takes much notice of his self-indulgence even though he sings well. A little further into the centre of the Square a troop of fire jugglers attract excited crowds. To the hypnotic beating of drums, flames shoot high forming feathery gold rings against the darkness. Memories best forgotten intrude as I watch the illuminated cigarette smoke swirl and rise like orange clouds against the city's night sky.

My thoughts switch to that New Year fiasco and recall how afterwards, Peter could not look me in the eye. Marek did not dare to look me in the eye - and Anne avoided me like the plague for weeks. And as for Marek's visits to our house, they grew much less frequent, although Father continued to meet him regularly after work for a drink in the pub.

Anne kept her distance for several weeks until things had settled down. This period proved hard for Mother who had grown to like and depend on Anne's friendship. Of course she blamed Marek entirely for the situation.

She would moan to Father, "Trust Marek. But for him, all would be well. Where there is Marek, there is trouble."

And there is more than a grain of truth in that, I thought.

Father said nothing, opting for the easy life.

Eventually, happy relations were restored between Mother and Anne; and despite Anne taking a part-time office job, they resumed their regular tête-a-têtes over coffee or tea. Uncle Greg remained as friendly as ever, always asking me questions about netball or my progress with the violin. One day when he was tending the rockery in his back garden he saw me, looked up and said, "You ought to pop across sometime. Pity you and Lisa don't get to see each other much any more."

"Okay, I will," I said feeling really sorry for him.

But I never went to the Harris's house unless it was essential; and neither did Peter or Lisa come over to ours - unless sent to borrow the odd onion or a cup of sugar. And I never got to see Whiskey again. Lisa told me gleefully over the fence one day in the middle of January that Peter had given him away to a school friend.

My personal Cold War with Peter persisted alongside the one between America and Russia; and both were unbearable in their own way. Surprisingly, I got used to this chilly relationship with our neighbours quite quickly; and indeed nothing changed until the summer of 1962 when all hell broke loose in Woodland Avenue.

Chapter 19
July 1962

It's the second week of Wimbledon. Maria Bueno has just won her match. Father's hooked on the doubles match following on from it; but I prefer to go into the garden and relax in the fresh air. Mother's in a sombre mood, baking in the kitchen. I can just about see her through the window, nodding and muttering as she kneads the dough with great vigour.

In the shade of the ash tree, I lounge in the deck chair. I watch a bumblebee nuzzle the honeysuckle and contemplate my exam results. So far I've gained 85% for English, for Maths 82% and 78% for Latin. I'm pleased and hope the rest of my results will be as good.

From the other side of the fence I hear Peter groaning as Lisa misses the shuttlecock yet again, and then they begin to argue about her wearing daft shoes for badminton. Restless, I get up, find my tennis racket and hit a few balls up against the wall of our house - I'm in the Wimbledon Ladies' Finals - winning the third set when the phone rings. But it seems no one can be bothered to answer it. The ringing finally stops only to begin again after a short interval. This time, thinking the call may be for me, I drop my racket and race indoors, but Father already has the receiver in his hand. Half looking at the television through the open door, he appears disinterested in what the caller has to say until…

"Nie! Co? Nie!! Gdzie jest Marek?"

"Where is Marek?" I ask myself. "Did Father really say where is Marek?"

Father's voice is loud, and angry. Is Marek at the root of the trouble yet again? Then everything happens at super speed. He rushes into the kitchen, gabbles something in Polish to Mother, ignores me, grabs the car keys and disappears, oblivious to the loud cheering of Wimbledon spectators in the sitting room.

At 9.15pm I've just finished practising my new violin piece in the sitting room when I hear the car pull up into our drive. Father gets out, opens the boot, removes a large brown suitcase which he carries to the house and leaves on the doormat. He returns to the car and takes out a small dark green holdall. Someone is sitting in the passenger seat, but I can't make out who it is.

"Mum!" I call, "Dad's back. I don't mention the luggage or that someone else is with him.

The passenger door opens and Bronia emerges, face puce, eyes red and swollen. Not a pretty sight. I drop the net curtain, quickly return my violin to its case and disappear, leaving Mother to greet them.

No one is keeping their voice down, but anyway I sit on the top stair eavesdropping. Although I'm unable to understand the exact sequence of events, my Polish is now good enough to grasp the gist of what's happened.

The long and the short of it, is Bronia had intended to visit a friend this evening after leaving the hairdresser salon where she works. However, this friend who lives in Slough, suddenly became unwell, phoned and cancelled. Unfortunately for Marek, he'd made "an arrangement" with his other woman (who unbelievably turns out to be Anne Harris) Gee! There they were, *at it* when Bronia returned home early. It doesn't take a lot of imagination to envisage the scene that followed.

From what Bronia is telling Mother at this moment, I understand the couples had become friendly on her return from Canada. Marek told Bronia he'd got to know Greg quite well while he was staying with us. Apparently, they meet up with Greg and Anne quite often these days. Anyhow, enraged at discovering Marek and Anne in bed together, she rang Greg at the hotel. Wow! Poor Greg! And then it would seem, in desperation she phoned Father. By the time he'd driven to Ealing, Marek true to form, probably dazed with vodka and in a cloud of cigarette smoke, had disappeared.

Bronia blows her nose. Mother says she'll make her some sweet tea before going upstairs to prepare the spare bedroom. While she's in the kitchen I hear Bronia start up again, her voice raised and conveying a certain relish. "At least she got her comeuppance. Would you believe it? That whore she kept shrieking at Marek, demanding him to tell *me* to get out. The bitch, she then turns to me and *she* tells *me* that Marek is going to marry *her.* But I tell you this. It is now *she* who is crying. Why? Because Marek he is pulling up trousers - and what does he say? Nothing. On and on that whore she yells, *Go on Marek! Tell Bronia. Tell her!* The blonde tart, she is hysterical, clinging to Marek's arm. And there he is, trying to wrench himself free, desperate to escape."

Bronia is now chortling and snorting like a horse. "So, what does Marek say? Of course, he tells her she must be kidding - asks the tart when marriage was mentioned? By this time, I tell you, she is wailing - especially when Marek shouts that she should be out of flat when he gets back. Serves her right, does it not, Stefan? And to think I left my husband, a good man, for this Marek Rogozinski."

Bronia is sobbing again and dabbing those swollen eyes. Some minutes later she reports with triumph that mascara was running down Anne's face, and she looked absolutely repulsive. By this time I'm halfway down the stairs and peeping through the banisters; and I have to say Bronia herself is no oil painting - with lobster eyes, blotchy complexion and shaking plump bosoms straining to get out of her tight low-cut pink blouse.

Mother returns with the tea and a plate of pastries. I scurry away once she heads towards the stairs on her way to make up the bed in the spare room. Just as well Bronia is ignorant of the fact that Marek and Anne also occupied that bed, I muse.

Once Bronia is settled in the front bedroom I slip down to the kitchen and pour myself a glass of milk. It's as if Mother and Father have forgotten I exist. They take no notice of me, but continue discussing the events of the evening. Father's saying that soon after he arrived at Marek's flat, Bronia started to throw her belongings into a suitcase. She then opened a large bottle of vodka, poured the entire contents all over the double bed before seizing bottles of beer and smashing them against the walls. Having vented her frustration and fury, Father managed to discover that Anne had also fled the sordid little scene in pursuit of Marek.

Mother listens, her mouth opening and shutting like a goldfish. I keep wondering when she's going to respond. Then she whispers, "All this time - Anne - with Marek - and I did not know it."

Well, I didn't know either. I imagined, after Peter and I saw them in the garage, they'd have thanked their lucky stars to have got away with it unscathed and gone their separate ways. But in truth, by now, I cease to be surprised by anything that this pair get up to.

I wait nervously all night for the bomb to go off next door. There is, I have to admit, something farcical about Bronia sleeping in the house right next door to her lover's girlfriend. But the expected explosion doesn't take place.

The next evening when I return from school Bronia's gone, and Mother and Father try to make a huge secret of the whole thing, clearly not wanting me to know much about what's going on. I ask where she is now, and their response is to act surprised as if they're amazed I'm aware she'd spent the night here. As always, trying to protect me - keep me in the dark; but this is truly ridiculous - where did they imagine I'd been hiding all yesterday evening? Unless of course they think I'm hard of hearing. I do think perhaps they've failed to realise just how much Polish I've actually grown to understand over the years. But for the sake of peace, I keep my mouth shut.

However, soon there's no hiding the fact that only two occupants are living in the house next door, Anne and Lisa. Mrs. Carr tells Mother that Peter has left home with his father - some sort of upset took place. "Somethin' gone wrong in the marriage," she says in a hushed voice. I learn some while later that they are both living in the hotel where Greg works.

Strangely, Mother is less shocked and outraged by the whole sorry affair than Father. She keeps appealing to him not to make judgements, but he's insistent that Mother should discontinue her friendship with Anne. And Anne is never entertained in our house again. But this afternoon when I return from school, I find Mother's not at home. Later she tells me she was next door having a cup of tea with Auntie Anne.

Chapter 20
July 1963

We're taking the apples to the shed. The nuns have an orchard in the convent grounds. Between the tall pine trees and tennis courts are a number of long sheds. Here they store the apples throughout the year. Rows upon rows of Coxes lie in straight lines on long wooden tables. Perfectly rounded, each the same green shade and tinged with a red hue - each one the exact same size. They stand in their immaculate uniforms like soldiers on parade.

The July sun, for a second day is beating down. It's late afternoon, the blackbirds are singing, and we should be on our way home by now; however the four of us have something we must do before leaving school.

Sinéad passes me her apple, offering to be lookout. Peeping from behind the shed, she informs us that fortunately no nuns are in sight.

"Must all be inside prayin'."

"Or having their tea," I laugh.

"I'm never stealing anything again," says Mary full of remorse and mad with us for having persuaded her to commit the mortal sin of theft.

In spite of our outward show of courage, I think all of us must have butterflies in our stomachs. Waiting, I'm imagining what Sister Mary Paul will say or even worse *do* if we're caught red-handed. But the coast is clear, and I'm safely through the open door with the other two hard on my heels. Krysia's whispers, "God, don't be so ridiculous Mary. It's not stealing. It's called borrowing. We just borrowed a few apples. No big deal."

Yesterday we'd been so hungry after staying behind to play tennis, that on a whim we crept into the shed and took four apples from the middle of a table. How delicious was that forbidden fruit.

"Blimmin' heck and what if the nuns notice?" Mary had asked gaping at the space we were leaving in our wake. "Just look at it."

"Never you mind," said Sinéad. "Oh jeez, tomorrow we'll each just bring an apple from home. Then after tennis practice, once everyone else has gone, we'll come an' put them back. With a bit of luck the nuns will be none the wiser, sure they won't."

"That's it," I had agreed. "I bet they don't come every day and count the apples. They won't know it was us anyhow."

So here we are apples in hands. We slot them into the long gap, one by one. Satisfied that the deed has been done, we step back to admire our honesty. The sight of those intruders fills us with horror.

"Hurry up, you three!" calls Sinéad.

"Here. Come in here, you Irish minx," cries Krysia giggling.

Even Mary's in stitches.

"God in heaven!" exclaims Sinéad when she sees the incongruous four. A large shiny red apple, an even larger bright green one, a golden yellowish specimen and a small gnarled one have taken the place of the beautiful Coxes. They look as out of place as a baby cuckoo in a sparrow's nest.

"Blimey what'll the nuns think when they find these?" asks Mary unable to stop laughing.

"They'll think, whoever's replaced their apples is mighty honest. Now, let's scram out of here. Come on," says Krysia.

It's already rush hour, so I'm pleased that this Friday, I won't need to travel on the stuffy bus and endure the sweaty smell of human bodies. In addition, staying the night with Kyrsia means no moaning from Mother about me being late home. I've learnt to sleep on my feet when she carries on and on; nevertheless, it's always good to avoid an irksome nag.

This will be the first time I've stayed the night at Krysia's, and I'm really looking forward to it; but I'm a little afraid that I won't be able to get to sleep and will simply toss and turn until daylight.

We turn into the leafy avenue with its large detached houses. It's still hot and close, so we've removed our ties. Our blouses hang open at the neck, and our school blazers are draped carelessly across our school bags - but still we wear the regulation school boaters.

"Oh by the way, I think the Liebermans are coming over for dinner this evening," says Krysia.

"That's nice," I reply *really* meaning it since I've met them here quite often and like them very much. The friendliness between these two families, Catholic and Jewish, never fails to impress me. Like Krysia's dad, Mr. Lieberman has the title of doctor, but unlike Dr.

Kotkowski, he's not a doctor of medicine, but of philosophy, (or as Krysia used to say in the First Year, a doctor of philo-something.)

"It's a sort of celebration because Dr. Lieberman's latest application to the golf club has been accepted."

This fires something inside me, and the words pop out so quickly that even I'm surprised to hear, "I'm Jewish."

Without taking a breath I await Krysia's reaction. I'm expecting her to stop stock-still, or to drop her bag in shock. But the birds keep chirping, the aeroplane flying above does not fall out of the sky, and the world's still spinning as she replies as casually as if I'd mentioned the purchase of a new pair of shoes, "Really? I didn't know that you go to the synagogue."

"I don't."

Krysia looks confused.

I explain to her as best I can, feeling awkward and anxious now the cat is out of the bag. With reserve I ask her how she thinks Sinéad and Mary would react if they knew.

"For heaven's sake, they're your friends. They wouldn't care two hoots." Krysia now sounds shocked, but soon she's smiling, and giving me a friendly nudge. "We're living in the 1960s not in Shylock's day, you know. It's no big deal. Honestly."

"No," I say, but am silently asking myself, "Why then has Dr. Lieberman only *just* been granted membership of the Golf Club?"

We're at the gates of her house. The broad front lawn smells of freshly mown grass, and I admire the tidy beds with co-ordinated pink, red and white flowers. Helena, Krysia's ten year old sister, is playing ball with Domino the dalmation. When they catch sight of us, both girl and dog rush over. Domino's ears and tongue are flapping and flopping as he runs. I'm pleased to be greeted with that familiar sloppy lick from their dopey dog.

"Cześć!" hails Mrs. Kotkowska who is laying a tea tray in the kitchen. "We're in the garden."

With a touch of pride I respond in Polish. I carry the plate of biscuits as we proceed out to the back lawn. Krysia's mother comments about our lateness, but no interrogation follows. I like Krysia's mum. She doesn't fuss. She doesn't nag. Her smile is warm and her manner friendly. She reminds me of how "Auntie" Anne used to be before she became Marilyn Monroe. Mrs. Kotkowska is, as Father describes Bronia, pleasantly plump. She's the warm, cuddly mum every child longs to come home to.

Next Friday the summer term ends, and with it, my third year at Our Lady of Lourdes. Over the next weeks I'll miss the Kotkowskis as I will my other friends who are off on holiday as soon as we break up. Krysia is to stay with her cousins who live near Pitlochry in Scotland. Mary's family are staying on a farm in Dorset whilst Sinéad's family is off camping in their native Ireland. "This year, me da said we're goin' to be adventurous," she declared.

Sinéad went on to suggest we lot would love it. "You should see our huge tents an' cosy sleepin' bags. We'll be eatin' out under the stars, so we will."

I burst out laughing. I can just picture it. Mother camping! Doesn't bear thinking about - Mother who begins to scratch at the first glimpse of a woodlouse or ant, and imagines rats when in the vicinity of the smallest hole or crevice.

Anyway, Sinéad is really excited because not only is she going "back home", but she's madly in love with President Kennedy, and as he'll be visiting Ireland while they are there, she's determined to get to see him. I, however, am madly in love with John Lennon, and am more concerned about surviving two weeks in Cornwall without being able to listen to my Beatles' "Please, Please Me" LP.

Chapter 21
Summer 1963
Cornwall

I'm sitting at the back of our recently purchased blue Ford Anglia, squashed between a suitcase that refused to fit into the boot and a bundle of bed linen. We're three hours into our journey, heading for Hayle in Cornwall. This is our first family holiday for seven years since the one to Bournemouth, which hadn't exactly been a success.

That year, rain or shine, whilst Father joined me in the sea with his trousers rolled up or helped to build castles in the sand, Mother, with a face like thunder, sat in a deck chair staring into the horizon. Father constantly tried to cheer her up, but to no avail. She wasn't happy; therefore as is the usual pattern, he wasn't happy. I was left believing that perhaps holidays are only fun in story books.

Nevertheless, I've a good feeling about this holiday. Even though Mother was a bit tetchy before the actual departure, she told Father yesterday over supper, that she's determined to have a good time. Determined to enjoy a holiday! A little odd in my book, but still, it bodes well.

Early morning. This is the time I like best, when hardly anyone else is about. Clambering down the sandy slopes laced with soft beards of grass, I begin to saunter along the beach towards the distant lighthouse. Miles of golden sand stretch ahead. Ozone fills my lungs; there's nothing quite like the smell of the sea. The ocean's a monstrous turquoise jewel, glinting and winking in the sunlight for as far as the eye can see. Thousands of fairy lights flicker on the crests of the waves which rise like the necks of swans. Today it purrs like a kitten, yesterday, the ocean roared like a ferocious lion. I paddle along the water's edge with sea lapping at my ankles. Above, seagulls squawk high in the sky and fly from the coast, waiting for the first signs of breakfast as they circle the fishing boats.

The solitude and sense of peace is bliss, that's until my thoughts turn to the politicians who could destroy all this beauty with a press of a button. However, the sun is high in the sky, the day bright with promise and the shadow of yesterday's chill has gone, so I refuse to be depressed and instantly dismiss these dismal thoughts.

We've been here nine days. It took Mother a day or two to adjust to the unfamiliar bungalow. A little grumbling here, a little fussing there and quite a lot of concern over the security of the house in Woodland Avenue. But now I'm happy to say, she seems relaxed and content - and naturally when Mother is fine, Father becomes a different person.

I love it here. The bungalow which stands on the cliff top already feels like home. It's clean. It's comfortable, if rather sparsely equipped. It has everything we need for a holiday. It even has a television which particularly pleases Father, albeit a coin-in-the slot one where sixpence purchases half an hour's worth of viewing.

In the evenings Mother prefers to knit after supper, then she winds her way down the sandy path to the rocks where she sits until dark, looking out to sea. She says that she likes to listen to the voice of the ocean. Of late I've been joining her. The first time I came, I stood from afar and watched. She knew I was there, as later she said, "You can come with me next time if you like, Child."

I said I'd like that very much. And it's here I learn that Mother had never seen the open sea until she was an adult. But mostly we sit in companionable silence, enchanted by the patterns of the water and hypnotised by the swirling chain of bubbles in the night rock pools.

The ocean with its constantly changing moods inspires me, so one evening when I return to the bungalow, I slip into my bedroom and recreate its music on my violin. Sometimes I hear John Lennon's words accompanying me, and sometimes the tune has the flavour of Brahms. For a moment I think of Marek who thankfully no longer visits our house.

Sitting in a tearoom in Marazion, my teeth sink into a scone filled with strawberry jam and Cornish cream. Mother says I look very funny with a white moustache. She's laughing which is so rare that I'm overcome with happiness.

On the table lies a bar of Bourneville chocolate. This, I bought to eat after supper. Father points to it and says, "That reminds me of when I was working in Birmingham chocolate factory." He chuckles a little. "So, on first morning, they take me to warehouse where I am to work. The men they are friendly, but it is difficult not speaking much English. Anyway, there I am loading onto lorries heavy boxes full of chocolate. Hard work you understand, but I was this strong young man in those days. I think everything is going so very well, until it comes to lunch break, and one man working in same team he asks to speak with me. And you know what he tells me?"

"What?" I ask delighted to hear Father chatting about old times.

"Well, this man he tells me to slow down, not to load so many boxes onto lorries very quickly. He says if I keep such fast pace up, they will all be expected to work that hard!"

"Really?"

"Really."

Mother's smiling, so I remark, "It's odd, isn't it, that Dad worked in a chocolate factory, when you hate chocolate so much?"

"I suppose," she says with a sniff.

I quickly revert to our previous discussion concerning the moon and its effect on the tides.

Driving back to Hayle we pass St. Michael's Mount I notice the tide is in. It's a hot afternoon, very hot and I'm longing to bathe in the sea. Father's surprised me this year. He's bought a pair of trunks and has been swimming too. Strange as it may seem, I had no idea that he could swim until we came away on this holiday. He now tells me of the risks he took swimming in the rivers and sliding down the waterfalls when he was a boy in Poland. Who would've thought Father to be so in love with danger?

Once on the beach Mother, fully dressed, settles in a deckchair reading the newspaper while Father and I change into our swim wear. The sun is very hot and I wonder how she's able to stand the heat. Impatient to bathe, I grab the surfboard and dive into the cold sea. Exhilaration! A huge wave rolls towards me like a mighty horse galloping across the ocean. I'm ready to ride. Before I reach the shallow waters, I'm rolling free; surfboard and I having parted company. My hair swirls round my body. This is heaven, I think, standing on the sand wiping the salty water from my eyes.

Later, when I'm sunbathing Mother becomes too hot and says she's going back to the bungalow. This I find a little sad because I know how much she likes it on the seashore. As the beach isn't crowded, I suggest she removes her cardigan. Father immediately looks uneasy.

"Mum, but there's no one nearby to see…"

"I will see," she says and stomps off.

I'm getting up to follow her, but Father advises me to leave her a while. As he drags his deck chair closer to me, I notice his brow is furrowed.

"Martina?"

"Yes," I reply. My heart sinks at the tone of his voice. I should've known that heaven couldn't last.

"You're fifteen this year, yes?"

"Of course. You know that. Why are you asking?"

"I want to tell you this. Mum she does not want it, but I believe you are old enough and should know. You have to keep what I say to yourself. It is most important that you do as I ask. Understand?"

"Okay, okay. Come on. What's all this about?"

He wastes no further time. "Mum, she has a sister."

"A sister? Mum's got a sister? I thought everyone in her family died in the war?"

"Well, not everyone. She has younger sister. Ewa. Ewa she is two years younger."

"Gee a sister! Well, why hasn't she ever said? And where's this sister then? Poland?" I'm kneeling on the sand with my hands resting on the side of the stripey green deck chair.

"Yes, in Poland."

It clicks. The mysterious letters. Since the first ones years ago, others followed, and no doubt were also destroyed. My thoughts now return to the conversation between Mother and Marek. The one I overheard on that dreadful New Year's Eve of 1960. The *her* they referred to, must have been Mother's sister. The *her* who met Marek's mother in Kraków. "But why doesn't Mum want any contact with her own sister?" I ask.

"What shall I say? You may not even believe such a thing, but I do not have answer to this question. Mum she refuses to discuss it - and

I gave up trying to make her years ago. It's like - her not wanting to talk about war - concentration camp - or even life under Communists before we came here to England. For her it all must be left behind, left in past, never to be mentioned."

"But when you two first met up again after the war? Surely she must've said something then?"

Father sighs. "A little… look Martina, it's not so very simple. Like many survivors of those terrible camps she did not want to speak of it. I suppose something, something very bad must have happened between them to destroy their relationship when they were in Auschwitz - what Mum did say, was that as far as she is concerned Ewa may as well be dead."

He pauses. I'm speechless. A seagull's harsh cry breaks the silence.

"You see, it was only through Marek I discovered Ewa played violin in some women's orchestra while in camp. So perhaps it has something to do with that, who knows?" He shrugs his shoulders.

I'm listening, listening intently. My toes are digging into the sand and Father's left hand is rubbing his cheek earnestly; and when he removes his fingers, a red mark remains.

"But why are you suddenly telling me all this now?"

"Because there is chance she may come to England. That is what Ewa wants, to visit. To see her sister - for purpose of reconciliation I believe. Quite recently Marek he told me this when we meet in pub. His mother in Kraków writes this in letter to him. It would seem she and Ewa meet now quite often."

"And Mum doesn't want to see her?"

"Absolutely not. She refuses. Of course travel abroad it still is not so easy in Communist countries, but things they are changing in Poland. So, who can say how soon…" Father's flow is interrupted.

When I look up, there, waving to us is Mother returning to the beach. She's changed, and is wearing a long-sleeved cream cotton blouse with her shorter burnt amber skirt patterned with khaki half-moons. In her hand she holds a bottle of orange squash.

There's a stony edge to the white clouds as we pack to leave Hayle. The relaxed silence of recent mornings is filled with unspoken tension while Mother checks we don't forget anything and that the bungalow is left clean and tidy. Father squeezes the last of the luggage into the car while I wander down to the shore to take a last glimpse of the sea before our long homeward journey.

Traffic jam follows traffic jam. The journey seems endless and by the time we turn into Woodland Avenue I'm almost asleep. Even before the car has come to a halt, I hear Mother gasp, "Oh no!"

It doesn't take long to learn the reason. There, large as life, in the Harris's front garden stands the sign "For Sale".

PART THREE

Chapter 22
Spring 1964

The SOLD sign is down and the Harris's house, as is customary for us to call it, is up For Sale yet again! Mother is *not* happy.

"Rats! I hear them. Scratching. I hear rats through the walls. Scratching all the time."

We're sitting eating breakfast. It's a fine morning in March. For once it's not raining and shafts of sunlight shoot through the kitchen window. They illuminate the dancing 'fairies', invisible on bleak days. Well, that's how I still like to think of motes. When I was little, Father told me those shiny floating flecks were fairies. Sometimes I would name them, and make up stories about Violet, Rose and Daisy. Yes, I think those were the names I gave to those heroines of my imaginings.

Musing upon this pleasant childhood fantasy, I spoon up the cornflakes from the bowl in front of me, and at the same time try to blank out Mother's most recent complaint. Ever since the Harris's house has gone back on the market, she's convinced thousands of rats have moved in. It's true that Mrs. Carr's black cat, Samba, was seen trotting across our lawn with a mouse, but a mouse is not a rat. But it's no use trying to persuade Mother. I for one have given up.

"Hania," pacifies Father who is already in danger of being late for work. "There are no rats, I tell you. The estate agent said this too. You know it. He went in house - twice, and looked. You must try to calm yourself."

Mother, petulant, is deaf to his words. "Such a pity, the man he had to have stroke, and they could not come to live in house. They looked so very nice people. Now it must go back on market before they even live in it for one day."

Father sighs. "That is life! We do not always get what we want. So, another nice family will come and buy it. But it is time I go. Saturday is always busy and I do not want to be late."

"In the meantime, we must suffer rats," Mother witters on.

Father offers to give me a lift to the netball rally as the venue is on his route. It's only ten past eight. I know I'll be early, but there's no way that I want to sit here listening to all this carry on about the rats. I would pay the Pied Piper to take away her rats if it were at all possible.

Without hesitation I accept his offer and leave the table. "Come back and finish your breakfast," Mother calls.

"Gee, I have."

"No, there is milk and flakes left. Come, eat."

I tut then stomp back. Standing, I consume the last dregs from the bowl and march out. All the while Mother reminds me about the starving children in India who would give their right hand for the food I always waste. "Well, put it all in a parcel and send it to them," I say callously in a deliberate attempt to needle her.

As we drive down the road, I feel ashamed, both on account of the children in India and for the way that I spoke to Mother; but recently she's *really* been getting on my nerves.

There's a traffic jam in the Broadway and Father's getting tetchy about the importance of being punctual. While we're at a stand-still I tie my hair back into a ponytail, put on some liquid make-up, then attempt to flick on a layer of mascara as the car begins to crawl along the road.

"Uh! Why put that rubbish on your face?" grumbles Father as irritated with me as he is with the traffic congestion. "A pretty girl like you does not need to cake face with all that make-up."

"Come off it, Dad," I say laughing. "I hardly put any on. You should see some girls if you think I cake on make-up."

"I know, I know. I see them at chemist. But you, you do not need make-up to look good…"

"Oh, you're dead funny," I say. "Last Sunday morning when I came downstairs without any make-up on, you asked me if I was feeling ill. Now, if I wore loads of the stuff, don't you think Mum would be on at me – never mind my form teacher?"

"Ah well, in my day…"

The traffic has begun to move faster and we're off.

By lunchtime our Under 16 netball team has won three matches and lost one. We have an hour to eat our packed lunches. Lady Jane Wellinford's, where the district tournament is being held, is on a huge campus dominated by a grand York stone building. Formerly, it was a stately home and is listed. Turrets rise up from its east and west wings, and the entrance at the front is a massive wooden studded double door. On arrival we were told explicitly, that this is only for staff and visitors, "Not girls."

Shielding my eyes from the sun's glare, we walk through the well-maintained gardens and I look at the main building more closely, I think, that it bears a close resemblance to Charlotte Bronte's Thornfield Hall. In my mind's eye I see Jane Eyre gazing out from an upstairs window. The grounds at Our Lady of Lourdes are a postage stamp in comparison. Milling all around like ants are the boarders and competitors dressed in a colourful array of uniforms.

Our last match was tough and we're late off court. We lost 13-10. Now it's proving difficult to find a bench where Krysia, Sinéad, Mary and I can sit together and eat. Unlike the little ones, we're reluctant to sit on the grass; especially as it's still damp from yesterday's showers.

Having scoured the place, we walk behind the new sports' hall. There we capitulate and simply plonk ourselves down on the cast-off desks stacked alongside the wall awaiting collection.

The big news is that Sinéad has a boyfriend. Niall. He's seventeen. It took her ages to get over President Kennedy's assassination last November, but now she's more than fully recovered, and is madly in love with this Niall. She met him some weeks ago when he joined her Irish band where they both play recorder. Love at first sight.

Wonder of wonders! Finally, a fortnight ago he asked her to the cinema. She says that he looks like Con from The Bachelors, and now she's bursting to tell us the next instalment in this romantic saga.

"T'was a bit of a struggle, but da in the end let me go with Niall to his friend's party. I promised, crossed me heart to be home by eleven. And t'was Michael's car we went in…"

"Your dad let you go in a strange boy's car?"

"Oh Mary!" chides Sinéad annoyed at the interruption. "He's not a strange boy at all; he's my boyfriend's brother." She emphasises *my boyfriend* with pride.

"And what a craic the party turned out to be. Fab! Loads of wine and beer. Babycham too. Better than all that, no parents, and to be sure, hours with Niall."

"Oh Yeah! I can just imagine," teases Krysia. "Bet there was more going on than holding hands and a kiss at your front door. Come on spill. We're all ears."

Sinéad is blushing, wiggles her hips a little and adjusts her bra under her aertex PE blouse. "Perhaps, but that's for me to know Krysh, and for you to guess." She giggles.

I'm feeling mighty uncomfortable and hoping that Sinéad isn't going to go into detail. Peals of laughter come from Krysia who herself has a crush on a boy. Someone she dances with from time to time at the Polish Club in South Kensington where she goes with her parents.

Scenes of Marek and Anne together ricochet through my mind. My cheeks are ablaze, and I'm sure soon the others will notice my embarrassment. But no one is looking at me. Sinéad is beginning to describe the dark room where couples were either dancing to slow numbers, or lying around the edge of the room. Again I can hear the gruntings and moanings slipping back across the years.

"I hope you don't get pregnant," says Mary.

"Don't be an eejit. God in heaven, we were only snoggin' - and things." She has this nauseating dreamy expression on her face; and I know full well what she means by *things.*

"You wait 'til you're in love." She shudders. With that Sinéad leaps up laughing and turns to Mary. "But don't you be tellin' me da - or mam for that matter."

Flinging her uneaten packed lunch into the nearest rubbish bin, she spins round whilst pulling the elastic band from her long blonde ponytail and tosses her head wildly.

"Well, course I won't, silly. What do you take me for?" There's a hint of a smile on Mary's face now, and I'm thinking that she's probably feeling a fool for coming across so priggish. With exaggerated enthusiasm she says, "Find me a dreamboat and we'll see. Are there any boys like Billy J. Kramer in that Irish band of yours?"

Krysia is leaning back against the wall with hands clasped behind her head, holding up her long brown hair. She's grinning, but her eyes reveal the envy she feels. I bet she's thinking it would take a miracle for her parents to allow her to go to that kind of party at fifteen.

I'm shocked. I'm shocked mainly at my own feelings of revulsion. A lead weight descends upon me as I wince at the thought of being slobbered over, pawed at, or being treated to animal gruntings while my ear is being nibbled away. And I'm afraid. Is there anything wrong with me? My day shades to a dull grey. I don't want to be here, but I remain where I sit trying to mask my feelings with a suitably interested expression. Like Sinéad I've no appetite. Mother would be furious to see all but a bite of a "good cheese sandwich" lying under the lid of a discarded school desk. Krysia asks me if I'm feeling okay as we hurry back to play the afternoon matches. I resort to my age-old excuse, "I'm feeling a bit sick" and it's left like that.

Sport has always been my salvation, but as I make my way home, the cloud of despair returns. Am I unnatural? *Wild beast* enters my mind. It's impossible to stop myself from crying and everyone on the top of the bus is trying not to look at me. I ring the bell and get off at the next Request stop.

Slowly as I tread my way towards Woodland Avenue, I think about Mother and wonder what she'd make of Sinéad if she knew what she was getting up to with her boyfriend. I picture the way Mother welcomes Sinéad to our home with a smile. She's taken to her Irish warmth and humour. Sinéad has charisma, and has certainly won Mother's affections. "Sinéad, she has not been here for some time. Why not invite her?" She'll drop into a perfectly ordinary conversation if my friend hasn't been over for a while.

She never says that about Krysia or Mary. When I point this out, Mother dismisses my words with, "What nonsense Child!"

Of all my friends, Krysia comes to our house most often. Just like when Marek used to visit, Mother makes a point of producing very English meals - grilled lamb chops or fried fish; and she never slips into Polish. With Mary, who comes least often, she asks the occasional question about school or holidays perhaps. But when Krysia is here, she only makes statements such as, "The meal is ready. Come, eat now."

I think because they are both Polish, Mrs. Kotkowska offered the hand of friendship to Mother on several occasions. But Mother, rather frostily, I thought, always made it very plain she wasn't interested. At first, I worried that this might jeopardise my own relationship with Krysia's family, but in actual fact, I think it's served to cement it; and I'm so grateful for the kindness Mrs. Kotkowska never fails to show me. Now as I walk along the pavement, I imagine talking to her about - this kissing - sex thing which is troubling me. I really wish I could. But somehow I know it'll never happen.

The shadows have lengthened in the evening sunshine. Although now quite late, I'm still walking up the garden path like a tortoise. Sinéad's romantic escapades have triggered such a strong reaction in me, that despite being annoyed with myself, I'm unable to drag myself out of the mire.

Mother's been baking, baking as if for an army. On every surface are large round tins, each over-flowing with cakes and buns. Forgetting my early morning shame, I spitefully ask, "Who are all those for? The rats?"

With contempt she replies, "No. They are to raise money for charity, Dr. Barnardo's Homes."

I say no more. She says no more. I don't believe her until our neighbour Mrs. Jones comes to collect them. Surprised to see Mother's mammoth contribution to her cake stall, she goes to give her a hug; but Mother quickly recoils unaccustomed to such shows of affection.

"Sorry," apologises Mrs. Jones.

Since Anne moved to Nottingham, Mother's been somewhat adrift. Mrs. Jones has become a convenient substitute, although, I think she's a little in awe of Mother. Indeed, they still refer to each other as Mrs. Jones and Mrs. Kalinska. I can't quite figure out how it began, but she has become fond of Mrs. Jones' four year old son Andrew, and seems to gain a great deal of pleasure from taking care of him when any opportunity arises. She's bought a red stuffed rabbit, some plastic cars, a box of picture dominoes and last week dug out some of my old nursery rhyme books so she can sing with him when he visits our house. He's a sweet boy with golden blond hair, and he dotes on her. I'm happy Mother has something else in her life to think about other than the empty house next door and the rats. I'm also happy that at least someone is capable of bringing real joy into her life; nevertheless I wish it could've been me.

"Is it, um, still all right to bring Andrew over for an hour on Monday afternoon while I take Sarah to ballet?" Mrs. Jones asks cautiously when she returns to collect the second batch of cakes.

"Of course," replies Mother. "Why ever not?"

As soon as the front door closes she imagines she hears noises coming from next door. Rats.

Later that evening while we're watching *Dixon of Dock Green* on television, Mrs. Jones returns. Anxious to show her gratitude, she's come bearing a large box of chocolates. "Thank you," says Mother with a forced smile.

Once the front door is shut, the chocolates are abandoned in the depths of the pantry.

After the programme is over I pull myself up from the sofa. Father glances at me from his armchair and says, "Why so quiet? Maybe disappointed your school only came fourth in tournament?"

"No, just tired."

Mother doesn't even take her eyes off the TV screen. I know she's irate, and only an apology for my rudeness will appease her. But her demeanour annoys me so much, I can't bring myself to do that; especially when her ears prick up and I wait for her to say the infernal word "rats" again.

"So," begins Father, "the weather forecast is good, and tomorrow it is Sunday. No work, and no sad faces. We go to Eastbourne for day."

Mother brightens up. "Eastbourne!"

"Yes, we will walk on sea front. Perhaps we will drive a little way then to see Wojciech? Yes, I will phone him."

Father immediately picks up the telephone book.

My heart sinks for I would dearly love a visit to the coast, and I know this is just the break from routine my parents need. "I can't, I've so much homework to do: Notes on three chapters of *Jane Eyre*, a Latin translation as well as an essay on the Agricultural Revolution for History. I just can't - and I've not done a note of violin practice yet this week-end."

I watch as Mother's expression of pleasure fades. It's then that I say sorry and suggest they go anyway, leave me at home. Father considers the proposal, whereas she rejects the idea out of hand, until I remind them that I will be sixteen in December.

Early the next morning I wake with heavy heart. Although I slept for at least eight hours, I don't feel rested. My head is fuggy and yesterday's fears linger. I'm worried. Worried about who I really am, and what the future will hold for me.

I lie on my side gazing at Mr. Bear, contemplating the dilemmas presented in life and searching for a reason as to why it's so consistently plagued with worry. Who should I blame? Is there a God? I'd like to think there is, otherwise why over the generations, would so many people have put their faith and trust in him? Yet if there is, how come he just sits back and lets everything happen and never intervenes to prevent awful tragedies?

At last, savouring the thought of a whole day's freedom, I endeavour to snap out of the doldrums, and I get up once I'm sure that Mother and Father are safely on their way to Eastbourne. It's heaven to be able to play my Beatles' records at full volume. No one to complain here - and the rats next door won't care. "I Wanna Hold Your Hand" reverberates throughout the house while I wash, and then I blast the walls with "Can't Buy Me Love" before singing along with my new "With the Beatles" LP. Looking at John Lennon's photo on the record sleeve, I consider the prospect of a kiss from him, and wonder how it would feel.

11 o'clock. Time to begin that stack of work. But as I skipped breakfast, first I warm up the Paprikas Mother left for my lunch. I can't be bothered to boil potatoes, so I simply chop up a tomato and proceed to eat the meal with a thickly buttered slice of bread. All the while, accompanied by The Beatles, I translate the set passage from *Caesar's Gallic Wars V*.

At 4.30pm, breathing a sigh of relief, I stuff all the completed homework into my school bag. There's still the violin practice to be tackled. I'm not entirely in the mood, but next week is my Grade 7 exam so I force myself to tune up and get started on the scales, only to be interrupted by a knocking at the front door.

As I take the stairs two at a time, I'm hoping I won't have to make polite conversation with some neighbour for ages.

When the door's open, I can't believe who's standing on the step.

Chapter 23
1964
Same day

He's in the kitchen casually leaning against the cupboard. I cannot believe that he's actually here and looking even younger than when I last saw him. The 5 o'clock shadow has disappeared and I think that being clean-shaven suits him better, as do the few additional pounds he appears to have gained. He's wearing smart denims and a bruised-brown suede jacket with upturned collar. Mother told me, when I'm alone in the house, I must not open the door to strangers. But he's not a stranger - although it feels as if he is.

Why hadn't I been quicker to shut the door before he'd finished even saying, "Cześć" let alone managed to get a foot over the threshold? Of course I was taken by surprise, and he was so insistent. It feels awkward, not at all like it used to when I was a little girl. I'm annoyed I missed my chance to fib, tell him that my parents wouldn't be back until after midnight. Now he's moved across the room and is ensconced on the most comfortable of the four kitchen chairs; the one with the soft red cushion that Mother prefers.

It's very hard to be impolite when someone's being friendly and they greet you with a wide smile. I'm bewildered, asking myself, how did he persuade me to make him a coffee? Picking up the kettle, I pour the boiling water into our only cracked cup; the one I've deliberately chosen for him.

I just do not need this. I'm infuriated mainly because I don't like being manipulated in this way, but also I'm anxious.

"Mum and Dad are in Eastbourne and won't be back 'til really late."

But being Marek, having wormed his way into the house, he seems determined to stay. To make matters worse, I hate the smell of Brut. Many girls may adore that aftershave, but I do not.

He's unnerving me with silence. I take longer to make the coffee than it needs. I don't want him to feel welcome, and having something to do, helps me to feel less uncomfortable. I make a meal out of obtaining digestive biscuits from the tin; all the broken ones are carefully filtered out and put aside for the birds.

"You have turned out to be a pretty one," he says. "You were a gawky little thing when young."

I make no comment and don't even look up from the task in hand.

Eager to engage me in conversation he says, "Bronia and I are hoping it will be possible to make a short trip to Poland in autumn." I make no reply. "Yes, things there are easing up a bit - with travel that is."

Poor dependent, soppy Bronia. I can see her sitting on our sofa snivelling; hanky in hand looking bereft of dignity and lost in desolation. How could she ever have taken him back, forgiven him after treating her like that? This is what I'd thought anyway when I overheard Father tell Mother, Bronia had returned to their flat having made the decision to put the whole sorry affair behind her. I couldn't believe my ears - less than two weeks after she'd caught him in bed with Anne. I recall thinking, I hope at least she waited until Marek had cleaned the beer stains off the walls and washed the bedding.

Grudgingly, I have to acknowledge that women do find Marek irresistible. He's able to twist them round his little finger with his sweet talk and lies. Of course he's no John Lennon, but he's got the rugged good looks of a middle-aged Hollywood film star; the kind that attracts both young and older women it seems.

No one would think that Father and Marek are the same age, forty-six. Father, with his grey hair, looks at least fifteen years his senior. Marek's thick crop is the shade of bitter dark coffee. But what really creates the divide is that Marek moves like a young buck whereas Father, although strong and wiry, is slower and more precise in his movement, giving the impression of someone much older.

To prevent further silence I say, "That's nice," referring to Marek's proposed venture to Poland. He reaches across the table to take the cup of coffee placed precariously near the edge. I push the plate of biscuits vaguely in his direction. In the guise of a dedicated violinist, I proceed to excuse myself, explaining that I'm anxious to return to the practice he'd interrupted.

"That is good to hear, this enthusiasm. I know your dad he is proud that you play so very well now. He tells me this often. Do you play the Brahms Violin Concerto yet?" He's jovial, trying to draw me into his warm cocoon.

"No, not yet." I aim to sound bored, hoping he'll get the hint and leave. Poor old Brahms. I've grown to dislike his concerto. It never fails to remind me of Marek.

"One day, Martina, one day. I know this, you will play so very well, like your aunt."

Anne springs to mind. Of course he doesn't mean her - besides she was always tone deaf. I realise who he means and I'm alive with curiosity.

"My aunt?"

"Ah! You are attentive now." Marek is victorious. From his pocket he takes out a pack of Embassy and offers me a cigarette.

"I am only fifteen," I remind him.

"Of course," he says, "you look so much older." Is he flirting with me?

So even though I long to learn more about this aunt who plays, or maybe once played the violin, I assume a manner intended to give the impression I'm not particularly interested.

"Your mum still has not spoken of her?" Like an owl, his eyes are wide and fixed on me.

I shake my head.

Maintaining my act of boredom, I begin to tidy up the leaflets and oddments that every kitchen surface seems to collect.

I sense a battle of wills emerging.

"You must ask her then. I think you must ask her soon."

Marek inhales the cigarette deeply. The prolonged silence which follows galls me. I'm not entirely sure, but I suspect his reticence to reveal further details is not so much in consideration for Mother's feelings on the matter, but more to pay me back for being so cold with him. But what does he expect? Who does he think he's fooling? He can't be so thick-skinned as to imagine I'm no longer concerned about what I'd witnessed on that New Year's Eve. He knows only too well, I'm aware he's both a scoundrel and a liar. I stare him in the face and insist on returning to my violin practice. Yet I'm unable to draw away.

"Family is important," he declares. "I will see my mother for first time after many, many years. That is, if I do secure papers, the official papers to allow me into Poland."

Not sure where this is going, I feel obliged to agree. It will be good for him to see his mother; and true, family is important. Fleetingly, I wonder how his mother managed to survive the war.

He stubs out his cigarette and grinds the butt into the saucer. "Look at me."

There's a steely edge to his voice and he's up, standing by the chair. Stubbornly, I turn my back on him, cupping my hands round an empty jam jar drying on the draining board.

"What is wrong with you?" He's very close behind me.

He knows full well.

Driven by a cocktail of hatred and courage, I swivel round. "Gee, are you stupid enough really not to know?"

"If it's that Anne thing - well, it was nothing…"

My voice is raised. "Nothing? It was something to…"

"Nothing to do with *you*, but your Aunt Ewa she *is* very much to do with you. She is family."

Refusing to let him seize the balance of power, I challenge his stare. With satisfaction I say, "I *know* about my Mother's sister in Poland. And I *know* she played - plays the violin. Dad told me!"

"Really," says Marek with cynicism. It's as if we're playing a game of one-upmanship. "So, then you know, that very soon she will be in England. She will be playing violin with Polish State Orchestra in London's Festival Hall; your dad he has told you that, has he?"

I didn't know. My defences are down and Marek is as usual the victor. An inner voice is telling me to go no further with this. A woman, coming to England, to play a violin in a concert; what's there to be afraid of? Yet dark clouds of foreboding are creeping up and over the horizon.

Leave well alone? The inner voice whispers, "If Mum and Dad wanted you to know, they'd have told you."

The other voice replies, "But they always keep things from you. Things you've a right to know - secrets."

Marek's retreated to his seat and my back is once again turned on him. I'm stunned, speechless and my eyes are fixed on the garden. I see Samba with a robin between his jaws. It's still alive. There's a flutter of wings. On any other day, I'd be out there making an attempt to release the poor creature from the cat's jaws, but today I do nothing, simply stare at its agony. Other than my own sobs, all that can be heard in the heavy stillness of the kitchen is the rustling of foil from the inside of Marek's cigarette pack, followed by the clicking of a lighter. The brightness of spring is fading with approaching dusk. My tears blind me. Samba, running across the lawn wavers in and out of focus until he disappears over the fence.

Marek speaks at last. His words are no longer harsh. "I did not come to see your dad. It is you I come to see this afternoon. You Martina. This business with Ewa, it has been on my mind. Yes, she is your mum's younger sister - but *your* relative too - and you do not have so many relatives alive. I think therefore, you must have a chance to know her. And that is it." He lights another cigarette before he's finished the one still burning in the ashtray. The smoke he exhales swirls towards the kitchen ceiling. "I am glad your dad has told you something at least."

I'm listening, but cannot bring myself to respond. My hand is searching my pocket for a hanky, but there's none. Marek continues, "Your dad, he phoned me last night. He asked for the phone number he'd lost, of our friend Wojciech, who moved near Eastbourne some months ago - told me your mum and himself they wanted to visit him today. Some hours after he call, I made up my mind - to come here - see if you were alone, and speak with you. Your mum, she refuses to acknowledge her only sister. Your dad - well, he prefers the easy road in life, so it is left to me."

My nose is running, I'm sniffing and using my clasped knuckles to stop the flow. Still I make a show of looking out of the window. The chair scrapes on the floor and Marek's there again behind me. I flinch as his hand touches my shoulder, brusquely I sweep it off. He offers me a man-sized handkerchief which I accept.

In gentle exasperation he sighs. "For God's sake, I'm not here to - cause trouble - or to - oh never mind."

He takes something out of his wallet - a sepia photograph which he places on the table as bait. Like a mouse unable to resist the cheese in a trap, I walk slowly across the kitchen and sit. "Go on," says Marek. "For God's sake take a look."

There are five children standing in that formal way people did years ago when posing for photographs. Three boys and two girls smile at the camera. They're wearing thick coats, knitted woolly hats and boots. It's winter. They're in a garden filled with bright white bushes and a leafless tree, its branches iced with snow. In the background is a house which looks rather like those chalets with shutters; the kind I've seen in brochures advertising skiing holidays in Switzerland. Everything seems light, white and pure. A perfect childhood moment captured for posterity.

It's not difficult to recognise the face of Father or Marek who's standing next to him right in the middle of the group. Marek, a tall strapping lad with a twinkle in his eye is holding skis, as does Father who's almost the same height, but thinner. Indeed, all those years ago when Mother was in hospital Father showed me a similar photo of the boys.

My attention turns to the two slender girls with dark plaits. They're much smaller than the boys. I surmise the taller girl must be Mother with her younger sister Ewa at her side. I'm enthralled for I've never seen a photograph of Mother as a child. And sometimes I've found it almost impossible to imagine her as ever being one. On the bookshelf in the sitting room stands a framed black and white photo of my parents taken on their wedding day. That's the youngest image of Mother I've ever seen - and even though it's the day of her marriage, there's only a hint of a smile on her lips - her eyes don't smile at all.

Marek watches me as I pick up the small photograph and look at it more closely. The girls are standing to the left of Father. The little one's holding his hand. Both are wearing the same style double-breasted coat; dark with broad collars. But it's the similarity in the girls' appearance that really strikes me. There is no mistaking they are sisters. Mother is surprisingly pretty and has an angelic, sweet expression. Ewa slouches a little, her tights wrinkle at the knees - I imagine her to be something of a tomboy. Nevertheless, both have wide smiles radiating the innocent joy of childhood. On that day, they wouldn't have had an inkling of what the future held in store for them.

"Who is the other boy?"

"Andrzej," Marek replies. "My younger brother."

I see the likeness in spite of the boy's fair hair and rounder face. I cringe at my lack of tact for I now have some recollection of conversations concerning this younger brother, who like Marek was an RAF pilot in Britain during the war, but unlike Marek, was killed in action.

"We were all friends. Our parents were friends, their parents were friends. No doubt some of our grandparents and great-grandparents were friends. We lived together, played together, attended same schools, same synagogue." Marek's voice has taken on an ethereal quality. "Of course there were many others who shared our lives - others we cared for." He stops and swallows.

The clock in the hall strikes the half hour. It's five thirty. Marek should have long gone, but I want to learn more, after all a little piece of Mother's life is unfolding here; and this is so important in helping me to understand - to understand the person whom I sense only plays the role of my mother, but in fact quite often wanders from the script.

The phone rings, and the spell's broken.

"Hello!" I'm abrupt and regret this once I recognise the voice. It's Mary who unlike Krysia and Sinéad never keeps me chatting for long. I surmise that the call concerns the violin exam we're both taking next Thursday, the day before the Easter term ends. But it's not about that. There's been a falling out between Sinéad and herself, over something Mary said about Niall. "I was only saying..."

All the time she's talking, I'm visualising Marek in the kitchen chain smoking and intermittently glancing at his watch. Incredible as it may seem, I actually want him to stay, so I interrupt Mary in full flow. "Sorry," I chip in, "but supper's on the table. Ring you later."

Scurrying back to Marek I find him gathering up his belongings, but before he's finished I tempt him with a beer; and he immediately sits down again. Without hesitation he says he'd prefer vodka. At once I oblige. Never having poured vodka in my life, I allow Marek to do this himself. It does the trick. His glass is almost half-full. He stays.

I waste no more time. "What was Mum like as a little girl?"

"Ah! Where to begin?" Pause. "She was kind, a nice girl. Good-natured and well liked. Tak, many times she would stick up for children who were weak, the ones who would get bullied. I suppose that is why when a young woman she had hoped to become a teacher. Of course, this was not to be. Make no mistake she was fun too - even if sometimes a little quiet and too serious - well, for my liking." He winks. "But as with the rest of us kids, she was not so very shy when it came to mischief."

I like to think of Mother getting up to mischief. "What kind of things did she do?"

"Oh let me think. Not so very bad things. Things maybe like - let me see - tak, pinching apples off farmer's tree; or maybe she steals out of house to have feast when she should be asleep. That kind of fun. Anyway, besides fun, just like Ewa loved to play violin, Hania she loved to sing. Wherever there was Hania, there was song. Just like a nightingale she sang."

I wonder when it was that the song left her.

"Also she loved to ski. Your grandfather too, he loved to ski. He liked to take all of us friends with him out of Kraków into the mountains. Naturally, we all loved those trips to Zakopane, but Hania the most. If only you could have seen how she sped down those slopes of the Tatra Mountains - one day you must go to see those magnificent giants for yourself. Yes, those times they were something."

Marek's glass is empty.

"Another vodka?" I slide the bottle across the kitchen table towards him.

"Ah! I quite forgot. This you may find, how should I say? Odd. But your mum she very much liked to go to the synagogue - and always was so afraid to disappoint God. You would not believe it Martina, that Hania, yes, when she was so small girl. This high." His hand is level with his waist. "Wanted to be rabbi when she was grown up. The girl wanted to be a rabbi! Such a thing! How we laughed - even the adults."

Mother wanted to be a rabbi? Going to the synagogue? Afraid to disappoint God? "Really? She doesn't even believe in God."

"That is true. For now is now, and then was then."

Marek stretches, stands, picks up the half-empty vodka bottle and meanders to the other side of the kitchen where he leans against the cupboard. Before carrying on, he replenishes his glass. "Na Zdrowie!"

He takes off his jacket, loosens the neck of his shirt and sits down again. "Now, your dad is good man. Yes, he is very good man. In truth he saved your mum. I do not exaggerate. Perhaps I should not say these things to you. But why not, perhaps no one else will. So anyway, he had fallen for this English girl; she was nurse he met in Northern Ireland while working as pharmacist in Royal Army Medical Corp. You may, or may not know, that he was posted to this Military hospital at Stranmillis - there they both worked - fell in love

- but life became complicated, you understand. He and Hania they had been friends, good friends before the war - like family. When he came home to Poland afterwards, he found her there, very much alone in Kraków - she had been taken in by Marta, a good woman who had helped many Jewish people. But Hania she was lonely, depressed and so very pleased to see Stefan. Seeing the state she was in, I think he felt desperately sorry for her. His heart then became torn. And so it goes. Well, after a little while he asked her to be his wife - a new life for her, with him."

"What about the nurse?"

"I know nothing more about this nurse - but anyway your parents, they were lucky to get out of Poland - I do not think Hania she could have coped living under Communists. What with such haunting memories - how should I say it - her mind it was already not in good state."

"Poor Mum," I say while Marek lights a cigarette; the last in the pack which he screws up before knocking back the remaining drops of vodka in his glass.

"And even when in England it was not easy for her, neither for Stefan. What with helping Hania to adjust - and then himself having to come to terms with guilt…"

"Guilt?" I reach for Marek's glass and place it on the draining board.

Marek retrieves it and pours himself another vodka.

"Knowing that he escaped from Poland, and she with so many others they stayed, suffered - murdered by them bloody Nazis…"

"But that's ridiculous. It wasn't *his* fault."

"Tak, tak Martina, of course it wasn't his fault, but when it comes to dishing out blame, or feeling guilt, where is logic?" He looks drained. "So, now I must go." Marek is decisive. "Your parents they soon will come; and it will not be good for them to find me here."

When he stands he's unsteady on his feet. He waits a second or two, clumsily puts on his jacket, reaches for the sepia photograph and slips it into his wallet. Then he takes out another. This one's not pre-war, but is a shiny black and white photo of a woman in her late thirties, or maybe early forties, bowing a violin. The woman clearly resembles Mother - and when I take a second look, I imagine I see a little of myself in her too. She has a certain mature beauty, which I think is largely down to those wide dark smiling eyes. And she's my aunt - my real aunt. Aunt Ewa.

"For you, for you to keep," says Marek. Once more he reaches into his breast pocket and this time hands me an envelope. "Inside there are two tickets for her concert. Bronia and I were to go, but it's more important for you to be there, to hear your aunt play - like one day, I hope to hear you play. I would like to take you myself, but somehow I do not think that is what you - or your dad and mum would wish. So, take your boyfriend?"

"I don't have a boyfriend," I answer, my voice taking on the previous prickly tone.

"Take them back," I demand thrusting the envelope at him. "I can't go. You know they'll never let me go."

I'm rushing after him, but he's already at the front door and it's a pointless waste of time and energy to pursue him further.

Ten minutes later I'm at the sink washing up when I hear Mother's voice in the hall. The almost empty vodka bottle disappears back into the cupboard, but there's little I'm able to do about the cigarette pollution.

"Pooh!" exclaims Mother on entry. "What is this?" She's frantically waving her arms through the blanket of smoke. Quickly, I stuff both photograph and tickets into my pocket and listen to Mother and Father in tandem rant about the dreadful smell and contamination of the house.

There's nothing for it but to tell the truth.

"Marek came round - to talk to you about something or other," I say confident that he will, if necessary, find the right things to say in order to appease the situation.

"What? Marek here?" gasps Mother who's still in the process of flinging open the kitchen windows.

"I will deal with this, Hania," Father interjects in a quiet voice. "Now, do not get excited. It will spoil what has been a very, very nice day. I will sort Marek out."

"Oh yes? I'm sure you will Dad," I say inwardly and leave before more fat can leap out of the frying pan.

Chapter 24
March 1964

Easter bunnies of every shape and colour glitter and shine from the displays at Selfridges. Their broad grins are so appealing that I'm unable to choose one. Mother's in a good mood today, and I'm tempted to suppose she's happy. She's offered to buy me one of the chocolate bunnies. Although as a family we partake in Christmas celebrations, Easter is completely ignored. I've never so much as received a small chocolate egg from my parents, so this for me is a real break-through. I choose one about the length of my hand; a plump rabbit with a powder pink dinner jacket, tall golden ears and very cute buckteeth.

Today, Monday, is the first day of the Easter holiday, and what Mother saw as we left for Oxford Street this morning catapulted her out of the doldrums. As we stepped on to the path, the For Sale sign next door was being replaced with Sold. Ever since the house became vacant Mother has been tetchy, but after Marek's recent visit, you would have thought the angel of death had cast its shadow over our household. Therefore, this piece of good fortune has not come a second too soon.

Mother had a very good idea as to why Marek had made his visit whilst they were conveniently out, and was livid. Violin practice became impossible after his departure. I was more tuned into their raised voices than to the 2nd movement of Tchaikovsky's Violin Concerto.

"See Ewa? Me? Of course not, and if I find he has mentioned this concert to the child… Huh! Nothing that man knows; he knows nothing. He was not there," she said. "How dare he speak of forgiveness when he was safe in England…"

A heavy thud followed; perhaps a book landing on the floor.

"It is *you* who knows nothing, Hania. I tell you this many times, your words are unjust. You may sneer, condemn Marek - accuse him of spending war drinking and womanising, but in this, it is *you* who knows nothing. You have your own agenda when it comes to Marek."

"And who was it who boasted always about women and such foolish nonsense he got up to? Marek."

"Well, maybe, but he is always full of bravado, and you were not there in England. Marek was…Hania, do *not* walk away," said father. "Enough is enough. You always shut your ears when I speak to you of this, but today you listen."

Rarely did Father break away from the road most travelled, but I could tell from the hardness of his tone that he was determined; and on such occasions when he really asserted himself, Mother quickly crumbled into submission.

I must admit that I'd never thought of Marek in terms of bravery or courage, therefore was surprised by what I learnt. As a young man in Poland, Marek had been accepted into one of the most prestigious officers' flying schools. I think Father said it was the Deblin School. Here, he said, the conditions were Spartan and the training extremely demanding. Marek, in Spartan conditions, obeying every command!

With unprecedented passion, Father continued to expand upon Marek's bravery. How, with great skill, he'd flown and shot down many Luftwaffe planes. "These German planes they were monsters in the sky - so much faster and more powerful than any possessed by our Polish air force," he said, and then referred to this taking place in "Black September". Mother, I presume, objecting to this accolade to Marek, must have made a move to leave the room because Father really shouted. "No. Hania you stay!"

I held my breath. Would she? Silence.

To my relief Father resumed more calmly. I dread to think of the repercussions had she defied him. He proceeded to say something about Marek, who with some eight or nine other airmen, had at great risk to his own life, flown one of the last air-worthy Polish air force planes out of the country, to Hungary.

My question as to how Marek's mother survived was then answered. Apparently, this too was as a result of his forethought and courage. Father reminded Mother that it was Marek who had arranged his mother's escape; secured safe passage. "This," he said, "involved great personal risk, and was achieved by gaining the confidence and the "aid" of some influential people who were in league with Nazi sympathisers. Father implied Marek "conned" them. That struck me as being very true to form. After the transit through Romania, for the duration of the war, she remained in hiding in the house of her married cousin who lived in an isolated mountain area some way outside Budapest.

Following on from this, Father spoke so fast that most of what he said was lost on me, but I did manage to ascertain, that Marek was commended for his bravery in the Polish section of the British Air Force whilst serving here in England. Repeating this fact, Father emphasised he never wanted to have to remind Mother of all this again. By then I'd heard enough. Exhausted, without washing, I undressed, flopped into bed with the light still burning. Drifting into sleep I glanced at my violin lying in its open case in the centre of the floor, and I thought it looked remarkably like an open coffin.

The wind outside soughed, and like so many years ago, I dreaded the night hours. In my dream, lashing bare branches of trees bent and groaned in the howling wind. They plunged downward, and like tentacles, coiled around me, making it impossible to move, impossible to cry out. I was lifted, lifted high. Below were black silhouettes, shapes of people - people walking. All faceless. Bathed in purple shadow, they were indistinguishable as they slowly followed the pallbearers and coffin. With a sudden jolt I awoke trembling; the lamp had been switched off and I lay there in the darkness feeling alone and afraid.

But here we are now on a shopping spree to buy me some new clothes for the summer months. The sun's out and the aura of gloom lifted. Hopefully, Mother in this positive frame of mind, will allow me to buy some mini-skirts more than just an inch above the knee.

I'm looking forward to staying overnight at Mary's house tomorrow. It's her birthday and since their falling out, she and Sinéad are not nearly so close. Anyway, Sinéad only seems to have time for Niall these days. Krysia's family have gone to spend Easter with their relatives in Scotland, therefore it's only Mary and I who'll be going to see Gerry and the Pacemakers, Cilla Black and Billy J. Kramer at the Granada tomorrow evening. It was a bit of a struggle to get Mother and Father to agree, but finally they relented after Mrs. Madeley reassured them her husband would be picking us up in the car straight after the pop concert.

Recently, Mother has been encouraging this relationship with Mary. Partly because she says it's good for me to be friends with the other girl in my Year who won a scholarship to Our Lady of Lourdes. Ridiculously, she prattles on about me getting intellectual stimulation from this friendship, and all that rubbish - as if all the other girls are pond life. Also she seems to approve of the Madeleys who are both teachers. Although Mary's dad teaches some P.E. he's in fact Head of the Science at a local grammar school; and her mum is a violin teacher. But more importantly, I think, they're not Polish.

Selfridges is packed with enthusiastic springtime shoppers. Weighed down with bags, they're milling around the attractive Easter displays and seem reluctant to leave without purchasing something from every department. Mother and I however, having traipsed around for at least half an hour, have done little else other than window-shop.

When she suggests going to the girls' clothing department, I groan inwardly for I'm convinced the latest teenage fashions will not be found in this store. But as we enter, I spot on the first rail a pale yellow mini-dress; and at once I imagine myself wearing it - tall and willowy, my long straight hair cloaking that fashionable pouting expression. In a flash, the image changes. And there's me standing on a seat in the Granada, screaming at Gerry Marsden and looking fab in the dress.

Holding it up against me, my reflection in the mirror heralds Mother's words of objection.

"Too skimpy," I imagine her saying.

Ecstatic is the only word to describe how I feel when she agrees to me trying it on. It has three quarter length wide sleeves and an empire line. Perfect. It's expensive so I offer to make a contribution from my Post Office savings. Mother is usually extremely frugal, and even though we aren't poor, she frequently reminds me, "Money it does not grow down at the end of garden."

"Nor on trees," I remind her.

When I emerge from the dressing room, pulling down the dress as far is it will go, she doesn't even query the length which must be at least two inches above the knee. Instead, she tells me that my fringe is too long and to brush it out of my eyes; then with no more ado, her purse is open and the item being purchased.

I'm praying that the Sold sign hasn't been removed by the time we get back to Woodland Avenue else the "decency" of the dress may be reconsidered. Perhaps ripping up the receipt would be a wise move? I laugh to myself as we march purposely along the pavement towards Woolworths where we plan to eat lunch. I like this self-service cafeteria as the food is tasty and the portions always generous.

Before queuing for our meal, Mother's intent on looking along the toy counters. She stops at the marbles. They're not the kind with one line of colour through the centre, but ones with rainbows, fried eggs or swirls of blues, reds and pinks captured like warm liquid in the round glass bulbs. She takes some in her hand, says she loves their firm coolness; and I watch as they run through her fingers like sand. Captivated, she examines individual ones, rolling each slowly between thumb and forefinger; and eventually, after much deliberation, she has selected ten. Having paid the shop assistant, they're popped in a small brown paper bag. Mother smiles and tells me Andrew will really like them.

Whilst she'd been choosing the marbles, I'd moved a little further along the counter and gazed nostalgically at the other toys and games - Pikasticks, Jacks and Five Stones. I remembered the hours I used to spend playing these with my friends. A tangled heap of small black rubber mice with spongy bodies and wispy tails lay near to them. I thought they looked like tarred, dead rats.

Now, holding one in my right hand, I move behind Mother, who having paid for the marbles, is putting her purse back into her handbag. As she turns, I gently shake the mouse a few inches from her nose. The head nods and the tail quivers. "You won't have to put up with these much longer now the house is sold."

I hear my childish giggles being overlapped with a piercing scream. Her bag drops to the floor and the marbles roll out in all directions, under counters and down the aisle. The colours blink and shine as they disappear from sight.

Hastily I toss the mouse back on top of its companions, and help Mother and a couple of small boys, who have appeared from nowhere, to retrieve the escapees. The shop assistant is bending down at Mother's side. "Are you all right, madam?"

I wonder if she thinks she has a customer here who's in the throes of a heart attack.

"Thank you. It is nothing," Mother insists. "Just marbles. They spilled from my bag when I dropped it." Her voice is tight with embarrassment. She looks daggers at me.

"Sorry, Mum," I'm repeating whilst on my hands and knees picking up another stray marble.

"And you think Child, that you are grown up enough to go to this Gerry Margan pop show, do you?"

"Marsden, Gerry Marsden," I correct her. "Look, it was a joke. Gee, Mum, just a silly joke with a toy mouse. That's all."

She's shaking and I feel genuinely sorry.

Mother's a dark horse; one who from time to time really surprises me. Despite the upset I'm hungry and am wolfing down sausages and chips when I look up to see her coquettish smile; and then I'm even more surprised to hear her admit how funny the marble episode must have appeared to bystanders.

"And it *is* good to think soon no rats next door," she says.

I wonder if I should take advantage of her good mood and voice the possibility of going to the Festival Hall. "Mum."

"What is it?"

"Oh, nothing much. Just that - I was wondering - if - you ever hear anything from Anne and Lisa?"

"Auntie Anne," she says with eyebrows raised. "From time to time she writes. Yes, they are doing quite good in Nottingham. Lives with her parents. Soon though Lisa and her, they will move into own house - she wants me to visit." Mother sounds enthusiastic. After a few more mouthfuls of lunch, she puts down her fork and looks at me, "But I think it better for divorced woman to live with her parents." She picks up the fork and resumes eating.

I'm curious as to what Lisa's like at fifteen. Is she the trendy teenager whose friendships blow hot and cold? Or has she returned to being warm and companionable like my primary school friend? And what of Peter? I wonder where he and Greg are living. Some time ago I heard Mother telling Father that Greg had been promoted and is working in a much larger hotel somewhere in central London. It seems eons ago since Peter accused Marek of being a stinking rotten Jew, but although I try, it's not easy to forgive.

"*Auntie* Anne," Mother continues as if I'm still a child, "she is working in solicitors' office. Lisa, like you, I expect is working hard in school with O'level exams coming next year."

I wonder if Lisa's really working hard, or is she like her old pals Norma and Hedgehog who whenever I go into our local Woolworths are serving behind the sweets or make-up counters? "And Peter?" Immediately, I regret asking the question since I have no interest in the answer.

"Auntie Anne does not write so very much about Peter. Only that he left school - did no longer want to go to the university. A sad boy Peter, I think he became."

"Families!" I say without thinking.

Mother's smile fades.

Chapter 25
March 1964

I'm staying an extra couple of nights at Mary's. It's Wednesday afternoon in Holy Week, the Madeleys have gone to the church to prepare for the Good Friday services. These, I understand, are to commemorate Jesus' crucifixion. This year, thanks to the new go-ahead young priest, there's not only to be an adults' service, but also one for the children. Mary's been roped into helping with the children's rehearsal whilst her parents practise the long readings.

When asked if I'd like to join them I replied, "Yes." But I must have sounded unenthusiastic, for Mrs. Madeley jumped in with, "You're most welcome to stay behind if you would prefer."

And I do prefer.

So here I am lying on the bed reading some magazines I found lying on top of the bookshelf in this pretty apple-green bedroom. Even though the sky is angry outside, I feel brighter than I've done of late. It feels okay to be alone in this room.

Mother rarely reads women's magazines. Her reading preference is newspapers and the occasional novel. Therefore having put aside *Jamaica Inn*, I flick through the glossy pages. First I read a story of how a girl falls in love with her older sister's boyfriend. Predictably, it has a happy ending when she finally finds a more suitable lad of her own age. Then I scan a page of somewhat amusing letters, mostly about pets, children's cute faux pas and several relating to uncanny coincidences. Lured by the photos of deep blue sea and white sands I proceed to peruse the article about travel through the Iberian Peninsula.

On the cover of one of the pop magazines is Billy J. Kramer looking exactly as he did on stage. Like Mary, I too think that he's really fab, but of course I'm still more crazy about John Lennon. My throat is quite raw and both of us have hoarse voices after all that screaming last night. I smile, imagining classical music fans standing on the seats in a concert hall yelling their heads off while a full orchestra plays Beethoven or Bach. This amusing image reminds me that Aunt Ewa's concert will be taking place tomorrow. The reality of her being in England is difficult to take on board. I wonder what she's doing this very minute. Rehearsing? Maybe doing something as ordinary as varnishing her nails? On the other hand she could be sitting in some hotel bar thinking about the sister who refuses to meet her. Feeling less cheerful now, I wonder if she knows anything at all about me.

I bend down, pull from underneath the bed my overnight bag, and remove the tickets from the side-pouch. The concert tickets Marek gave me - the gateway to my aunt. But the gateway, I know, will not be opening for me. So why keep them? My fingers twitch. I might as well tear them up and chuck them away. However the urge passes, and instead I place them on the bedside cabinet.

Unlike at Krysia's, where we share a bedroom, here at Mary's, I'm sleeping in Roxanne's room. Mary's older sister Roxanne is at university in Liverpool during term time, but is away for Easter staying with her boyfriend's family in Bath and won't be back until after Bank Holiday Monday.

Mary has the small bedroom overlooking the road. The design of the house is very similar to ours - a three bed-roomed Cutler style semi with two large bedrooms and a box room in the front. Her house however, is overflowing with tennis rackets, golf clubs and all sorts of sports equipment, never mind the unbelievable assortment of musical instruments, including a piano, which dominates the dining room. Full size, half size and even the odd quarter size violin can be found in almost every room. Volumes of sheet music, old newspapers or copies of the *Scientific American* lie in piles everywhere - even in the toilet.

The back room is devoted to Mrs. Madeley's violin lessons, and therefore the crowded front room serves as dining room, sitting room and a study for Mr. Madeley. Standing in the corner is an oak desk, its green leather surface virtually undetectable beneath the piles of exercise books and folders. A pair of almost worn-out greyish plimsolls, a silver whistle and a huge bunch of keys, lie in a heap on the desk's left-hand side. What little space remains in the room accommodates a large comfortable green sofa and a small brown armchair wedged neatly between sofa and beige wall. The fireplace has been plastered over to make room for the television set. Mother would have apoplexy to see the number of used cups and tea plates left scattered around the house. From time to time Mrs. Madeley badgers the family to harvest the abandoned crockery. Laughingly she scolds everyone, including herself, for such slovenliness.

Most days a constant hubbub of comings and goings continues from morning to evening. Pupils arriving, Mrs. Madeley rushing off to teach someone or other; Mr. Madeley off to coach the boys' local football team, the phone ringing and neighbours popping in for a chat.

It's difficult to understand why Mary's such a worrier - a stickler for rules and frequently comes across so prim and proper. When we first became friends, I imagined that she came from a staunch Catholic home with strict Victorian discipline, but nothing could be further from the truth.

Indeed, Mary's a great thinker. She has her fun side, but she's passionate when it comes to good causes, and is a bastion for righteousness and justice. At one time she wanted to be a PE teacher, now she's determined to study medicine; and on qualifying intends to go out to Africa or India to help those communities in dire need. Yet this same girl last night was screaming hysterically with the best of us.

Mary, like me, only loves boys at a distance. She's not got a boyfriend either. I'm still worried, and there's that sinking feeling constantly lying beneath the surface. The idea of kissing and petting, let alone having sex fills me with fear and revulsion. I've been dwelling on the possibility that Mary feels the same way, but as always with things deeply troubling me, I'm too cowardly to initiate the necessary conversation.

Seizing a couple of the teen magazines, I lean back on to the pillows and relax into the Problem Pages.

My best friend says that I can get pregnant from heavy petting. Is this true?

Age 13

Age thirteen! I gasp.

I have been having sex with my boyfriend for nearly nine months. My parents caught us one evening when they got back early from a

party. Now they have banned me from seeing my boyfriend. I really don't think I can live without him.
How can I get my parents to change their minds?

Age 16

Well, if her parents are anything like mine there'll be no chance, take it from me, is my reply to that letter.

I long to have a boyfriend, but I'm very fat and no boys ever ask me out. I feel very jealous of my friends when I see them kissing boys.

Age 14

Gee! Am I the only girl in the world who is not obsessed with all this kissing and sex? With little enthusiasm I read through more letters written in a similar vein until I reach the last letter on the page.

I did not want him to kiss me on this first date. I let him and I hated it. Now I am terrified that I am abnormal...

Age 16

I sit bolt upright and re-read the letter. What's the reply going to be? Go and talk to your GP? Make an appointment to see a psychiatrist? Or commit suicide? I burst into tears as I absorb the advice.

...don't worry...you are perfectly normal...everyone is different in matters of relationships and sex...you just have not met the right boy yet...

Sinking back into the pillows, I look out of the window as the iron-grey clouds separate to reveal a pale blue wash. A branch of the beech tree brushes the window. It feels as if a dead weight has been lifted off me and I begin to doze to the voice of the kindly wind outside.

I awake to find Mary, wearing her red PVC mac, sitting on the edge of the bed. "You were dead to the world," she says.

Still sleepy, I wrap myself into the cosy folds of the eiderdown and moan a little, but make no reply.

"It's okay, stay there for a bit if you want. No hurry. We're not eating, not for at least half an hour."

Chapter 26
1964
Next Day

The orchestra's tuning up. A cacophony of discordant notes rings through the auditorium. Once or twice I've been to the Festival Hall with Mother and Father; however my last visit here was with the school when I was in the Third Year. We came by coach one evening to hear a selection of baroque pieces - mainly Handel and Bach. I think that concert was intended for schools because the place buzzed with young people. But this evening's concert seems only to have attracted the elderly and middle-aged, so far Mary and I appear to be the only teenagers present.

"Ooh! Glad to rest my pins," puffs an old man in front of me as he drops into the seat and his walking stick crashes to the floor.

"Tickets are at a premium for that play. Truthfully, I'm not in the least bit surprised to hear they're sold out. Remember it's the Shakespeare festival next month," pontificates a woman from behind.

The auditorium has a fresh new, airy feel and unlike the hard wooden seats audiences are treated to in the town hall; these are soft, very comfortable and well tiered. From Row F, the view thankfully is devoid of heads. I hate having to strain my neck, bobbing from side to side in order to catch a glimpse of the conductor.

Mary's opening a packet of mints without a care in the world, whereas in spite of the thrill of anticipation, I feel like a naughty child who's sneaked out to play in defiance of her parents' wishes. In fact, this is precisely the situation. The only difference being, I'm not a child and I've every right "to play" this game.

The clock on the wall indicates there's about five minutes to go before the performance begins. So far only men sit in the string section. They exchange the odd word and sift through their scores. While I wait for my aunt to appear a thought occurs to me, and my eyes begin to dart round the auditorium. My imagination is running wild. I picture the scene as if a film sequence. There's Mother bursting through the entrance, rushing down the aisle towards me in an attempt to drag me out before the house lights go down. My feet begin to shuffle. Mary's smiling.

"I think the concert's going to be okay - actually more than okay - excellent," Mary says with a reassuring nudge and then offers me a mint. I accept. My mouth is dry. "Lucky for us your uncle couldn't make it, eh?"

"Um - yeah - him deciding to go away for Easter, I guess, was lucky for us." My words sound unconvincing. I feel so uncomfortable lying to my friend.

"You know what? We'll also get to hear how that 2nd movement of Tchaikovsky's Violin Concerto should really sound like, yeah?" Mary giggles.

"True," I agree, but I know Mary will have made a brilliant job of her Grade 7 violin exam.

Despite feeling guilty, I'm thinking how fortuitous it is to have been staying with Mary on the very evening of Ewa's concert. And what luck that she spotted the tickets on the bedside cabinet. Fortunately, Mary has a wide taste in music and is happy to rock as well as to take in a classical piece or two. By my own admission, I know it's devious not to have put Mrs. Madeley in the picture when the subject of the wasted tickets was raised during yesterday's supper, but the window of opportunity was opening, and it was too good to miss.

"Mum, Martina's got these tickets to a concert - classical not pop - Shostakovich, Tchaikovsky, you know, that sort of thing - for tomorrow evening. They were her uncle's, but he can't go now. Don't suppose we can? It'd be a pity to waste them."

Actually even for Mary I was taken by surprise at such enthusiasm.

"But where is this concert?"

"Festival Hall."

"The Festival Hall," Mrs. Madeley said whilst cutting off the fat from her lamb chop. "That's on the South Bank. You can't be out in London on your own so late."

Hopes dashed I continued forking up my peas.

"Okay, no probs, just a thought. We're not that bothered anyway, are we? I mean, it's not like it's the Beatles or Billy J. is it?"

"Gee no! 'Course not," I agreed.

Mr. Madeley was the first to collect up the dishes. Before long all four of us were in the kitchen washing and drying up while discussing whether we could be bothered to watch *Coronation Street.* Mrs. Madeley said all at once, "I've had a thought. If there are still any seats left for that concert you were talking about, then I'll take you. I'd really enjoy it. It's the holidays, I've no lessons tomorrow. What do you say girls?"

And here we are. Mary and I in Row F and Mrs. Madeley three rows back. A woman dressed in a white blouse and long black skirt catches my attention. Engrossed in conversation with another who carries a viola, she weaves her way through the chairs to the string section.

Is it her? The hair is too light; too long. I look again, more intently this time. She has the look of Mother. Like a ballerina she stands with straight back, appearing lean and strong. Yes. Yes. It is her. Her appearance is a little different from the photograph, but it's definitely her. She finishes the conversation and turns to face the auditorium, her eyes surveying the audience. I think perhaps that for a few seconds they rest on me, or is it my imagination? The moment passes and soon her attention is taken up with the fine tuning of her instrument.

I'm aware that Mary is whispering something, but I'm deaf to her words. The lights dim. There's tumultuous applause as the conductor enters, bows, and then acknowledges the leader of the orchestra. But I give them only a cursory glance before fixing my eyes upon Ewa. Lights down. The silence is alive with anticipation. As the first notes from the violins fill the auditorium, I simply cannot believe I'm here in the Festival Hall, where right in front of me, my aunt is playing the instrument I love.

Chapter 27
2008
Kraków

Last night I fell asleep quickly only to wake before the first light of morning. I lay wide-awake in the stuffy hotel room and gradually the walls began to close in on me like a prison. How annoying it would be to be married to a light sleeper. Fortunately for me this isn't the case. Slipping from beneath the duvet, I dressed, scribbled a quick note, and here I am outside in the fresh air; the sky a tapestry of night and day.

Low lying mist veils the Vistula. It's mystical. Before me is a picture from the centre page of my childhood book, *The Tales of King Arthur*. That sharp light of early morning winks on the still river as it winds round Wawel Castle like a mirrored ribbon. A lone rowing boat is moored on the opposite bank with a family of ducks close by, weaving across the water in the sunshine. Daybreak. Devoid of people, it's hard to believe that Kraków soon will be bursting with tourists. Yet I know it won't be long before the city awakens and the spell of tranquillity broken.

Sodden with dew, the soft grass sinks beneath my feet. Dawn brings yelps from the city's dogs who vociferously demand their first romp of the day. A young man, clad in a loose charcoal grey tracksuit passes me. His hair stands spiky and his jowls remain unshaven. The collar of his blue-striped pyjama jacket peeps from the zip-top, hinting at his reluctance to be out walking the lively brown and white mongrel at this unearthly hour. I turn from the river into Zwierzyniecka Street, a nurse acknowledges me with a tired nod. A couple of burly men in overalls, engaged in conversation, stride past. The sun dances between the tall buildings as I stroll in the vague direction of the city centre.

And here I am on the corner of Straszewskiego Street; I see the Philharmonic Hall. It never fails to impress me - that magnificent building with its huge pillars and inviting balconies. I know Ewa played violin in many concerts here. How many exactly? I've no idea.

I picture myself, aged fifteen, in Mary's house. The bathroom door is locked, and I'm on the floor, kneeling on the green lino secretly scribbling a note to this aunt I've never met; and hoping against hope that after the concert at the Festival Hall I'll be able to find a way of getting it to her.

However, the note never left my bag that evening. I had no idea what to do with it; and since the concert tour moved to Birmingham the next day, my chance was lost.

On reflection, I should have sought Marek's help. But I was too proud to ask; and perhaps deep down, afraid of the consequences. Indeed, I wonder how the future would have played out had we met at that point in our lives. If I'd made a different choice maybe - just maybe, events wouldn't have turned out the way they did.

Chapter 28
1964
Easter Holiday

"A postcard for you," says Mother handing it to me as Krysia, Mary, Sinéad and I play Monopoly on the kitchen table. We gossip more than we play.

"You know, it looks a bit like you with that fringe," jokes Krysia who's returned from Scotland before the card she posted had arrived. The picture on the front is a buxom horned highland cattle, its fringe almost entirely covering its eyes.

"Ha ha Krysh!" I say pretending not to be amused.

"Your friend she is right. It looks like you," echoes Mother who's unable to resist a dig at my hair. But this morning she refrains from giving the usual sobering piece of advice about having my unruly fringe cut before it damages my eyes.

Today sees her in good spirits as she and Mrs. Jones, (whom she now calls Angela) are taking Andrew to a puppet show at the Baptist church hall; and Mother's been invited to their house afterwards for a spot of lunch. She's quite perky and full of vitality. Even though her hair is still scraped back into that rather old fashioned style, recently her expression has grown softer. She smiles more often, and projects an inner peace that I've only previously witnessed when we were by the sea in Cornwall. In spite of her disapproval of the mini, she actually is adhering, just a little bit, to the current fashion; and today wears a dress which is a bright coral blue and just above the knee.

Before passing "Go" I land on Park Lane, and while I'm in the process of purchasing the property, Mother rushes back to pick up the lemon cheesecake she made last night. "Almost forgot."

She's tense and excited like a girl going off on a first date with the boy of her dreams. I'm pleased her friendship with the Jones family has blossomed; it seems to have made a real difference to her life.

"You have money?" she asks me. "Money for this lunch at Wimpy Bar?"

"Yes, Mum," I reply offering the dice to Sinéad who's leaning on the table, head on hand, and showing not the slightest bit of interest in the game.

"Pity to waste money. You could have good sandwich here. But that is what you young people want, I think - this Wimpy Bar. But now I am off. So, goodbye girls."

Sinéad's the only one who makes no reply. "Wakey, wakey," says Mary stretching across the table and waving her hand like a fan in front of her friend's face. "What's up with you? As if we didn't know."

"Shut up!" bites back Sinéad.

Krysia and I exchange glances as Sinéad thrusts herself backwards into the chair and sits morosely with arms folded and eyes downcast.

"Okay be like that, but I don't know why you put up with it?" Mary says.

"Like what?"

"You know perfectly well. Saying he'll phone and then he doesn't. Well, not 'til the last minute on a Saturday night - if he's got nothing better to do that is. Then you jump. It's really pathetic …"

"Why don't you just belt up about Niall. Anyway, it's not like that at all, sure…"

"Okay? So why, last Saturday, were you round my house as manic as a blimmin' jack-in-the-box and crying your eyes out then? And isn't it true, when your mum rang to say he'd phoned, you're out of the door as if all that waiting on tenterhooks, and all those flippin' tears never happened? Hell Sinéad, where's your pride?"

"T'was just the once you stupid bitch. Because we've been seein' each other a while, he just takes it for granted that we'll be goin' out so…"

"Don't you dare call me stupid bitch! And yeah, too right he takes you for granted, you idiot…"

"Shut your big mouth. You're just so jealous because you can't be gettin' a boyfriend…"

"Wouldn't want one who treats me like that."

Sinéad is out of her chair screaming into Mary's face. "You be takin' that back, you bitch. Are you a-listenin' to me? Take it back."

It happens so fast. Mary leaps up and pushes her hard against the cupboard. Sinead, crying, in turn violently flings the chair out of her path and stomps off into the sitting room. Krysia and I stand amazed at the sudden venom.

"Hey! That was pretty rotten Mary," Krysia intervenes. "You didn't need to wind her up like that. You know how crazy she is about that boy."

"Look, Krysh, you and I both know he's a waste of space."

From the sitting room Sinéad yells, "I hate you Mary Madeley. You're just a sanctimonious little cow…"

Mary refuses to be drawn further. Stony faced she addresses Krysia and myself.

"For bloody hell sake, I'm not just bitching. I just can't stand seeing him treat her like that. It's obvious he doesn't really care, isn't it? I mean, he couldn't even be bothered to let her know he was going away over Easter. So okay Krysh, take her side, but you're not always there to see how damned upset she gets. It…"

I leave Mary to Krysia and go to Sinéad who's no longer crying, but standing by the bay window in the sitting room looking out into the avenue. "Don't *you* be sayin' anythin'," she snaps as I approach. "None of you understand, right?"

"Right," I repeat knowing full well it's true. I have no idea how it feels to be in love.

Neither of us speaks. After a short while Sinéad begins to calm down and staring into the net curtains asks, "So would you be thinkin' that I'm an eejit too - you know - with Niall an'all?"

I don't want to start her off again, but I need to be honest, yet diplomatic, "Well, you know - er - maybe he doesn't realise - er - how much all the hanging about - er - waiting to hear from him is upsetting you."

"I sort of tried tellin' him, so I did. But you know what fellas are like. Don't like girls makin' a fuss."

No, I don't know what fellas are like, but I say that I do.

For several minutes, I stand with my hand on her shoulder waiting for the renewed bout of crying to subside, and then I see it, a coffee-coloured mini-cooper pulling up into the drive at number 66. In the driver's seat sits a woman, and towering in the back, is a shadowy shape with a tail. Once the car door opens, the woman climbs out, and within seconds, bags are being unloaded while a collection of lampshades tumble from the packed car. The woman is tall, slim, and of a similar age to Mother, perhaps a little younger. Her fashionable red dress with broad buckled belt is approximately an inch above the knee. I think Mother would agree; a suitable length for someone of middle age. She has a neatly cut fringe. Her dark blonde hair is straight with a kiss curl either side of her chin, much in the style of Mary Quant. From the back of the car appear two hands passing out cardboard boxes which she in turn stacks on the path.

"They must be our new neighbours," I say.

A loud barking comes from inside the car, and then it appears - an enormous fluffy brown and black Alsatian. The panting dog is followed by a George Harrison look-alike. He's not however a dead ringer for the Beatle, a bit younger, taller and with a slightly fuller face. He wears mid-blue denim jeans and a well worn black leather jacket which gapes open to reveal a white T-shirt plus a thick roped golden chain round his neck. His dark hair, a little wild, hangs below his collar.

Sinéad brightens up. "How old would you be thinkin' he is?" she asks still snivelling into her handkerchief.

"Eighteen, nineteen maybe," I reply watching him lead the mighty dog up the path. I'm pleased to see the boy, but apprehensive as to how Mother will feel about the dog because she's never liked them much - and detests Alsatians. She says they are vicious, unpredictable creatures; and one should not even attempt to befriend them. The boy, nevertheless, may be worth getting to know.

"Maybe, I should consider chuckin' Niall," Sinéad says with a giggle, then bursts into tears all over again.

We're interrupted by Mary's apology to Sinéad. Explanations. Truce. Peace. And they're friends again. Well, at least for the time being. The day can now go ahead as planned.

Later, when I walk up the path, I know the family has finally moved in. The curtains upstairs are drawn. As yet there are none downstairs, enabling me to see the blonde woman and a man with spectacles, dark peppered grey hair and a short cut beard eating at a table in the bay. There's no sign of George Harrison, but I hear a deep bark, and a doggy face with alert pointed ears appears at the window.

Winter's reluctant to relinquish its hold on the spring, hence the moon's greenish gold hue; however the sky is clear and boasts a million stars. It's a chilly evening and I've been out long enough. Having consumed burgers and Knickerbocker Glories at the Wimpy Bar, Sinéad persuaded us to take the bus to her house. She said it wasn't the case, but we all knew that she was hoping for *that* phone call.

Niall still hadn't rung when I left. Well, Saturday's tomorrow, and as they usually don't go out until about 8 o'clock, I guess he's got another twenty three hours or so. Poor Sinéad, I'll never let myself fall so pathetically in love like that, I'm thinking as I enter the kitchen to see Mother's distraught, whitened face.

"It is a beast, a huge beast. Have you not heard the barking? How can I live with that next door, Stefan?"

Mother's seen it - or maybe, just the barking was enough.

"Hania, Hania," Father consoles. "We have good fences. The dog will not come here. I will go to these new neighbours, I will explain about you and dogs…"

"Me and dogs? Not dogs - this kind - this kind that bites - tears people's flesh - rips them apart. Wolves in disguise! Wolves in disguise…"

"Oh don't exaggerate," I interrupt. "He's just a dog, an Alsatian - maybe a big one, but he's not going to rip anyone apart for goodness sake! Come on, Mum. At long last the house next door isn't empty; we've neighbours - and no more rats."

Mother throws down her baking bowl. While it spins like a top, the unmixed flour rises in a cloud as the milk and eggs splash across the floor in every direction. Finally the bowl comes rattling to a halt by the back door. "Don't speak like this to me!" she shouts. "You have not seen what these dogs can do. If you had seen them pouncing, tearing necks, arms - even faces off people, then you would not smile so rudely and tell me I exaggerate."

Cracking the wooden spoon on the draining board, she treads straight through the congealing mess, marches through the hall, upstairs and into her bedroom slamming the door behind her. Intermittent barking from next door's garden punctuates the silence she leaves behind. Father looks at me as if to say, "Now you have done it."

Chapter 29
1964
Next day

Saturday morning. Father's left for work by the time I come downstairs to find Mother making a pot of tea. She looks tired and I suspect she didn't sleep well. I don't expect her to speak to me after last night's display of emotion; therefore I'm surprised when she asks if I'd prefer cornflakes or a slice of toast. Despite not being hungry, I accept the toast, appreciative of the peace offering.

We sit opposite each other struggling to find anything to say. It strikes me, these days, there can't be many kids sitting with their own mother feeling so uncomfortable. I want to ask her about the dogs - the vicious spectacles she must have witnessed. I want to know about that camp - Auschwitz. I need to understand. But as usual I'm tongue-tied.

Krysia's mum says bottling things up isn't good for you. "Talk about problems. Get them out into the open. It's healthy. After all, a trouble shared is a trouble halved," she says. If only Mother could do that. I'm convinced Ewa is the key. But the opportunity's been missed.

I've no real plans for today other than finishing the last of my holiday homework before term starts again on Monday. There's still the diagram of the human digestive system to draw; and I've put off learning a list of French vocabulary for days. A documentary about the recent Winter Olympics is on BBC this evening. Gee, won't that sound really fab when the girls at school ask me what I did last Saturday night. Sinéad will no doubt have had her last minute phone call from lover boy; Krysia's going to the Polish club in Kensington with her parents and Mary's out for the day visiting cousins in Coventry.

By 11.30 I find myself in the library paying the fines for the overdue books I should've returned last week. The crusty old dragon rebukes me for this heinous crime and instead of choosing new books I escape as quickly as possible.

Passing the Wimpy Bar, on impulse I wander through the door. It's crowded, mainly with teenagers. I see that Norma no longer has a Saturday job at Woolworths, but is behind the counter making milkshakes and coffees. I long for a strawberry shake, but ask for a coffee as it seems more grown up. "Coffee!" says Norma smiling as if we are long lost friends. "I prefer milkshake myself. Coffee's so bitter. By the way, heard anything from Lisa?" she adds handing me my change.

"No. Have you?"

"Nope. Not a thing, but I saw Peter a couple of weeks back. He said he was over this way to see a mate from his old school. Before I got a word in 'bout Lisa, he's off. His hair's dead long now. A total mess if you ask me."

"Oh!" I say to Norma who still makes me feel dowdy and square.

As I sip the bitter dark coffee I wish I'd stuck to my guns and not worried about appearing grown up. That's until I spot him. There he is in the far corner by the toilet sign drinking Coca-Cola and reading the *New Musical Express*. He's wearing the same jeans and leather jacket as yesterday. He's not noticed me, and of course has no idea that I'm his neighbour anyway. But should he look this way, I'm pleased he'll see a girl who drinks coffee. Well, at least now I'll be able to say I went to the Wimpy Bar, if anyone at school asks what I did on Saturday.

The weather has brightened up by the time I get home. Mother wastes no time in handing me the washing basket. She asks me to do the small task of hanging out the wet clothes because she's so very busy. Indeed, she's up to her elbows in dough. She then confides this next piece of information as if it's a decision of maximum importance. And it is this. She and Father have agreed to invite the new neighbours in for a drink. "Not the dog," she adds rather unnecessarily. The plan being, that Father will go over and invite them after supper. She divulges that at quite an early hour this morning, from her bedroom window, she caught sight of the neighbours walking down their front path. Mother stretches her neck and stands erect. "Very respectable people. You can see it by the way they dress."

Humph! I think. She obviously hasn't yet seen the boy.

The last of the socks is pegged on the line and I stand back to look at the washing's frantic dance in the wind. Shirts are billowing with invisible men, the tea towels flap furiously, and Father's pyjama bottoms struggle to pull free and fly away. "Freedom," the washing in my mind cries. A peg from a white shirt drops to the ground, bounces on the patio and lands by the fence. Stooping to pick it up, I hear a snuffling, followed by a throaty low bark. There, in a gap where the fence is a little broken appears a large, black nose, sniffing. Then I hear, "Bruno, Komm her."

"Komm her? German," I whisper to myself, curious as to how that will go down with Mother. Better than the dog? Or worse?

Chapter 30
1964
Same day

"He won't hurt you. He's curious, that's all," a voice comes from the other side of the wooden fence. The English is good with only a hint of an accent.

The heavy pounding and scratching at the wooden panels continues nonetheless. Bruno's barking is constant. It's guttural and rhythmic. Six short woofs and a lengthy low-pitched growl. I'm beginning to take Mother's point about a wolf in disguise and wonder how long it'll take before she calls me in. But the window of the kitchen is being closed and then the back door shuts. Unable to see him, but from the youthful tone of voice, I suppose it's George Harrison speaking. "Okay, thanks," I reply.

"Hiya!" he says a couple of seconds later as I'm stretching to replace the clothes peg on the shoulder of the white shirt waving on the line. Bruno has stopped his incessant barking, and his claws can be heard tip-tapping on the path as he scampers off. He reaches the lawn and then through the wire fence, I'm now able to see the dog at the bottom of our neighbours' garden. His head's down sniffing the plants in the overgrown rockery which at one time had been Greg's pride and joy.

"Hiya," I respond.

"Can't hold a conversation with that great wooden barrier between us," George Harrison says with confidence, and he's there, peeking over the lower wire fence, the one which separates the second halves of our gardens.

Thank God, I've not yet taken off my new suede jacket, I'm thinking as he comes into view. I reckon I don't look too bad in the navy trousers, but the jumper is definitely too chunky. Not wanting to seem over-keen, I pretend to struggle with the flapping shirt, and deliberately fumble with the clothes peg. Anyway, I'm uncertain what to say next, not having anticipated a conversation with George Harrison quite so soon. I need not have worried for he's already asking my name. Although his eyes are playful, I think he's a little forward when he follows up my reply with, "I'm pleased to see such a pretty lass living next door."

Nevertheless I'm flattered.

He introduces himself as Kon. "Kon with a K, short for Konrad." Then he informs me that, although their family originally comes from Cologne, they've been living in Manchester for the past eight and a half years. Taking a pack of cigarettes from the pocket of his leather jacket, he offers me one.

"Not at the moment," I reply wondering how old he thinks I am. We chat for a while about this and that. As a ploy to establish his age, I ask him where he goes to university or college.

"I don't."

"Sorry," I say quickly not wanting to offend.

"Don't be. I'm only seventeen, but I've left school. Hated it most of the time. Got the *required* five O'levels, then ditched it. Couldn't wait. Aye, well my parents flipped their lids when I told them I wasn't going back to the dump. Made a big fuss and all that for a while - like parents do. Then Dad found me this job - with *prospects* - in a bank. Really uncool. Well, I can tell you that bored the pants off me. So when they told me we were moving down here, I told *them*, no transfer - no more crashingly dull days in a bank."

He bends down to stroke Bruno who's now lying majestically with paws outstretched in front of him and tail thumping on the grass.

Kon looks up. "And what about you?"

I watch his eyes for the reaction when I reveal that I'm fifteen and still at school. "Our Lady of Lourdes." I'm astounded to hear the pride in my voice as the name of the school slips out.

"Catholic?"

"Yeah." I know there's the underlying intention to mislead, but I can't bring myself to deal with this Jewish thing. All at once I feel anxious, anxious about Mother. It doesn't bother *me*, but perhaps it would be wise to tip Father off about the nationality of our new neighbours before he delivers the invitation.

Bruno is up and barking again. I see Samba bolting from under the gooseberry bushes, the dog hard on his heels. The terrified cat scrambles up the blossoming apple tree, jumps onto the shed roof. With a fretful bark of defeat the Alsatian slinks over and flops at the boy's feet. Kon pats the dog's huge head in consolation. Time to go.

As I lift up the empty laundry basket, Kon leans across the fence. "For you," he says holding out a daffodil. Most boys of his age wouldn't hand a strange girl a flower, but Kon isn't even sheepish. I take it and with some reserve thank him.

"Hey, how about one day when I take Bruno for a walk you come too?"

"Yeah, that'd be nice," I reply. And mean it.

Hidden once again by the tall wooden partition, Kon calls, "We'll make it soon."

Walking back to the house, clasping the single daffodil, I feel victorious, joyous and beautiful. What a romantic, I think, and then feel a pang of fear as I consider where this could lead. I tuck the flower in my jacket pocket before going inside.

When I step into the kitchen and see Mother's sour expression, the implication of having these new German neighbours really begins to sink in. I've a sixth sense about this, and it doesn't bode well.

I wait for the inevitable question, "Who were you speaking to?" But it doesn't come. Mother starts muttering under her breath. "Tear your hand to pieces if they get chance. Yes, Stefan he will have to speak with neighbours. That dog it is too big for these small gardens - too big." Outside Bruno barks again and Mother tenses. Her head rises and momentarily her upper body stiffens.

Something delicious is baking in the oven. In fact I could already smell the apples and pastry before reaching the back door. Mother throws down her oven-gloves, goes to the kitchen sink and begins the washing up. She starts with spoons; then the mixing bowl (which incredibly has weathered last night's fall) before tackling the whisk which she washes over and over again. The blades twist on. They're sparkling silver and squeaky clean, but the dish-mop wipes and wipes. And all the while, seemingly unaware of what she's doing, Mother discusses with herself the problem of the dog.

Juke Box Jury has finished and still there's no sign of Father. Nervously I wait, determined to impart the information that our neighbours are German before he discovers it for himself - on their doorstep. But he's late from work. For once it's me as well as Mother who's annoyed about this. Meeting Marek for a drink, I bet.

I keep bobbing up and down, peering out of the window. This irritates Mother who wonders why I'm unable to sit still. Rain is threatening so I use this feeble excuse to explain my restlessness. She says that she's trying to follow a complicated knitting pattern and finds my constant movement a distraction.

Then I see him; Father coming out of the neighbours' front door. It's too late for intervention. Mother lowers the jumper she's knitting once the key rattles in the lock. It's as if relaxing were a crime. She leaps up from the armchair and is in the kitchen immediately re-lighting the gas on the stove. Father calls hello and apologises for his lateness. Mother doesn't bother to enquire why he's been delayed, only mumbles that the meal will be ruined; and within seconds she's serving up crumbling potatoes. Father's taking off his raincoat as I stand beside him in the hall. Even though I'm aware the casserole has already been placed on the table, I whisper, "I need a word." For once I've not stalled.

Father surely must have failed to hear me, for he's climbing the stairs whilst calling down, "Hania, I will not be long."

"Dad," I say with quiet urgency when he reaches the landing. "You know our new neighbours are German, don't you?"

At first he looks at me out of the corner of his eye and says nothing, but then with lips pursed, he confirms that he does know - he's invited them anyway. He explains he decided to go and invite them before coming home - to save having to go out again after supper. With little trace of emotion, he admits he was shocked when he realised they were German. "But I expect they too were a little surprised when they heard Polish accent."

Mother calls, "I tell you a second time the meal it is on table."

We continue to ignore her. "They are Mr. and Mrs. Wilner - um - Kurt and Renate they tell me - and seem very nice people." Matching my whisper Father says, "They ask me in for sherry. It would be unfriendly to refuse. While we take drink, I offer invitation. But they are not able to come tomorrow. So, they come next Sunday. I think Martina, it is important to let bygones be bygones. The war is over a long time now, after all."

It's not me who needs convincing. I'm one hundred percent with that.

"The meal!" shouts Mother.

"Coming," Father and I answer as one.

Filled with apprehension I say, "But you'd better tell Mum before she finds out for herself." I then ask if the boy is included in the invitation, and try not to sound particularly concerned one way or the other.

Father nips into the bathroom whilst I head towards the kitchen where Mother sits at the table tapping a fork on her place mat. "Do you know why I bother to cook good food when no one wants to eat?" Fuming, she gets up from her chair and dollops beef and vegetables onto my plate.

I wish Father would just come out with it, get it over and done with. The dread and suspense is unbearable. It's killing my appetite, but I chew my way through the meat and long for conversation. Eventually I'm unable to shovel any more food into my mouth, so I push a mound of carrots and potato to the side of my plate.

There's apple cake for dessert. I love this and miraculously my appetite is back. I take the jug of cream and begin to pour as Mother speaks. "Stefan, remember you must go next door. Invite them for tomorrow evening. It is important that we make them welcome - but not the dog. When you are there, it will be a good time to mention this dog is problem, yes?"

This is the moment. How long until the explosion? But Father only states that he's already been, and that the welcome party is postponed until next Sunday due to the neighbours having some previous arrangement. I know now from whom I've inherited the gift of procrastination. I wait for Father to reveal their names. Nothing is said. Preoccupied with the topic of the Alsatian, Mother doesn't ask, and in a way I'm relieved.

We've missed the TV review of the Winter Olympics and Father seems more intent on what President Johnson has to say about the progress in Vietnam than in disclosing to Mother the fact that she has German neighbours. I wonder if she'll prefer her rats when she finds out. I hope at least Father will tell her before next Sunday.

The *News* provides an update on the survivors of the Good Friday Earthquake in Alaska, after that item I decide to go upstairs; Father may find it easier to drop the bombshell with just the two of them present.

The ringing of the phone makes me jump. I answer it as I'm in the hall and right beside it.

"Cześć!" says the caller as soon I chant our number. It's Marek.

"Hello!" Without hesitation I say, "I'll get Dad."

"No need, Martina. Only tell him, he left small package on pub bar. I see it only has aspirin and shaving cream inside. I give it him when we meet. You tell him this?"

"Yes," I say abruptly.

I'm about to put down the receiver when he asks how I am. Not wanting to get involved in a protracted conversation I answer, "Fine thanks."

"What about violin exam?"

"Haven't got the result yet, but yeah, I think it went okay, thanks."

Without thinking, I begin telling him that I used the concert tickets he gave me; saw my aunt in the Festival Hall - listened to her playing violin. There's no surprise in his voice. "That is good. I will write to her, tell her you were there. Definitely she will be pleased. I know this."

"No, don't tell…"

But Marek is already saying, "Do widzenia."

When I return to the living room Mother and Father are conversing although the television's still on. Has he told her? Or is he about to? Perhaps they're not talking about the Wilners at all? But then I see Mother shrug her shoulders and churlishly she says, for my benefit, "You think I did not know? *Komm her* that boy said to the dog, was it not?"

I remain silent.

Father's biting his lip. We exchange glances and we wait. "Well?" Mother's addressing me directly now. "Well? - Well? You were there - were you not?"

"Yes." I turn to go.

Father's not helping me by staying silent, and I don't know what to do or say.

She's interrogating me like a police sergeant. Suddenly she does not look like my Mother. Her eyes are hard and cold. She does not sound like my mother. Her voice cuts like sharp stone. I feel afraid. "Well?"

In the time it takes to flip a coin, everything's changed. The twisted mouth has a hint of a smile, and the voice is warmer. "Well, not all Germans are Nazis, are they?" she says and relaxes back into the armchair.

I see Father's eyes close for a second and I detect relief in his sigh.

The title music of some old 1950's spy thriller follows on from the end of the *News*. Mother tries to coax me to stay and watch it with them. "This film it is full of intrigue," she says.

My head is reeling with more intrigue than anyone would wish for. "No thanks," I reply before conveying Marek's message.

I'm feeling relieved as I cross the sitting room to go out. That's until I hear Mother's chilly voice. "That scruffy German boy with the long hairstyle and jacket like teddy boy - it is better you keep away from that type." For a fleeting moment the icy shard returns to her eyes. "A hot drink?" she then asks in her everyday voice.

Chapter 31
1964
One week later

Gee, it's been a tough week, I think on my way home from a Saturday tennis tournament at St. Anne's. We've only been back at school five days - six if today counts. Not only have I had all that extra homework due to me taking O'level English Language, Maths and Music a year early, but Mother's moods have been so unpredictable - and Sinéad being down since Niall chucked her last weekend hasn't made life any easier.

A pity that Sinéad and I lost every match in straight sets this morning. Last year we prided ourselves on our constant wins throughout the whole season. Today though was a disaster, an embarrassment. Sinéad's mind was far from tennis.

Muscles ache that I didn't even know existed, and my spirit is low. It's not scorching, but the April sun is warm. My hair hangs in long high bunches; I'm hot, perspiring profusely and wearing a version of the school uniform. On my arrival home, I swing open the front gate and my tennis racket tumbles out of my loosely packed satchel, bumps across the path, landing on the flowerbed where it flattens a number of crimson tulips.

"Oh dear, very careless."

I look up to see Kon leaning out of the box room window and laughing. "What school did you say you go to? St. Trinians?"

"Hilarious!" I return hating to be a figure of fun and wishing the ground would swallow me up. Wasting no more time, I head for the front door. Before the key's out of my purse, he's there standing right beside my sweaty body, smiling.

"I'm off to take Bruno for a walk? Want to come?"

"Hardly," I say, "dressed like this"

He scrunches his face, makes a cheeky expression. "Okay lass, give you ten minutes."

"You're joking. I'll need more than ten minutes."

"An hour then?"

We shake hands on forty minutes.

I glance at myself in the mirror. It's taken some time to decide what to wear. Not wanting to be overdressed, I decide it's more in keeping with taking a dog for a walk, to wear blue slacks and my lemon ribbed top. My hair, freshly washed, has a pleasing sheen. Lipstick - just a dash of pearly pink - and a little mascara. Don't want to look as if I'm advertising myself for a date. I peep from behind the curtains of the spare bedroom. He's not there, and it's gone forty minutes. I've no wish to be seen hanging around, waiting on the pavement. Feeling slightly nauseous, I'm not quite sure what to do. Now in some small way I can relate to Sinéad and feel sorry for her waiting for Niall's phone calls time and time again.

Mother has the vacuum cleaner out; she's been hard at it since breakfast. She calls it spring cleaning, I call it preparation for tomorrow's visitors. I'm about to tell her I'm going to the shops, but she glances up from her task with a look in her eye that makes me change my mind. Anyway, I know there'll be no fuss if I tell Father instead. He's gardening, making the most of the good weather during his few days holiday from the pharmacy.

Leaning on the spade, he is talking to Mr. Wilner over the fence. The smell of freshly cut grass greets me as I step into the garden and cross the lawn towards them.

I've not seen Mr.Wilner at close quarters before, and as I draw near I see the resemblance between father and son. The older man is taller, more solid than Kon. The darkness of Kon's hair obviously comes from the paternal side of the family. However, Mr. Wilner's pale blue eyes seem incongruous with someone with his darkish complexion. He's smiling, and I think what a friendly face this man has. Catching sight of me, he immediately waves and calls, "Hello!" with a broad German accent.

After polite introductions, I take advantage of Mr.Wilner's presence and inform Father that I'm off to walk Bruno with Kon - and add for good measure that we won't be very long. I don't wait for his reply. As soon as I leave them, the men resume their conversation about the dreadful weeds in the Wilner's garden, and I hear Father offer to get his special, strong weed-killer from the shed.

Not wanting to return to the house, I lift the latch of the back gate and decide to take the bull by the horns; do the grown up thing, knock on Kon's front door and say that I'm ready. But as soon as I'm through the gate he appears on the pavement, Bruno pulling at the lead, raring to go.

Too hot for leather jackets, Kon looks casual and cool in jeans and a mustard T-shirt with *Make love not war* on the front. Thankfully the aftershave he's wearing is not Brut. It's fragrant, not too sweet and definitely "manly". I like it. On seeing me, Bruno begins to bark. He leaps up. I recoil. Kon laughs and says what all owners of big dogs say, "He's really a gentle giant."

As he restrains Bruno, I note Kon's arms are muscular and strong. We walk with the dog tugging constantly at the leash, yearning no doubt for freedom. Our speed being dictated by the dog's pace, we proceed very quickly along the pavement. Kon, not knowing the area very well yet, suggests we go to what's rapidly becoming "his usual haunt", the park.

Now that we're supposed to make conversation, we seem lost for words, so Bruno becomes the conversation piece. I babble on about the sleekness of the dog's fur, how massive he is, ask how much he eats and how many walks he needs each day, until Kon obviously having had enough of this trivia interrupts, "I've got a job."

"Well, that's fab! What is it?"

"Down at the record shop in the High Street. The drag is I've got to work Saturdays, but the plus side is I get Monday and Wednesday afternoons off. So now you'll be able to come along whenever I'm there, stay in the booth and listen to all the latest hits for as long as you like. And you know what? I won't even insist you buy them. How about that then?"

"Yeah. Yeah. That's - er - cool."

"Aye well, I won't be working in a shop forever, but it's music - it's a start - and I get paid - every week. And miles better than a bank. Surprise, surprise, my parents don't think so. *No prospects*, said the old man."

I'm with "the old man" on that one, but I don't say so.

The park's crowded with people and dogs. It's been some months since I've been here. It must have been last November when Krysia and I decided winter walks are sometimes preferable to being cooped up indoors. Vacant swings swayed with ghostly riders; the childless roundabout pointlessly turned in the wind. The pond was clogged with empty Coca-Cola bottles; and scrunched up sweet wrappers lay trapped in the reeds or danced in the wind across the icy surface.

Today however, every swing is occupied. Numbers of impatient children stand eagerly awaiting their turn. The roundabout is overcrowded with youngsters, shrieking and screaming as it spins faster and faster. I'm pleased to see that the pond's free from litter and the ducks have returned.

We follow the pathway along the edge of the field where groups of boys and girls are playing various ball games; football, cricket or Piggy in the Middle. A Jack Russell amuses us as he wildly dashes in all directions, seizing balls and running off with them. There are many dogs romping free so Kon concludes it's safer to keep Bruno on the lead.

Once we arrive at the other side of the park where the mammoth oaks and horse chestnuts grow, we're alone. "Tired?" Kon asks.

I say that I am a little, so we make our way over to the wooden bench, shaded by the leafy canopy of the largest tree. It feels good to sit while Bruno, panting loudly, lies down. "To look at him, you wouldn't think it, but he's getting on. Had him since we came to England. The brute's nine this year - quite old actually for this breed of dog."

I agree that he is a magnificent creature for his age. Then neither of us speaks for a time.

"Was that you I heard playing the violin the other evening? Beatles' tunes - so I reckoned it wasn't your mum or dad. Heard you when I was in the garden with this mutt."

"Yeah," I reply pleasantly surprised to realise that he'd listened long enough to recognise the music. "It's a medley. I've sort of been working on it a while - ever growing as the Beatles release new songs - just do it for myself - not for anything special. For fun, I guess."

"Well, it sounded pretty special to me."

"Thanks."

I'm a bit embarrassed and am glad when he changes the subject, tells me that he plays guitar - rhythm and lead. He's got a Fender Strat. After that it's easy. The conversation flows. He explains that he has ambitions, ambitions to put together a group - which will have something of the Manchester sound - a bit like the Hollies, but with his own stamp on it - original songs - original line-ups and great harmonies. I explain that I love pop; then confess unashamedly, that I love classical music too. And he's okay with it; says it's really groovy and he hates people who just go with the crowd.

I talk about school, friends, my indecision concerning my own future career until Bruno grows restless and wants to be up and away. "Come on," I say getting up.

Kon's reluctant to move. "Give me your hand. Help this poor tired lad to his feet." He's play-acting, but I simply look up to heaven and offer assistance. He grasps my hand, I pull, he resists; we're really laughing. Then suddenly he springs to his feet, but without releasing me.

Walking hand in hand through the park with a boy feels good. Walking hand in hand with *this* boy feels ecstatic. I can't quite believe my luck when I notice Norma and Strawberry Blonde coming towards us. Once we're face to face, I make a point of not smiling too broadly, but do say hello, trusting I sound friendly, yet suitably laid back. Their eyes are on stalks. They greet me, but can't take their eyes off Kon.

The wind's picking up as we approach the tennis courts. My hair blows across my face, and Kon stretches out to sweep it away. There's a doubles match. The players, dressed in white, three women and a man, aren't very good. They seem to know the rules, but a game rarely gets going before one of them belts the ball out of court or into the net. Nevertheless, we stand and watch.

I can feel Kon's arm moving against mine. His hip is lightly touching me. From the corner of my eye I see him turn, and I know he's looking at me. I continue pretending to be engrossed in the match as yet another ball is called out. It's not long before I feel Kon's left hand on my upper arm, and with that I turn my head a fraction; and we're looking at each other. He moves. Now we're so close that I can feel his warmth. Leaning forward, he places his right hand behind my head. I'd always thought that romantic authors write the cliché, *She could feel her heart beating faster* just before a first kiss, to create suspense for the reader, but here I am with chest tight and heart thumping. Kon's right hand reaches out and strokes the hair behind my ear. He's looking into my eyes as he draws me closer to him. Embarrassed by such intimacy, I close mine. I expect his mouth to be hungry and strong, but his lips are barely brushing mine…

Wham! We jump in fright. "Dummkopf!" Kon yells.

A tennis ball is wedged in the wire fence inches from our faces.

The man on court yells, "Sorry" to a background of female giggles. The ball is retrieved and play immediately resumes.

My old fear of physical contact leaves me feeling a little relieved, but there's more than a flicker of something else inside me which is greatly disappointed. The moment is lost.

"Cretins!" Kon says as he takes my hand and we walk away listening to yet another, "Out!"

"How about me taking you to the cinema tonight?"

I need no time to consider this. I absolutely know this would be a problem with Mother - and most likely Father too. The subject of me dating has in fact never been discussed with either of them, but they often remark that Sinéad is far too young to have a boyfriend. Mother says she's surprised that the daughter of a dentist is allowed to do whatever she likes. Sadly, Sinéad has slipped out of favour as far as she's concerned. A date with Kon, a German teddy boy, as Mother already refers to him, is definitely out of the question. I just know it. Maybe in the future, when I've done a little work on Father - maybe if tomorrow's visit proves a success; but this evening, it's inconceivable.

Quickly I remind Kon that my friend Sinéad is distraught over this break up with her boyfriend - and then resort to lying, say I've promised to be at home in case she wants to come over for the evening.

Kon's face drops, but he keeps hold of my hand. "Aye," he says, "well, maybe another time?"

"Okay, that'd be good," I say wondering if he'll risk another rebuff. "But of course you're coming to our house with your parents tomorrow, aren't you?"

"Sure," he says without the enthusiasm I was hoping for.

Chapter 32
1964
Next day

"We do not want the Germans to think us to be filth, do we?" Mother says in a chirpy tone incongruous with the sentiment of her words.

"But, you've already hoovered the whole house yesterday - even the rooms they won't go into." I say this while flicking through the pages of the recently delivered Sunday paper. Homing in on the article concerning race riots in America I add, "And Mum, I wish you'd stop calling the Wilners, the Germans."

"Well, they are, aren't they? Even the dog it is a German Shepherd."

Father, sleepy, hair uncombed and generally looking dishevelled, comes into the kitchen wearing his dressing gown. He glances at Mother, tuts at her words and leans towards me; I reluctantly hand him the newspaper and switch to reading a rather battered edition of *Murder in the Vicarage*.

"Hania, perhaps this visit it is not such a good idea. It is not too late. With some suitable excuse it still can be cancelled," he says.

My heart skips a beat; this is the last thing I want to happen. Even though she says it in a manner more appropriate to a person having to undergo serious surgery, I'm relieved when Mother replies, "No need. It is important this is done - even if it is just once." She continues to prepare a platter of cold meats and cheese for breakfast. Tomatoes are chopped into bite-size pieces, and a jar of unopened gherkins is taken from the cupboard. This, she places on the table between the damson preserve and the basket of brown seeded bread. Standing back as if scrutinising a display for an art exhibition, she then rearranges the loaf so it's beside the jam and close to the butter dish.

"But I think that Martina is right, Hania," says Father in his soft, typically tactful way. Seated, he looks straight ahead as he helps himself to bread and a slice or two of cheese.

"It is better, I think, that you do not keep referring to them as the Germans. They are after all, our neighbours."

Mother wants flowers for the sitting room, so during the afternoon she asks me to go into the garden and pick some. Despite the recent dry weather and warm temperatures, she rarely goes out there these days. I think this is a pity, for she's always enjoyed the garden so much.

Bruno is outside barking heartily, and I can hear Kon speaking to him in German. This, I consider a little odd since the dog to all intents and purposes is English - born and bred here and has never been to Germany from what I understand. If the dog was spoken to in English, would Mother perhaps be able to come to terms with it more easily?

"I'm busy practising," I call from the dining room. "I'm trying to get to grips with the new Grade 8 violin piece before my lesson tomorrow." In fact it's my Beatles' medley I'm anxious to perfect, and I feel certain Mother knows this; however she makes no comment when she enters the room.

"Have I not enough to do without this too?" She's already setting out the plates, glasses, cups and saucers as well as folding napkins for this evening. It's only 4 o'clock and our guests aren't expected for another three hours.

I don't want to encounter Kon until later, so I simply take the scissors and wicker basket Mother holds out, and say I'll go shortly. Satisfied with this, she returns to her own tasks.

Once the barking has ceased, I put down the violin and do what I've been asked. Boy and dog thankfully seem to have gone inside, so I proceed with the cutting of flowers. I choose tulips, only those in shades of pink, crimson and deep purple. I think too many colours can be garish. The daffodils are past their prime so I leave them to enjoy what remains of their lives in the sunshine. A tulip petal flutters down from one of the blooms like a blood red snowflake. It lands on the tip of my shoe. I pick it up. It's like velvet, and I think it feels more like the ear of a tiny puppy. Two vases in the sitting room, filled with this selection of flowers, I decide will look very tasteful.

Pleased to have finished gathering the flowers without interruption, I hurry back into the house. “Ooh, chasin’ Samba was he?” It’s Mrs. Carr’s voice. She’s wearing her floral overall and standing in the doorway of our kitchen holding an onion. “Well dearie, Samba can run very fast. Anyways, he seems to be all right.”

“The next time, the cat might not get away.” Mother’s words sound daunting. “This dog it is a dangerous kind. Too big for these gardens.”

“Oh well, we’ll just have to wait and see. Thanks for the onion, dearie. It’s very kind of you. Don’t know how I could’ve forgotten. Gettin’ old that’s my trouble. Brain like a sieve these days. I’ll bring you one tomorrow - just as soon as I get back from them shops. All right?”

“Do not worry about onion Mrs. Carr. I have got very many.”

“’Course I’ll bring it back. Always pay me debts so to speak. And don’t you be worryin’ yourself about Samba. He’s got nine lives, he has. Just won’t go near their garden when the dog’s around… Germans you say they are?”

“Yes, German.”

“Oh well! We just got to put the war behind us; and that awful old Hitler. It’s for the best. All that hate and killin’. No good to anyone.”

“And all Germans are not Nazis,” says Mother in her frozen voice, smiling.

“I’ll be orf now, mustn’t dillydally. Thanks again dearie for the onion,” says Mrs. Carr already halfway down the hall.

Mrs. Carr gone, Mother comments that the tulips look very nice and she passes me two vases. But we end up arranging the flowers together, one vase each.

As we do this, Mother tells me cheerfully that the Germans will go away satisfied with their welcome; but the look in her eye is dark, and it makes me wonder if in actual fact, this will be the case. I’m beginning to really dread tonight’s do.

Chapter 33
1964
Same day

Anyone would think that we were entertaining royalty. There's Father dressed in an immaculately pressed light grey suit, white shirt and an unfashionable navy blue tie. Mother toys with the current style, wearing her newly purchased shift with swirling patterns in different shades of blue - its length, just above the knee. She would look really attractive, but for the buttoned up fawn cardigan and matronly hairstyle.

Half an hour to go and she's like a cat on hot bricks. One minute she's sitting in her chair, upright, hands locked, unable to settle to anything, the next she's up fussing over the positioning of the open sandwiches on the plate. Should the salami alternate with the cheese? Would they not be better separated entirely, cheese to the left and salami to the right? Seconds later she decides slices of tomato bordering the sandwiches would improve the spectacle.

"They look lovely," I reassure her. "Honestly they're fine just as they are." The television is on, but only Father is attentive to the lions' exploits on the African grasslands. I attempt to read my Agatha Christie, but in reality I'm an hour into the future, picturing with trepidation, this room and the six people who will soon be sitting in it.

I think I must have missed the doorbell when Mother all of a sudden leaps to her feet. But it's not that at all. In panic, she's decided the mountain of food is insufficient.

"We do not want the Germans to think we are mean," she says as she rushes off.

Not only are there already enough sandwiches to feed an army, but in addition there are mounds of little pastries and homemade biscuits. A lemon cheesecake forms a magnificent centrepiece on the table which has been moved from the dining room into the bay of the sitting room for this special occasion.

I'm about to speak when Father frowns, puts his finger on his lips and mouths, "Shh!"

"But who will eat all this?"

"Say nothing," he whispers. "This entertaining it is so much effort for Mum. And she is trying so very hard for it to be right."

This is true, but I'm pretty sure the Wilners will only be expecting snacks; and besides there's only so much food a person can consume. Nevertheless I refrain from saying so. The lions roar on in the background and proceed to tear chunks from the carcass of yet another antelope.

Mother's back, carrying a plate containing a whole sliced fruitcake. This she attempts to squeeze in between the Twiglets and the chopped green peppers. She flinches as Bruno's barking can be heard through the adjoining wall, suggesting perhaps that the Wilners are preparing for departure.

Ten minutes to go. Mother's seated herself on the hard dining room chair close to the window; restlessly she keeps watch. When the barking resumes, her eyes flash at Father. He raises his eyebrows as if to say, "There is no point. They are not going to get rid of their beloved pet."

Mother knows what he means. "Do it Stefan. He barks too much apart from anything else."

I know Father will say precisely nothing about the dog, so on that count I feel totally unconcerned.

They're here. Well, Mrs. Wilner and Kon are here, ensconced in the sitting room. Mr. Wilner's been delayed by an important business phone call, but won't be long. There is an exchange of pleasantries and plenty of chatter as to whether coffee, tea or something stronger is preferred. I've vacated the sofa leaving it free for the Wilners. She's dressed in mid-blue slacks and a short-sleeved pink blouse with a currently fashionable Peter Pan collar. The first thing that strikes me about Kon is his intoxicating aftershave - but I do wonder how often he actually has to shave. He's wearing jeans and a black polo neck top. Mother tried to nag me into wearing a "decent" length dress, but as I no longer have anything but minis, apart from my school uniform, I'm "forced" to wear my brand new denims. The ones Mother laughably calls, "teddy girl wear", her term for anyone or anything she considers scruffy or unsavoury.

I make a point of sitting on a chair some distance from Kon and remain aloof. He in turn, speaks very little to me. It's difficult to know whether he's annoyed due to me refusing the date, or is simply inhibited in the presence of our parents.

Earlier this morning, I'd been fantasising; imagining that after a respectable interval, Kon and I would slip away to take Bruno out for a walk; but from a fine day has emerged a very wet evening. A while ago a light shower started, now the rain is lashing against the sitting room windows. Rolls of distant thunder and the dark bruised sky suggest a storm is brewing.

Mother won't sit down for long. She's buzzing around with drinks and bowls of crisps, her face a smiling mask. Even though Father already knows the answer from chatting with her husband over the fence, he inquires how the family are settling in; and Mrs. Wilner in turn explains that the decorators are due next week. "Vot a nightmare!" she says. "Ze house needs a complete overhaul, redecorating from top to bottom."

"I see that," says Father sympathetic to her plight. "It has been empty for so long."

"You would not believe zis, but in ze pantry zer vas a rat - dead in ze corner, under ze bottom shelf."

With that Mother almost drops the cup and saucer she's carrying. "Rats! I knew it. Rats!" she cries.

"No more rat. All gone. Only ze von." Mrs. Wilner is out of her chair taking the cup and saucer while attempting to put pay to Mother's fears. "Maybe I exaggerate a little. I meant, ze house needs to be decorated, not zat it is dirty. It is zat ze taste of ze people who lived zer before is not ze same as ours. Zat is all. Please, you do not vorry yourself Mrs. Kalinska, zer are no more rats." She retreats to the sofa and gulps down her coffee.

Mother says she's not worried, and it's easy for me to realise that she's no longer filled with horror, but is indeed triumphant. Turning to Father she's extremely brusque. "You see, not everything is in my imagination."

Her poisonous glare instantly changes into a smile and she asks Mrs.Wilner the very same question as did Father. "And how are you settling into Woodland Avenue?"

This time comes the reply, "Oh very vell. Ve like zis neighbourhood very much - and ze house - very nice."

Father has produced two glasses of fizzy lemonade, one for Kon and the other for me. Without being asked Kon's helping himself to the crisps from the bowl placed on the small table right in front of him. He munches away without a glance in my direction.

Mrs. Wilner is amiable. Father, who's returned to his usual armchair, leans forward and enquires what she does for a living. She says that formerly, "at home" she was a teacher - taught English and French in the Gymnasium - what we would call in England, a grammar school she explains - but is hoping soon to gain the necessary British qualifications to become a translator. Her dream is to open her own translation agency in London. This strikes a chord with Father who relaxes into the topic of starting one's own business, and he proceeds to tell her that he's recently bought the chemist shop where he runs the pharmacy. For a while the problems of such financial ventures dominate the conversation.

She then turns to me, smiling. "And you, Martina? My husband, and Konrad have had ze pleasure of speaking vis you, but zis evening is ze first opportunity for me. Konrad tells me zat you play ze violin very vell, yes?"

No longer feeling like a spare part in my own home, I welcome this attention, and ignore the fact that her son is behaving like a spoilt brat. But Father anticipates my answer. "Martina she is excellent player. Starting work on Grade 8, it is highest music examination students can take - and we are hoping soon she will take up piano too." He sits tall and looks at me with pride as he carries on to speak of my intelligence and excellence in sport. In sufferance I sit blushing; ironically I detest all this praise.

Looking away, I catch sight of Kon who's now leaning forward. His elbow rests on his knee and his hand partially hides a grin. "Parents!" he mouths to me. And I feel much better.

The thunder rumbles louder and louder. Bruno barks louder and louder. Mother looks tense. A strand of her hair has escaped the clip and is hanging down alongside her right cheek. She makes no attempt to do anything about it. The barking reaches a crescendo as Mr. Wilner finally arrives. Now he's actually here, Mother's matching his smile. "Come. Come sit," she says directing him to the sofa even before he's through the sitting room door. He has a slight limp which I'd not noticed before. I wonder if he was injured during the war, but I know no one will ask since the subject of World War Two is definitely taboo.

A loud clap of thunder. Everyone jumps. It's very close. Bruno barks into action. "The dog…" says Mother looking at Father.

Mr. Wilner interrupts, "Not to worry, Bruno vill calm down once zis zunder has passed. My, vot a vonderful feast!" he exclaims noticing the spread. Immediately the room is filled with Mr. Wilner. He brings with him an atmosphere of liveliness and good humour, and I for one am grateful. Accepting the beer on offer he says, "It is gut."

The storm is gathering and the sky is suddenly a sheet of flashing fire. Bruno begins to bark again. Mother's smile collapses. Mr. Wilner notices at once. "Perhaps ze barking disturbs you?" He addresses Mother since Father is drawing the curtains.

Kon breaks away from our prattle about crisps and the snacks we prefer, and makes the same point as previously about Bruno being a gentle giant.

"A wolf in disguise more like," Mother blurts out to my horror.

"No! No!" objects Mr. Wilner. He sounds sad - friendly sad. "He is guter Hund. Noisy perhaps sometimes, but Bruno never hurts any people."

Unconvinced, Mother grunts.

"You do not like dogs?" Mr. Wilner asks.

"I do not like that kind of dog, Alsatians…But, let us now eat." She's over by the table, and picking up the tea plates she dishes them out as if they're hooplas at the fair.

I'm shocked because Mother's usually such a stickler for politeness and social etiquette.

Curtains closed, brings Father hastily to the middle of the room. With anxious fingers padding his cheek, he quickly intervenes, "I am sorry. Um - please understand - my wife she had very bad experience in past with this breed of dogs. Again I am sorry for offence."

"No offence taken," declares Mr. Wilner, his friendly smile back.

Mother's look at Father is darker than the stormy skies outside. She sits.

The silence is filled with World War Two.

Mother with a flounce and a flurry is up again. "Come, come, it's time for food."

"Such a feast!" exclaims Mr. Wilner again as he piles sandwiches high on to his plate.

"And so much verk!" declares his wife helping herself to two salami sandwiches and several gherkins.

"Not so very much," fibs Mother.

Mother eats nothing. Like a servant she hovers discreetly over her guests ensuring that their plates are constantly replenished and their cups or glasses full. Plenty to eat, and the fare thankfully provides plenty of safe conversation.

Father eventually insists Mother sits herself down and eats something. He asks me to go and make her a coffee. Relieved to break the monotony of small talk, I'm delighted to oblige. Mother sits on my chair and I hear Mrs. Wilner asking her what she does. I hear her begin to describe how she cares for a little child called Andrew, and then I'm in the kitchen refilling the kettle.

A rumble of thunder is followed by an electric sky and a further crack. Waiting for the water to boil, I stare out of the window at the torrential rain, simply amazed at how quickly the weather in England can change. One minute a friend, the next a foe.

My back is to the kitchen door. I jump when I first feel them; his hands lightly on my waist. The aftershave betrays its owner. When I turn Kon's face breaks into a quizzical smile. I try to reciprocate, but my lips won't cooperate, they begin to twitch. It's as if I've got some sort of dreadful tic. I'm once again that nervous child. My heart is thumping so much I can't believe it's inaudible. Out of the corner of my eye I see that the kitchen door's been closed, and I know neither of my parents will like it; they'll be suspicious. But I forget about that once Kon's stroking my cheek. Slowly he draws me to him and his lips are lightly brushing mine. His kisses are short and teasing until he can resist no longer - and I don't want him to. And then I want this kiss to last and last.

A rattle of the door handle brings me back to reality. We jump apart. Father's there, standing in the doorway. Did he see anything? He's asking why the coffee's taking so long. I reply weakly that the kettle took ages to boil. Anticipating his unspoken question, I tell him that Kon offered to help. "Oh really!" he says placing used cups and saucers on the draining board. "Well, hurry up - and by the way, the door it stays open."

When we return to the sitting room with Mother's coffee, the food has stopped flowing and the conversation is flagging. Father, keen to fill the vacuum starts to impress upon the Wilners the dangers, both to lawn and dog, of using too much of the weed-killer he's given them. "It is most important to read the instructions." After Father has repeated this warning several times Mr. Wilner brings up the forthcoming summer Olympics in Tokyo.

"Pity there's no tennis in it," I say.

"Tennis. I too love tennis," Mrs. Wilner remarks, "It is sad, but tennis vill never be an Olympic sport, I think."

"Why not?"

"Too many ozer popular sports - and easier to provide space and facilities. So many courts needed for tennis."

"One day maybe," I say.

As Father pours more beer for Mr. Wilner and himself, he adds that at least there's Wimbledon every year. "And you enjoy watching it on television; and one day Martina, you will be able to go yourself to watch the matches. Play there perhaps?"

Kon and I share a chuckle.

"I am hoping to get us to ze Olympics in Japan zis summer," Mr. Wilner states.

"Really," responds Mother as if she doesn't quite believe him. Her eyes don't look up from the cup in her hand.

"Yes, it is not so difficult to book when you verk in ze business."

"And what is *the* business?"

"Did I not already tell you, Mr. Wilner he works for the German Tourist Board, Hania?" Father pipes up.

Mother raises her head and pecks at the Twiglet she holds between finger and thumb, and says innocently, "Um! And do many people wish to holiday in Germany these days?"

Not to be baited Mr. Wilner tosses his head back and laughs, but says nothing. Mrs. Wilner's no longer smiling. She shuffles in her seat, and I spot her glimpsing discreetly at her watch. Father ignores Mother's remark, but offers still more beer. Kon accepts, but his father prefers him to stick to lemonade, much to Kon's silent fury.

After too much alcohol and a determined avoidance of any topic remotely connected to the war, Mr. Wilner suddenly reaches down beside the sofa. He picks up a large paper bag. Delighted his gift hasn't been forgotten, he produces several bars of chocolate. "Ze best in ze vorld, Lindt," he declares quickly unwrapping the chocolate and breaking it into squares. "Bought at Schmidt's," he says offering it around.

I wait for Kon to accept a piece before taking a square. This reminds me of our childhood picnics, and how "Auntie" Anne delighted us by pulling out the chocolate bars from a bag - just like a magician does a rabbit.

"Gut?" he asks before noticing Mother has none.

There are still a few pieces lying in the wrapper.

"Take it," he presses Mother. "It is very gut chocolate." He's a little tipsy, and not anxious to be thwarted. "Take it," he insists.

"No thank you." Mother's reply borders on rudeness.

Her adamant refusal fires him, challenges him. "Oh Hania," he says playfully. "No girl can resist a little piece of chocolate."

"First, *Mr. Wilner* I am not a girl. Second, I never eat chocolate!"

"Never?" He's still smiling and playing the game.

"*Never*." Her eyes are ice. "Now would you excuse me, I have headache."

She's gone - and no one's smiling.

Chapter 34
1964
Next day - Monday

"It's because I'm German. Aye, it's because I'm German that you won't go out with me, isn't it?" Kon says when he meets me after school the next day.

"It's because of my mother," I reply with a wry laugh. "You've met her - and after yesterday, I'm surprised you want anything to do with me, really I am."

We're strolling hand in hand in the opposite direction to Woodland Avenue on our way to the park. Last night's torrential rain continued throughout the morning, but has now stopped, leaving the pavements wet and glistening. The umbrellas are down and the April sun is creating misty orange halos around the heads of the distant tall trees. A speeding black saloon car splashes muddy water from a stream running in torrents alongside the kerb of the main road. A small girl wearing the Manor Lodge uniform squeals with delight as it soaks her legs. The woman with her, wearing a yellow PVC mac, clips her over the head and tells her to stop making such a silly noise.

"That's parents for you. They'll freak you out, if you let them. Do *not* let them," Kon stresses grabbing hold of my school bag and chucking it over his shoulder. "Bloody 'ell! This thing weighs a ton."

"Loads of homework to do - and I've also got a violin lesson later, so I can't be too long or *my* mum will freak out. Anyhow, why do your parents freak you out? They seem dead nice to me."

Kon is slow to answer. "Aye, *nice* is the operative word. If you want to be an accountant like my dad, a teacher like my mum, or go to university, you know, be something *nice* and respectable, then you're an okay person. Anything else - you might as well be telling my parents that it's your ambition to clean floors for the rest of your life." He mimics Mr. Wilner. *"Vot vould your grandvater say if he only knew that you verk in a shop.* Shock! Horror! Well, you know what I want to ask the old man? What's important? Grandfather's flippin' thoughts on the matter, or my future happiness? I tell you lass, do *not* let them get under your skin. Parents they just freak you out if you let them." He's holding my hand so tightly that it's beginning to hurt.

Don't I know it, I'm thinking. I'm still furious with Mother after her little performance last night. Father's always reminding me how much she's suffered in the past, and therefore we must make allowances - but having had such resolve earlier in the day, a determination to build bridges, surely she could've shown a bit more self-control - behaved better - after all she is an adult.

I must confess to having great admiration for Father's diplomacy. He certainly handled the situation better than I would ever have imagined - not easy after that melodramatic exit of Mother's. He explained how his wife has been suffering dreadful headaches of late, hence the aggression and intolerance to the barking of their Bruno; and of course the necessity to avoid certain foods, ones that trigger pain.

I couldn't quite believe it. Mr. Wilner began to blame himself for offending Mother, and apologising for being so forward in calling Mrs. Kalinska by her *Christian* name. Mrs. Wilner recommended a variety of common cures for headaches quite forgetting Father's a pharmacist. On remembering, she blushed and quickly changed the subject, suggesting Mother and him call them Kurt and Renate from now on. Father, not used to such early familiarity, coughed before replying, "That might be nice."

To cement good neighbourly relations, further coffees were served to Kurt and Renate. Kon declined the offer, but helped himself to a bottle of beer.

All this, while I just sat there, a voyeur, thinking that my first kiss with Kon must surely be the last after such a fiasco. But as the Wilners made their exit shortly after coffee had been served, Kon lingered in the hallway and whispered, "Meet you at the bus stop after school tomorrow."

"Five thirty. Got tennis practice," I replied.

Anyway, here we are today, in the park, sitting on a damp bench. I look down at the reflection in the deep puddle at our feet. I see a boy. I see a girl. That girl is me, and I'm so glad. We sit in companionable silence. It feels as if I've known Kon for longer than just a couple of weeks, yet I can't bring myself to share my misgivings concerning Mother. How she is *really* "freaking me out".

How when Father and I were clearing up after last night's "do" she appeared on the stairs clad in her long-sleeved cream nightdress, hair tumbling across her shoulders and arms flailing like Lady Macbeth.

"It's him," she repeated.

"Who?" Father demanded, his hand on her shoulder. "Who Hania? Who?" He tried to coax her down the stairs, but she remained firm, eyes looking blindly ahead, and I knew she was far from Woodland Avenue.

I shouldn't be so angry, but it's so difficult not to be. This morning at breakfast, she's the same old Mother, back in Woodland Avenue, instructing me to pick up my dinner money, pressing an umbrella into my hand. A wince when Bruno barks, but not the slightest reference to last night - nothing at all is mentioned until I'm calling goodbye at the front door.

"Come here, Child," she commands.

Thinking she's going to remind me again about my violin lesson with Mrs. Riverton, I shout back, "I know, violin lesson tonight, I've not forgotten."

She's out of the kitchen in the hall, teapot in hand. "It's not that." Her voice is hard. "It is that German boy. His father he is Nazi. Do not have anything to do with the boy. You hear me? You listen to me very well."

But I *am* going to have something to do with the boy.

"Look, it'd be tricky going with you to the cinema," I say to him later across the table of the Wimpy Bar. "But, how do you fancy going to a dance next Friday?"

"Take you to a dance?" His eyes brighten up.

I twirl the plastic tomato ketchup container and explain that the dance is being held at the school where my friend Mary's father teaches.

"A school dance?" He finds this amusing.

"Well, don't bother then, if it's so damn beneath you - if you're too grown up…"

"Hey there! Get off your high horse, lass. Any dance with you will be cool."

The plan is for me to purchase the tickets in advance, and we meet there. He's a bit disappointed when I tell him we won't actually be going together, and in addition that I'll be staying overnight with

Krysia whose dad will be picking us up after the dance. But he agrees it's better than nothing. He moves across to the seat next to me and seals the deal with a kiss.

"Better not tell your parents," I say. "Just in case they let it slip to mine." But somehow I feel pretty certain there won't be too many encounters between our respective parents in the near future.

My Bender arrives. I sip a little more of the Coca-Cola, open the bun and squeeze tomato ketchup on the sausage.

"Isn't there pork in that sausage?" Kon enquires.

"Don't know really. Never thought about it. Why?"

"No reason, just thought Jews didn't eat pork."

I don't reply at first. Then I look up at him and ask, "Is it a problem, being Jewish?"

He bites into his Wimpy. "Don't be daft, lass, 'course not," he replies and pops a fork full of chips into his mouth.

"What makes you think I'm Jewish anyway?"

"Give me credit for some intelligence," he says with raised brow then pecks me on the cheek.

A fine drizzle begins to fall from the bleached sky. It's almost quarter to seven when we reach home much later than intended. I know Mother will kill me. It would've been prudent for us to have walked separately down the avenue. A hurried kiss sees me up the path. Did the net curtain twitch?

I dread my reception. Step into the house - wait. I take a deep breath. But all is still. No sound except for the clock ticking in the hall. No smells of cooking. Usually on a Monday, it's an early meal due to my violin lesson. This unfamiliar deadness gives me a sense of foreboding. I drop my bag in the corner of the hall next to the coat stand. "Hiya!" I call, my voice light and friendly.

No response. The sitting room door is open. No Mother. She must have slipped into the kitchen. But she's not there either. Neither is there any food prepared; and the table's not been laid. Father will be home any minute now, expecting a meal. A full basket of wet washing stands by the back door. Where is she? I don't like the eerie silence pervading the house.

I hear a faint noise coming from upstairs. Something drops to the floor. Something light I suspect. "Mum," I call. "Mum, is that you?"

No answer. I venture up the stairs.

When I open the bedroom door, there she is, sitting on her unmade bed counting sticking plasters into an old blackcurrant pastille tin. As well as the mound by her pillows, several lie scattered on the floor by her hairbrush, between the bed and the dressing table. She's still in her nightwear. Her hair's carelessly pulled back, held by two or three small brown combs.

"Hello," she says looking up, and then carries on with her counting.

It feels as if a ghost has invaded our home.

Chapter 35
1964
Next Thursday

"Nazi. Nazi means nasty. The words sound much the same, don't they Andrew?"

Mother uses that patronising sing-song voice adults manufacture when telling stories to small children.

Having slipped off my school blazer, I sneak a look into the sitting room, and there, kneeling on the floor is Mother. Her smile is radiant as she builds a tower with coloured blocks; the ones she recently purchased for her little angel. I notice the neglected vases of wilting tulips; some little more than lifeless stems with crew cuts, their curling petals littering the carpet.

"Brm! Brm!" Andrew's not listening to mother now, but is more intent on pushing his chunky red fire engine round and round. Its bell jangles louder and louder as it picks up speed, circling the growing wooden edifice with gusto. With a roar, Andrew revs it up, "Brmm! Brmm! Brmmm!" And crash. Squeals of sheer delight rise as the tower collapses and the bricks scatter across the room.

"Am I a nasty Nazi?" Andrew then asks.

"No, no my little one..."

Without even a hello I steal into the kitchen, make a coffee, snatch an iced fairy cake from the plate beside the kettle, and creep up the stairs to my bedroom. I hate to think what Mrs. Jones' reaction will be if Andrew's bath-time chatter tonight includes nasties and Nazis.

Through the adjoining wall a guitar twangs to life. Kon must be home. The throbbing bass notes reverberate. It's loud, as if the music is in this very room. It's "Johnny Be Good". Oh God! I think, acknowledging that at least it's being played well. I'm pleased however when the tune changes.

I can't wait for the dance tomorrow. To be with Kon. Not a stolen walk in the park, or a hurried snack in the Wimpy Bar - but a real date, our first proper date. My spirits lift as I picture the Endsley Grammar School hall alive with rock and anticipation. There on stage is the Sixth Form Five in matching black polo neck sweaters, smart suits and those ankle boots the Beatles wear - no longer sixth formers, but a fab pop group. I recollect how at the last dance I was with Krysia, Mary, Christie and Elaine. I see us doing the Twist, dancing in a circle round a pile of handbags. And there's Sinéad with Niall. The lights are dimming, and it's almost as dusky as the world outside - that is until the coloured spot lights begin to swirl across the ceiling and dance around the floor. An image emerges of Sinéad and Niall wrapped in each other's arms, dancing to a slow number, followed by an image of the rest of our group, sitting on the chairs with plastic smiles in hope of catching the eye of a half-decent boy. Then I think about tomorrow, and other pictures replace those grey depressing ones. This time there I am, wrapped in Kon's arms while the group plays their version of "Do You Want to Know a Secret?" and I'm not one of the wallflowers.

Reluctant to knuckle down to my pile of homework, I prefer to listen to Kon's guitar rocking on, but eventually common sense prevails and I begin with Chemistry. The background music makes the homework bearable. *Music While You Work.* But this is nothing like the radio programme Mother occasionally listened to some years back.

Intermittently the guitar stops. Phrases are repeated, chords changed. I like the beat, and the melody is catchy. Nevertheless, it feels as if I'm an intruder, an uninvited guest, eavesdropping on a composition in the making. Labouring one section, Kon plays the same bars over and over again; I think this must be the middle eight. I'm overwhelmed with the urge to pick up my violin and complete the next phrase, but I refrain. Kon may think it impertinent, and he'd probably resent such a smug invasion of both his creativity and privacy.

I'm guessing that his inspiration is exhausted when the music stops with no satisfactory musical resolution accomplished. Chemistry experiment written up, I draw a line under today's work, stuff the exercise book back into my bag and with a sigh take out my English homework; our new GCE set book for English Literature. The doorbell rings. I jump, letting the novel fall shut. Could it be Kon? Opening the bedroom door a fraction I listen, determined to rush down and speak to him before Mother has the chance. God knows what she might say; what with all this talk of Nazis and nasties.

However, it's not Kon and I'm not sure whether I feel relief or disappointment.

"Angela!" greets Mother. "Come, come. Take a small coffee. I have some very good pastries."

But Angela seemingly is in a hurry, and declines the invitation. From the landing I'm able to see Andrew in the hall. He's on his hands and knees pushing a green dinky car. Suddenly it spins out of control and collides with Mother's leg. Mrs. Jones admonishes him at once, but Mother declares that it's of no consequence - it doesn't hurt very much. Andrew has retrieved the car. It's again hurtling through the air and this time takes a chip out of the skirting board. Mother smiles on and pats him gently on the head. "Never mind, it only takes lick of paint to make it all nice again," she says.

I know that's not what she would have said to me had I done the same thing at Andrew's age. And I would have certainly received more than a gentle pat on the head.

"Brmmm!" He's off again. As I'm about to step back into my room I catch Mother's words, "... the Germans… I have suspicions..."

"Brmmm! Brmm!" Crash.

"Really," cuts in Mrs. Jones. "Come on Andrew..." I hear the door closing seconds later.

I'm at my desk trying not to dwell on the implications of what Mother said to Mrs. Jones. The evening sun's now low in the sky, and shafts of light stream through the window disturbing my vision. I look up from the blinding whiteness of Page 1 of *A Tale of Two Cities* and am taken aback by the unnatural brightness of the red-tiled roof tops. A stout pigeon dives towards the house opposite, landing full force on the television aerial; it begins to bend precariously. Will it withstand the weight of this bird? Fortunately, before disaster strikes, the pigeon spreads its wings and flies away into the feathery white clouds.

It's when I go to draw the curtain in order to block out the sun's glare that I see her. Her back is to me. Halfway up the garden beside the flowerbed, she stands close to the fence which separates our garden from the Wilner's. It's surprising to see her there, especially in light of the fact that Bruno's outside sniffing the lawn and giving the occasional bark. Like a pup he starts to gambol and prance, chasing any butterfly daring to flutter his way. Eventually the Alsatian slows down, prowls for a while before lolloping over to the rockery where he engages in one of his favourite pursuits, the nuzzling and nipping of plants.

Mother remains erect and still as if in a trance. I feel uneasy. For the first time this week her hair is neatly fastened into a French roll, but I despair to see her wearing that calf-length pleated navy skirt she's not worn since the fifties; and of course her faithful fawn cardigan is buttoned up over a plain white blouse. A blackbird flies down to the lawn, hopping inches from her feet, but she doesn't falter in her stillness.

"Komm Bruno. Komm!" Mr. Wilner's out. He tempts Bruno with a bowl filled with meat. "Guter Hund, guter Hund," he says with affection, at the same time stroking the dog's solid head. They disappear into the house.

Mother jerking to life as if a switch has been flicked on, turns round; her taut face coming into view. The afternoon smile has been replaced by a dour evening expression. Quickly her fists unfold revealing a small tin. She prises open the lid. Then as if she has no idea what's inside, she examines its contents. What on earth is she up to?

From next door blasts the familiar composition. Kon quickly resumes working on the middle eight. He's got the last part sounding pretty good. A bum chord. He starts again - from the opening bar. Sometimes he strums, sometimes he picks. The music's loud, intrusive, he must have turned up the amp; I wonder if it's for my benefit. But I can't afford to be distracted.

Mother moves with purpose towards the fence. She places the tin on the soil between a rose bush and a cluster of nodding late snowdrops; then takes out a single sticking plaster. Carefully she peels off the strip from the underside and lets it fall where it may. Leaning across to the wooden fence, she attempts to stick the plaster over a hole. But it doesn't do the trick, a chink of light still peeps through. Bending low, she removes a second one from the blackcurrant pastille tin, and then presses it hard over the same gap. Methodically, meticulously she proceeds, working steadily towards the house. Another hole. Another plaster. Bend. Stick. Bend. Stick. Soon there are at least ten plasters gummed to the fence.

"My God!" I exclaim when the horror of the thing fully dawns on me.

I'm anxious to put an end to this nonsense, but desperate not to draw the neighbours' attention as to what's going on here. Mother's not seen me. My stomach feels like clay, frozen and heavy. My throat aches and my mouth is parched. Now that I'm in the garden I'm at a loss to know how best to deal with this. I want to tear the plasters off the fence, scream at her to stop. Make her. With brute force if necessary, get her into the house. By hook or by crook, I have to stop this madness. But a voice inside me says, "Be gentle."

"Mum," I keep my voice just above a whisper. I'm shivering although the evening temperature for this time of year is warm.

She jumps. Her head swivels round. She stares with vacant eyes.

"What?"

"Mum, what on earth are you doing?"

"I see them - when I am out here - eyes they look at me through holes - that German dog - and him - him - he spies on me - he thinks I do not notice - that I will not dare to go out - to hang out washing - I see eyes, always they are looking. But I am not afraid of him. No. Not any longer."

"What *are* you talking about?" My voice although very quiet borders on the hysterical. I try to pick up the tin, but she's not having it. We're jostling for possession when it tumbles to the mud.

Abandoning the struggle, I start to rip the plasters from the fence. Mother struggles to restrain me. "Dad," I plead inwardly. "Why are you always so bloody late from work these days? Come home soon, please. I really need you. *Now.*"

"Be it on your head. You will see. I know him. That beard, those glasses they cannot deceive me." Mother's voice is raised, shrill and vindictive. My head's reeling. Damn it, if Father doesn't come soon, I'll have to seek help from another quarter, I know this, but from where? Definitely not from the neighbours and especially not from Kon. But from whom? Possible adults flash through my mind. They appear as photographs, each on a separate page of an album. As I dismiss them one by one, the pages turn until there's no one left except Marek. Perhaps I should phone him? Perhaps I should go and phone him right now?

My train of thought is broken with the sound of Bruno's return. He pads to the far corner of the Wilner's garden, close to where our shed meets the apple tree. Recognising me, he tries to summon my attention with friendly woofs. But I'm occupied with more important matters and take no notice of him. Refusing to be ignored he stands on hind legs leaning against the wire fence, his weight placing strain on the section which has been working loose from the post for some time; and indeed has been weakened further by the recent storm. The section, which for days Mother's been nagging Father to repair.

"Get in, Mum!" I beg. But she continues to scrabble and grope on the ground, picking up those plasters that have fallen out of the tin.

I'm beside myself. My sympathy for Mother wanes as I imagine Kon looking out of his bedroom window, as surely he will soon, and what will confront him?

"Stop that and go inside," I hiss with ferocity, at the same time keeping an eye on Bruno who's not to be deterred by my lack of attention. But Mother refuses to budge. Having stood up, she's now trying to stick more plasters over more holes.

Bruno, barking incessantly, begins to leap and pound. The fence no longer able to withstand the dog's might, buckles. He's through the gap, running towards me. His giant paws are up on my shoulders and his tongue licking my face. I pat him a little, stroke him, and then try to grasp his collar, but he's not to be held. Tail wagging, he runs off again. Discovering one of my tennis balls by the ash tree, he bites into it and scampers off with it to the other end of our garden. I try to reassure Mother that he'll not harm her; that he really is a big softy; but deaf to my words, she's crouching down, face in cupped hands. "Mum," I say disarmed by her distress, my hand on her arm. She mutters in incoherent Polish. I speak to her in simple Polish, but it's useless, she's lost in her own world of fear and misery and refuses to let me in.

No one's looking out of their window. A stroke of luck. I decide to leave Mother where she is for the time being and take Bruno home. He's now lying down by the French window chewing the ball as if it were a cherished bone. I plan to take him to the Wilner's front door. This, I anticipate will prevent them from witnessing what's going on in our garden. Hopefully, when I've dispatched this errant dog, it'll prove easier to coax Mother back into the house. It crosses my mind, that without the presence of Bruno she may even be able to pull herself together, and will have beaten a hasty retreat indoors by the time I return.

Too late. Mr. Wilner's face appears on the other side of the fence. "Bruno!" he calls. "I apologise," he says once realising Bruno's whereabouts. "Bruno, bad dog!" he scolds in English. "Sorry Martina, Bruno is a bad dog to be in your garden. But how is zis possible? Did he jump ze fence? No, he could not."

I point to the gap.

Still scolding Bruno, he catches sight of Mother in the flowerbed hunched and muttering. A tell-tale furrow over the bridge of Mr. Wilner's nose reveals his anguish. He pushes the coiling wire to one side and sidles through. As quickly as his limp allows he walks over to Mother. Extending his hand, he offers a comforting touch, but at the last moment thinks better of the gesture, and simply kneels beside her on the soil. His voice is soft and kind. "Mrs. Kalinska, I apologise for my dog - for ze distress - I am so sorry. Give me your hand. Let me help you up."

I'm right behind him clutching Bruno's studded collar.

Suddenly Mother's hands are withdrawn from her face. Her fingers spread and pull away as if she's withdrawing a mask. Her eyes snap open. Wide-eyed, she rises proud and stern.

"I apologise for my dog," repeats Mr. Wilner, the furrow in his brow visibly deepening as his words fail to be acknowledged.

Walking towards the kitchen door, followed by Mr. Wilner, she marches without turning. Once her foot is on the step, as if she's had a change of heart, she bolts round and looks directly at him. Mr. Wilner begins again, "Mrs. Kalinska..."

I see splinters of hatred in her eyes. "I am not to be so easily fooled *Herr Obersturmführer Weissner* - not by you, neither by your gentle giant."

She wastes no time in slamming the door, leaving me feeling mortified and in dread of Mr. Wilner's reaction. Surely he'll be outraged?

I feel so hurt for him when all he says is, "I apologise Martina. I am sorry. The dog has frightened your mother - but zis Obersturmführer Weissner I am *not*."

His eyes are glinting. I'm embarrassed and don't want to see this grown man cry, so without delay I hand over Bruno. "I know that Mr. Wilner - and I'm so sorry. Please forgive her. My mum doesn't really know what she's saying. The dog - Bruno shocked her - confused her - I don't think anything's making sense. She doesn't mean it. I'm really sorry," I say watching them disappear through the back gate.

Willing myself not to cry, my legs shaking, I stand on the balding patch of grass where my childhood swing stood until recently, and from there I stare at the surreal image before me - sticking plasters; some stuck, and others flaccidly hanging from the fence.

I know I should go inside the house and concern myself with Mother's wellbeing, but I can't. I just can't. It's impossible to rationalise my dizzy emotions. At present I'm feeling deeply ashamed of my mother. Loathing and pity are entwined; but in truth, anger overrides every other emotion. If Kon doesn't show up at the dance tomorrow, well, I know I'll never, ever forgive her. And Father, where is he? It's almost 7.30. He should be the one dealing with all this, not me.

The thought of sharing the same breathing space as Mother is abhorrent, so I don't return to the house. Instead, I harvest the plasters stuck to the fence, then sit on the low wall bordering the bed where parsley and sage grows.

Kon's peering over the fence. I'm not in the mood for him. What does one say to the boy you love when your mother has but minutes ago insulted his father with unprecedented vengeance? There are no words, only tears. He's through the gap and holding me. "It's not your fault," he says.

After a while, he leaves me, goes into the Wilner's shed, takes out a toolbox and repairs the fence. Admitting it's no work of art, he assures me that at least it's now secure.

"See you tomorrow," he says before kissing me.

The house is silent. I expect Mother to have taken refuge in her bedroom. I turn off the oven, for no one has laid the table and the house reeks of burning casserole. Then I see her in the shadows of the dining room. She sits on a chair, elbows resting on the table, her hands as if in prayer. I wonder what spectres haunt her - have left her so insensitive to anyone else's feelings. Turning to me, she opens her mouth to speak. I want her to reach out, to comfort me, to tell me that everything will be all right. However, the momentary spark of recognition is gone, and I'm invisible to her again. I walk away and all I feel is Kon's kiss on my lips. Switching the landing light on, I return to my homework.

It is the best of times. It is the worst of times.

I re-read the opening sentences of *A Tale of Two Cities* and begin to sob. It's as if Charles Dickens has written these words especially for me.

Chapter 36
1964
The day after the Dance

This morning I wouldn't have thought I'd still be at the Kotkowki's so late in the day. Yet here I am sitting on the staircase reading a report in the Sunday Times about the futile battles between mods and rockers on Margate beach while Father has a "quick chat" with Dr. Kotkowski. Krysia, Helena and their mother should be standing for the opening prayers at evening mass by now.

The smell of roast chicken hangs in the air, competing with the aroma of the rose polish I always associate with Krysia's house. It's particularly strong in the hall where there's parquet flooring.

"Roast chicken for lunch," announced Mrs. Kotkowska at Sunday breakfast. I couldn't believe my luck. "Especially for Martina's visit," she had said laying her hand on my shoulder. I know she understands how difficult life is for me at the moment.

The grandfather clock in the hall strikes 6 o'clock. In bounds Domino. Just like Bruno, he never wants to miss out on strokes and pats. He gallops forward. Encountering one of the light brown oval mats, he slides towards me, leaving dirty paw prints on both wood and mat. It's extraordinary how the house manages to appear so immaculately clean with this loveable ungainly creature constantly tramping in and out. With colossal doggy force, he pushes his hefty wet nose into the pages of the newspaper; instantly it crumples in submission. I succumb to his quest for attention. "Dogs," I say to him with affection. "Dogs," I repeat with less enthusiasm remembering Mother.

On the wall hangs a newly framed print of the very same painting we have in the corridor by the school hall. Each morning, just like the traffic jam on the main road, there's congestion while the whole school files into assembly; and I always seem to end up standing next to 'The Light of the World' by Holman Hunt. I'm definitely not, what Father terms, a connoisseur of art, but I do know what I like. Actually, when I first saw the painting, it struck me as being nothing more than one of those unwanted, dingy pictures so often put up on walls of school corridors, for no reason other than to make the place look less stark. But, I must admit that 'The Light of the World' gradually became a familiar acquaintance, and with the passing years, a desired friend. I can't imagine how many times I've read the words on its dog-eared label:

Behold I stand at the door and knock; if any man hear my voice, and open the door, I will come to him, and will sup with him, and he with me.

To be frank, I think it's the words I've grown to love more than the actual painting itself. I know the words by heart and cling to them for hope when I look at the image of Jesus knocking on the hallowed door. It's my secret. I've told no one, not even Krysia. Although I hope it's no secret to God; that he hears me knocking and will open the door to me - and of course to Mother, even though she doesn't believe at all.

What was it that Marek once told me? Mother was afraid to disappoint God? How strange to be so devoted to him, and then to lose one's faith altogether. What a vacuum that must leave in a heart. Sometimes when we're alone, Father and I share thoughts on this complex matter of religion. He tells me he prefers to remain open-minded as to the existence of God, but is adamant that if such a powerful deity exists, it cannot possibly be concerned with the lives of individual human beings. This naturally is in absolute contradiction to all we're taught at school.

Me, I think there is some kind of God. To be honest, I'm not sure how it all works - whether Jesus is the Son of God, or if there's a Holy Ghost. Three in one… it sounds a bit over-complicated. But I do believe in a loving God. And what I feel certain of is, that God is the same God whatever religion. The nuns of course would faint with horror to hear me say this. Sister Mary Frances would hold up her hands and cry, "Blasphemy!" But personally I don't think it matters a jot where you pray - church - synagogue - wherever - because if he's there, he'll be listening.

My cynicism of Sister's blind faith diminishes as her words come flooding back, "Girls, God never gives anyone a cross heavier than they are able to bear."

Please, please, let that be true.

The door of the lounge is more than half-open. Father, purple shadows beneath his eyes, sits hunched in a heavily cushioned armchair. It strikes me, watching his forefinger stroking his lower lip that he looks like a man twice his age. Dr. Kotkowski stands a short distance from him with his elbow resting on the mantelpiece. Both sip from their glasses of vodka. I'm pleased my comprehension of Polish is now reasonable and I'm able to understand most of what passes between them. Father's a proud man, and I know what it must be costing him to seek advice from Dr. Kotkowski, who after all, is little more than a stranger.

"...Definitely Stefan your wife needs to talk about her time in Auschwitz… It is essential that she comes to terms with those experiences… it seems so much she is suppressing… she *must* face her demons."

Demons. The word rings an unwelcome bell.

With that I retreat until I hear Father's voice sounding defensive. I move a little closer. He explains his fruitless efforts over the decades to get his wife to share her past with him… the "difficulties" since the German family's arrival… his concern about me with important exams coming up… the demands of the recently purchased chemist shop… having had to take Friday and Saturday off work following his wife's "little episode" last Thursday. (This is how Father has come to refer to it.) All this punctuated with his gratitude to the Kotkowkis for inviting me to stay the entire weekend.

It's a relief to know Father's unburdening himself, and I feel sure that Dr. Kotkowski will offer sound advice. Having shifted Domino who was sprawled across my feet, I walk to the chair by the hallstand, sit, and think that despite everything else, this weekend has been "the best of times". The dance indeed worked out much better than I'd dared to imagine.

Throughout Friday at school I had difficulty in concentrating, but during Maths at the end of the day, it became impossible. I don't think I took in one word Mrs. Matherson said as the chalk in her hand flew back and forth across the blackboard. "So you see if "a" equals "c" then it's plain that..." Well, it wasn't plain to me. By the time "a" was supposed to equal "c" or indeed anything else, my joyful anticipation of the dance had vanished, for I'd convinced myself that Kon wasn't going to come after all.

Later that evening, tense and aloof, I waited with Krysia and Mary by the tall metal gates outside Endsley Grammar School. Like a bride on her wedding day, I was praying that I'd not be stood up. Kids bubbling with excitement and flaunting the latest fashions made their way to the hall where the Sixth Form Five had finished warming up and were playing their opening number.

Ten minutes into the dance and we're still outside. "I was dead right. He's not coming," I announced. The memory of Mother, frozen in her twilight world came back to haunt me. A surge of anger found me blaming her.

"'Course he's coming," Krysia reassured.

"He's not Krysh, I know it."

"Typical of boys," said Mary. "Always late. But - er - he'll be here."

And there he was, walking fast. But not fast enough.

"Wilners..." Father's amplified voice rapidly brings me back to Sunday evening. I become alarmed. He's understating mother's reaction to the dog, and even more so, making little of her endeavours to cover the holes in the fence with sticking plasters. This madness is virtually being glossed over. But I cringe when he speaks of his wife's insistence that Mr. Wilner is Obersturmführer Weissner.

At this point in the conversation the voices become so quiet that I'm unable to make out anything they say, until Father with emotion confesses his embarrassment at having to go and apologise on Mother's behalf. I gather Mrs. Wilner's reaction was somewhat cool; however Mr. Wilner generously dismissed "the episode" as being just one of those unfortunate things, fuelled by her terror of dogs. Because of this, he's offered to pay for a sturdy wooden fence to replace the wire one.

I breathe a sigh of relief. Perhaps neighbourly relations, like a fence, can be repaired after all. Thank goodness, I'm thinking as I recall Kon's phone call from the record shop at 10.00 yesterday morning. In fact Krysia and I were still in bed chatting when Mrs. Kotkowksa called upstairs, "Martina, phone."

"Miss you already," Kon said. *Miss you already.* The words have been echoing through my mind ever since. We were supposed to meet today at 6.30, to take Bruno for a walk, but thanks to Father's protracted conversation with Dr. Kotkowski, I'll not be home in time.

My ears prick up, and my heart sinks. "The Wilners they neither are keen on this relationship… he seems like nice enough young man… but under such circumstances…"

No! Every fibre in my body is in revolt. More often than not I'm compliant. It makes life easier - but in this, I'm resolute. The former anger I'd felt towards Mother re-surfaces. I'm determined she'll not destroy the one really good thing in my life. I may be impotent to help her, but I'm sure not impotent in being able to help myself.

Jittery and unable to sit still, I begin to walk up and down the hall. The tapping of my shoes on the hard flooring should be enough to remind Father of my presence. Hasn't the conversation gone on long enough? But I'm ignored.

"Stefan, I feel very certain that your wife needs professional help. Psychiatry as you know is not my field of medicine, but I can recommend a good man…"

"Psychiatrist? Oh no! That will not be necessary," interrupts Father. "Perhaps holiday? I think perhaps it is necessary for her to take some rest - surely a break from what troubles her will help? The sea she loves. It is maybe better not to rush into this thing."

"Rush? Well, that's a joke. He's kidding himself," I say to myself. In fact I'm dumbfounded, stunned by Father's reluctance to take such a glaringly obvious step forward. "Get Mother the help she plainly needs!" is my silent scream.

"My wife she did seem more her old self this morning, Dr. Kotkowski. She got dressed, ate small sandwich at midday. It is encouraging surely, that as I left to come to collect Martina, she was chopping up beef steak?" The cadence in his words has changed. "Yes, I think some days, or perhaps a week or so away will do trick." His false cheeriness signals our imminent departure.

I see Dr. Kotkowki avert his eyes. He slowly steps towards Father and takes the empty glass.

"Hmm," he sighs, "Well, of course I am a physician not a psychiatrist. Stefan, you know your own wife better than I do, so ultimately the decision has to lie with you. I feel obliged to say… although of course it is only my opinion, a short break is not the long-term solution. The essential thing, I believe, is for her to face her demons…"

"Surely a change in environment might help?"

"Not… well, possibly."

Father thanks him for his time and says that he feels so much better having obtained the doctor's advice, and we're in the car ready for the drive home.

A quarter of an hour into the journey, the car is growling up a steep hill. I actually hope it'll grind to a halt, delaying our return home. Now that I've missed my rendezvous with Kon, the prospect of facing 64, Woodland Avenue is much like anticipating a morgue. I feel no inclination to make conversation, although Father is verbose. As he drives he converses largely with himself, planning a break for Mother. He considers the possibility of her staying a short while with "Auntie" Anne in Nottingham. "Nothing they have in common, but still Mum is fond of her. So maybe this would work out. What do you think?"

Surprise is my initial reaction. For Father took great pains in discouraging their friendship after that Marek business came to light. But needs must I suppose, and that's what I tell him. What I would prefer to hear is a change of heart, and Father being resolved in seeking the professional help advised. Nevertheless, he's intent on setting things in motion - and soon.

We still have several miles to go when an unhealthy chug, a croak, followed by a deathly splutter from the engine forces us to pull over to the kerb. After tinkering a while under the bonnet, Father's expression is blank; he obviously hasn't a clue as to what the problem is. I watch his fingers beat his lips. The bonnet is shut.

"Need 'elp, mate?" shouts a motorcyclist clad in black leather, posting a letter in the pillar box opposite.

"I cannot find what is wrong… the car is not old… I must confess, but I am no mechanic."

The bonnet again bounces open. Father, like a spare part, hovers on the grass verge making a token suggestion from time to time.

Taking out my Maths book I regret my oversight, or rather neglect, in not having finished this homework. I had intended to find half an hour sometime during the weekend, but it never quite happened. Merely looking at the algebra problems doesn't help; and I begin to wonder why on earth I've been entered for Maths O'level this summer. Deep down, I know that with perseverance I could do this work, but at this precise moment, my head feels as if it's stuffed with cotton wool. I need a Peter to come to my rescue. Possibly Kon is good at Maths?

All that talk of demons, not to mention Anne Harris, has brought Peter to mind. In spite of everything that's happened between us, I know Peter is intrinsically an intelligent, kind and sensitive person, and feel sorry to think of all his potential going to waste. That's if Norma's got it right. Screwed up by parents - or at least one. Rather, I should say, screwed up by mothers. I'm then reminded of the wisdom according to Kon - *Parents will freak you out if you let them.*

Well, I'm damned if I'm going to let mine.

But my fighting spirit is dampened when I consider what it must be like to be imprisoned. Daily, to live in fear of the gas chambers; tormented by constant hunger and to endure the unimaginable. Horrors so dreadful that Mother's unable to share them with anyone; and all this, when she was not so very many years older than my fifteen. It doesn't bear thinking about. Mother's not herself, and all the time that I have known her, she's not been her true self.

The depressing atmosphere dominating our house is no doubt paradise in comparison to Auschwitz, and I feel ashamed to have been so intolerant. I picture Mother on Friday morning, standing two thirds of the way up the staircase wearing that worn cream nightdress, her lank hair loosely tied back by one of my elderly white ribbons with zigzag threads of cotton straying from the ends. Like a sculpture she stood in her halo of sadness. Then, as if suddenly metamorphosised into life, she gingerly descended. Every step, laboured. Clinging to the banister, she crept like someone bed-ridden for months.

"Have you eaten breakfast?" she asked looking over my head at the ceiling.

"Yes," I replied pleased to have a modicum of normality back in my life, yet fearful as to what was round the corner.

I must be the only girl at Our Lady of Lourdes who actually looks forward to school after the weekend. There normality reigns. The certainty of Sister Mary Paul moaning at us in assembly, and then praising God for his goodness; Sinéad prattling on about Mark, the boy she met at the dance; the routine of a timetable, and having a fair idea as to how most people are likely to react. All this comes as a welcome relief from home.

"No probs, mate," I hear. "Plug lead come off. That's all. On now though. Shouldn't give you no more bover."

Father offers to give the lad a little something for his trouble, but he flatly refuses. He gives me a wave, hops on his motorbike, and after some noisy revs is away - in minutes we are too.

Chapter 37
1964
Same evening

The car approaches Woodland Avenue and there they are, Kon with Bruno heading in the direction of the park. He catches sight of me sitting in the front seat and pulls a face. "Sorry," he mouths and points to his gentle giant who is tugging at the lead. I give a discreet wave. Father sees, I wait for a comment, but he pretends not to have noticed.

Mrs. Wilner is tackling the rather overgrown flowerbed running the length of their privet hedge. The puffy gardening gloves make her arms look artificial and ridiculously stick thin. In contrast, her orange striped shift looks pristine; it's the kind of dress most women would prefer to keep for a party. In fact, she reminds me of a marionette I once owned when I was about nine. I get out of the car and smile. She does not, but she manages a curt, "Hello."

Simultaneously, Mr. Wilner, face bright red, bursts through their side-gate shouting, "Wo ist Konrad? Ich hab's ihm gesagt…" Obersturmführer Weissner is standing before me donned in Nazi uniform, complete with forbidding jackboots. Seeing us, he comes to a sharp halt, breaks into a smile, lifts his right hand in greeting and says to Father, "You know vot zees kids are, never do as asked."

Herr Obersturmführer has disappeared and once again stands Mr. Wilner wearing grey slacks and a pale green open-necked shirt. In a quiet, pleasant voice he rephrases the question to his wife who replies with exaggerated sweetness. Even without much knowledge of German, I work out, that Kon's taking Bruno for a walk at last, after having been told many times.

I'm dreading entering the house. Will Mother be dressed, or will she have changed into some ancient creased nightie and that moth-eaten brown dressing gown she's been vowing to throw away for donkeys' years?

The front door opens. Not a sound. I creep in as if entering a haunted house. Then I spot her in the sitting room relaxing on the sofa with slippered feet on the footstool. With relief I see she is dressed and reading the Sunday paper. The same one I'd been reading at Krysia's. She lifts her head when I say, "Hello."

After a cursory greeting she tuts, "These terrible mods and rockers - teddyboys - teddyboys - or what do they say now? Bitniks. It does not matter, all should be behind prison bars."

Mother's herself. Perhaps Father's right. A break away from familiar territory may prove to be the best solution after all. I'm praying however, that he doesn't procrastinate and contacts Anne as soon as possible. Meanwhile, I'm determined not to delay putting my own plan into action.

"Sandwiches. With cheese." Mother points to a plate on the sideboard covered with a tea towel. "Seed cake too."

I'm relieved. Having heard Father say to Dr. Kotkowski that she'd been chopping beef earlier, I'd anticipated feeling obliged to eat another heavy meal today. "Fab, sandwiches," I say. "I thought we were going to have some kind of meat and vegetables…"

"And why would you be thinking that, Child?" she snaps.

"Well, no reason - except Dad said you were cutting up some beef, that's all."

"No!"

"Dad said…"

"No... No meat tonight. Just eat sandwiches."

"It's fine, I love sandwiches. Sandwiches are fine," I say while lifting off the tea towel and helping myself to more food than I really want.

Unable to settle down to Sunday evening television, I go up to my bedroom. Dusk has brought a lilac hue to the sky. Heavy grey clouds frame the roof-tops. The promise of a fine day tomorrow hangs in the balance. I think about my plan; however do nothing, simply sit at my desk staring into the shadowy garden. The shed door has been left open; it swings to and fro, banging in the wind, but I can't be bothered to do anything about it.

On the desk in front of me lies a blank sheet of paper. Not only am I finding the planned task much more difficult than I'd expected, my good intentions are fading. I've something else on my mind. The boy next door. So instead of putting pen to paper, I prefer to keep watch for Kon.

As time marches on I begin to feel somewhat aggrieved. Having missed our walk, I thought he would have at least popped into the back garden in hope of a chance meeting. The ecstatic joy I'd felt in the wake of Friday's dance is disappearing fast. Perhaps the prospect of a Romeo and Juliet style romance fails to appeal to him. But knowing Kon, I'd have thought it would add spice to the relationship. So where is he? Strains of guitar music can be heard through the wall, but it's not loud enough to drown the constant banging of the shed door which is beginning to drive me mad.

I shiver with the unexpected chill of the evening. A misty arc of the moon appears high above the cloud casting a celestial light across the pathway to the shed. The wind is whipping up, and it bites cold. Nevertheless, I walk slowly towards the end of the garden. Kon's bedroom curtains are drawn, but I can tell by the glow his light is still on. I'm hopeful that he may open the curtains and see me. Actually, there's a good chance he'll soon lean out of his window smoking a cigarette.

I stop halfway down the path; and with my foot push away the intrusive clump of forget-me-nots spreading across the paving stones. Samba, hearing my footsteps, bounds over the fence from the Wilner's garden, providing me with further excuse for delay. I bend down and take some time stroking him luxuriously from head to tail.

The door's wide open when I reach the shed. In the dim moonlight I see that a couple of objects are out of place, so I step inside. Straightaway my shoe makes contact with something solid. When I glance down, it appears to be a packet which has fallen on its side. A step forward and I'm stumbling on a stray garden fork, and then kick a hand spade. With my foot I shuffle the packet to one side. When I look at it more closely, I see it's weed-killer and a fair amount has spilt from the open corner. How careless of Father. But then I consider how tired he must be, worn out after these traumatic last few days - never mind the car breaking down on our return journey from Krysia's. It's hardly surprising that when Mr.Wilner gave back the remains of the weed-killer this evening, he failed to return it safely to the top shelf.

Rather than leaving the packet on the floor, I decide to put it back where it's usually stored. Moving slightly to the left, I catch sight of another packet, blanketed in the shadows. It lies somewhere between the old leaky watering can, a cardboard box filled with old newspapers and stacked deck chairs. This packet too is torn open, and a mountain of powder lies like heaped salt. God! Father can deal with this lot, I decide.

An intrusive strong gust of wind catches a double page of a *Daily Herald*. Like a tent loosened from its pegs, it billows and sails out of the open shed, coming to rest in the branches of a nearby rose bush. I see now the wind has swept away the sheet of cloud in the sky, revealing a host of stars and a perfectly rotund golden moon. Shining like a new penny, it lights up the night garden.

Anxious about the weed-killer, I check that the shed door is securely bolted before returning to the house. All hopes of an encounter with Kon dashed, I march briskly past the rose bush, seize the flapping newspaper page and screw it into a ball. When I reach the dustbin I snatch up the lid, only to find it's full to the brim and a parcel wrapped in darkish paper is close to falling out. Tentatively, with two fingers, I push the soggy mass back into the bin; the damp paper tears exposing its contents. I take a closer look. Is it meat? Perhaps the beef Father said Mother was chopping earlier today? I recoil. The dustbin smells foul; nevertheless, curiosity takes over.

It must be the meat. Tiny patches of flour lace the edges. Why would Mother throw away perfectly good beef when she's always been so fiercely against wasting food? It must have been tough. But then why deny cutting it up? It makes no sense. This doesn't sit well with me as I picture those plasters sticking to the fence. I look up at the full moon, sigh, and wonder.

Chapter 38
1964
Next day

I spot him even before the bus has arrived. Casually leaning against the side of the shelter, he holds a cigarette and stares across the road. On the pavement beside him lies his guitar in its battered black case. Despite the high temperature Kon's doggedly wearing his faithful leather jacket and denim jeans. His dark hair's now quite long. It hangs well over a raised collar while his thick fringe sweeps across his forehead. For an instant he appears like a model posing for a magazine shoot. I imagine the black and white shot on a page of *Nova*. Kon, with that sultry expression, so like George Harrison's in those photos taken in the smoky Hamburg clubs where the Beatles had played a few years ago.

Gloom is transformed into ecstasy when I leap off the platform literally into Kon's arms. The unexpectedness of this encounter makes his kiss all the more welcome. Indeed, the tight knot which has been restricting my chest all day is loosening, and a sweet stirring throughout my body begins to take its place.

"You're blockin' the way. Move orf, yer ruffians," moans an old woman. "Kids today. No decency!" She waves her walking stick in the air and stalks off.

Ignoring her, Kon asks, "Want to hear a bit of good news?"

Cheered by the prospect of good news, I say I do.

"Guess what? From this very day, I'm officially the lead guitarist in a group - the Black Widow Spiders."

"Black Widow Spiders?" I hoot with amusement.

"Aye. Well, that's the name for now." Momentarily he seems deflated. "Anyway, I saw the ad in the *New Musical Express*. Some lads over in Harrow, at the tech - are getting this group together - so took myself off - really, really early this morning - first bloke there I was - auditioned - and guess what? They want me big time."

"Gee that's fab," I say, not sure whether I believe my own enthusiasm, for I'm wondering where I'm going to fit into the jigsaw of Kon's new life.

He takes my hand and we begin to amble homeward. Electric with excitement Kon describes how they played all day in the bass player's garage - getting to know each other's styles and making a start at working on some original material.

"Weren't they meant to be in college?"

With an explosion of laughter, Kon stops still and looks at me as if I'm insane.

"Bloody 'ell! 'Course they were Miss Goody Two Shoes. But sometimes, just sometimes in life there're more important things than study, you know."

My cheeks grow warm, and I know he can't fail to notice me blushing. What a fool, he must think me. Just a stupid little kid. I'm so annoyed with myself. That's until I see the superior, insolent smile on his face. Fury takes over; but before I voice my annoyance, Kon tells me he thinks I'm so cute, and not to take any notice of his teasing. His kiss convinces me.

Later when we pass the billboard which for as long as I can remember has displayed adverts for chocolates or a grinning Santa at Christmas, I notice a new one. It's tempting the public to drink pale ale with *gentle summer rain,* whatever that is. The caption reads, *Made for each other.* That's Kon and me, I think with pride, and he's forgiven.

"Hey, I'll take you to a rehearsal. Even better lass, a dance once we've really got ourselves on the road. Like that eh?"

"Yeah, Fab! Will you be giving up your job at the record shop then?" I try to make the question sound casual.

"Now that'd really go down well with the old man, wouldn't it? Don't think so, not quite yet anyway. Not 'til we make it to at least er - 100 in the charts." He laughs, but I sense in reality he's serious about this musical venture.

"You don't get on that great with your dad, do you?"

"He's all right most of the time, but he nags. Bloody hell, they say women nag, but God, my dad could win first prize for nagging, especially nagging me." He drops my hand, takes out a pack of cigarettes from his jacket pocket and lights up. "Constant orders. Do this. Do that - and with no delay."

There, before my eyes stands Mother's Obersturmführer. Immediately I feel ashamed and the image disappears.

"I mean, take yesterday," he continues. "I tell him that I'll take that bloody dog for a walk about ten times, but no - it's *Ven? Ven? Ven are you going to take Bruno out?* Again and again. If it was so sodding important to go that very minute, why couldn't he bloody well take the dog himself eh? Then *he* leaves the back door open; finds Bruno sniffing the flowerbeds full of weed-killer - yeah, that *he'd* put on a while back - and guess what? Blames me."

"You?"

"Aye, 'cause I hadn't buggered off yet with the dog. I mean, it'd send anyone round the bend, wouldn't it?"

We're now walking at quite a pace. "You know what? All that fuss. Bruno was only out there a second or two, not a whole bloody day or anything."

When we approach home it's 5.40pm. We're no longer walking briskly and Kon makes a huge thing about the weight of my bag on his shoulder. Coupled with carrying his guitar, he says the wretched thing's wearing him out; however he refuses to give it back to me. We play tug of war and laugh a little too loudly. I half expect to see Mother at the window checking I'm not with "that German boy", but it's Mrs.Wilner who rushes out of their front door just as Kon and I are kissing goodbye. Her eyes are red, her hair uncombed, and her usual immaculate appearance non-existent.

"Bruno ist tot!" she cries.

"Nein! You're joking - Bruno dead? Shit! He can't be. Nein, not our Bruno," Kon shouts looking from his mother to me.

Mr. Wilner thunders forth from behind his wife. He points a finger at Kon. "Konrad! Er is tot! Du hast ihn vergiftet!"

"Vergiftet? Dead? Bruno poisoned? Ich?" Kon turns to me. "Hey, did you hear that? Now I'm bloody well being accused of killing our dog."

Mrs. Wilner's hands are cupped over her mouth, and I watch the tears cascading down her cheeks. "Bruno, oh mein Bruno!" Addressing me she says in English. "Poisoned. By veed-killer. Ze vet said poisoned." Distraught she slips back inside the house.

"Weed-killer," Kon echoes.

"Konrad. Ins Haus!" orders Mr Wilner, obviously embarrassed by such a spectacle.

"Fuck you, I'm *not* going inside."

It would be tactful and kind of me to leave the family to their misery, but I don't want to abandon my boyfriend to the wrath of his parents. So in spite of Mr. Wilner glowering at me, I remain until Kon storms off down the road.

"Kon! Kon!" I call running after him. But he's not stopping. At the corner of Woodland Avenue he spins round, "Please, not now. I just need to be on my own."

Like a heroine in a romantic film I rush towards him, "But…"

"Not now. Please - please Martina just go home, okay?" His voice cracks and he's holding up his hands to signify that he really wants me to come no closer. I can see he's struggling to keep back the tears, and I feel helpless. There's no romance in this moment. He turns and speeds off without looking round, and I'm standing alone with only the squirrel clambering up the nearby rowan tree for company.

When I return home, I see his guitar propped up against next door's wall. Without wanting to alert his parents, I furtively walk up their drive and carry it away. One thing I feel quite certain about is that at some point Kon will return to collect it.

As I unlock our front door my thoughts turn to poor Bruno, the gentle giant. The memory of him pushing his head into my hand fills me with sadness. I can almost feel his soft fur, and smell the doggie scent he had on wet days. Although Kon often called him "bloody" and made him sound like an encumbrance, deep down I know how fond he was of the dog. In fact, I'd grown to feel much affection for him myself. Poisoned. Poor innocent Bruno, poisoned. What a horrible, agonising way to die. And then it strikes me that perhaps Kon's delay in taking Bruno for a walk was due to him waiting for me.

The smell of apple cake hits me when I step into our house. Mother, wearing a new red and white spotted apron, stands by the table in the kitchen transferring small golden cakes from an oven tray to wire racks.

Often on Monday afternoons she looks after Andrew, but not today. Yesterday evening, Mrs. Jones dropped a note through the letter-box explaining that she didn't need Mother to mind him for the next couple of weeks, and she'd let her know when Andrew could come again. Having read the note, Mother scrunched it up. "Herr Obersturmführer Weissner's doing," she snarled.

I decide not to mention Bruno's death, she'll find out soon enough. She's more talkative than I have known her of late. Not having had Andrew for the afternoon I'd anticipated her to be morose and uncommunicative; but instead she offers me one of the warm cakes and proceeds to tell me how much she enjoyed shopping this morning. This, I regard as a real breakthrough since lately, either Father or I've had to squeeze the task into our own busy schedules.

Yet the recent news of Bruno's tragic death weighs so heavily on my mind that I'm unable to contain myself any longer and blurt out, "Bruno's dead," and follow this up with the important detail that the Wilners are devastated.

"Really!" She might as well have said, "Good." Her half-smile suggests the news is sweet. Mother turns her back on me and embarks on washing a wooden spoon. "Pity it is not Obersturmführer Weissner too," she adds in a brittle whisper.

Horrified by her callousness, I no longer recognise the woman who is my mother. From the annals of my mind come the words, *Jews are worse than wild beasts,* and I'm terrified.

The sink tidy is full. When Mother places it on the draining board I volunteer to empty it into the dustbin. It comes as no surprise to see that the dustmen have flung the bin back through the side-gate, and it is several feet away from its customary position; the lid upside down, lying close by. As usual they've left a trail of refuse in their wake. I reach out for a sizeable piece of eggshell, and then grab a soap wrapper which carried by the breeze hops along the patio. I fling them into the bin before dragging the thing two or three yards. In bending to pick up the lid, I catch sight of a cube of beef sticking under the lip. The beef I'd seen coated in flour?

I begin again to wonder. Bruno was in the Wilner's garden for seconds - according to Kon. This may or may not be the case, but what plays on my mind is the two opened packets of weed-killer in the shed. After all, Mr. Wilner had returned one, but who had taken the second from its usual shelf? Mother? No. But why did she deny chopping up the beef? Was it really traces of flour on the meat? Or was it something more sinister? There's no visible evidence of anything resembling flour on this soggy piece of meat. No, I cannot believe Mother would - could do such a terrible - *criminal* thing. No right minded person... The lid drops from my hand and clatters onto the metal bin. I *do not* want to think about this anymore.

I feel cold and sick. It surges from the depths of my stomach as I rush to the toilet, making it just in time. Mother's standing behind me while I kneel and vomit violently a second time. I feel the tips of her fingers rest on my shoulder. I quiver and heave again. "Did you eat something not good?" She sounds worried.

"Not sure." My voice is weak, but feeling a little better I get off my knees.

I say nothing about my suspicions and complain that the foul smell of the dustbin is probably responsible.

"Make sure you wash hands properly, Child," Mother says handing me a handkerchief before turning to go.

"I will," I say and disappear into my bedroom.

Hugging Mr. Bear, I sit on my bed contemplating the horror of the situation. I'm torn between possibilities. Bruno poisoned as a consequence of the delayed walk and Mr. Wilner having failed to keep him out of the back garden; alternatively, Bruno being deliberately poisoned by Mother. If I were a gambler, I know where I'd be placing my bet. After all, hadn't Samba jumped over the fence from the Wilner's garden yesterday evening? And didn't I see the cat, right as rain, strutting across the road on my way to school this morning? What should I do? I can't let Kon shoulder the blame, yet if what I suspect is true, what will happen to Mother? This is something I should share with Father - but not yet. However, I can't just sit here. This "thing" will not go away simply because I want it to. It's clear what I have to do, and I must do it this very evening.

Chapter 39
1964
Later that evening

Ealing Broadway station is busier than I would have expected at 7.40 on a Monday evening. A constant flow of commuters exits the station, many diving in and out of the nearby laundrette to collect their service wash, while the Wimpy Bar buzzes with hungry workers snatching a burger or coffee on their way home.

Summer is in the air. I look with envy at the laughing, carefree young couples who stroll along the pavement towards the main Broadway and I wish Kon and I could be like them rather than *star cross'd lovers*.

With the evening being so humid, a crowd of youths, glasses and cigarettes in hand, prop up the wall of the pub on the corner where the old man selling papers cries, "Ev'nin Standard!" I'm already a little late and all this waiting is making my stomach feel like a basket of butterflies. I know it. I've already missed him. Perhaps he'll think I've changed my mind. Cars stream past, yet his is not amongst them. My mind reels back a couple of hours to when I was creeping downstairs determined to make my escape.

I poked my head round the dining room door to see Mother bent over the table, deep in concentration, writing. "The going's good," I said to myself. Pushing the door ajar, I tiptoed backwards across the hall, picked up the receiver and waited while the endless ringing continued. About to give up, I heard a voice on the other end reciting the phone number.

"It's me, Martina," I whispered in a manner not reflecting the bleakness of my spirit. I asked if he'd be able to meet me this evening - a matter of urgency. My voice must have sounded in keeping with someone arranging a birthday party; but nervous in case Mother was listening, I carried on in this vein. He told me he'd just locked up and was about to go to the pub. Although somewhat irritated by my refusal to elaborate, half-heartedly he agreed.

"7.30," I said even though I knew I was unlikely to make it in time.

I grabbed my purse and braced myself for any protest from Mother. Doubtlessly, she would vehemently object to me going out "so late" in the evening without adequate explanation. Too bad, I'd already decided to go anyway and deal with the consequences later.

My heart sank when again I peeked in the dining room. "Oh my God!" I gasped catching sight of the pile of Elastoplast boxes towering in the centre of the table. Once aware of my presence, Mother's head jerked up, pen poised and eyes vacant. Letting the pen fall from her fingers, she began to paw some of the screwed up balls of paper strewn across the polished surface. I didn't want to hang around for an interrogation, and in truth hardly dared to look at what she was writing; but the unmistakeable letters, "NAZ" jumped up from the paper in front of her.

I left as soon as I could with Mother's sharp questions resounding in my ears. "Where? Where is it you go? Not with that German boy - that Nazi's son. *Do not go* when I tell you this."

He will not let me down. Whatever his other failings, I feel sure of this. I'm shockingly aware that Marek is the only person I can depend on for the kind of help I need - or should I say, the help Mother needs? He's the one person I know who understands our family background - the only one who'll be able to see this thing clearly; unlike Father who at present can't see the wood for the trees. And in truth Marek's probably the only one who *really* cares enough about our family. Nevertheless, we have history. I realise therefore, that I'll have to eat humble pie, and this makes me feel more than a little uncomfortable.

And there he is, smiling as he leans out of the open window of his Austin Cambridge, white with an orange stripe across the flank.

"Cześć!" he calls.

"Cześć," I reply, trying to smile.

I'm impressed with the turtleneck off-white shirt he's wearing; and his new trendy Beatle haircut actually does suit him. For the umpteenth time in my life, I'm staggered to realise Marek and Father are more or less the same age.

"Like the car?" he asks as he opens the passenger door for me to hop in.

"New?" I ask before thanking him for coming at such short notice.

"Quite," he replies. "So, Martina, what brings you to *me*? And what is that is so very urgent?"

I cannot fail to notice the hint of victory in his voice as we pick up speed and head up the hill; the quick way he tells me, to West Ealing where he now lives.

I tell him what I have to discuss is serious - private - therefore I'd prefer not to go back to his place. "I don't want to be rude - but Bronia will be there and…"

"There is no Bronia. Not anymore. We have split." With an unfamiliar sheepishness, he informs me that he has a new girlfriend, Irena. "She is in fact not so many years older than you. Well, in her twenties anyway," he boasts. "And almost as pretty as you."

He's more than a shade too cocky for my liking. I'm not interested in this new girlfriend; however I am interested in whether or not, as a consequence of his new situation, he's changed his plan to visit his mother in Poland later this year. Amused by my sudden concern about his trip, he says, "Why? Are you thinking of joining me, want to keep me company? Because you see, now I have my beautiful Irena, so I am not able to accept this - er - so gracious offer."

I hate his idiot talk. And it's this banal repartee that finally does it.

I find myself sitting in the passenger seat trying to stem a flow of raging tears. Obviously he has no concern for me. How crazy was I to think he would have. Crazy even to have imagined him being instrumental in Mother's salvation. Marek's mocking me. Just a Jack the Lad whose preoccupation is with his fresh conquest, Irena.

But I'm wrong. The car screeches to a halt at the nearest kerb and Marek moves across the seat and places his arm round my shoulders; but before I have time to object, it's withdrawn. Chucking his cigarette out of the window, he passes me a clean man-sized handkerchief. Without the flippancy he says, "Sorry. Perhaps joking's not so good today. So come, tell me why you cry?"

I make no reply.

"Tell me. Tell me Martina. What has happened that is so bad?"

My sobbing is so violent that I can barely breathe, let alone speak.

"Your mum?"

I nod.

Right there my pent up feelings come pouring out. About Mother's reactions to our German neighbours - the death of Bruno - the sticking plasters gummed to the fence - Dr. Kotkowski's advice - Father putting his head in the sand - the proposed trip for Mother to stay with a friend. I feel stupid when I reveal my abortive plan to write the simplest of letters to Ewa in Polish, in spite of having no address for her. Finally, I explode, "For goodness sake Mum needs professional help - she must face her demons. Dr. Kotkoswki told Dad that. And what's Dad's remedy? A break with a friend. That's no answer at all. I'm only fifteen and even I know it."

Marek reaches across and gives my shoulder a friendly rub, just the way he used to when I was very young. He draws heavily on his newly lit cigarette, opens the window allowing the curling smoke to escape. "I must say, the plasters and the dog business come as surprise, but otherwise what you tell me, really it does not. When your dad he told me Germans had moved next door, I knew it would be like when red rag is put to a bull - an omen - and you know, I thought something like this it would happen sooner or later." More to himself than to me he says, "For so long Hania has been a time-bomb ticking away - waiting to - er - well, never mind."

He pounds his thigh with a clenched right fist, and expresses regret in not having managed to persuade Mother to meet Ewa when she'd been in London for the concert. It strikes me that in all the years I've known Marek, this is the first time there's no bravado. Having flung the unsmoked cigarette out of the window, he stretches his fingers across his knees and turns to look at me. "The sisters, they must meet. Somehow they must meet. Really I do believe it, that once Hania sees Ewa in the flesh, there will be change of heart - not straight away, but after little time, she too will want this reconciliation. They are sisters for God's sake. The same blood - and such friends as children. I don't know why, or what happened, but however terrible, I am convinced deep down…"

"And Ewa? Did you meet her while she was in London?"

"Of course, but just for vodka in pub."

"And did she say anything about what happened between them?"

"No. You have to remember I have not seen Ewa for many years. Things like this they are not so very easy to speak about."

We sit silently, drained of words. Marek takes out another cigarette, rolls it between his fingers for a couple of seconds before lighting up.

Eventually I mutter, "Well, Dad says Mum just wants to leave the past behind - and I can sort of see that - but now…"

"But now it seems it cannot be possible. So, we have to do something," he says with energy and resolve. Marek having reverted to his former more flippant self reveals that because he no longer has to wait for Bronia's official papers to come through, his forthcoming trip to Poland has been brought forward. In fact he'll be flying out from London Airport on Thursday. "And no Irena on this trip," he adds.

As if I care one way or another.

Marek starts up the engine. After only a few of minutes we are parked in front of a large Victorian terraced house. The garden's small, bordered by a low brick wall and a fence which is in urgent need of repair. The flowerbed is a matted carpet of weeds with little other than a single neglected rose bush growing there. Three or four sad orange blooms hang limply from the branches, outnumbered by a host of deadheads. Marek unlocks the front door and I follow him through the dingy hallway to a large high-ceilinged room at the rear end of the house.

I recognise some of the heavy rather old-fashioned pieces of furniture from Marek's previous flat. Above the mantelpiece hangs a huge modern painting in the style of Picasso; I'm just about able to make out shapes representing human forms of different genders, shapes and sizes, entwined and melded. He tells me he finished painting it only last week. Beneath, standing in an empty wine bottle, is a multi-coloured candle overflowing with solid torrents of wax; and on either side of it are two framed photographs. The larger is a colour one of a handsome, smiling woman with a full head of greying hair. She has the same twinkle in her eye as does Marek. His mother I assume. To the left of the candle is a sepia photo. It's a head and shoulder shot of a young pilot in uniform. I feel sad, for I recognise Marek's brother from the photographs I'd once been shown; and it strikes me Andrzej probably hadn't lived much longer after this had been taken. He smiles at me across the decades, and the tragedy of so many lost young lives really hits home.

The walnut table is littered with sketch books, tubes of paint and newspapers, but otherwise the room, although reeking of stale grey ashtrays is surprisingly tidy. In the centre is a large high-backed beige sofa. Here I sit. I feel lighter, as if a burden has already been lifted from my shoulders - even though I don't yet know what Marek's words *we have to do something* will entail; the *we* comes as a relief.

Marek flings open the French windows. I'm pleased, for this both cools and airs the room. He stands with the garden as a backdrop and the doorframe his proscenium arch, and tells me that when he returns from Kraków, Bronia will have removed most of the hideous furniture, and then he'll set about modernising the whole house. He exits quite suddenly leaving me to contemplate the overgrown back garden. When he returns after some time, he hands me a mug of tea, and then pours a large vodka which he downs in one go.

"I phoned your dad."

"You did what?"

"So they do not worry."

"Worry? Huh! It's not me who Dad should be worrying about."

After a pause, Marek guardedly warns me that there's been some kind of upheaval because Mother was convinced I'd gone off with "that German boy", and apparently when Kon knocked asking if I had his guitar, she became quite offensive.

"Oh God! What exactly did she say? Tell me!"

"Exactly, I do not know. Your dad he did not tell me, exactly. But this is why it is so important to get things into motion as soon as possible." With that he pushes a pen and paper into my hands and beckons me over to the table.

He proposes that I write a short letter to Ewa. "First you write in English. Then I translate. Say you were at her concert perhaps: something about yourself. Then why her sister she now needs help. Of course, you can make it brief. Leave details to me. I tell her these things when we meet in Zakopane soon."

Once the letter is written, although still anxious about what Mother has said to Kon, I feel hungry. Marek having relaxed into a less sombre mood puts on a record while he rustles up a small meal. I've not enjoyed the Brahms Violin Concerto for so long that it comes as a surprise to find I love it again. "Perhaps I will yet come to hear you play this piece," calls Marek from the kitchen.

After ten minutes he returns with various cheeses, brown bread and large white soup bowls containing thick gherkins and tomatoes roughly cut into halves. I'm now ravenous and tuck in as soon as the food is on the table. Mugs of coffee plus Wypiekane follow. I adore these little ginger cakes coated in chocolate. Mother never buys them and as they're such a treat, I help myself to two immediately. Once settled in an armchair Marek says, "You didn't tell me that this friend your mum is to stay with is Anne."

"No," I reply feeling awkward.

"Anyway, I understand she'll be off to Anne's in a day or so. And then we shall see if it will make some difference."

A little later while Marek searches for his car keys I realise I'm glad that Mum's going soon. At least we'll get a breather for a while, but I dread the days before she goes almost as much as my reception when I get back home.

Chapter 40
May 1964

"I'm not going all the way."

"Don't worry, I've got something, so you won't get pregnant," Kon says kissing my neck as we snuggle up on the sofa. Not feeling quite so comfortable now I begin to wriggle free.

"It's not that - well, not only that. I - I just don't want to, that's why," I say extricating myself from his arms. Standing, I comb my hair with my fingers and stuff my top back into my skirt.

Kon remains lying stretched out, wide-eyed and flushed. "I do love you Martina, really *really* love you," he pleads with a saucy grin all over his face.

I take the cushion from the armchair, and playfully, but with some force, throw it at him. It lands hard on his face.

"Hey, you little vixen," he cries bounding up and chasing me round the room. Before I know it, he's holding me and we are laughing and kissing at the same time. My back's leaning against the wall. Our caresses become more than flirtatious pecks, his hand again wanders under my T-shirt and I feel his urgency as he presses against my hipbone. Gradually his chuckling dissolves and the breathing grows quick and heavy. I sense the beast in him is aroused and that he's in a different place from me. It's time to stop. Firmly I pull away, but he's not to be so easily deterred. He clings to me, keeping me imprisoned in his strong arms while at the same time determinedly holding our kiss. I feel a little afraid, frightened that things are getting out of control, so I give him a sharp decisive push. Immediately his arms fall away, and I'm free. Startled, he stares at me like an alien who's just landed on Earth.

"Dad will be home soon, and he'll be dead mad if I haven't put the dinner on," I say making a move towards the door. I don't want to give the impression I'm annoyed, therefore I turn and ask, "Do you want to help me? Peel the potatoes, yeah?"

"Not my scene," he says, but without a trace of sulkiness in his voice. Lazily Kon leans forward, reaches for his guitar and begins to strum a simple run of minor chords while I make my way to prepare the potatoes and carrots before opening a tin of mince.

Father's later than usual, so when I return from the kitchen, Kon suggests I get my violin and we play my Beatle medley, a duet for guitar and violin. Even if I do admit it, our duet has begun to sound pretty okay. "Maybe that group of yours could have a violin in its line-up?"

"Oh aye, the others would think that really groovy, I don't think."

"Joking," I say and I swipe him across the head with the tea towel.

The memory of last Saturday flashes into my mind. Kon managed to persuade Father to let me go with him to the group's first gig. Having told him the venue was a school, and that they were playing at a dance, Father finally agreed. In fact, I felt quite guilty watching him wave us goodbye as we drove off in the taxi to a pub in Acton.

The pub turned out to be a dive, smoky and dingy. On entry I was almost bowled over by the stench of stale beer and over-flowing ashtrays. The evening had hardly begun when I found myself virtually abandoned, left on a musty dusty chair, while Kon hunched in the tiny performance space, turned from me and began tuning up. This was *not* the "in" place to be on a Saturday night. It boasted mostly of middle-aged or older men with Irish accents, who with cigarettes and pints of beer welded to their hands, propped up the dark wooden bar. In the corner, sitting under a well-worn dartboard was a woman who reminded me of that bespectacled Martha Longhurst from *Coronation Street*. Next to her sat a rather sullen balding man supping Guinness whilst never taking his eyes off the pretty blonde barmaid who cheerily served her regulars.

After a few minutes, I spotted, crawling out of a dark corner, what turned out to be the other Black Widow Spiders. (Every bit as creepy as their namesakes.) Roll-ups hanging from their mouths, and without eye contact, the three of them reluctantly grunted what I took to be some kind of greeting when Kon deigned to introduce them to me. I had to keep reminding myself that these lads are actually college students.

The first riff twanged to life and they were off. Really off! Eyes averted, and backs bent, they were lost in the magic of their music; and there was I, sitting like some dumb groupie sipping Babycham and pretending to be enthralled by their sound.

Although I told them during their break, the music was fab, in actual fact it's a heavy tuneless kind of rock, and I hate it. It sounds nothing like the music I hear Kon playing through my bedroom wall; and definitely nothing like the Hollies. I'm curious as to why Kon has joined a group producing this excuse for music.

Anyway, towards the end of their second set, Kon mouthed to me, "My song coming up."

But I didn't recognise his composition swamped by the heavy drumbeat, the thumping bass and sung by a vocalist who sounded as if he'd swallowed half a gravel pit. I smiled and Kon smiled back. By the time they'd reached their final number there was only Martha Longhurst left in the main bar reading the *Daily Sketch*.

Next day I hinted to Kon that their music is not the Manchester sound he'd talked about producing. Infuriatingly he patted me on the head calling me square. "We're before our time. You wait and see, our sound will be all the rage a couple of years on."

"Rubbish," I replied forgetting to be tactful. "You're dead wrong, that - er music - will *never* catch on." And then I scolded him for patronising me.

Well, that was the weekend, and here we are ready to make a very different sound. The shift from romance to music comes as a relief. I didn't want to "go all the way" but neither did I want Kon to go home in a mood. Kon strums "Please Please Me" while I hurry to get my violin. During the last fortnight since Mother's been away, life's been so easy. Although I pretend to be looking forward to her homecoming, I absolutely am not. I'm quite sure Father's also savouring the respite albeit that almost every day he says how much he's missing her. His complexion is no longer ashen and the skin on his face less taut; also it's gratifying to see that he's not walking round the house like a blind man nearing a precipice.

The break's definitely doing her good. Perhaps he knows best after all. In fact, Mother's so content that she wishes to stay a bit longer, and it seems Anne's happy for the visit to be extended. She reports that Mother hasn't once made reference to the German neighbours - or the dog.

"Funny," Anne said to Father on the phone, "it's as if Woodland Avenue doesn't exist for her."

And no date has as yet been fixed for her return.

What has been the icing on the cake, as far as I'm concerned, is that Kon's no longer banished from the house; but I've noticed that Father arrives home from work earlier than usual most days. He claims to trust me, but I doubt if deep down he trusts Kon. Anyway, this evening he'll enter the house to find us in the innocent pursuit of music making.

We begin with "I Will" which comes in the middle of the medley, because last time we played the piece, it was at this point that we kept going out of time with each other. I'm thinking how "together" we are today, and how the balance between violin and guitar is getting better and better, when we're interrupted by a knock on the front door. We stop in the middle of a bar. A bum note screeches from my violin, and Kon and I share a look of annoyance. It has gone 6.30, and I wonder if Father has forgotten his key yet again; or maybe it'll turn out to be Kon's mother ostensibly summoning him home for his evening meal. That doubtlessly will cause another ruction.

Indeed, the events of recent weeks haven't only left the Wilner family bewildered and grieving, but have served to create much friction between Kon and his parents, even though he's been exonerated from causing Bruno's death. A few days ago, unperturbed by my presence, mother and son exchanged heated words in German, and then when his mum had stormed off, Kon exploded. "The old bag! Treats me like a bloody kid. Can't wait to move out! Just can't wait."

But when I open the front door I see it's neither Father nor Mrs. Wilner, it's Mrs. Carr. "Hello, dearie," she says. "All right?"

"Fine, thank you."

"Phew! Hot today. Hot for this time of year."

"Yes."

"And how's your mummy?"

"Oh! Okay, thanks."

"Not home yet then?"

"No," I say and don't elaborate, in the hope she'll be satisfied with my answer and go. Then I notice she's holding some letters.

"Here, dearie," she says handing them to me. "Postman stuck these through my letterbox by mistake this mornin'. Blessed nuisance. This new postman's always doin' that."

I stand politely listening to her complain about how the postal service has deteriorated and how much more reliable it used to be. All the while I'm conscious of the clock ticking, and just want to get back to Kon before Father makes his appearance.

While I'm considering how to kindly draw this conversation to an end, a lad walks up the path. Typical. Just my luck! God, what now? Some bloke selling encyclopaedias. Although Mrs. Carr is partially blocking my view, I'm able to see that he's tall with longish, slightly unruly brown hair. She moves to the side and I notice his jeans are well-worn; the royal blue T-shirt looks new enough, but creased, and his fore-finger is hooked into a navy parka draped over his shoulder. I think he's probably a wretched student trying to earn a bob or two as a door-to-door salesman. At first glance he seems familiar, and then a stranger once more. But at second glance I'm certain he's no stranger.

"Well, dearie," sighs Mrs. Carr at last coming to the end of her diatribe about how much better almost everything was before the war. "Standin' here gossipin' with you won't get me tea cooked, will it? Must be off. Cheerio." And she bustles off home leaving me gawking at a ghost from the past.

For a second or two we remain speechless; the awkwardness still there after all these years. The unresolved hostility is palpable, and it's Peter who eventually breaks the ensuing silence with a cough and says, "Hello." He doesn't waste time on pleasantries, but skips straight to the point. "I've come to collect the bag for your mum." Avoiding eye contact, he gazes at my forehead.

"Bag for my mum? What bag?"

Father never mentioned anything about Peter coming to collect anything for Mother.

Another awkward silence reigns. Obviously somewhat irritated at the prospect of a wasted journey, he continues, "Your dad said it would be ready. Said if I called round today at about this time, it would be ready."

I have to confess that being confronted with Peter after so many years has taken the wind out of my sails. *Stinking rotten Jew.* I try to erase the words from my mind, but the image of Peter standing in the Harris's garage yelling those ugly words refuses to fade.

"Didn't you know I was coming?"

"No. No, I didn't. My dad must've forgotten to tell me. Anyway he's late. Probably thought he'd be back in time to deal with it himself."

Anyone overhearing our chilly conversation would assume that some very recent conflict had taken place. Now I feel at a loss as how to proceed, but I do notice Peter isn't the wreck Norma described.

"Well, the thing is… I'm going to Nottingham tomorrow - staying a few days. I don't know… Mum asked if I'd get the extra stuff for your… look, never mind if…"

"Hang on," I put in quickly as he begins to walk away. "I'll go and look. My dad may have got a bag ready."

Peter sighs and retraces his steps. He's leaning on the doorjamb when Samba trips across the flowerbed and begins to rub his head against Peter's leg. Bending down, he strokes his sleek black head and affectionately tells the purring cat how good it is to see him again.

And as I turn, there's Kon behind me. "Who's the lad then?" he whispers giving Peter the eye of suspicion. I explain that Peter used to live next door, where he now lives, and that he's come to collect a bag of things to take up to my mum in Nottingham. Am I imagining it? Is he actually jealous? Jealous of Peter? Just as I'm entertaining this absurd idea, Kon strides forward, revises his frosty tone and light-heartedly admonishes me for leaving the lad standing on the doorstep. Full of camaraderie he invites Peter in; then suggests I run upstairs and find the bag. Walking through the hall, Kon offers Peter a beer as if he was the master of the house, and it's accepted.

On reaching the landing, I'm still clutching the letters Mrs. Carr handed me. There are four. I dart into my room and toss them carelessly onto my bed. The three official ones in brown envelopes are most likely boring bills, but I note that the fourth, which had been sandwiched between the others, is addressed to me - and it's from Poland. Marek's writing is on the envelope. He's certainly taking a chance sending me a letter here at home. Even though I'm excited and want to open it straight away, I resist. The white envelope is tightly packed; I turn it over and over. I feel a thudding under my ribs and my face feels warm and tight. Yet the moment to open it is not now.

All I want is to rid the house of people so that I'm able to read the letter in peace. But I need to sort out this business of Mother's bag. So I leave it on the bed and go into my parents' bedroom. Fortunately, beside her bed lies a small brown and cream holdall. And thank heavens it's filled with Mother's clothing. Hurrying down the stairs, the heavy bag bumps against the wall leaving scuffs in its wake. I make a mental note to sponge them off before Father notices.

The lads are established in the sitting room. Kon, re-lighting a cigarette, is on the floor between the abandoned guitar and violin, lounging against the sofa. Peter, like a candidate awaiting interview sits opposite on a dining room chair.

"...play lead guitar in a group. How about you?"

"Hoping to go to university - next year, that is - had a year out - it's complicated - so I'm still only 1st Year Sixth even though I'm eighteen..."

"Must make you feel a bit of a retard," Kon cracks.

I surprise myself when instantly I leap to Peter's defence. "He's anything but a retard. Brilliant at Maths and..."

But Peter doesn't need me to fight his battles, and I feel a bit of a fool as I look across to see him smiling. "Doesn't bother me. Anyway, there's tons of people at tech doing A' levels and they're a lot older than eighteen."

"No offence mate." Then to me Kon says, "I *know* how it feels to be thought a retard, Martina."

I don't quite see the logic of this response, but I detect the edge in his voice as he looks at me with daggers. I wonder if he'll get into a strop and go - but he doesn't budge.

With that Peter puts down his half-finished glass of beer, stands and reaches for the holdall. "Thanks. Be on my way now."

"Finish your beer," says Kon offering a cigarette. Peter declines, but sits down again.

The letter will have to wait.

The atmosphere warms, and there follows some chat about The Beatles and the Liverpool sound. Making no contribution, I sit on the floor close to Kon and observe Peter. He's in fact quite good looking in a studenty kind of way. The spots he'd sported as a youngster have all but disappeared, and now in his more relaxed pose, he comes across as being quietly confident.

They run out of conversation. Following an awkward silence, Peter in an avuncular manner turns to me, "What about those friends of yours? What were their names Siobhan and…"

"Sinéad, Krysia and Mary." I mention that Krysia is struggling with Maths - and laughingly put in that she could do with a patient teacher like him. Peter smiles. Kon does not. Then I carry on to say that Krysia can't decide whether to train as a nurse or go to university to study modern languages. When I get to Mary, he says he doesn't actually remember her, but I still carry on and tell him that she's intent on going to medical school after A'levels. And then there's Sinéad. He's not forgotten what she looked like, and refers to her as the pretty blonde Irish one. "She's hoping to be an air hostess, work for Aer Lingus…"

Kon chips in as if Sinéad was a great pal of many years, saying that she changes her mind as quickly as she falls in and out of love. With that Kon puts his arm around me and adds, "Unlike Martina."

Peter proceeds to tell me that Lisa has really pulled up her socks, and is planning to go to Teachers' Training college after A'levels. I'm delighted and ask him to say hi to her for me.

And there is Father in the doorway excusing himself for his unavoidable lateness - something about a pharmaceutical rep turning up late for the arranged appointment. He swears he told me Peter was coming to collect Mother's bag, but I know he didn't. Peter converses with Father while I wander down the path with Kon who's suddenly become inexplicably peevish. Now he seems in a rush, saying that he's got a rehearsal; and without a kiss, he disappears through his garden gate.

Later, while Father and I are sharing supper, I consider how little I really understand what makes Kon tick, but mostly I dwell on the letter upstairs.

"Mum's progress is good. A break, that's what was needed," Father says with satisfaction. Thankfully he eats quite quickly - even the tinned chocolate sponge pudding he brought home is consumed faster than such a treat deserves. As he places his spoon in the empty dessert bowl, he says that he now wants to enjoy what's left of the balmy evening. Having helped me wash the dishes, he changes out of his suit and begins weeding, and then digs the beds towards the back of the garden.

Alone at last. I can no longer resist the temptation to open the letter. But once holding the sealed white envelope, I shiver, and begin to fear its secrets. I hesitate. Then my fingers move. Slowly, very slowly I begin to slit open the top of the envelope with my nail file. Shaking, I'm unable to proceed, so I place it on my desk, rub my damp palms together and walk to the window.

Father, half-illuminated stands in what remains of the sunshine. The other half of his body appears as an indistinguishable grey silhouette in the evening shadows. A portrait painted by an artist who has captured the essence of Father perfectly. Yet he's not an inanimate picture, he's a man - a person who feels things just as I do. In our family Mother's needs have always been paramount. However, I wonder what are his latent needs? I can't remember him ever complaining about his lot in life; and with Mother, his life can never have been easy. His foot rests on the lug of the spade as he gazes at the shed. Is he contemplating impossible dreams, or is he entertaining darker thoughts he dare not voice?

All at once my hands take on a life of their own. Frantically, they snatch and tear at the envelope until it gapes wide open, releasing its contents onto the desk where the unfolding leaves seem to beckon to me.

Chapter 41
2008
Poland

No seat is left vacant. The door shuts and the coach drives off through the suburbs of Kraków. Soon after we leave the city, numerous concrete monstrosities steal the pleasing vista. These huge ugly blocks, which still provide homes for thousands are a sobering reminder of the bleak Communist era.

There reigns an unusual quietness in this coach packed with tourists; only an undercurrent of conversation can be heard above the engine's steady drone as we travel south. The Krakus Mound flashes passed my window, but I'm not really taking in much of what I see since my thoughts are elsewhere. I imagine everyone here has their reasons, their own agenda, for embarking on this trip. For me it's a personal pilgrimage, something over the years that I've intended to do, but kept putting off.

My sixtieth birthday looms on the horizon, and this serves to remind me that I'm not immortal. So here I am, preparing at last to face what I've shied away from for so long. Today will be painful, and I'm unable to imagine how I will feel by sunset.

My fingers twist the handles of my soft black leather bag before straying inside to reassure myself that the small posy of rosebuds I've brought along with me is still intact. I'm not sure where or when I shall have the opportunity to lay them, but I've seen photos of candles and flowers left in memory of those who died in Auschwitz, and I'm determined to do the same. The tip of my thumb now brushes a corner of an envelope. It's the letter, the one I received over forty years ago. The words "Woodland Avenue" have faded somewhat, but the handwriting of both Ewa's scribing and Marek's translation on the pages inside, remain bold and clear.

The countryside and villages zoom by as the coach picks up speed, and I feel like a sentenced prisoner in transit to death row as I sit transfixed and incapable of communication.

After a few more miles, at the front of the coach, a small TV screen flickers to life and the guide who welcomed us aboard, explains in a sombre voice that we're about to see a film which should prepare us for our visit. The middle-aged couple in the seats across the aisle continue to munch away at their sandwiches while I swallow hard and make a determined effort to be brave, but already there's a lump in my throat.

We are reminded that six million Jews were exterminated by the Nazis; and vast numbers died in this very camp. But not only Jews, gypsies and the mentally ill - any marginalized group considered sub-human by Hitler suffered the same fate. The facts and figures never fail to shock me.

Grainy film footage reveals the victims arriving at the main gate of the concentration camp. *Arbeit macht frei - Work makes you free.* Unsuccessfully, I blink away the tears whilst focusing on the train where the old and young en masse tumble from lines of enclosed freight carriages. All exhausted. All bewildered. All clutching cases or bags of some kind. It's dreadful knowing that if these people had felt any relief in reaching their destination, soon their hopes were to be shattered.

I'm unable to take my eyes off the faces. However, would I even recognise Mother and Ewa. Would I? But I simply cannot stop myself from scrutinising the multitude of young female faces as the frames rapidly change and the figures before me become emaciated skeletons draped in striped ill-fitting garbs. Eventually I give up. I don't think I could bear to witness their suffering anyway.

The film continues to tell its evil story while I sit staring at the screen, hoping everyone else in the coach is so intent on the horrors of Auschwitz, they'll not notice me crying, really crying. My stomach's a tight ball. I sit frozen in the seat and fear that I'm going to hyperventilate.

His hand reaches out, he places it over mine. He wants me to know that he understands, but I'm not ready for the spell of Auschwitz to be broken, and I need to prepare for its reality alone, so I pull away.

I'm conscious that this whole thing is also difficult for him. The regrets and demons, which from time to time rear their ugly heads, must be riding high in his mind. Today however, I'm unable to deal with his ghosts. Staring out of the window, it takes only seconds to regret this self-indulgence, and I take his hand.

The sun goes in. One minute the sky is eggshell blue, the next a blotchy grey. In fact I know that we're almost here before anyone says so. I sense we're entering territory shrouded in evil. A permanent shadow has crept across this place where the burden of guilt has seeped through every inch of its soil. The evil legacy of the Holocaust saturates the very foundations on which Oświęcim stands.

Stark dispirited buildings line the route we travel. There's an uncanny air of abandonment. Where are all the people? It looks like a ghost town. The few I do see seem ravaged and lifeless. It's as if they're personally burdened with guilt. I have to say that it amazes me how anyone could live in this town. How are they able to carry on day after day knowing what took place just a stone's throw away?

Two small scruffy boys, caps pulled low over their foreheads, loll against a shabby building, bicycles at their feet sprawled across the pavement. Walking in their direction, on the same side of the road, is a woman with the face of an old crone yet the gait of a young matron. On her arm hangs a wicker basket and she's dressed entirely in the black clothing of a widowed peasant. As in all towns, men frequent bars and cafes, passing the time of day drinking and smoking, Oświęcim is no exception. The coach comes to a standstill and there they are; the lunch-time workers who prefer beer to a sandwich or a bowl of soup. Three men dressed in loose dark, tired clothing share a drink, but throughout the five minute delay I never see them exchange a word.

With a shudder the coach resumes its journey, and I feel the sting of anticipation, these last minutes before arriving at the museum of Auschwitz.

We are here. And as I step down from the coach, I think of those words:

I walk through the valley of the shadow of death.

Chapter 42
2008
Poland

Now that we've arrived, I feel strangely calm. An aura of sunshine brightens the sky, but there's a biting wind; it's definitely colder today than it's been of late. The Polish tour guide is Matylda. Stocky with short immaculately styled copper hair, she's smartly dressed in a tan suede coat and wearing polished brown ankle boots. In greeting she smiles, then immediately sets the tone for the day. Just as I'd been perplexed as to how the local people could live in Oświęcim, I'm now wondering what kind of person can face showing visitors round Auschwitz. Then she speaks.

Her English, although heavily accented, is good. She keeps her voice soft, maintaining a quiet respect. "Is there any person who can visit this place where so many men, women and children were murdered, tormented, starved, and not be shocked? I do not think it possible… more people lost their lives here than the entire number of Americans and British who died in the Second World War… The museum of Auschwitz - Birkenau stands testimony to the cruelty of which man is capable... it stands so that the next generations should come… witness… learn... so the world will never see such inhumanity again. Here we preserve the past in order to protect the future."

We're surrounded by a drone of voices as other parties listen to similar introductions in a host of different languages. The numbed hush of our group is marked as each person hangs on to the words of our guide. She continues, "Please do not forget when you look at the piles of spectacles, the mass of human hair, the mountain of shoes, the stacks of cases, that all these once belonged to people, real people like you and me."

I know now why she has undertaken the job.

The main gate is smaller than I'd imagined, but I'm filled with awe as my thoughts turn to all those people who passed under the inscription, *Arbeit macht frei* - all those people including my mother, Ewa, my grandparents. In that moment Ewa's letter comes to life.

My legs had no feeling, it was a real struggle for me to put one foot in front of the other. The relief at reaching our destination was soon superseded by fear. Being packed into cattle wagons, virtually starving and overcome with the vile stench of humanity and death, was intolerable.

When the freight train at last had come to a halt, we heard the loud snarling, "Alle raus!" The sides of the carriages were violently opened to a blinding day; and before even having had time to adjust to the light, we were brutally torn from the train and thrown to the ground by the SS guards. Those who had died on the journey were, to our horror, flung on to the awaiting wagons - one body piled on top of the next, regardless. So harsh and venomous rang the German orders that I lay where I fell frozen in terror and disbelief. Hania bent down and pulled me up. Immediately a guard was behind her shouting, "Steh' auf!" Mercilessly he began to beat her with a stick, yelling incessantly to move along quickly, "Mach schnell, Judenschwein."

You cannot imagine how many thousands of people streamed from the endless rows of carriages... I was nineteen and crying like a baby.

Confusion as far as the eye could see. Overwhelmed with terror, I was unable to proceed. To the annoyance of those walking behind us, I had dropped my precious violin which had instantly been kicked away under a forest of legs. It was disappearing fast. Everyone was in so much hurry, pushing and shoving their way, to what? No doubt towards hope of something better than the ghetto we had left behind in Podgorze.

"See, it's a work camp! They are not going to kill us! They want us to work for them." I heard a man reassure a howling young woman as he pointed to the inscription "Arbeit macht frei".

Hania bent down struggling to retrieve the violin case, whilst at the same time tugging my coat sleeve and dragging me on. She kept warning me that if I fell behind, the SS guards would be upon me with their whips. And from the smirk on some of their faces and their ice cold eyes, I knew they needed little excuse for indulging in such punishment. Handing me the violin case, she whispered in my ear, that I must not lose heart, to keep faith in Yahweh. "Yahweh will be our salvation, you see, he will look after us," she consoled as we tried to catch sight of our parents who had been carried forward in this seething crowd...

"Judenschwein!" Soldiers yelled repeatedly at our mother as she begged not to be separated from Tatuś – my father. "Rueben! Rue-be-n!" she cried. And all around us as selection took place, tormented, uncontrollable screaming pierced the air as we were pushed into random columns. I had never before seen my mother, your grandmother, shed more than a tear or two, and here she was wringing her hands, on her knees begging and wailing hysterically. A soldier, with a huge Alsatian appeared and stood above our mother pointing his rifle at her head, whilst the dog barking incessantly, bared his teeth, and then viciously went into attack. Shielding her face, your grandmother raised her hand. Her hand, badly bitten, it ran with blood. Hania intervened risking the wrath of both soldier and dog; and somehow she managed to pull our mother to her feet, soothing her and reassuring her that the separation would be temporary, and soon we would all be together - once the official business was complete - but we never set eyes on Tatuś, your grandfather, again...

As we stand now looking towards the chamber where thousands upon thousands were gassed after selection, I recall what Ewa wrote concerning her own ordeal; how following the induction period she was separated from her mother and sister, ending up in Buno-Monowitz, a sub-camp within the Auschwitz complex. Saved through her ability to play the violin, she was forced to become a member of the Auschwitz women's orchestra. She vividly describes the mixture of relief and guilt she had felt in coming to terms with being a privileged prisoner. I visualise that paragraph in her letter where she writes of her shame at having to play welcome music at the main gate; at being party to that Nazi deception of giving false hope to the new arrivals. This, Ewa wrote, was in fact far worse than having had to entertain the SS officers at their concerts and social gatherings.

...I did not see my mother or sister for a long time after the separation... perhaps weeks, months... not until I had become cunning and discovered how to absent myself for short periods from the orchestral playing... if caught, I would have been shot... and

opportunities only arose when we musicians were left unguarded, mostly during the days of chaos and commotion when vast numbers of new victims were arriving... it was like living on another planet. If I tell you, that I probably would not have recognised my own mother and sister had they passed me by, I think you would find it difficult to believe; but I can assure you it is true. With shaven heads, and dressed in those almost identically striped garments, we were not only dehumanised, but were not the same people as before, in appearance or spirit...

Our group enters the gas chamber, the gas chamber that masqueraded as showers, and I try to imagine how it must have felt when those doors slammed shut, and it began to dawn on those trapped inside that it was gas, not water pouring in from above.

I notice an area cordoned off by a rope, and there, flowers and lighted candles have been left in memory of victims. But I spend too long in contemplating where I should place my posy, and by the time I've decided to ask the guide if it's permissible to unhook the rope and enter the enclosure, the party's moved off.

As an adult I've made it my business to acquaint myself with the horrors of Auschwitz-Birkenau, so I'm no stranger to the details, but being here is very different from reading about it. It's heartbreaking to picture your own mother an inmate of this satanic place. I recall recently reading on one website that some survivors stated, the very earth at Auschwitz moaned with the voices of the victims - and now with every step I take I become more and more convinced they are right.

Trekking along the railway track Matylda tells us Birkenau means a place with birch trees. She adds that the grass stretching before us was not there when the camp was in operation, there was only mud. As we follow her, the wind moans, and I contemplate this dead zone as it would have looked in 1943. In her letter Ewa writes, that the day the family arrived it was exceptionally cold; the sky a patchwork of gunmetal grey and red mist. Then as we walk further it strikes me that not a single bird flies here even though the surrounding area is quite rural. Do they sense the inherent evil too? The rail track is long. I imagine the freight train packed with bewildered humanity. How would I feel arriving in such a God-forsaken place as Mother did at just twenty-one? I recall the photo of the children taken in her garden; she a child, standing under the branches of a tree, smiling. Then I remember the one of her as a bride looking sad and vacant as she stands beside the groom, my father. I'm no longer puzzled as to why her eyes are not smiling, even on her wedding day.

Bunches of flowers, some fresh, others already dead, lie scattered along the rail track. I lay down my red rosebuds and say a silent prayer. We seem to move so quickly. Perhaps it would've been better to have come here alone instead of with an organised tour. But when we reach the International Monument to the Victims of Fascism in Birkenau, we're given time for personal reflection.

I walk towards the plaque dedicated to the memory of Polish victims of the Holocaust. Written in Polish are the words:

Forever let this place be a cry of despair and a warning to humanity where the Nazis murdered about one and a half million men, women and children, mainly Jews, from various countries in Europe.

The lump in my throat is back.

My thoughts are running wild. I drift away from the crowd, sit on one of the large grey stones behind the plaques and take Marek's translation of Ewa's letter out of my bag.

...Marek and I have discussed your mother's recent disturbing behaviour and I agree with him, it is essential for her to "face her demons"... Perhaps you have been hoping that my letter will divulge the reason for the rift between my sister and myself. I must apologise if this is the case. Marek tells me that you are an intelligent young lady; therefore I am sure you will understand when I tell you that it would be wrong of me to reveal such a thing without your mother's consent... My intention is to achieve reconciliation. But so far over the years my attempts have failed... Your mother remains adamant in not wanting this... however I am planning to come to England anyway. I know a meeting with my sister will not be easy to arrange - perhaps more difficult than I imagine, but instinctively I know it is the right thing to do - it simply must happen... At this stage I think it best though not to inform her of my intentions...

So many years ago. Yes, Ewa's visit did eventually take place. Sometimes the memory seems so distant that I have to ask myself if it really happened at all, but today I remember it as clearly as if it were yesterday. And it's with heavy heart that I recall the testament - Mother's testimony, written after Liberation; its existence unbeknown to me at the time.

It was recovered by chance; found under the mattress in the house of Marta, a kind woman who had offered Mother a place to live on her return to Kraków after the war. These thin sheets of paper covered in Mother's spidery scrawl were given to Ewa on Marta's death after the house had been cleared out; and in turn, Ewa left them with her sister when they finally met.

Not only did the testament open my eyes, but it proved to be a catalyst in the downward spiralling events that followed.

PART FOUR

Chapter 43
August 1965

"Come on lazy bones!" shrieks Sinéad from the side of the swimming pool. "Sure, 'tis not cold, not at all." Even with wet hair she looks gorgeous in her new orange and pink psychedelic swimsuit.

"Chicken," laughs Krysia who is still only waist deep. The loose knot of dark hair at the top of her head threatens to spill from the elastic band as she bobs up and down in the blue water.

"In a minute," I call from the nearby grassy area where I'm lying on a towel, relaxing.

I lean back on my elbows, and slowly stretch out my legs. Mary's already halfway down the length of the pool, swimming breaststroke at Olympic pace. Despite their cajoling, I stay put, preferring the heat of the August sunshine to the cool water. I feel far from glamorous in my unsexy dark blue costume with my hair tied back in a kiddie pony tail - although this afternoon I simply don't care, I'm truly happy.

The four of us are in a good mood. It's results' day, and we've all passed the GCE O'levels we need in order to embark on what we want to do next. Sinéad, who claims to have done a minimum of revision, is relieved to have scraped six passes, which means she can take up her place on the BBC secretarial training scheme in September. Her unexpected fear of flying during her first flight to Cork last Easter put paid to her ambition of becoming an air hostess. Krysia has seven O'levels, and will now be able to study for A' levels in Polish, French and Biology. Mary and I, counting those we passed last summer, both have ten, and have opted for the Science route. Mary, as predicted, has achieved A grades right across the board, but I've only managed to gain 7 A's and 3 B's. Nonetheless, I'm delighted considering the traumas of the past year.

Usually time flies by, but it feels longer than twelve months since Father had to almost forcibly bring Mother home from Nottingham. As her visit to Anne became more and more extended, the prospect of the homecoming became less and less appealing. Moreover, she had outstayed her welcome by the summer holidays, since a romance was brewing for Anne, and this hadn't gone down well with Mother. Yet Father still maintained that the break was the very thing she needed.

The "little break" over and done with, quickly saw the renewal of Mother's sombre moods, and gradually her irrational behaviour returned. Some days she would seem her old self, reminding me to take my dinner money, or nagging me about eating sufficient breakfast. However, by the time term was well and truly underway, frequently she could be seen sitting staring into space; or rhythmically chopping endless supplies of vegetables whilst ranting and raving about the Nazis next door - complaining they had brought back the filthy rats. Rats, she said, were running in profusion at the bottom of the garden. But I never saw any rats. Of course the old chestnut kept coming up about Obersturmführer Weissner's son playing his awful music too loud.

Kon once again was banished from our house. When I appealed to Father he refused to listen and supported the rule. Therefore the easy relationship Kon and I had enjoyed over the many weeks became more difficult to sustain. His parents, who had slowly warmed to me during Mother's absence, grew distant and wary, especially after they received an anonymous letter, complete with Swastika saying, "Nazis go home."

Mother claimed to have no knowledge of this, suggesting most of the people in the neighbourhood, in fact in the whole of England, hate Germans. "Anybody," she repeated, "anybody could have written the thing."

Still, I had my suspicions. For the sinister look in her eye was back - and it hadn't escaped my notice, she had begun to hoard packets of sticking plasters again.

"Mum," I said one afternoon while she was baking a million apple cakes for no one in particular. "Look at this."

And from an old brown paper bag I removed a head and shoulder portrait of a soldier, a young German soldier in army uniform. There could be no mistaking who was sketched in charcoal - Mr. Wilner, a young, thinner Mr. Wilner with a thick mop of dark hair and an uneasy smile.

"Painted by another German soldier who was in the *same* prisoner of war camp as Mr. Wilner."

Mother looked blank.

"Mr Wilner, *a prisoner of war*, so he couldn't be this Obersturmführer Weissner."

"Why do you show this?" She then began to shout a barrage of incomprehensible Polish.

Eventually I managed to calm her. Silence her. Sit her down in an armchair and point to the writing on the back of the framed portrait that Kon had sneaked out of the Wilner's spare bedroom. All to prove to Mother that his dad was no SS guard. The writing, after so many years remained perfectly legible. *Portrait of Kurt Wilner by Josef Schneider 13th May 1943 - Glen Mill POW.*

"And you think I am stupid?"

"No, Mum of course I don't. But for heaven sake look, look at the year, 1943. Mr Wilner was a prisoner of war in 1943. He was a prisoner of war in Glen Mill Camp in Oldham - all the time you were in - in Auschwitz."

"Do not speak to your mother as if she is stupid. It is you Child who is stupid. Stupid to believe this deceit." With an angry fist she knocked the portrait out of my hands. It fell in a spin to the floor, and to my horror when I looked down, I saw the frame was broken in three places.

Naively, Kon and I had assumed this portrait would provide the necessary evidence to stop all the Obersturmführer nonsense. But quite the opposite. Coupled with the arrival of Ewa, it served only to exacerbate Mother's mental decline.

An unwelcome splash of cold water on my arm, the patter of wet feet on paving stones, accompanied by children's yelps of playful banter make me jump. Sitting up, I look for my friends, and immediately see Mary and Krysia queuing at the steps of the diving board. Sinéad's lolling on the grass on the other side of the pool, engaged in animated conversation with a group of girls and boys I don't recognise. I know I should shift myself, join them, but the sun's heat is so seductive that I lie back again and succumb to sleep. Soon I'm drifting into the turmoil of an unforgettable Sunday evening last autumn.

There's Ewa standing in our hall wearing a stylish cream raincoat with big pockets and bright red pointed stilettos. Marek pops into the picture. Father, with crumpled smile moves forward to welcome his sister-in-law with a formal handshake; but she sidesteps the hand and gives him a hug. It's as if I'm watching a silent movie. The front door is closing, it shuts out a gloomy day more akin to January than October; but it's unable to shut out the gloom lurking inside the house.

Ewa's visit has not turned out to be the surprise originally intended. Father refused to be party to such a plan; however with much effort and manipulation, he managed to persuade Mother to meet with her sister. But just like a shrewd politician she stipulated certain conditions. One, the encounter be short and two, the pair of them be left entirely alone throughout.

Unfortunately, Mother's having another bad day. Last night she took to the bed in the spare room and is still not up today. She's uttered not a word to either Father or me, and the cup of coffee I brought her earlier remains untouched on the bedside table. Now here's Ewa all the way from Poland determined to be reconciled, and Mother doggedly uncooperative. Father disappears upstairs while I take tea and cakes to Ewa and Marek who are talking in the sitting room.

"Dziękuje, oh, I am meaning thank you," Ewa says accepting the cup and saucer. She tells me how delighted she was to receive my letters. Although this is the first time we've met face to face, there's already a rapport.

While we drink tea, I fill her in with some details of my life, after which Ewa describes her world of music and tells me about her husband, Jakob. A lull in the conversation prompts her to confide that it would've been good to have had a daughter, indeed children; but regrettably she married so late in life. All the time we converse, in our strange mixture of basic English and Polish, Mother hides away upstairs and Father flits in and out reassuring Ewa that Hania will soon be ready to see her. As for Marek, he sits back and smokes, while paging through *Olympic Games Tokyo 1964*, a gift for Kon from his parents on their return from Japan.

At 6.30pm Ewa stands, brushes the crumbs from her navy blue skirt, straightens the matching linen jacket and braces herself. Her absent smile and the flick of her hair suggest she's recognised defeat. Marek, changing the flint in his cigarette lighter, airs the fury he's so far restrained. "For God's sake do something about that wife of yours!" he barks in Polish. Getting up, he strides into the hall, returning with Ewa's coat. This, he dramatically holds out waiting for her to put it on.

Pushing both coat and Marek aside, she turns to Father and says, "No more delays, Stefan. I must be in Paris tomorrow. The concert will not wait for me." With Father following like a meek lamb, she's out of the sitting room and her footsteps are heard marching up the stairs.

"Well!" exclaims Marek surprised by Ewa's forcefulness. "If Mohamed won't come to the mountain, then the mountain must come to Mohamed, one supposes. This is how the English saying goes I think, Martina?" I carry a few cups and saucers through to the kitchen. He follows me and bolts out of the back door. "Need a breath of fresh air."

When Father reappears he's frowning and biting his lip. He moves to the window and watches his friend walking up and down the garden. It's not long though before Marek's back inside, complaining about billowing smoke coming from next door.

"Mr. Wilner likes to make bonfires at weekends - burns garden rubbish," explains Father.

"Yes, Germans always liked to make fires," remarks Marek with a surprising touch of sarcasm.

"Shouldn't bother you, - all those cigarettes you smoke," I put in.

"Ha! Ha! So funny," he replies shoving the pack of Embassy back into his pocket and slinking off in a huff.

Restless, I begin to remove the remaining cups and plates from the sitting room. No one's eaten much. We have an excess of cakes filling several tins, so I dispose of the leftovers, chucking them straight into the dustbin; and all the while I hear Mother's voice from years gone by, reminding me of the starving children in China, Africa or India.

Through the open door, I hear Marek toy with the idea of going to the pub - leaving them to it. "We come back, maybe in an hour say."

But before Father has a chance to reply, Ewa's footsteps can be heard tripping down the stairs. An hour proved a gross over-estimation. There's no need to look twice to see the encounter didn't go well. "So?" asks Father.

"I speak to her, but she has nothing to say. Hania lies in the bed with her head facing the wall. She refuses even to acknowledge my presence, let alone speak to me. She says nothing, absolutely nothing. I am very sorry, Stefan, but what else can I do?"

"Please Ewa, maybe tomorrow if you return..."

"Tomorrow, I fly to Paris. I told you, I have to be there for the concert. Maybe in the future. Who knows how things will pan out. Anyway, I have left a few of her personal belongings on the bed. They were recovered from Marta Taduska's house. You may remember Marta? She lived close by our streets when we were children."

"Of course."

Father's already helping Ewa to put on her coat. I can see she's most anxious to leave. "As I said, I hope it will be possible to come again, and soon. But I tell you Stefan, in the meantime, she urgently needs professional help, of this I am very sure."

A shriek rouses me. "Don't you dare splash me, you pig!" cries a podgy young girl in a red swimsuit.

"Pig eh? Well! See, I dare," laughs a boy of about the same age, chasing her. For a moment I'm aware it's a sweltering summer day and not that miserable autumn one, yet I'm unable to prevent my heavy eyes closing again; and the replay of the past resumes.

Now an undefined shape materialises. It nears the ash tree and moves towards the fence at the end of our back garden; the section repaired, but never, as promised by Mr.Wilner, replaced after Bruno's death.

It's dark, intensely dark, but as the clouds clear, the silver-gold moon provides the garden with a glow. Stars come to life, painting a fairytale picture in the sky. Movement. The shape appears to be no more than a bulbous shadow. Is it human? Yes. I'm now able to see it more clearly, and it is; it's unmistakeably Mother. From my bedroom window I'm watching her pick up an object. She raises it to shoulder level. Even in the strengthening light it's hard to make out exactly what's going on. I strain my eyes. What's she holding? A largish can? What's she doing? I stare until it dawns on me. No, it can't be true. Not even Mother would do that. But it is true.

In a flurry of excitement she's throwing paraffin over the Wilner's shed - and then, as if this were not shocking enough, to my horror, firefly after firefly ride the fence sparking the darkness - and I realise she's striking matches. The shed explodes. Tongues of orange and yellow flames lick the night sky with their crackling laughter, and before long a smoky canopy smothers the stars.

I see Father rushing into the garden. I'm not in the picture, but I know I'm not far behind. When we reach the furnace, it's not Mother who gloats over the burning edifice repeating, "Obersturmführer Weissner! Herr Obersturmführer Weissner! Komm! Komm Saumensch. See the fire I make for you!"

It's someone who wears a mask, a mask of Mother. She turns, looks at Father with a fiendish smile and states, "You see, those Nazis love fires."

The mingling images grow unreal - the colours a pale wash. A collage of people waver and fade into indistinct figures. And like a ghost from another plane of existence, I'm a helpless spectator. Now I can just about hear Mr. Wilner's echoing voice call, "Konrad, ring ze fire brigade, ze police. Quick! Quick!"

A sequence of chaotic fast-forwarding events ensues which in due course slows down - and there's Mother, serene and silent in the spotlight walking down the path between two police officers. Father, head bent, crestfallen and grey with shame, follows.

Laughter? Another water fight at the pool's edge. In spite of being glad to return to the cheery world of leisure and swimming pool, it's not easy to dismiss such daunting recollections. So once more my thoughts slip back to the end of 1964; and for the thousandth time I'm asking myself, what could have triggered Mother's antic to burn down the Wilner's shed on that particular day? Rats? Second World War film footage on TV? Discovering from Mrs. Carr that Mrs. Wilner was now caring for little Andrew? Who knows? Not only were we lucky, but indebted to the Wilners for not pressing charges.

But one positive thing resulted from that nightmare, Mother having to accept the professional help she needed. In addition, on the very evening of the fire, once Father had phoned Dr. Kotkowski, he announced, "We move house as soon as is possible."

And the next day, I had to sit my Chemistry mock exam.

Now I will swim.

The water is silky and shockingly cold. It takes my breath away, but not for long. Soon I'm off, under the water swimming like an otter, only surfacing occasionally for breath. Down I plunge again. Rolling and swimming. Rolling and spinning. Blind to everyone, I swim and swim until exhaustion kicks in, and I paddle my way to the steps. There I see the other three frantically waving, beckoning me to join them, and I do.

Like First Formers, we sit chatting and giggling round the wooden table. In front of us stand glasses of melting strawberry and vanilla ice-cream. Beside them, bottles of Coca-Cola warm in the sunshine whilst we chatter on nonsensically. It'll never be quite the same again. It feels like the last day of our childhood. For a start, the "Four Marys" will only be three when the new term begins in September. Sinéad says it's not going to happen, but I know that once she enters the world of work there won't be much time left for us school girls; especially with all that new talent just waiting to be conquered at the BBC.

With the O'level result business over and done with, holidays are soon to be taken. Tomorrow Krysia and her family are flying to Lido di Jesolo in Italy for a fortnight; and Sinéad will soon be "back home" in Ireland. The following Monday sees Mary off for a week to South Wales. And the Kalinskis? Well, for us it will be moving day.

"You'll be missin' Kon so you will," says Sinéad who seems to have forgotten that he's rarely home these days since ditching the Black Widow Spiders and moving back to Manchester to form a new group with some old mates.

"Tactful as ever," sighs Mary.

"'Course she'll see him - well, as much as she does now anyway," bites back Krysia.

"Yeah! You know absence makes the heart grow fonder and all that," I say noticing a blob of strawberry ice-cream on the front of my costume.

As I wipe it off with the corner of my towel, I think about Kon, and it comes as a surprise to realise that in actual fact, I'm genuinely not worried. Since the Kalinski-Wilner Cold War began, we've always managed to find a way through - if it's meant to be, it's meant to be, I conclude.

Mary interrupts my thoughts, "Hey, Martina don't forget we've got that Youth Orchestra residential thing to look forward to before we go back to school."

Sinéad and Krysia immediately begin to rib her about Paul, the trumpeter she's fancied from the day we joined the orchestra last spring. Mary looks up to heaven, blushes and smiles as she sips her empty bottle of Coca-Cola. For a little while longer we're laughing school friends, but all too soon it'll be time to pack up and go our separate ways.

Chapter 44
August 1965
Same Day

As I turn the corner into Woodland Avenue, I'm aware this could be the very last time I return home to number 64. I'm not sorry to be moving even though it's hard to imagine living in any other house. It is, I know, for the best, and after all it's only a twenty-minute bus ride from here. In fact the new house has a very similar layout to this one; semi-detached with two large and one small bedroom. 12, Winterbourne Crescent has slightly bigger rooms, and isn't pebble dashed, but Tudor in style. What Mother absolutely adores is the purple wisteria climbing up and above the front door. For me, it has the advantage of being nearer to school, and to where most of my friends live - most importantly Krysia and her family, who yet again proved Good Samaritans in my time of need, inviting me to stay during the mock exams after Mother had set fire to the Wilner's shed.

Like many people, I was ignorant and assumed mental illness to be synonymous with madness. Certainly after seeing both the fire and my mother raging side by side, I'd come to the conclusion she had to be insane. But during my stay at the Kotkowskis, Krysia's father took the trouble to explain a few things which gave me some insight into the workings of the human mind.

After supper one evening, about to go upstairs, I spotted Dr. Kotkowski in his study. He was dressed in a charcoal grey suit, starched white shirt and tie; the clothes he'd worn to work. Sitting at his desk, he was reading *The Lancet*. "Come in," he called.

"Oh no! What's Mother been up to now?" I asked myself.

I felt like a pupil entering a headmaster's office. Smiling, he indicated for me to sit on the chair next to his desk.

"So, how are the mocks going?"

"Fine, thank you."

Surely Dr. Kotkowski hasn't invited me in to enquire about my mocks? But quickly he changed the subject.

"See," he said, getting up and leafing through *Gray's Anatomy*. "See this diagram of the human brain." He pointed to an area labelled sub-cortex. "It is here where the emotions are stored." Then his finger moved to what he referred to as the Neo-cortex. "Now this is the section more concerned with rational thoughts, the area of the brain, some psychoanalysts believe, has a lesser capacity for depression."

He stopped, perhaps reminding himself that he was not lecturing to medical students and began to simplify. "So, a method to help someone, like your mother who has endured terrible experiences, is to get them to talk about what they have undergone, and once this has been accomplished, the idea is to bombard them with positive happy thoughts. You see, this chemically stimulates the brain, enabling the person to move on from traumas of the past."

I realised this was an over simplification, nevertheless I was grateful to Dr. Kotkowsi for his concern and endeavour to help me understand what was going on with Mother.

"Definitely when one is working with the human brain, nothing is ever a certainty. You understand that?"

I nodded.

"But always we must remain hopeful - always. People who have been damaged - broken as a result of personal trauma - er - very bad experiences, protect themselves by… How should I put it? They hide from themselves as well as from the rest of the world. They are disillusioned and no longer able to trust others. Sadly, often these people they end up hurting those closest to them; usually without even realising the pain they cause. You know, although they appear to be functioning quite normally, behind the daily mask they wear, they remain deeply troubled." Dr. Kotkowski stopped, swallowed and clasped his hands.

"Let me explain something else," he said, lightly beating his hand with a pencil. "A further difficulty for such victims is they find it hard to make human connections in the way most other people do. Is what I say clear to you?"

"I think so."

"And definitely Jewish victims of concentration camps, like your mother, fall into this category."

I like Dr. Kotkowski as much as Krysia's mother, but for a different reason, she's the mother of my dreams whereas he talks to me, talks to me like an intelligent adult.

There's no doubt that Mother's been a lot better since her days as an in-patient; and perhaps her current counselling sessions will continue to make a positive difference - although I have to say, she cancels more than she attends.

Since the shed burning incident, she largely keeps herself to herself, rejecting social contact with neighbours. She never encourages, nor receives visits from anyone other than Mrs. Carr who knocks for the occasional chat; no doubt to break the monotony of her own lonely days. Marek though, has become a regular visitor again, dining with us at least once a fortnight. He always comes alone. For the first time for as long as I've known him, he has no girlfriend. Mother still refuses to admit it, but he does bring a sparkle to the evening.

She and I seem to have reached an understanding. This involves not mentioning Kon's name, but we both know who it is when I say that I'm going out with "a friend". The Wilners maintain a low profile, and apart from polite words of greeting we avoid each other whenever possible. The uneasy truce so far holds. But I'm sure when the removal van arrives outside our front gate they'll breathe a sigh of relief.

I still haven't told Kon about my good O'level results, and as I enter the house thinking about when would be the best time to phone him, I stumble over a tea chest in the hall.

"What the hell's this doing here?" I exclaim rubbing my leg.

"Is a mother expected to do all the packing herself?" I hear from the kitchen where I smell Chicken Paprikas cooking.

"Chicken Paprikas. My favourite."

"Well, if a girl gets good grades in exams she deserves her favourite."

Mother wearing apron and cooking spoon in hand, and daughter with bag of damp swimming togs on shoulder, are in the hall exchanging smiles.

Chapter 45
1965
Saturday. Two days before moving house

"There are two letters, Child," points out Mother cheerfully over breakfast. "One for me and the other for you." She hands me the blue envelope. Straightaway I recognise Kon's handwriting. It's large and distinctive with the tall narrow letters close to each other.

Mother's in a good frame of mind. The anticipation of Monday's move from Woodland Avenue seems to have raised her spirits. She's delighted to receive this letter. Forgetting about her full cup of tea on the sideboard, she sits down and looks at the address on the front of the envelope.

"Is it not Auntie Anne's handwriting?"

"Anne," I say ignoring Mother's reproachful glare; then state that I'm not sure, even though I am. I begin to pick off tiny pieces of shell from the top of my boiled egg. What Anne has to say is of no interest to me. The only thing that interests me is what's in the blue envelope, but I refrain from opening my letter with Mother there.

"A wedding! In October," she declares holding up a card decorated with tiny silver bells. "Auntie Anne is to be married. We, the Kalinskis, are invited *...to the wedding of Anne Harris and Mark Labett - October 23rd 1965 - and to the reception afterwards at The Sherwood Hotel..."*

I'm surprised to see her so thrilled since that boyfriend destroyed the harmony between Anne and herself during her "little break" in Nottingham last year. However, it seems to be of no consequence now, and Mother's overjoyed at the prospect of attending the wedding.

"It is another new outfit I expect you will be wanting, yes? But not so short skirt as those dreadful minis you girls like to wear nowadays. Also I buy new frock... Your father, he too will need new suit, the ones he has they are looking as if moths have been eating them..."

"Moth-eaten."

"Yes, moth-eaten," she echoes.

Nothing for ages has cheered Mother up like the news of Anne's wedding, but I'm only half-listening to her chatter. Even after all these years, the thought of Anne with a man has unsavoury connotations for me, and I'm not the slightest bit interested in her wedding. More importantly, it's been over a week, maybe ten days, since I've heard anything from Kon - not even had a phone call - so I'm itching to open his letter. While Mother prattles on about the wedding and new clothes, I can't resist opening it. The envelope hasn't been glued down very well so the triangular flap at the back pulls away with ease.

Dear Martina,

Sorry I've not been in touch lately, but been dead busy getting the group on the road. It's a good sound - like the Hollies, a bit. A lot better than the Black Widow Spiders, I can tell you. You'd like this music. Find it groovy.

I know it's a bit sudden, but we've got the chance to go and play over in Germany. Got some last minute bookings in clubs in Cologne and then in Hamburg. It all happened in a buzz. Probably gone by the time you get this letter.

Now comes the hard bit. I've been thinking a lot about us. As you're moving house soon, and I'm off to Germany, I reckon it's best for us to split. You know things haven't been easy for a while, with family and all that. Sorry if this comes as a bit of a shock, and I'm really sorry if you're upset, but I really do think it's for the best even though I know we'll miss each other. Maybe sometime we'll meet up again, and then who knows?

Thanks for your last letter telling me your new address. Sorry I've not returned your calls. Been dead busy. I'll write and let you know how The Roof Rats are doing. Maybe you'll get to see us on telly one day, who knows.

Thanks for everything. We definitely had some good times. You're also definitely a hot chick. Hope you're okay and that you got good O'level results. (Hundred percent know you will have.)

Look after yourself.

Kon

PS. Hope A' levels go well too.

"From that Ger… never mind," sighs Mother.

I ignore her, just sit there staring at Kon's letter not knowing whether I'm devastated, relieved or simply numb with the shock of being dumped by the boy who only weeks ago told me I was his everything, the only girl he'd ever loved. Mother bridles a little then perks up again. "We must hurry with this breakfast. There is still much packing to be done. All to be done by Monday, Child."

Despite the words of panic, her tone is one of excited anticipation. I know that she cannot wait to wave goodbye to this house, this street, and more especially to "the Germans".

"Let's hope we don't find Germans living in Winterbourne Crescent," I whisper turning the uneaten boiled egg upside down in its cup and hammering the life out of it with my teaspoon.

It's 9am. Through the window I see a solitary white cloud floating like a feather across a clear blue sky, and I know the day will be fine. In order to air the house, Mother's left the back door wide-open. She wears a baggy plain green shift with a burgundy cardigan buttoned up over the top; the beads of perspiration on her forehead indicate that the temperature is already high.

"Your friend upsets you?" she says glancing at the letter lying face down on the table under my right hand.

I hear a note of satisfaction in her voice, and I take great delight in replying, "Not at all, good news, his group The Roof Rats are doing really well now."

"Rats," she scoffs and goes to the cupboard taking out a shopping bag. "So much to do today. You must now carry on with that room of yours. Goodness knows why it takes you so long to pack."

Mother tells me she's off to the shops to buy those last minute items needed for the new house, and that she'll be out all morning, but I know she's also off to deliver a small gift to Andrew. It's a rare treat these days for her to see him, but today Angela Jones is letting bygones be bygones and has invited Mother for morning coffee.

Once she's left I turn on Radio Caroline and mash the cold egg into a pulp as the Righteous Brothers sing, "You've Lost that Lovin' Feeling", then squash it right down into the egg cup while Sonny and Cher's "I Got You Babe" reminds me I no longer have a boyfriend. A core of pain has settled in the pit of my stomach. Should I be crying? No more Kon. Am I annoyed he chucked me, got in first? I close my eyes, and already I miss the sensations that take over when we kiss, when he touches me; and I know why I'll miss him.

When I go into my bedroom, I'm staggered at Mother's accusation that there's still so much to pack. The room looks like a warehouse and my made bed looks incongruous amid overflowing tea chests. Polly and Mr. Bear, I shan't pack until the last minute. They sit on an otherwise bare shelf looking lonesome. Stretching up, I take down my beloved teddy and bury my face into his soft tummy; and only then do I feel the tears well up. I wish Krysia wasn't on holiday. Should I phone Mary or Sinéad? No, I can't face all the sympathy and well-meaning advice.

There's nothing else left to do in my room so I wander across the landing and pop my head round the door of the spare bedroom. Very little packing has been done here. True, the single wardrobe's empty, and the elderly, rather musty, hardbacks have been removed from the shelves. They lie in small piles by a partially filled tea chest. Picking up a stack of six, I go to put them inside when I change my mind. Surely they're intended for the dustbin? So I let them drop and begin to wrap up some of the out of favour ornaments, those which over the years have been relegated to this room.

Why Mother keeps the bright red and green leprechaun with a stupid smile is beyond my understanding. Sinéad gave it to me at the end of the First Year, and Mother took such a fancy to it that she rescued it from my waste paper basket, and now refuses to part with the garish object. Then there's the beautiful cut glass vase from Poland, a gift from Marek following his trip there last year. I'm surprised to discover that has already found its way to the spare bedroom. Or should I be?

I pick up the tiny brown and white china kitten with one chipped ear, and recall buying it at the school bazaar during my last year at Manor Lodge Primary. I smile, remembering how proudly I gave it to Mother as a Christmas present - bought with my own money. All of these pieces and more I wrap in pages of old newspaper and place into the tea chest until it's almost full to the brim.

Actually, I hate this room. Not only because its shabby, and its furnishings are old fashioned, but mostly because of the memories. When I open the door and look inside, it all floods back - my feelings of shock and revulsion at seeing Marek and Anne lying entwined on this very bed; doing what then to me was unimaginable.

Of course, older now, I'm less naive, but within these walls I'm always that child.

I tug the worn green candlewick counterpane from the bed and fold it. Then bundle up the flat multi-coloured eiderdown. Under these, lie a few musty spare blankets awaiting the overnight visitors who never come. No one has slept in this room for years apart from Mother when she took refuge here during Ewa's visit to England.

As I've no idea where to put this lot, I flop down on the bed and ponder. My thoughts turn to Kon and I wonder what he's up to - this very minute. I feel sure he's having a lot more fun than I am. In due course I pull myself together and shuffle off the bed. In doing so, I somehow shift the mattress from the base. Bending down to readjust it, I notice a short piece of string on the carpet; its ends are tied together. Then I notice paper protruding from beneath the mattress. I pull it free and see that I'm holding a collection of thin pages, stapled together in the left hand corner. With great care I smooth the crumpled, yellowing sheets. Written in a spidery scrawl on the front is *Hania Strykowska*. Mother! Mother before she was married. This is irresistible. At once I begin to read the first pages. But the Polish is too difficult for me to fully comprehend.

The doorbell. Oh No! Bloody hell! I ignore it.

Chapter 46
August 1965
Same day

It's dated April 1945. Some words like *Auschwitz* leap off the page, and although I'm able to understand many phrases, it's frustrating to realise the sense of lots of the passages are lost on me. For the second time this morning, I'm wishing Krysia was not on holiday. She'd have no problem in translating this.

I realise this must be one of the personal items Ewa left for her sister during the abortive visit. After her departure, Father and I went upstairs to Mother. Curious as to what these personal items would be, I thought it strange to find nothing. Spectre white, she lay in bed, catatonic; face to the wall. There Mother remained for another hour or so before making an amazing recovery. In the blink of an eye she was downstairs in the kitchen, seemingly no headache; and very soon debating whether to cook a full meal or simply to serve cold meats with a healthy soup.

So great was my curiosity, I couldn't resist searching for the mysterious items. I scoured both the spare room and my parents' bedroom, but oddly enough never thought to look under mattresses. I guess Mother had intended to remove the pages, perhaps destroy them, and no doubt as a result of the events that followed, it got forgotten.

The doorbell starts again. This time it refuses to be ignored. Infuriated by its persistence I relent and race down the stairs.

On the doorstep, large as life is Marek. How providential!

"Come in. Come in," I say.

His smile drops and his eyes meet mine with suspicion.

"Come in," I repeat.

"Why so keen?" he replies stubbing out a cigarette butt on the wall before entering.

Handing me a box of milk chocolates and a large glossy hardback entitled *The Liverpool Sound - Classics of the 60s*, he congratulates me on my excellent exam results. I thank him. He walks into the kitchen, puts the kettle on the hob, and from the cupboard takes one of the few remaining unpacked cups and saucers. He then helps himself to a heaped teaspoonful of Nescafé from the jar which is barely a quarter full. I avoid mentioning that Mother was hoping the coffee would last until moving day.

"So, little one - well, not so little one - ten good grades in exams. Your dad, he explains it is Sciences you will study in those A' levels. I do not think now I will ever hear you play Brahms Violin Concerto in concert hall."

"You never know," I say anxious to move on to the more pressing matter.

I'm about to speak when he tells me he's surprised to find Mother out, for he'd fully expected to find her steeped in preparations for the big day. "Business is a bit quiet with many people on their holidays, so I leave Margot to look after shop today and come both to say to you, well done, and to help with packing since your dad must work Saturdays. I thought…"

"Marek," I interrupt, "I need you to translate something, something from Polish…"

"Oh! And what is it? Something important?"

"Yeah, very."

"For God's sake calm down. You seem so - how do you say it? Uptight."

"I'm fine. Fine. But it's something I found. I need to know what it all says. Something Mum must've written - about the war."

"Your mum? Well, I suppose you better get it - let me see this thing. Then perhaps I take it and return it in a day or…"

"No! No! Not in a day or two. I want to know now. I need you to do it now, while Mum's out. She'll be gone ages, the whole morning. Please it's important. Well, important to me - and there's not that many pages anyway. Please Marek."

Without waiting for an answer, I rush away returning with the collection of handwritten pages. I hold it up so he can see the front page - *Hania Strykowska 1945*. Like a docile sheep he follows me into the sitting room where I virtually push him onto the sofa and thrust Mother's reflections into his hands. Pulling a chair up next to him, I make sure that I'm able to see out of the window. I wait impatiently, shuffling and shifting while he scans the first pages. Then he begins.

April 1945

I cannot believe it! The marching is over. Death marches, that is what people here are calling them. It is amazing to realise that against all the odds I have somehow survived and am at last free. I cannot take it in - the fact that we - I, am actually free; that the daily torment is truly over – yet what does this freedom actually mean? No more Nazi SS guards or cruel Kapos? But what of our nightmares, the evils that constantly haunt us, twisting our spirits inside out? I do not think it possible to be free, to be absolutely free again, ever.....

I have to tell myself - remind myself over and over that these kind people, the ones who care for us in this former prisoner of war camp, are here to help us - ease us back into the world. They are our friends, our allies and not our captors. But even knowing this, I freeze in panic with any sudden or unexpected physical contact from another human being.

A dog barks - and I am in Auschwitz, my back pressing against a wall as one of the drooling beasts with an open cage of gnashing teeth bounds and bites at me. I am back in the ice-cold Kojes spending a wakeful night, six to a shelf in the wooden bunk bed with a background of screams terrorising the darkness. How ironic that when in Auschwitz, I yearned to wake in a soft bed, snuggle into the folds of clean sheets and warm blankets, but now I lie awake under the stifling layers of bedclothes disconcerted by the softness of the mattress. It is incredible that I find it hard to fall asleep without companions lying together like tight spoons neatly placed in a drawer. Liberation. Liberation! I never thought I would again see innocent light shining through a deathly grey sky. The word liberation constantly teases me. It is not that I fail to understand its meaning, but I cannot feel its truth.

"Home," They keep repeating gleefully. "Soon you will be home." They say it as if we are homesick children returning from a long holiday without our parents. Afraid they may think us ungrateful, we smile.....

But where now is this place, home? Poland, I suppose; but exactly where in Kraków will I go? Podgorze, the Jewish ghetto? Or to

Kazimierz? But what of our old family house? Who lives in it now? Where will I live? I do not think Tatuś could be alive; there has been no news of him since we were separated at that God forsaken gate. There is no one. Well, Ewa, but I do not count her. We are no longer sisters. I am dead to her and she to me.....

Of course I am glad to be alive, but at the same time I feel so afraid - it is as if I am floating like a lone star in outer space. In limbo. Floating in limbo.....

So much food. More than one "feed" a day we receive here - and every day! More than a bowl of watery bean soup, the odd potato, perhaps a lump of fat and a hunk of hard black bread. Here we are served bread I dare to look at without the fear of what may creep from between the stiff crusts. Yes, every day there is not only food, but fresh food. Some of us here cannot quite believe it is really happening. I have seen people openly stuff bread under their jumpers, up their sleeves - thinking it inconceivable that in just a couple of hours more food will arrive. It is true, and hardly surprising - for in fact my stomach can barely remember when it last enjoyed such luxurious living. How we survived! Adults playing make-believe so that the stale bread tasted like beautiful, fresh challah; the cherished fat, we imagined to be tender morsels of veal.....

Sometimes during daylight, I pinch myself to check I am safely awake and breathe a sigh of relief when reassured that all this is not an illusion; but at night it is more difficult. I ache with terror and starvation in my dreams. In the black early hours, I frequently wake, quaking at the sound of the silence punctuated with the same piercing screams that laced our time in the camp. Beneath the covers I lie scratching, habitually clawing skin from my bones in order to remove those layers of caking lice which cover my entire body. It is essential to avoid touching the festering boils, ripe with pus. I feel the wetness of my own blood coating my fingers before it dawns on me that I am no longer infested, no longer in that hellhole.....

Until this morning, I slept in a bed by a window - one of the windows overlooking the gardens. I like to think of them as gardens although I suppose they are more like run-down grounds in reality. Nevertheless, I love to look out and see green grass rather than endless stretches of sluggish brown mud. I will never forget that a blade of grass was indeed a rare treasure in Auschwitz.

A few yards from the window is one of the beds where the prisoners of war had once cultivated peas and runner beans. Pendulous and neglected, they anticipate death unlike the healthy weeds surrounding them.

Gerda, a Dutch woman, has kindly agreed to swap beds with me. In a way I regret this changing of beds as I will miss the view, but I can no longer tolerate being next to an outside wall. Waking at night, I hear tapping, and know it must be rats. They tell me it is only mice, and that there are no rats here, but I don't know. Today I was awakened by hideous screeches. In the light of the early morning, it took several seconds to come to and realise the ear-piercing cry was in fact coming from me. In a sweat I yanked back the covers, fully expecting to see, as in Auschwitz, a rat nibbling my toes. The deep ragged purple scar on the big toe of my left foot I could not ignore; but there was no rat, only the tapping which instigated my request to move to a bed on the other side of the room.....

In Auschwitz I always dreamed of being at home. Tatuś was there, wearing his kipa, Mamusia, dressed for a celebration as were Ewa and I. We were not in that awful one room slum in the ghetto, but in our lovely dining room in Kazimierze. Each dream opened with Hanukka. The candles stood proudly, providing a wealth of light. Mounds of wood crackled in the hearth, and we were always sitting round the table covered in our best white lace cloth with a veritable banquet spread before us. The dream began with us singing God's praises. However, the voices gradually became distorted, and faded once we had opened our presents. I was always being given that present, a gold bracelet; the same one I received for Hanukka just before the Nazis forced our move to Podgorze. But I have to say, no gift could ever be as precious to me as the bracelet, the string gem, Mamusia gave me for our first Hanukka in Auschwitz. Yes, my dream was always of Hanukka - at home where we were safe - at home where our stomachs were full. Indeed, these dreams served me well. They were my salvation - oh how I hated waking. It is extraordinary that now there is no glaring electrified fencing to imprison me, my nights are haunted by nightmares of being back in Auschwitz.....

Rehabilitation? Is it possible for us to pick up the life we left behind so long ago? Still I have to admit there is a certain comfort in being with others who understand what it means to have been a captive of those Nazi swine.

Yet we all react in different ways. Some people here talk endlessly. For them, reliving their personal horrors again and again helps; but most only want to talk about who survived and who did not. There are others who rarely speak at all; they prefer to sit in silent contemplation. Then there are those who write - some from sunrise to sunset, day after day. Me, well I think I want to forget the past and will endeavour to do that once this irksome urge to write has left me.....

Mostly we are Jews here - thousands of us. Actually I am surprised to see so many survivors. Jews from Poland, Czechoslovakia, Russia - Jews from every corner of Europe - but none of us will ever forget our fellow brothers and sisters who are not here, those who have not had the fortune to survive. Each Friday evening at dusk, the candles are lit for Shabbat. Candles to thank God. Well, I cannot give thanks to God. I would prefer to smash the best plates and pour away the wine. I no longer celebrate Shabbat.....

It is hard to understand the naivety of mankind. I hear people expounding that after this war, persecution of Jews will never happen again, but I do not believe it. Look at the pogroms. Since the crucifixion of Jesus Christ, Jews have been hated and damned. Persecution, it seems, is inevitable if you are Jewish - an unwelcome birthright.....

Of all things, Ewa is here, I saw her today. But we did not speak. She ignored me and I did the same. How dare she judge me! She, who was privileged, played her way to comparative comfort and survival. Did I blame her when she was selected for the women's orchestra? No. Condemn her for benefiting from the additional food and better conditions than Mamusia and I received? No, I did not. Setting eyes on Ewa has brought it all back. I am restless, unable to settle... In spite of my resolve to put everything behind me, I feel compelled to write about what happened. It has become an unwanted obsession. Who knows? Maybe it will help me - maybe.

Chapter 47
Testament of Hania Strykowska continued

The first time I saw him it was a raw evening in the heart of winter, and he was standing close to our Koje supervising proceedings. In fact I distinctly remember thinking how innocuously pleasant he looked for an SS officer. The brown hair escaping from under his cap was untypical of an Aryan Nazi, but on that occasion, I thought him not quite as forbidding as most of those hardnosed guards. Zählappell was being called - yet again. They had already lined us up three times in the biting wind because two women in the next Koje had made a bolt for freedom. Despite an intensive search they could not be found - and no one was talking. As usual with an escape, food was being refused us until the number of prisoners tallied with the guards' figures. The Rapportführer, with a face like thunder sat at his desk throughout the roll calls spitting venom and threats of insufferable punishments.

"Judenschweine" "Saujuden" - "Get up - move out!" rang throughout the camp. The whips were whipping and the sticks beating.

That fat bitch Kapo Zosia kept coming at me with her whip, commanding me to move my arse more swiftly. I swear she got a real thrill out of using that thing. There, in the bunk bed next to ours lay Ruti, our neighbour from Kazimierze. She writhed in agony clutching her aching stomach, swimming in her own crap because the Scheisskapo refused her entry to the latrines -"Wait until it is your time!" she would yell.

An hour later, too sick to move, the whip was doing its work, and not long after, Ruti was shot for refusing to attend Zählappell. And what did the rest of us do? Absolutely nothing. We looked on, helpless. You know what? I admit it. I was relieved to see her die. At least she was out of her misery.

I had worked for more than twelve hours - all that damn sorting in a shed in sub-zero temperatures. My freezing fingers ached. My legs felt like jelly from standing so long without food. The day before, having turned my back for an instant, I found my food bowl had disappeared. Some thieving little shit had stolen it. But yes, I still had a piece of bread hidden under my loose clothing, right by my breast. It had to last me into the next day - no one, but no one was going to get the chance to steal that. How can I ever forget it was dog eat dog in that place of perpetual starvation? If I'd got my hands on whoever left me with an empty belly, they would have been lucky to survive and tell the tale.

Mamusia tried to persuade me to share her soup, but she was weak, getting weaker by the day, and if she became ill and could not work, then she would be taken - like all those others too sick for labour - she would disappear.

Marek stops. He's still reading, but not aloud. Looking up at me he says, "I think this has to be enough." He rolls up the testament. "Your mum will be back soon - and besides I am not sure that…"

"Marek! You're joking! Don't stop now. She won't be back for ages, I told you. Anyway, just in case, I'm sitting by the window. There's no need to worry, I promise. I'll see her ages before she comes anywhere near the house. Now, come on, get on with it. Please."

"I don't think so." His voice is hoarse; his face grave.

Before he's able to rise from the chair, I've snatched the pages from his grasp.

"Well, don't worry then," I say with fury. Calling his bluff I say, "I'll go over to Krysia's, she'll be able to translate it, no trouble."

"For God's sake, Martina!" To my relief, ignorant of the fact that Krysia is far away in Italy, he snatches it back and resumes reading.

Some girl told me that he was Obersturmführer Weissner, come straight from the Russian front and had been seen snooping round my place of work. Kanada they called it - land of riches - how sickening - anyway it was the place where I stood day after day sorting out piles of clothes and the belongings of those who were soon to, or had already "disappeared". So, when an opportunity arose I never threw it away - a risk here, a risk there - to steal unnoticed a few bits and pieces to make life easier.

That night, he was standing by the Koje watching - watching and brutishly smiling as we made our way out into the penetrating wind for yet another roll call. With resignation, like somnambulists we walked to our correct places in the line. Everyone knew that there would be more roll calls until someone betrayed the escapees, or the guards got fed up, chose random prisoners and shot them. Yes, the exact same number of prisoners as missing. This was routine.

Later, on our way back from yet another fruitless roll call, I noticed Obersturmführer Weissner had been joined by a young guard. They appeared an odd contrast. He was short, dumpy with a broad, ruddy face, black hair and small glassy eyes - the kind that suggests a drinking habit. With such a dark complexion, deep brown eyes and a toothbrush moustache, I thought he looked remarkably like Hitler.

We loathed passing the SS guards with their suggestive and crude comments, but the route back to our Koje made it impossible to avoid them. I despised the creatures. I could feel their eyes undressing me.

Instead of joining the other women, I crept off behind the Koje so that I could eat in peace without having to put up with the begging and the threats. I pulled open the top of my garment and snatched out the savoured bread; ravenously I gnawed. Relief!

"Du!"

I ignored it. Chewed fast. Wasn't going to let any bastard steal away this bit of food. Wasn't going to waste a crumb. The last dry pieces grazed my throat as I swallowed hard.

"Judenschwein, did you hear?" the guard bellowed.

"What?" I retorted still not looking up, but afraid not to reply.

"Komm her!" Obersturmführer Weissner ordered, the whip flicking in his left hand.

I obeyed, but not too quickly.

He leant down, and roughly pinched my chin between his thumb and forefinger, while staring at me with those piercing blue eyes. "Uum! If she was not a filthy lice ridden Jewish whore, she would be quite attractive," he stated.

"But without hair, she is nothing but a shaven Jewish pig," sneered his companion.

"True," replied the senior SS guard examining me closely like a slave master weighing up a prospective purchase.

They exchanged wry smiles. A pause. I stood like a statue hardly daring to breathe. Suddenly Obersturmführer Weissner's hand dived into his jacket pocket and pulled something out - something dark. In the shadows it was impossible at first to see exactly what.

But then - who would have thought it? Could it really be? Yes, it was. It was chocolate. Not only did my gut ache from starvation, I loved chocolate. Nonchalantly he opened the wrapper, broke off a square and pushed it into my face - right under my nose. I had not set eyes on chocolate for years. How many years, I could not even remember. My mouth was no longer dry. I could already feel the tingle of temptation under my tongue.

"Ah! The Jewish whore likes chocolate, I see!" he said laughing and waving the tantalising piece less than a centimetre from my lips. Like a beggar my hand shot out, grabbing wildly at the delicious piece. Even as my hand flew from my side, I knew it was a mistake, but hunger had got the better of me. I was simply grabbing at air, for the chocolate had already disappeared into that Nazi swine's pocket.

That fat little Hitler bastard was now butting me in the belly with his rifle and kicking my backside whilst I was doubled up in pain.

"Do you think you deserve chocolate, good German chocolate, Judenschwein?" Weissner taunted when eventually I managed to stand.

I refused to answer. The pistol was raised.

"Well?" he asked again.

"No," I whispered.

"I cannot hear you. Louder Jewish whore."

"No."

"No, of course not," said the Obersturmführer very sweetly, and then spat in my face.

Saliva dribbled down my cheek as I stood filled with shame and indignity, watching the guards go their separate ways; Obersturmführer Weissner with a slight limp that I will never forget.....

Two days later, I was desperate, still not having managed to obtain a bowl. My best bet of course was to wait until someone died; however I was always too late, some vulture seemed to have nosed out the corpse before me. Ruti's bowl had long gone, even before her body had been removed from the bunk bed. How hunger changes a person. Yes, it was stealing or nothing. With eyes like a hawk I lurked in the shadows of the latrines, waiting my chance, waiting to pounce like a heartless thief in the night - but no one was stupid enough to allow their bowl out of sight. I vowed then, that when I did eventually manage to get another, it would stay tied round my waist, night and day - even in the showers.

Next day Mamusia insisted in sharing her soup and lump of dry black bread with me. The ration was particularly meagre, and I am still able to recall her voice scolding me for picking out the insects, emphasising the importance of not wasting anything nutritious.....

In 1943 Kanada had not yet moved from the main camp. Even though it was slave labour, I have to confess, we were marginally better off than most of the other prisoners. True, I felt guilty, uneasy at first, but that soon wore off; especially as Mamusia kept reassuring me that we were not doing wrong. "The living have to do what they can to survive." I remember she said. Besides if we turned down the offer to work in Kanada, there would be no shortage of volunteers to take our place. I still console myself, knowing that even those small items we managed to sneak out made some difference to the lives of others. And as far as I was concerned, the bank notes served as toilet paper, and on a lucky day, my soiled knickers could be substituted for a clean pair from the huge pile.

Looking back, I suppose as Kapos went, Jola who usually supervised our shed, wasn't too bad. Maybe she couldn't stand our stink, but for whatever reason she seemed to turn a blind eye to the pilfering of knickers. Perhaps the SS woman in charge of us also could not stand evil smells. Well, certainly she had an obsession about us being presentable and "clean". The outcome being that we were allowed extra showers. Who knows, perhaps that privilege in some way contributed to my downfall?

Wheelbarrows laden with clothes and other paraphernalia arrived daily. The girls who brought them poured them out onto the mountain waiting to be sorted at the end of the long shed. The higher the pile grew, the better we prisoners liked it. For then we could sneak away, take a short sleep within and behind the mass of confiscated belongings, without being noticed. On the other side of the wall was an extension used as a staff room by the SS. There, both men and women guards relaxed. When I had the opportunity to snatch a nap, I lay there, able to see them through a gap in the wooden slats, laughing, smoking and swigging down beer - and all the while the gramophone played vile patriotic Hun songs. And then one day, my eye met his - Weissner peeking through from the other side.

As Mamusia and I were leaving the shed after work the same day I heard, "Komm her!"

Without turning I knew who was addressing me. Mamusia's eyes dropped. She froze. Surreptitiously, I squeezed her hand to reassure her that I would be fine, and then slowly I walked over to where he stood. And waited. While the rest of the women filed from the shed the Obersturmführer ignored me, pretending to be scrutinising the official papers he held. I watched as the others marched out of view, and then it was just him and me standing at the doorway. He ordered me to step back inside. My heart began to pound. I dared not disobey. Without Mamusia and my companions, courage was failing me, and I knew I would have to rely on bravado to see me through.

It seemed a long time that we stood in silence, enough for it to register that outside the light shower had changed to teeming rain. What did he want? "Schokolade," he said holding out a large bar.

Chocolate! I remained silent, my eyes set on the beautiful mouth-watering thing.

Smiling, he began to strip away the wrapper. Strip it seductively, as a man would the woman he loves.

"Take," he said now offering a square in the same way a father would to his child.

Thinking, like before, it had to be some kind of trick, I resisted the temptation, willing myself not to even glimpse at the delicious little piece.

"For you," he said and put it on the edge of a workbench. There it sat; the temptress beckoning. "Go on," he whispered.

No. I was determined not to demean myself. Why would this Nazi SS officer possibly want to give me a piece of chocolate? Me, whom he had called a filthy, lice ridden Jewish whore. As extraordinary as it seemed, there had to be only one reason. I was <u>not</u> going to oblige.

Time did not seem to be of any consequence. We stood. And stood. Me, weak with hunger trying to convince myself, that I was looking at nothing but a lump of Alsatian shit - and there he stood with outstretched hand holding another sweet morsel. All the time my stomach burned, protested vehemently at being starved. I looked at the jackboots. I shut my eyes.

"Schokolade," he repeated lovingly.

I could stand it no more. I exploded in face of temptation and was upon it. Ambrosia! It melted, and the deliciousness coated every region of my mouth. To this day nothing has ever tasted so good. I devoured the piece and lusted for another. I wanted more. More! My taste buds were aroused. More. I just had to have more. I was addicted. But the chocolate was no longer in sight.

"You would be surprised what a girl would do for a bite of chocolate," Weissner said, "but it is not surprising if she's a Jew girl. You know what? You can have more. Carelessly he threw down the remaining pieces. All you have to do," he said, walking to the other side of the shed, tugging me by the sleeve and pulling me across to the soft mountain by the far wall, "is this." His trousers wide open, left me in no doubt as to what he wanted in exchange for the chocolate.

"Chocolate!" I begged.

He laughed. "Chocolate? After."

Willingly I lay on a pile of tangled clothing. All I could think about was the sweet, sweet taste.

I did not resist. It was so easy for him. He pulled up my garb. I barely knew what he was doing - or cared at this moment. All I wanted was to eat - and more than anything, to eat the promised chocolate. My mouth was salivating at the very thought of it.

His knees prised me apart, and then he was inside me - the searing pain brought me to my senses – a burning poker tearing my flesh. How could I? How could I let this happen? Me, a virgin who had never even allowed a boy to steal a kiss. I closed my eyes, unable to look into his face as his heavy breathing changed to unrestrained groans. But fortunately I did not have to suffer long because he was quickly satisfied. "Get up! Get up Jewish whore and eat your chocolate."

And there they were, by a workbench, the few small pieces he had cast to the floor. However, I did not bother to stand, but quickly crawled, grabbed, and gobbled them up at once.

"And Jewish whore, lazy Jewish whore, no more sleeping when you're meant to be working." He limped out of the door, leaving me in the middle of the floor feeling like a heap of garbage.....

It rained all night. By morning the place was running like a sewer. Mamusia had been coughing, coughing like a trooper, and I was really worried because it was impossible to get our sodden clothes dry. The straw we slept on was steaming, and it stank like an unkempt farmyard. Yet we had to press on, keep on with the struggle to survive. By now I did not only hate that Nazi bastard, but also myself for giving into the lust for chocolate .....

The vile stench and bleating of the sick was unendurable, I had to get out of the Koje for a while, just had to. I was so hungry that it was almost impossible to remain sane while watching others eat, and I was adamant Mamusia should not share her food with me again. As if bewitched, as if under some evil spell, my thoughts kept drifting to the chocolate.

Rumours spread that there was chaos at the gate - masses of new arrivals. Perhaps this will give Ewa the opportunity to slip away unnoticed today? I thought. I was so hopeful, realising it must have been months since I had seen her.

And for me, new arrivals meant more work, more sifting and sorting. Hanging out behind the neighbouring Koje, I was thinking about all the items soon to be within my hands, wondering if I dare risk pinching anything that could be used as a food bowl; and should I become lucky, where on my person could I safely hide such an object?

A shadow shrouded me. How strange not to have heard the sound of heavy boots or guttural hard German. Weissner! It was Obersturmführer Weissner flanked by two young guards of lower rank. One was lean, fair haired with spots like a schoolboy; the other was that "Hitler" who had accompanied Weissner the first time I came across him. Had they been following me? They exchanged glances, walked with slow deliberation in my direction, blocking my path.

"Ah! Here is the whore," the Obersturmführer said triumphantly while holding me in his gaze. "Judenschwein. The one who loves chocolate."

The chocolate was already unwrapped in his hand. I feasted my eyes upon it. No! This time I would resist - after all, my reward had been so tiny. Not worth the effort. I looked again. I was fooling myself; I was aching for it, the worm of hunger rekindled.

"Here," he said holding out his hand.

I wanted it. Would do anything for just this one small piece.

As I went to take it, he threw down the chocolate. I thought it had fallen on the iron-hard ground. At first I could not see it, camouflaged in a deep muddy, partially frozen puddle, but then it caught my eye, a little corner protruding, calling to me. I was down, grovelling; once again hunger had turned me into a shameless beggar. Unceremoniously, I scooped it up; mud and chocolate were the same.

"Today, there is even more," laughed Weissner.

By this time I was crouching, lusting for the promised "more".

"Chocolate afterwards," he said raising an eyebrow and giving the blond guard the nod.

He tossed another piece to the ground, and I dived towards it like a cat into a tank of fish. With that, a jackboot crushed my fingers. Dazed, I looked up into the spotty, leering face. Hate and fury suddenly burned within me.

He wasted little time. I remember he was slight, yet surprisingly strong as he grabbed my clothing, yanked me up and slammed me up against the wall. However, I was not as acquiescent as before - biting and kicking - a knee for the groin - an elbow for the stomach - until the end of a rifle barrel was rammed above my ear.

Voices. Female voices? Whose? A turn of the head. Faces? Faces of Janna and Elena! "Get out of here!" I managed to yell, desperate for these girls from the Koje not to witness my shame.

"Want some chocolate too?" I heard Weissner shout.

They were gone. The rifle slid down from my ear, I could feel it quivering against my neck. Laughter. The bastard holding it was chuckling - until he was overcome with coughing - and then silence.

My attacker proceeded to pull me away from the rifle, violently dragging me a little further along the wall. He was ready. I was not. But I thought of the chocolate to follow and became a willing rag doll. His face was turned so as not to look into my Jewish eyes; not to smell the stink of me while he pulled the striped garb up above my thighs, ripped open his flies and thrust into me. Yet again that searing pain burned between my legs, and my head rhythmically thudded against the wall. I could not believe how heavy the monster was. He stopped, gave a satisfied grunt and his breathing grew quiet and slow. Yes. It had finished. But no, like a recharged motor, he was off again.

Not for long. Harsh words in German. Plainly a rebuke from the senior officer, and he was dragged off by his comrade who eagerly awaited his turn. Having given up on the struggle, I stayed still, dreaming of chocolate. But it was not Hania Strykowska, it was a different whore who waited intoxicated with the pain, and aware only of the occasional star winking through the hanging winter mist. And then a bull of a man was upon me, smothering me - wheezing and groaning. He fumbled and mumbled. Suddenly I received a tremendous push. I landed on the ground at the edge of the puddle, winded, lying with my hand touching the forming buds of soft ice.

This bastard did not turn his head or close his eyes. His face, with its ugly contortions was as repugnant as his stale beery breath. That huge red face filled me with loathing as he laboured and trembled with effort. Foul smelling sweat dripped like a tap as he thrust up and down. I closed my eyes - just wanted him to get on with it, get it over and done with - thought my ribs would crack under his great weight if he didn't get satisfaction soon.

When I opened my eyes, I saw Obersturmführer Weissner standing a little way off, his stone blue eyes glued on the proceedings. He rocked on his heels, his hand in his pocket and the tip of his tongue slowly, rhythmically licking his lower lip.

Jackboots began kicking both of us - the thin guard was not discriminating. "Hurry up!" he shouted at the slobbering hulk on top of me who began to pummel my stomach in frustration.

"Judenschwein, Saumensch, du Drecksau, you filthy pig!" It was not me he hit repeatedly, not me, because I no longer felt pain, was numb - had removed myself. I was far away, above the blanket of clouds listening to the song of distant birds, the ones that refused to fly anywhere near this satanic place.

A woman screaming! I snapped back to Earth. Janna or Elena back? Surely not. I blinked. Twisting round as best I could, I saw it. A different face. No! No, it could not be!

"Hania ! Not Hania. Get off! Get off her! I beg you. Please! Leave my daughter alone!" She was above us, her fists wildly beating my abuser - his back, his head, his arms.

"Mamusiu!" I cried feeling a mixture of shame and relief. "Mamusiu!" I wailed like a child relieved to know that at last her mother has come to the rescue.

"No, please. Not my darling daughter..."

The thin guard marched across, savagely tore her off and flung her to the ground where she lay stunned, taking a lashing from the whip. Undeterred she persisted in begging them to leave me alone. The distant barking of Alsatians grew closer and closer.

From then on, when I have the courage to recall what happened, I see everything that took place in slow motion. The panting guard still unsatisfied, being dragged off me, struggling to pull up his trousers and then stumbling away. Me not daring to move, lying still, watching in trepidation as Obersturmführer Weissner smirked, strode towards Mamusia and held out the chocolate, "A little piece for Mother?" he asked politely before ordering a rifle to be pointed at her head. "Now you look," he said as the barrel of the gun came closer, resting beneath her jaw. "You look very carefully, and see what your Jewish whore daughter will do for a piece of chocolate."

It was his turn, and he had his audience. He hauled me up from the ground, and had me there against the outer wall of the Koje; coldly without a moan or a sigh.

"Why does he want to rape a bald, lice ridden woman who is nothing but skin and bones?" I asked myself, and I am still asking myself that question. I am mystified for I had never before heard of Nazis wanting sex with Jewish women - in fact it was strictly forbidden for Germans to defile themselves in that way. But it happened. Yes, it happened. And as long as I live I will never be able to forget that it happened.

His excitement was quickly appeased. Deflated, he looked at me, and for a fleeting moment there was a look of puzzlement on his face. Perhaps I imagined it, but it was as if he was wondering where he was, and what on earth he was doing - and in that instant my body returned to me; I winced in pain, then I spat, spat him in the eye, But in truth, I was not spitting so much at him, but into the eye of God that day.

"Shoot!" I heard Weissner call.

"Mamusiu!" I shrieked at the sound of the rifle.

Then a second scream - as if from nowhere. And there was Ewa. Ewa on her knees beside Mamusia, howling. I had so longed for her to come today, and now I wished she was miles from this place.

"Mamusiu!" I too was howling. "Mamusiu!"

Obersturmführer Weissner ordered the gathering crowd to disperse, and the remaining guard began shooting warning shots into the air - but before walking off, he threw a couple of pieces of chocolate onto the ground in front of me.

"Your reward," he said smugly. "Filthy Jewish whore! Enjoy."

But I did not go near them, left them for the insects.

"Mamusiu! Mamusiu!" Ewa and I both sobbed. But our mother lay oblivious to our anguish - just another corpse, just another statistic, just another human being who did not survive Auschwitz-Birkenau.

"Ewa," I wept falling into her arms. But she pushed me away.

"Leave me alone, you whore. You killed Mamusia! You killed Mamusia!"

The guards were already there heaping our beloved mother on to some wagon as if she were a sack of rubbish, while I, on my knees begged Ewa to at least listen to what I had to say, to try to understand - but she fled without a backward glance, shouting that as long as we both lived, she would never forgive me - and for good measure added, she hoped I rot in hell with all the other whores who sold their bodies for chocolate.....

Chocolate belongs to that place. It dragged me down to the depths of degradation; and now I cannot see a piece, smell a piece or even touch a piece of chocolate without feeling sick to my stomach...

"And what is this?" cries Mother standing in the doorway of the sitting room. What is *this*?" she repeats. "What is going on?"

I'd been so absorbed in her testament that I'd quite forgotten my promise to keep watch.

"Hania," pipes up Marek already off the sofa and by her side, "Hania, come. Sit. It is probably... how to say it... good you have come back at this..." He's depending on his usual charm to smooth troubled waters, but she's having none of it. Like a tornado she sweeps across the room and seizes her testimony. The thin paper tears as she extricates her secrets from his hand.

"Where did you get this?" Her voice is steel. Her eyes aflame with rage, flash from Marek to me.

"Under the mattress," I reply terrified by her reaction.

"Under the mattress?"

"Under the mattress in the spare bedroom - when Ewa… I mean, you must have forgotten that you put it there…"

"Under the mattress?" she shouts. Then, more to herself than to us she whispers, "Oh, under the mattress - in - in the spare room."

I'm crying.

"Mum," I say running to her and taking her hand. "Mum. Maybe it's good that I found… that I know what happened. Now I understand…"

She screws up her eyes and pulls her hand from mine.

"Understand! Understand? Let me tell you this thing. A mother does not want her daughter to know, let alone understand such terrible things. How can *you* understand these things? How? How? When I do not even understand them *myself*."

She backs out of the room, her torn testament flapping in her right hand. Marek and I, stunned, stand silently staring at one another as the front door slams shut.

Chapter 48
August 1965
Monday. Moving Day

The removal van's here, but Mother is not. No one has seen her since Saturday.

Final contracts have been exchanged. The house no longer belongs to us and we have to be out by this afternoon to accommodate the new owners.

When Father returned from work on Saturday evening with a bundle of fish and chips wrapped in newspaper, I was waiting full of accusation. "Why didn't you tell me? Why didn't you tell me what happened to my own mother in that awful... that vile Auschwitz place?"

"Martina, stop! What is this you talk about? You know quite well the kinds of dreadful things that happened in Auschwitz."

"But you didn't tell me about Mum. That - Mum was - was - raped, did you? No, you didn't tell me *that*, did you? That she..."

"Your mother raped? What are you talking about? Raped? Do not say such a terrible thing."

And then it all came out. The secrets she'd been keeping all these years - even from her own husband; the shame that had transformed her into a stranger, even to herself. I'd never before seen Father so distraught; it was both terrifying and heartbreaking to see him wilt like a sick plant as he wept.

"Another fine August day," the disc jockey exclaimed brightly on Radio Caroline. I switched him off. Outside the voices of children playing happily on the pavements could be heard while I sat on the sofa beside Father.

"I know now why Hania did not want to see her own sister, but did she really think it would make any difference to how I felt about her?" he asked. "And Ewa, Ewa she said nothing, nothing at all to *me* about any of this."

It was hard to tell which was greater, his anger or his hurt.

"It wasn't her secret to tell," I heard myself saying, and suddenly felt very old and wise, for *I did* understand. True, Ewa knew this revelation could ultimately help her sister to come to terms with the past, but at the same time, I knew how she felt about divulging such a thing without Mother's agreement.

The fish and chips lay unwrapped, its smell pervading the house for hours - and still there was no sign of Mother. I was jittery, unable to think straight, to do anything except linger by the bay window watching; praying that I would soon see her coming round the corner. A black abyss of despair filled me one minute, and in the next I was feeling confident she'd be back before we moved - or maybe that she'd simply turn up at the new house. The children laughed and shouted in the street oblivious to my distress.

As the old cliché goes, minutes really did pass like hours as we waited endlessly. Where would she have gone? To Angela Jones? Mrs. Carr? No. Well, who then? Who might she tell about all this? Anne? No. Anyway Nottingham's too far away. When she left, all she had with her was her shopping bag, the clothes she stood up in and her torn testament.

Saturday had been bright and warm with the evening retaining the heat of the day. I convinced myself it was perfect for outdoor wanderings and she would be home by nightfall. But as the temperature dropped and darkness fell, it didn't happen.

"Shouldn't we phone the police?" I had asked Father, when pale and uncommunicative, he returned from searching the neighbourhood.

"No. Not the police. That is not necessary." Instead he picked up the receiver saying that he would see if Mum had perhaps made her way to Marek's. But Marek was out and the phone continued to ring. I badgered him to try neighbours, friends and any other possible acquaintances.

"Not the neighbours, not so soon," he said, but made some other phone calls.

However, no one had seen or heard from her, not even Anne.

Dawn on Sunday. Still nothing. The police refused to acknowledge her as a "missing person" claiming that she'd left of her own volition - "the result of a family barney," the constable on the desk said. "You'll see, she'll be back, they always do after barneys. She'll be home when the heat dies down, sir."

And that was that. Father made a somewhat garbled attempt at explaining the circumstances of her disappearance, but it made no difference. "Auschwitz? The war! That was all a long time ago, sir," the young police constable said looking puzzled. He offered us a cup of tea, but we refused and made our way home to continue the waiting game.

Neither of us had eaten anything since Mother's disappearance, and at midday Father made us a milky coffee and presented me with a few digestives he had found at the bottom of the biscuit tin. I didn't want anything to eat, but I took the coffee back to the sitting room. The seat by the window was a magnet; I couldn't keep my eyes from the street for long.

Then I spotted her. Right down at the end of the road. Not the end that leads to the main road, but the other end. It was the green dress and burgundy cardigan that caught my eye. She was walking at snail pace. Was it deliberate? Perhaps she was afraid of Father's reaction when she eventually reached home. After all, where had she been all night? Worry quickly changed to anger. "Wait 'til I see her," I said to myself. "How dare she put us through all this."

But in the next breath I changed my mind, deciding love and understanding were what Mother needed most right now.

Just when I thought Father was going to crack up, he'd decided to get on with the packing, and while he was removing a number of old concert programmes from the magazine rack. I called, "Dad, come here. Look down the road. It's Mum!"

His eyes lit up. The programmes fell from his grasp and he hurried across to the window. I felt his hand squeeze my arm. She was getting closer, still walking slowly. "You won't be mad at her, will you?"

He tutted in reply, his face beaming.

A group of small boys playing cricket on the road were now blocking the view. A car coming. They skipped up onto the kerb, and we could see her again. I began to imagine the scene when she actually did get through the door. Would she still be outraged, furious with me? What would she say to Father? Would she talk about the testament? Would he try to make her?

With relief we watched her draw closer. But then my heart sank. For I saw that although the green shift was much the same colour as Mother's dress, its length was shorter; and besides, the cardigan was plum rather than burgundy. The woman now approaching number 35 was younger and not really like Mother at all.

Yesterday's fish and chips were still on the table when Peter arrived.

"My mum rang. Told me… is she back yet?"

"No," I replied trying to hold back the tears.

"Hell, I'm really sorry."

He sat himself down on the footstool, and for a while no one spoke. Father, shifting the concert programmes from one surface to another, was getting nowhere. He fumbled and grouched, growing ever more indecisive as to whether they were worth keeping or not. In exasperation he eventually tossed them onto the coffee table and stood stroking the side of his nose, staring at the half-empty tea chests. Peter leapt to his feet. "What about me doing that?"

"No, no - well - that would be kind," Father conceded.

Swiftly getting into action, Peter disposed of the programmes plus a stack of elderly, curling magazine recipes; also thanks to Peter, the foul smelling fish and chips joined them in the dustbin. This encouraged Father and I to stop being idle and help him with the rest of the packing.

The larder proved difficult. What to keep? What to throw away? What will Mother expect us to bring to the new house? I kept thinking she'll be annoyed if I've thrown away any of her special herbs, no matter how out of date. Several ancient tins of tomato and chicken noodle soups bit the dust along with half a cauliflower and a couple of new potatoes. I couldn't be bothered to take back the empty bottles to the newsagent. So what? It was a waste of effort for a few pennies. A packet of mixed fruit Spangles cushioned in a cocoon of dusty fluff lay in the far corner. Peter and I were in the process of deciding the fate of two packets of crème caramel and four tins of rice pudding when we heard Marek arrive.

His voice sounded more annoyed than concerned when Father explained that Hania hadn't been home since Saturday. I thought maybe he was being defensive because of the role he'd played in her disappearance. Without saying hello, I stayed in the kitchen and began filling Peter in on some of the details regarding Mother. Although I told him about her coming home to find Marek translating what she'd written about her experiences in Auschwitz, I deliberately omitted anything alluding to chocolate, sex or rape.

Scowling, Marek burst into the kitchen searching for something to use as a makeshift ashtray. I stopped mid-stream, dropping a sprouting onion. Having picked it up, I looked at Peter and immediately sensed his discomfort. I was glad when Marek, with Father in tow, stormed off to the police station. "Barney," I heard him repeating loudly as they left. "I will give those detective men, barney!"

Chapter 49
1965
The Move

The move is underway - without Mother.

Peter surprises us by turning up at number 12, Winterbourne Crescent shortly after Father has unlocked the front door. Today, instead of yesterday's fashionable jeans, he's wearing old black trousers and a short sleeved white shirt that looks as if it has been put in the dark wash once too often. "Thought you might be able to use some help," he says. He does not ask, and I sense it's unnecessary to tell him Mother's still missing.

"Nice to meet you," greets a middle-aged brunette with a tight perm and bouncing bosom. She walks briskly up our path and already her hand is extended towards Father. "Mrs. Harding, your new next door neighbour. Oh! And this is my gorgeous little boy, Preston." She introduces a frisky golden Labrador pup who begins to bark and paw my legs. Having shaken Father's hand, she turns to Peter and myself, and proceeds to state with the authority of a Brown Owl, that we're most welcome to the crescent. Father, keen to avoid conversation hastily introduces himself, and is almost through the door when she offers a choice of hot or cold drinks. "Maybe a little later," she says somewhat deflated.

"Thank you," I reply following Father and Peter.

When the door is shut, I see Mrs. Harding's shadow through the frosted glass, and I know she's still standing on the step.

It's an agreeable house. Not only do I like the black and white Tudor style, but inside the sun floods each empty room with light. If Mother were here, I'm certain she would feel its good spirit. But sadly she's not.

Thank goodness the previous owners sold the house with curtains and fitted carpets. "Fitted carpets!" exclaimed Mother, impressed after the first viewing. "What woman would not want fitted carpets? An unpractical light beige, but *fitted* throughout the house."

As Peter and I stroll from room to room, I imagine how depressing it would be to hear the echo of our feet on the wooden floorboards; and how awful to wake up to stark naked windows. The wallpapers are plain, embossed, without patterns. They are of various pastel shades and although some may consider them non-descript, I think they enhance the bright, airy feel of the place.

Father makes no real effort to look around. He doesn't even go into the spacious kitchen with its modern orange and white fitments. This, he'd advocated was a wonderful feature of the house, a selling point. But fitted kitchen and fitted carpets hold no interest for him today. For a while he looks disorientated, makes a beeline for the window in the front room, and stands gazing out into the crescent, tapping his fingernails on the windowsill. Is he looking for the removal van that lost us at the traffic lights half a mile away, or is his mind on Mother?

He doesn't have to wait long, for the huge imposing monster on wheels soon appears, trundling into this narrow residential road, dwarfing every other vehicle in sight and clipping the branches of the trees. It's another five minutes before the removal men emerge from their cab, ready to unload.

Soon there are four of us standing amongst the same forest of tea chests as filled Woodland Avenue not so very long ago, but now they're planted in a different glade.

"Any news of Hania?" Marek asks Father.

Father's expression answers his question.

None of us do anything except get in the way of the removal men who already seem tired. They puff and grumble about the day being particularly hot. Are they trying to make us feel guilty for standing about whilst they do all the work? I remind myself that they *are* being paid to do this. But I take the hint about the soaring temperatures, and go to find those items necessary to make them a drink. As luck would have it, the first tea chest I stumble upon in the kitchen happens to be the one containing the kettle, the tea caddy and cups; all very badly packed at the last minute and now sticking out through a layer of shredded newspapers. With reluctance, I'm beginning to think that I'll have to go and ask Mrs. Harding for some milk; and as I'm wondering what to say if she should ask me about my mother, one of the men hands me a small flask of milk.

Having provided the thirsty men with refreshment, I return to the front room. Peter, looking like a spare part lounges on the tea chest near the door, ignored. On seeing me, Father says there's nothing yet to do; nothing he wants us to do. "Better wait to see where Mum wants to put things."

Marek raises his eyebrows and lights a cigarette.

The room becomes hot and exceedingly stuffy; cigarette smoke adds to the unpleasantness, so I suggest a window be opened. Peter agrees, and goes to do it. As he does, Marek stops speaking to Father mid-sentence and throws Peter a look which unmistakeably says, *What business is it of yours?*

With no more ado he takes a pound from his pocket and thrusts it towards me, "Go and buy yourself - and the young pup - some chips, Wimpy buns - or something - your dad and I need to talk."

I feel about ten years old. Father jumps into life, brushes Marek's money aside, and hands me a ten shilling note asking me if it's enough.

I'm glad to escape the atmosphere pregnant with foreboding. But as Peter and I leave, I'm mortified to see the clumsy way that the removal men are handling our piano. They heave and wobble it down the van's ramp with a cacophony of jangling notes ringing forth. The grey-haired removal man, who's grossly over-weight for someone with such a physical job, has perspiration pouring down his brow, and both men have extensive, unsightly wet patches on their shirts under their armpits. If only Father had listened to Mother's advice, and had hired a specialist firm to transport the instrument. What will she say if it's permanently damaged? I'm pleased to think of my violin lying safely on the floor of my new bedroom having travelled with me in the car.

Peter's quiet, which is good since I'm in no mood to chat. We dawdle past the houses towards the local shops, where on our journey here, I'd spotted a Wimpy Bar opposite Woolworths on the far side of the main road.

On entering, I guess this branch must be a recent acquisition to the parade, what with its redder than red logos and glinting, pristine surfaces, plus the absolutely litter free floor. "Try a Bender!" The posters scream from three of the four walls. I have, and I do again today, whereas Peter orders the regular Wimpy beef burger with cheese and French fries.

But not hungry, I just nibble the moulded round sausage I've removed from the centre of the bun. Absentmindedly, I gulp my Coca-Cola so fast that the bubbles fizz painfully behind my nose.

An easy silence reigns as Peter eats and I pick. Being with him feels comfortable, like putting on an old familiar jumper. It's a relief to be able to be myself, and not to worry about whether I'm boring my companion by not speaking enough; or whether the boy I'm with maybe comparing me unfavourably to a model from a teenage magazine. Sitting here with Peter is nostalgic. It takes me back to our childhood, when uninhibited we shared summer picnics and teatimes round at the Harris's.

Then as if from nowhere rears a pang of guilt; that same old guilt which troubled me for years following the New Year's Eve party of 1960.

"Peter," I say. "I - I - I kind of need to tell you something."

He looks up licking ketchup from his thumb and throws me a comforting smile. "What is it?"

I'm sure that he is expecting to hear some further revelation concerning Mother's disappearance.

"I'm sorry Peter, I lied…"

Immediately he's tuned in, the warmth gone from his face.

"Let's not go there," he cuts in, his voice hard. Picking up his fork, he shunts the remaining few fries around his plate.

"Okay, but I just want to tell you this. It was you calling Marek…"

"I know, I know, a stinking, rotten Jew."

"Well, actually - it was the word "typical" that really got me."

Peter's head is bent. He sounds cross.

"Oh - er look - I don't know what to say, but - I'm sorry about all of that…"

He drops his fork; his elbow's on the table and his cheek rests on the palm of his hand. There's a pause before Peter speaks again. "Hell! Look, I wasn't thinking - just wasn't thinking straight that night. That's all. You probably won't believe me, but I don't have anything against Jews - never have done. I didn't - God, I hardly *knew* any. I'm not even sure I knew you were Jewish then - if I did, I didn't mean anything by it. Look, it was that man - with my mum. I just yelled the first bloody insult that came into my head."

"But why - why *typical* of Jews? That's what I don't understand."

"I don't know."

Two teenage girls have taken the table next to us, prompting Peter to lower his voice. This still proves unsatisfactory so he moves across the table and sits next to me. I can now smell his soapy freshness and the pleasant scent of his aftershave. The fact that the girls are exchanging smiles and eyeing Peter makes me aware that I'm with a good-looking boy, but to me it's irrelevant.

"Look, thinking about it now, it was probably because…" He hesitates, decides to carry on. "How can I put it? - Okay. Here goes." Speaking in a raised whisper he says, "Dad's hotel was exceptionally busy before New Year's Eve that year, so he asked if I'd do a bit of casual work - to earn a bob or two doing basic kitchen tasks and stuff. You know, washing up, that sort of thing. Anyhow, one day things were pretty dead, really quiet, so the bloke in charge said I might as well go home after lunches were over and not worry about evening meals. So I did." Peter clears his throat.

"Well, Lisa was staying overnight at Norma's - or some friend or other. When I got home I let myself in and I was surprised to hear voices because I was expecting Mum to be at work. It was Mum's voice, but I barely recognised it at first because it was all high pitched and flirtatious - like silly teenage girls in films, you know what I mean?"

I nod, knowing exactly what he means.

"And then I recognise *his* voice - Marek's - and he's laughing. She's laughing too…"

The girls across the way are speaking loudly now. So I have to listen carefully, for Peter's talking at some pace. His flushed cheeks, plus the way he's beating the teaspoon against his Coca-Cola glass suggest that he's uncomfortable with this. He hesitates. Bites his lower lip and continues. "Then Marek comes up with, *So, you are the lucky girlie, aren't you?* Well, I ask you how yukky… anyway, he tells my mum that she's lucky he chose her because he's the best looking Jew in West London, would you believe? And then bloody hell, the best looking Jew in the whole of London. Soon they're talking more rubbish and… well, I don't need - don't really want to go into it much more. You don't need to be Brain of Britain to work out what was going on there, do you? Huh! I can tell you, I was out the door quick as lightning." Peter pauses. "You see Martina, I'd more than a suspicion before that goddamn party."

Should I confess that I knew about Anne and Marek's affair before that goddamn party too? On reflection, I think it prudent to keep it to myself.

"Look, I'm sorry I offended you, honestly I am," Peter says. "But it's all water under the bridge now."

"Yeah, water under the bridge," I repeat. Then anxious to change the subject, "How's your dad these days?"

"Oh, he's fine. Amazingly fine. Got this new girlfriend, Sandra. Might've told you that already. Funny though, how parents mess up their lives then they just sort of spring back real fast."

"And what about you?" I venture to make eye contact.

"Me? Oh I'm fine. Had a pretty rough patch, but I'm absolutely fine now," he replies a little too quickly to be entirely convincing. This time *he* changes the subject and tells me about his plans to study architecture at university. As we converse my concentration wanes. Butterflies are beginning to create turmoil in my stomach since my thoughts have returned to Mother. More than an hour has passed and I'm anxious to get home in the hope of being greeted with good news.

However, the closer we get to the crescent, the less positive I feel. I relive the moment when Mother entered the sitting room; remember her expression of horror when she knew her secret was out in the open. I see her face, those fiendish eyes spitting venom when she realised what Marek had been translating. Could this be enough for a relapse?

I recall Dr. Kotkowski's ominous words:

...although they appear to be functioning normally, behind the daily mask they wear, they are deeply troubled...

Filled with trepidation, I wonder where Mother is at this moment, and indeed what she may be getting up to. My mind turns to poor Bruno, Bruno who was poisoned. By Mother? I envisage the fence dotted with sticking plasters - her screaming abuse at Mr. Wilner - *Obersturmführer Weissner!* How she despises Germans - the poison pen letter - the Wilner's shed ablaze, tongues of fire leaping into the sky.

When we get back, Marek's car is still parked outside the house, behind the removal van.

"I'd better be off," Peter says when he sees it.

"Oh!" I exclaim not attempting to hide my disappointment.

"Sorry, but I just can't stand the bloke. I'll ring you - soon."

The house is already beginning to look more like a home than a warehouse. Marek must have somehow fired Father into getting started on the job of unpacking. The front room resembles a sitting room with sofa and armchairs suitably positioned. Some ornaments and books have been haphazardly placed on the shelves, and this helps to create that "lived in" feel. There is though a gaping space begging to be filled, and it's where the television will be positioned tomorrow when Radio Rentals brings the new bigger, better set than the one we previously rented. No tea chests, they're now crowding out the back room.

Activity in the kitchen. I enter to find the two men filling the cupboards with packets and tinned foods. They've already made a start on the crockery and saucepans. These lie strewn across the table. "Where shall I put them, Dad?" I ask wanting to do my bit.

"Leave them for the time being. I think Mum will want to do that herself," he replies.

Marek gives me the kind of look that tells me not to challenge his hopeful expectation.

Upstairs, the removal men are piling suitcases onto the floor, yet strangely both twin beds have been made up in what has been designated the parental bedroom. The back room on this first floor is to be mine. It overlooks the garden as did my bedroom in Woodland Avenue. I'm delighted with the view in spite of the lack of flowers growing in the beds and the unruly mass of foliage in need of taming.

Sheets, my usual blanket and the eiderdown have been stacked, waiting for me to make my own bed. But I can't yet be bothered to do anything so mundane, so I unpack some bits and pieces, then rescue Mr. Bear from incarceration, spread out the eiderdown and stretch out on top of it looking up at the ceiling; and there I lie with him in my arms, crying. It's unnerving to consider all those times when I'd been pleased not to have had Mother around; and now I miss her, and would do anything to have her here fussing around this new house. It had never been voiced, but all three of us knew that the move heralded a fresh start for Mother - for our small family. I'm no expert when it comes to prayer, but I close my eyes and begin with "Our Father who art in heaven…"

My thoughts are elsewhere when I look up to see Marek in the room. "Hey, did you hear what I said?" His voice is kind. He's not talking to me like a ten year old now.

"I shall be off soon. But I have made omelettes for both of you. They are on kitchen table. You must eat. You hear me, Martina? It is not good in these situations not to eat. Oh! And you make sure your dad he eats too."

"Yes, yes I will. Thank you."

I'm conscious that my gratitude sounds meagre and a little grudging, but the conversation Peter and I held in the Wimpy Bar is still all too fresh.

What do people do when waiting for news of a "missing" loved one? In films they seem desperately sad, but somehow after a while, they manage to carry on much as usual. With Marek and Peter gone, we are lost. Father makes noises about us getting on with the unpacking, but does very little. "Explain how a wife she can live with her husband for so long and keep such secrets," he says pouring vodka into a teacup.

Every time the phone rings I jump, I freeze, I wrestle with hope and dread. During the evening Anne phones twice, Wojciech once, and we are greatly touched with the concern shown by the Wilners. Whilst Father is speaking to Mr. Wilner on the phone, I wander into the kitchen. "Does Kon know about Mother?" I ask myself. Seeing the cold, and for the most part uneaten omelettes, I feel guilty and scrape them into the sink-tidy. Then as I begin to rinse the plates under the hot tap, the doorbell rings.

Father ends his telephone conversation abruptly. I'm drying my hands when from the kitchen I see them standing on the doorstep - two police officers, one male and one female.

Chapter 50
September 1965

A single red poppy is on the front of the card. The words beneath read *With Sympathy*.

I open it.

Dear Mr. Kalinski,

We were very sad to hear of your wife's tragic death. She will be sadly missed. Please accept our condolences.

We will keep you and Martina in our prayers.

Ronald and Angela Jones & family

I replace the card amongst the many others standing like an army of soldiers on the sitting room windowsill. Neither Father nor I can be bothered to draw the curtains at night. It's almost daybreak, a golden sheen glimmers through the broken sky of night. I'm praying that the sun will shine throughout the morning. Later today I should have been returning from the Youth Orchestra's residential, instead I've woken knowing that within hours I'll have to face Mother's funeral.

It seems longer than a mere fifteen days since we received the shattering news that Mother's body had been discovered near Beachy Head, washed up on a beach. Apart from her bag retrieved as flotsam, no personal possessions were found. How she reached there, or the details of her final hours remain a mystery. Had the idea of suicide been planted in her subconscious during those walks over the cliffs when she and Father had visited Wojciech in Eastbourne? The post-mortem concluded a verdict of suicide, and the coroner stated that no foul play is suspected.

Recrimination and guilt consume me. If only I had shown more sensitivity, considered how Mother might feel, not rushed into uncovering her private reflections. If only I had not coaxed Marek into providing an immediate translation. If only I had been more attentive in looking out for Mother as she came home early that day. If only - if only…

At first Father was a broken man and I despaired. But in the last few days he's been a rock, cradling my grief and reassuring me that "If only" is a waste of time. Strangely, he seems to have found renewed strength from my vulnerability, and he impresses on me that I must not hold myself responsible for the tragedy of Mother's death - nor indeed any of the tragedies of her past life.

"Your mother was a victim - a victim of Fascism - of Nazi prejudice - a victim of the worst possible atrocities that human beings are capable of inflicting upon each other. So it is. Such gross evil has far-reaching repercussions - and you know Martina, the effects are lasting; they pass from one generation to the next."

As the funeral closes in on us, I see a further change in him. He stands taller, has taken control from Marek who was stalwart in his support; and in truth has been instrumental in orchestrating the funeral arrangements.

The hall clock strikes the hour. It is 6.00am and I've already been up so long. The dawn chorus won't let me sleep, neither will my dreams. Since learning of her death, not a night has passed without Mother appearing in them. Sometimes they contain images of her lifeless body in a coffin, or her drifting away on a stormy sea, with me on the shore calling in vain, "Mum! Mum! Don't leave me." Other times I see myself opening the front door and there she is. I wake with relief, momentarily fooled into believing her death was but a nightmare - then the black cloud of truth descends.

This morning, I gave up on any further attempts to go back to sleep. After aimlessly pottering around downstairs, I've now resorted to organising the large reference books, randomly shoved into the bookcase. The first one I pull out is on art, a gift from Marek.

My hands are unsteady and the book heavier than I'd anticipated, so it falls to the floor opening at a page that reveals a painting called "The Scream" by Edvard Munch. I'm staring at a contorted, bald woman who's covering her ears with her hands, attempting to shut out her own screams. From the sheer torment in her eyes, it's obvious she's failing. I recognise her at once. This is - this was Mother. A woman hiding behind the daily mask she'd worn ever since her years in Auschwitz. At least now she's at peace, I think, picking up and gently closing *The World of Surrealism*. Nevertheless I ache for my own loss.

Father, Ewa, her husband Jakob and I travel to the funeral in a black limousine which follows the hearse. As with the coffin, the roof is a mass of colourful wreaths, and I'm stunned at how many people care.

I met Jakob two days ago when he arrived with Ewa. As typical of Communist countries there arose the problem of obtaining travel documents, and at one point, it seemed as if he might not be able to make the funeral at all. He's older than I'd expected. His hair's thinning and almost white. Being tall gives the impression that he's very slight; and his craggy face points to a past filled with hardship and suffering. Quiet and unassuming, he, like Father gazes out of the window as we proceed. Ewa sits close to her husband with her hands neatly folded in her lap, eyes downcast; however, her occasional perfunctory glances at her brother-in-law do not escape me. I wonder if he's forgiven Ewa for not revealing Mother's secrets. With Father it's hard to tell because he's always so polite and correct. Ewa from time to time throws me a sympathetic smile; it's uncanny, but the rapport we'd once had is no longer there. I feel as if I'm with strangers, and wish that Peter could be here.

No one says much as the cortège makes its slow journey, passing shoppers and commuters who wait at bus stops on this, an ordinary day for them. As our car pulls up at a zebra crossing, an elderly man doffs his hat and curious people take furtive glimpses at our suffering. I feel like a goldfish in a bowl and resent their pity.

The high temperatures of the last week have dropped, and already I notice a hint of autumn. On the branches of some of the taller trees a number of leaves are beginning to yellow and curl. I'm pleased it's cooler since I'm wearing a grey winter skirt, the kind Mother would have approved of, and a black cardigan under the light black summer coat I'd purchased after much painful searching alone.

The crematorium is a functional building - a conveyor belt for disposing of the dead. We wait outside by the wide trim lawn in the well-kept garden. The previous funeral is not yet finished. We've been instructed that when it is, the front doors will be opened, and we may enter once the other funeral party has left through the side.

As with the wreaths and flowers, I'm delighted to see so many mourners gathered here to pay their last respects to Mother. Marek is striding towards us from the direction of the car park. With him is Wojciech accompanied by his daughter Gabby. On reaching our party Wojciech vigorously shakes his friend's hand. Following his words of sympathy he says in English, looking from Father to me, "I know what it is to lose a wife as does my daughter Gabby, a mother."

But he can only imagine what it must feel like when a wife and mother takes her own life.

Dr. Kotkowski holds back until Wojciech, Gabby and Marek move away. Then he and Mrs. Kotkowska approach us. He speaks in a quiet intimate manner, offering condolences on behalf of his family. "If there is anything, anything at all that I - we can do." He glances at his wife. "Definitely you must not hesitate to ask."

Krysia's mum puts her arm round my shoulder and tells me that I must come over to their house. "And don't leave it too long," she says. "You hear me, Martina?"

"Yes," I reply. "Thank you."

Krysia's not here, but at the periphery of the crowd, standing beside her mum lingers Mary, face pale and drawn. I'm touched to see her here, especially in view of the fact that she must have left the Youth Orchestra residential early in order to attend. She catches my eye, but is undecided what to do under these strange circumstances. We're on different sides of life's experience; and when the opportunity to speak presents itself, we've nothing to say.

Greg Harris arrives. He's strolling from the over-spill car park across the neat lawn oblivious of the "Keep off the grass" signs. Holding Greg's hand is a blonde who's a younger version of Anne. A little distance behind them, walks Peter looking uncomfortable in a very obviously new, smart black suit. And there, standing on the other side of the funeral cars, dressed in dark brown is Angela Jones with Mrs. Carr who has already begun dabbing her eyes. Some of the other neighbours from Woodland Avenue are huddled together in conversation, and then I recognise some of Father's colleagues, Lena, Paul and a lady only known to me as Mrs. Knight.

The waiting seems endless. I'm unable to stop my eyes from straying towards the coffin, and although I will myself not to, the imagined image of Mother's mutilated body refuses to disappear. I have to say I was relieved that there was no question of me viewing Mother while she lay in the chapel of rest. I don't want that picture to haunt me for the rest of my life. I prefer to remember her as in the photograph I've placed on my dressing table; the one of her sitting on a rock on the beach in Cornwall with a wisp of hair flying in the breeze, and her eyes, as well as her lips, smiling.

Peter breaks ranks and slowly walks over to me.

"How are you coping?" he asks.

"Okay," I reply. And it's true because I feel like an actress on a stage rather than Martina at her mother's funeral.

His smile is kind, and when he lightly squeezes my arm, I know he really does understand what a terrible ordeal this is for me.

Activity. The pallbearers are moving towards the funeral cars. A flood of people are coming our way from the other side of the chapel. Father interrupts my thoughts. "It is time," he says in an unnatural hoarse voice, taking my arm. We're ready. As I turn, I see, still some way off, Anne and Lisa veering right from the car park and rushing along the path.

The coffin is bathed in an aura of sunlight and the rest of the chapel seems dark in comparison despite the many windows. I prefer stained-glass windows like the ones in the school chapel, and the ones here are plain.

After the canned music of a Chopin Nocturne and a brief introduction from the appointed minister, Marek stands to deliver the eulogy.

"Born in Kraków… devoted wife and mother… friend to us all… pillar of the community…"

As he steps down and rejoins the family in the front pew Father rises. This isn't in the plan and I'm surprised, and in fact begin to feel nervous, wondering what on earth he can say that's not already been said.

When he reaches the lectern, he stops. The atmosphere is alive with tension. "My wife Hania was a victim," he begins, "a victim of the most terrible - evil form of prej…" He falters. "She was brought up a…" His voice cracks and he lowers his eyes. I'm willing him not to break down. The silence is deafening. Then he takes a deep breath, pulls back his shoulders, stretches and emerges from that shrunken man. From his pocket he takes a card. Putting on his spectacles he reads, his voice now strong.

"The Kaddish Prayer," he announces with pride. "May His illustrious name become increasingly great and holy in the world that He created according to His will, and may He establish His kingdom and flower the redemption bringing Moshiach closer, in your lifetime and in your days and in the lifetime of all the house of Israel speedily and soon. And let us say amen.

May His illustrious name be blessed always and forever. Blessed, praised, glorified, exalted, extolled, honoured, raised up and acclaimed be the name of the Holy One. Blessed be He, beyond every blessing, hymn, praise and consolation that is uttered in the world. And let us say amen."

"Amen," echoes Marek.

"May abundant peace from heaven, and life be upon all Israel. And let us say amen. May He who makes peace in His high places make peace upon us and upon all Israel. And let us say amen."

"Amen," repeats Ewa, Jakob and Wojciech along with Marek.

"Amen!" My voice rings out after the others have finished.

Father looks straight ahead as he walks from the lectern, and fleetingly, as he passes the casket, his hand rests upon it.

In the final moments of the ceremony, after the coffin has passed through the curtains, I find myself silently saying the prayer for the dead, the one I learnt at Our Lady of Lourdes. "Eternal rest, give unto them O Lord, and let perpetual light shine upon them." I change the "May they rest in peace" to "May she rest in peace."

A Jewish prayer. A Christian prayer. It doesn't matter. I know it's the same God who listens to both.

Father walks to the car with Marek, Wojciech and Gabby. I hang back preferring to be alone. Mrs. Carr catches up with me, "Here dearie," she says handing me a box of chocolates. "I know it's not much, but… well…"

"It's very sweet of you," I interrupt, touched by her kindness. But the thought of chocolate these days is repugnant to me. Peter's waving goodbye to his mum and Lisa who are rushing away without having spoken a single word to anyone else. Soon Peter is walking alongside me, and my hand slips into his. At that very moment I spot him coming out of the chapel, wearing a black leather jacket and midnight blue cords. Had he been there all the time? I hadn't noticed him sitting in the pews when I'd entered. Perhaps he arrived late.

On seeing me, Kon hurries in our direction. I drop Peter's hand and stand still. Peter has seen him too and says he needs to speak with his dad.

"Sorry about your mum," Kon says.

"Thanks."

"Is there going to be a wake, or whatever it's called?"

"No, just a few sandwiches for family and close friends at home. We couldn't get it together to do anything else."

"Aye, I can see that. Um - right. Well - well, I'm around for a couple of days. Maybe cool for us to go for a drink - or coffee?"

"No thanks," I reply without hesitation. Not so much because of the "Dear John" letter, but ironically now that Mother is dead, a date with a German boy would feel like betrayal.

Later that evening as the sun sets on the day of my mother's funeral, I lie on my bed exhausted. Tomorrow I must think about preparing my school uniform since thankfully, the beginning of term is fast approaching. I'm certain that I've made the right decision in taking up Science subjects at A'level, for I know now what my career shall be - medicine. Unlike Mary, I'm ultimately not so interested in healing the body, but more intent on healing disturbed minds.

I can hear the irritating bark of that Labrador puppy Preston coming from next door; the friendly little dog I pass and choose to ignore. I cast my eyes across the room to the waste paper basket and see, poking out, the box of chocolates given to me by Mrs. Carr. A minute or two later, I think about my abrupt rejection of Kon's invitation to meet him for a drink - then I remember Father's words about the evil effects of prejudice and how they are passed from one generation to the next. How bitterness festers. And I decide it must end with me. Like an injured sparrow, I stretch my wings - know that I must fly, for if I fail, Hitler wins.

I move off the bed, force myself to open the box of chocolates, pop a strawberry cream into my mouth - and enjoy it. Scrawl a quick note to Kon, saying on second thoughts I'd love to meet him for a coffee. And as I walk down the garden path on my way to the pillar box, Preston's scampering on his front lawn; I make a point of stroking him.

Chapter 51
Kraków 2008

Our last night in Kraków. This hasn't been the happiest of our visits to the city over the years. It has brought back so many memories; painful memories, which have forced me to face my own demons - but perhaps at last they may be laid to rest.

At the beginning of the week when Jakob returned from the synagogue, he appeared more sickly and world-weary than I ever remember him. Nine days ago, before Ewa's stroke, who would have thought he'd outlive her. I put down the glass of slightly over-chilled white wine and text Philip.

Still ok 4 u 2 pick us up at gatwick 2moz? Mum xx

Popping the mobile phone back into my bag, I admonish myself for having yet again failed to post the card of Market Square to Father and Lena. Father and Lena! It now rolls off the tongue, but this hasn't always been the case. At twenty-one, I'd resented Father marrying again; however I've grown to delight in the peace and contentment he's found in this marriage.

"A telephone call for you, Dr. Harris," calls the hotel receptionist. Bewildered, I get up from the brown leather chair in the corner of the small bar and cross the lobby to the desk.

"Your husband," she says handing me the receiver.

"Sorry darling, left my mobile in the room, and as I still can't remember your number, I had to ring the hotel. Anyway, just to let you know we're running a bit late. Marek's being his usual cantankerous self. Don't worry though, shouldn't be too long now."

"Oh dear," I say to myself, wondering whether this birthday surprise perhaps was not such a good idea after all.

The apartment Marek bought after he retired and returned to Kraków, in order to live off the fat of the land on his English pension, isn't very far from the hotel, so with a bit of luck it shouldn't even take them ten minutes to get here. Much to everyone's surprise, within months, he married some Polish bombshell at least twenty five years his junior; but tragically she was killed in a skiing accident near Zakopane soon after.

Marek walks slowly. Frail and hunched over a walking stick, he mutters and grumbles. "I may be old, but I am not helpless. I can still get up steps without help you know, young pup."

Peter sighs with exasperation and looks up to heaven knowing the futility of arguing with this stubborn old man.

"Cześć," I say.

"Tak, tak, cześć," he replies giving me a peck on the cheek.

"Come, now. Time for the surprise."

"Surprise? What surprise? I am too old for this thing, a surprise. At my age birthdays are better not remembered. The birthday is not until tomorrow anyway."

I remind him that we won't be in Poland tomorrow, and hastily steer him towards the cab I see pulling up outside.

The clement weather encourages people to walk; hence the traffic is unusually light for the evening, so fortunately we arrive at the Philharmonic Hall in time. The pavements however, are seething with tourists admiring the building's splendid architecture, leaving concert-goers like us to battle through the crowd.

I'm convinced that Marek will know what the surprise is as soon as we enter the foyer, but his eyesight is not as good as it once was; and he's so determined not to walk at snail pace that he doesn't look at the posters on the walls advertising tonight's programme.

We have front row seats. Peter sits to my left, and Marek who's on my right wastes no time in asking me what the music will be. I tease him a little. "Ah, you just wait and see."

He doesn't have to wait long to find out. The auditorium is almost full and the orchestra tuning up.

"Anya!" exclaims Marek a little too loudly as a slender young woman with long dark hair, holding a violin, enters with the conductor to thunderous applause. Peter and I have attended many of her concerts, all over the world; and I have to say that I'm just as proud of our daughter today as when we attended her first solo performance aged seven in primary school.

Brahms Violin Concert begins. Marek turns to me, winks; then gives me that saucy smile of his younger years.

Author's Notes

The historical context of *A Little Piece for Mother* is true; however the story and all the characters are imagined. The Kalinski family is not mine; although being the daughter of a Slovak Jewish immigrant, who escaped the Nazis in 1938, has helped me greatly in setting the scene and giving authenticity to the feelings and reactions of the characters, especially Martina's.

The inspiration for the story came from the poem "Real Chocolate" by Stewart Florsheim author of *The Short Fall from Grace* and winner of 2005 Blue Light Book Award. This poem you will find printed after Acknowledgements.

Much time went into background reading, researching at London's Imperial War Museum as well as on websites, and I have visited Auschwitz-Birkenau twice. Indeed, I have made every endeavour to capture the horror of the place and to ensure facts and details are correct. Throughout writing the chapters concerned with Auschwitz, I worked alongside maps and diagrams of the camp. If by chance, the logistics are not quite right, please forgive me, be lenient and keep in mind that this is a story.

The autobiographies and accounts by survivors of Auschwitz were always shocking; but the details and personal reactions varied. Kitty Hart, in her book states that she only knew of one occasion when an SS guard had sexual relations with a Jewish prisoner. After all it was strictly forbidden. However, other evidence reveals the contrary and situations as portrayed in "Real Chocolate" were not rare occurrences.

Thank you for reading my novel. I do hope you got as much from reading it as I did from writing it.

Acknowledgements

A huge thank you to my wonderful husband John, for his endless encouragement, mentoring and proof reading – not to mention his tireless efforts helping with the IT!

Thank you to my daughter Caroline for having written such a useful and accurate History dissertation.

Thanks to Marianne Leeson and Rosmarie Nettleton for their encouragement, suggestions and help with the German. To Vera Suoloe for her assistance with the spelling of Polish words.

A big thank you to author Siobhan Curham, and members of the Harrow Writers' Group for their support and encouragement throughout.

Thanks to Bill Hunt for the use of his Auschwitz-Birkenau photograph in the cover design. *(Also see Bibliography)*

Last, but not least, a massive thank you to Stewart for writing such a powerful poem which touched me and inspired *A Little Piece for Mother*.

"Real Chocolate"

They lured me out of the barracks
with promises of chocolate
and words like *Schätzchen*
but the other women knew,
and called me soldiers' whore
even before they heard the noises outside.
I knew as well,
but hunger has a way of changing you,
of causing you to forget who you are.
Funny, how there can be hope in desperation.

They threw the chocolate to the ground
and laughed: *da Freß*. I lunged for it,
and tasted mud, *Dreh dich rum, Judenschwein.*
I saw big black boots, pairs and pairs,
and the ground was so muddy,
it seemed to give way to my body
I hiked up my prisoner's garb and spread my legs.
They were so light and opened so easily
that I thanked God because I knew
I wouldn't resist.
This body is no longer mine, this hunger;
at last, there is no reason to fight.

I wonder now if their desire for me
was a desire for death,
fucking a bald woman who was only skin and bones,
whose only salvation would be a cup of watery soup
for dinner, a slice of stale bread,
and maybe, if the soldiers wanted her again,
this time, a piece of real chocolate.

by Stewart J. Florsheim

"The practice of gang rape of female prisoners by soldiers was a common occurrence in the camps"
anonymous inmate of Auschwitz

Bibliography

Pack up Your Medicines by CV Hammond - Publisher: Purnvic Books (ISBN-10: 0953233006 - ISBN-13: 978-0953233007)

The Poles in Britain, 1940-2000: From Betrayal to Assimilation - Editor: Peter D. Stachura - Publisher: Routledge (ISBN-10: 0714684449 - ISBN-13: 978-0714684444)

The Forgotten Few by Adam Zymoyski - Publisher: Leo Cooper Ltd (ISBN-10: 1844150909 - ISBN-13: 978-1844150908)

Reflections: Auschwitz, Memory, and a Life Recreated by Agi and Henry Greenspan Publisher: Paragon House (ISBN-10: 1557788618 - ISBN-13: 978-1557788610)

Return to Auschwitz by Kitty Hart-Moxon - Publisher: House of Stratus (ISBN-10: 0755101367 - ISBN-13: 978-0755101368)

Eva's Story by Eva Schloss with Evelyn Julia Kent Publisher: Castle-Kent (ISBN-10: 0951886509 - ISBN-13: 978-0951886502)

The 50s and 60s - The Best of Times by Alison Pressley Publisher: pub. Michael O'Mara Books (ISBN 1-84317-065-5)

Ghosts of the Holocaust: An Anthology of Poetry by the Second Generation Editor: Stewart J. Florsheim - Publisher: Wayne State University Press 1989 (ISBN-10: 081432052X - ISBN-13: 978-0814320525)

How did the invasion of Czechoslovakia and the subsequent threat of anti-Semetic policy affect the Jewish population? Dissertation by Caroline Zaluski 1995 - University of Derby

A History of the Holocaust by Yehuda Bauer (ref Chapter 8 quotes pages1 and 2) Publisher: Children's Press(CT) (ISBN-10: 0531155765 - ISBN-13: 978-0531155769)

Bill Hunt: http://www.muddyclay.com/ and http://auschwitz-birkenau.org/

http://en.wikipedia.org

http://psychology.jrank.org/pages/71/Behavior-Therapy.html

About the author

Kraków Market Square
(Polish: Rynek Główny w Krakówie)

Barbara Towell lives with her husband and cat in North West London. Until recently she was teaching English full-time in a local high school; however now she teaches part-time and enjoys the luxury of having more time for music and writing. She has had articles published in national magazines and some years ago, sold a series of children's stories to Dial-a-Telephone Story. She was the winner of the Harrow 2000 Millennium Carol Writing Competition, and with her husband John, wrote the musical "Faith is the Key". This was staged in Harrow and currently is in production in Dumfries, Scotland. *A Little Piece for Mother* is her first novel.

Barbara Towell's E-mail: alpfmauthor@sky.com

Questions for Reading Groups

Why do you think that it was so important for Martina to know about her family background?

Do you agree with the Kalinski's decision to become British and to leave the past behind them? In your view how successful were they at achieving their goal?

How do you respond to Hania?

What do you think about the way the Wilners respond to the Kalinski family?

Do you feel that Stefan evolves throughout the book? How, and for what reasons?

How important is Marek's role in the story?

How do you feel about the way Martina reacts to the affair of Marek and Anne? What would you have done in her position?

The novel has a number of different settings with regards to place and era. Which of these appeal to you the most?

How did the chapters concerning Auschwitz affect you? If you have not been already, would you now visit the Auschwitz-Birkenau museum?

What in your opinion are the most important themes?

In what ways does the novel reveal what it was like to be a child and teenager in the 1950s and early 1960s?

Which character interests you most, and why?
If you could interview one character, who would you choose and what would you ask them?

How do you respond to the ending of the book?

What points do you think are being made in the final chapters?

Lightning Source UK Ltd.
Milton Keynes UK
UKOW05f0234260214

227150UK00002B/13/P

9 781906 755461